AUTUMN COMES T

and

VIEW FROM A BALCONY

Born in Darlington, Co. Durham, Louise Bradley's family moved to Scarborough when she was four. During the war she served in the WRNS as a teleprinter operator, at the same time learning to type! She has worked in the editorial department of a provincial newspaper and has written a number of novels based in the North-East of England.

AUTUMN COMES TO MRS HAZELL

and

VIEW FROM A BALCONY

Louise Brindley

Pan Books

Autumn Comes to Mrs Hazell/View from a Balcony

Autumn Comes to Mrs Hazell first published 2000 by Severn House
View From A Balcony first published 2000 by Severn House

This edition published 2001 by Pan Books
an imprint of Macmillan Publishers Ltd
25 Eccleston Place, London SW1W 9NF
Basingstoke and Oxford
Associated companies throughout the world
www.macmillan.com

ISBN 0 330 48670 5

1 3 5 7 9 8 6 4 2

A CIP catalogue record for this book is available from
the British Library.

Printed and bound in Great Britain by
Mackays of Chatham plc, Chatham, Kent

AUTUMN COMES TO MRS HAZELL

Prologue

Spring, 1971

"You mean to say this man you're thinking of marrying doesn't believe in God?" Aunt Grace stared at her niece disbelievingly.

Lisa had been dreading this moment; breaking the news that she and John wouldn't be having a church wedding. "I'm sorry, darling, but you had to know sooner or later. At least he has the courage of his conviction."

"*Conviction*? To admit that he believes in – nothing? And you brought up Church of England! I can't help thinking how pretty you looked in your confirmation dress. You wore a white veil, white shoes and socks, and carried a posy of lilies-of-the-valley."

"I know, but that was a long time ago."

"What has time to do with it? Or are you telling me that you have also stopped believing in God?"

"Of course not. It's simply a matter of – compromise."

"On your part, not his! Why couldn't *he* have done the compromising?"

They were at breakfast together that Sunday morning, Lisa and her Aunt Grace, seated at a table overlooking the back garden, an old familiar ritual, soon to end.

"Eat your egg before it gets cold," Lisa suggested quietly, determined not to quarrel.

1

"I don't want my egg! I'm too upset! This man, this John Hazell. What do you know about him when all is said and done? You've scarcely known him five minutes. You've had a dozen or more men friends in the past. What's so special about this one?"

Smiling, gazing out of the window at a blue-tit pecking nuts from a wire-container, Lisa said dreamily, "He reads poetry to me."

"*Poetry*! Well, now I've heard everything! Poetry indeed!" The old lady sniffed her contempt. "And what about all the shirts and socks he'll want washed; the food he'll want cooking when he's not reading poetry? And what about the age difference between you?"

"Please, Aunt Grace. I've already explained – the age difference is really no problem."

"Not now, perhaps, but it will be, in time, just you wait and see!"

"Don't you want me to be happy?"

Aunt Grace looked shocked. "How can you ask such a thing? Your happiness means everything in the world to me. You couldn't mean more to me if you were my own child. All these years I've taken care of you – ever since your parents died . . ."

"Please, darling, don't say any more. I know you love me, and I'm sorry if I've made you unhappy. It's just that I've never been in love before."

"It's come as a shock, that's all. You might at least have become engaged first; given me time to get used to the idea of your leaving me." Tears blurred the old lady's eyes. "We've been together for such a long time. I thought we'd go on being together. You seemed so happy; so settled in your new job. Then suddenly, out of the blue, you tell me you're getting married; going away to live."

"Oh please, love, don't cry!" Pushing back her chair, Lisa placed a protective arm about her aunt's shoulders. "It all happened so quickly. When John told me he was leaving

2

Wheatford, and asked me to marry him, I couldn't bear the thought of losing him. I *had* to say yes. Please try to understand."

"Oh, I understand well enough, and I'd rejoice in your happiness if I thought he was right for you. Oh, he's good-looking, and clever, I'll grant him that, but there's something about him I can't cotton on to. He's – cold, Lisa. Cold and calculating; lacking a sense of humour."

"No, honestly, you're wrong. He's just shy, a little unsure of himself at rock bottom. That evening he came to supper, he gave the wrong impression; sent out all the wrong signals, and he knew it. Come on, Aunt Grace, admit it! You had made up your mind beforehand not to like him, to find fault with him whatever he said or did. I'm right, aren't I?"

"I'd have disliked him even more had I known at the time he didn't believe in God," Aunt Grace said sharply. "But never mind that, and stop trying to strangle me! You know I can't bear being fussed!" Miss Grace French had a mind of her own, and a will to match. "Just tell me, where do you and your agnostic poet intend to live when you're married? Cloud Cuckoo Land?"

"Of course. Where else?" Laughter bubbled up in Lisa as she began clearing away the breakfast things. "John's found a cottage to rent not far from the school – at least, not far enough away from it to cause problems in the bad weather – just far enough away to ensure our privacy. It sounds idyllic. He described it in his last letter as being a fairy-tale cottage: long, low and rambling, with diamond-paned windows, ivied walls, and apple trees on the front lawn."

"In other words, Cloud Cuckoo Land!" Aunt Grace smiled wistfully. Rising stiffly to her feet, she said, "Well, Lisa, since there is obviously nothing I can say or do to make you see sense, I wish you all the luck in the world." She added ascerbically, "And believe me, you'll need it!"

Lisa said happily, piling the pots into the sink, "Trust you, Aunt Grace, to add the sting in the tail!"

3

"Ah well, my girl, I may be old, but I'm not daft. Far from. I know when it's time to stop beating my head against a stone wall."

Turning eagerly, "So you will come to my wedding?" Lisa asked.

"In lieu of the Lord and Creator of Mankind, you mean, in a register office, as a representative of the Church of England? No, Lisa, I'm sorry. All I can do is wish you luck, not give you a blessing! I'm a churchgoer, not a hypocrite! And that's where I'm going now: to church. I take it you'd rather not come with me?"

"No, Aunt, I'm sorry. I'd rather stay here; wash up the breakfast pots; prepare the lunch. Believe me, Aunt Grace, I really am desperately sorry," Lisa said quietly. "The last thing I want is to leave you. I love you so much, so very much, but what else can I do? This is my last chance of a home, a husband, possibly even a child to call my own. If our roles were reversed, what would *you* do, Aunt Grace? What would *you* do?"

"Why, the same as you, I imagine," the old woman admitted. "I'd follow my heart all the way home, as I did with you when you were just a small bewildered child in need of love and understanding after the death of your parents. Marriage is different, I know, but love remains the strongest force known to the human race, and if you really love John Hazell, who am I to stand in the way of your happiness?"

When the old lady had gone upstairs to get ready for church, her hands deep in washing-up water, Lisa thought about John Hazell, and the poem he had read to her the night he had asked her to marry him:

'A snake came to my water trough.
And I, in pyjamas for the heat,
To drink there'.

Afterwards, holding her, fondling her hair, he said, "You

4

mean that you're still a virgin, Lisa? That you have never had sex?"

"No, never," she answered, smiling, smoothing his cheek with her hand.

"Why not? Why haven't you?"

"Difficult to explain. Let's just say that I never felt inclined to give my body without the rest of me – my heart, mind and spirit."

"You're a strange mixture, Lisa. Young, old, foolish, wise . . ."

"Too old?" She had a sudden, odd premonition.

"Not for me. Heaven preserve me from my own generation."

"Heaven? But you don't believe in – heaven. And ten years, that's a big difference, John. Really a huge gap!"

"In which case, don't marry me! Let go of me now before it's too late."

"It's already too late so far as I'm concerned."

"So you will marry me, Lisa?"

"If you really want me."

"*Want* you? Oh, my darling, I want you and need you more than I have ever wanted or needed anyone in my life before."

"In which case, my love, I'm yours entirely from now on! Oh, Johnny, my darling Johnny, with all my heart and soul, I adore you!"

'And I have something to expiate –
A pettiness . . .'

Chapter One

Autumn, 1981

She hated having to wear glasses. Without them, she could not see properly to apply her mascara and eyebrow pencil. Eyeliner, she considered to be far too *outrée* for a plain everyday person such as herself. No way did she wish to resemble the Serpent of the Nile, or Theda Bara – the vamp of those 1920's silent movies seen occasionally on TV. Worse still, holding her glasses away from her face to gain a magnifying effect, she saw, with horror, the tiny lines round her eyes running together like tram-tracks to a terminus. What one might call a no-win situation.

And yet, if only she might have a little time to herself, thought Mrs Hazell, if she were free to run along the beach at early morning, as she had once done in the springtime of her life, the seagulls flying overhead, and the shining rock-pools at her feet, the tiny crabs, starfish, and the waving sea-anemones might suddenly, miraculously swim into focus without the aid of glasses.

Strange how she longed to be alone near the sea, when she was so often alone on the beach. But never in the way she envisaged, uplifted by a magical feeling of youth. Not now, not ever again. 'Youth's a stuff will not endure', as Shakespeare had it, and he was right. Youth melted away like mist on a summer morning, beyond recall.

Besides, staid middle-aged women who paid the earth to have their hair permed, set and lacquered, and wore headscarves to ensure that the perm didn't turn frizzy, did not seem to belong to the seashore. Not like girls in blue demins, lithe and lovely, their hair streaming back from their faces in the salt air, letting the sea wash over their feet.

Moreover, Mrs Hazell wasn't free any more, inasmuch as she had a job of work to do; money to earn – and she was expendable. Her boss, Mrs Fogarty, had made that abundantly clear to her.

Constantly came that carping voice of her employer, reminding everyone within earshot that members of staff who did not pull their weight at The Bay View Residential Hotel, faced instant dismissal.

"Mrs Hazell! Mrs Hazell!" There was Mrs Fogarty now, calling to her down the basement stairs.

In the hinterland between sleeping and waking, Lisa felt disorientated, uncertain of the time. How long had she been in her room? Not more than an hour. Surely not more than an hour? And this was her afternoon off.

Putting on her shoes, she struggled up from the armchair near the ancient gas-fire, smoothed her hair and went up to the kitchen.

Mrs Fogarty was there, thin-lipped, with shoulders like wire coathangers, peering into the bread bin.

"I want you to go to the shops for me," she said without preamble. "Fetch two large whites and two browns, and hurry! You know how quickly they sell out on a Saturday. And if the bakery *has* sold out, try the supermarket! Well, don't just *stand* there! *Hurry!*"

"Yes, Mrs Fogarty." No use reminding her employer that this was her afternoon off. Jobs were hard to come by, and Mrs Hazell desperately needed a roof over her head.

Unhooking two linen shopping bags from the store-room door, Lisa set off for the shops, leaving Bay View by the basement door leading to the back gate set in a high red brick wall of Victorian vintage.

On the garden path, she paused suddenly to sniff the air – scenting that first, unmistakable tang of autumn in the rising smoke from a smouldering bonfire near the kitchen garden, where the ancient gardener was burning the summertime detritus of runner-bean stalks, spring-cabbage leaves, and the wizened fronds of the sweet-peas which, for a brief moment in time, had run riot in the other part of the garden, scenting the air with their fragrance.

Strange, this ability of hers to scent the seasons as they came and went, Lisa thought, remembering how, often, on cold winter mornings long ago, she had sensed the coming of spring, at the cottage, long before the daffodil buds appeared. It was to do with a subtle change in the atmosphere: a thread of birdsong from the tree-tops; a certain knowledge that, despite the winds and rains of winter, spring was here at last.

The cottage. Mrs Hazell's aching need of home, of belonging, tugged at her heartstrings as she hurried towards the busy shopping thoroughfare to buy bread for The Bay View Hotel.

This was just a small seaside resort, described in the travel guide as 'ideal for family holidays', which was the reason Lisa had come here after the death of her Aunt Grace – for the quiet charm of the place and its memories of childhood.

There were still visitors about, enjoying the warmth of early September. Soon they would all be gone, and the sea would wash away the last of the children's joyously-erected sandcastles.

Entering the bakery, she stood in the queue, wondering what she should do if left with the choice of bread rolls or butter-lumps when she reached the counter. The girl told Lisa she was lucky. Orders were supposed to be picked up by four o'clock at the latest on Saturdays. She could let her have one large white, two browns and a French baton someone hadn't bothered to collect.

Gratefully, Lisa packed the bread into the shopping bags, and paid the assistant from her own purse, not thinking to ask for a receipt. Not thinking clearly at all because of her headache – a dull, throbbing pain at her temples.

Coming out of the bakery, standing near the pelican crossing, looking across the road, suddenly she saw John. There was no mistaking his walk, the way his hair fell across his forehead. How typical of her ex-husband that he should be leaving a newsagents.

Newspaper bills had been astronomical at the cottage. There had been papers everywhere: what she thought of as 'the heavies' strewn over chairs on wet Sunday afternoons; piles of papers to put out every week for the refuse collectors.

She watched him fold the newspaper he had just bought: saw him cross the pavement towards a dark-haired woman holding the handle of a push-chair in which lolled an equally dark-haired child. John's new wife wore navy slacks and a red cardigan. Her free hand held the child's bucket and spade. Her face was sharp and pointed, like a pixie's.

"Oh Christ," Lisa said aloud, as John and his family moved away together, heading for the beach. Her legs began to shake, tears to trickle down her face. She had come to terms with Linda's existence in John's life. The child was a different matter entirely. The child they had created together.

A man came up to her. "Excuse me. I couldn't help noticing. Are you feeling unwell?" he asked. "Do you need help?"

"No. I – I'm fine. Really."

The pain that engulfed her was worse than any she had known before. Oh, not physical pain, not of the kind she had endured when the gynaecologist had carried out his

9

initial internal examination to discover why she had not conceived. She could bear physical pain, but mental anguish was far worse.

"Excuse me." The man was at her side once more, persistent this time. "I can see you're not well. There's a café across the road. A cup of tea might help."

Clasping her firmly by the elbow, picking up the shopping bags which had fallen, unnoticed, to the pavement, he steered her across the road as the captain of a ship might steer a crippled vessel into harbour.

Any port in a storm, she thought inconsequentially as he led her to a table near the window, ordered tea for two, and offered her a cigarette.

"No, I don't, thanks."

"Mind if I do?"

"No. Why on earth should I?" She wondered if he was beginning to regret his rashness in hauling a strange woman into a tea-shop: involving himself in a situation which he could neither solve nor remedy.

"My name is Edward Miller," he said. "I hope the tea's all right. My wife says I never give it time to brew properly."

"It really doesn't matter one way or the other."

"Sugar?"

"No." My God, she thought, John is out there, and I am sitting here drinking tea with a complete stranger.

"My wife says I should use sweeteners," he said. "She thinks too much sugar is bad for me. Personally, I hate the damned things. They leave such a bitter taste on the tongue, don't you think?"

She didn't answer; simply wished that he would go away and stop bothering her.

"Feeling better now?" He had a pleasant, unspectacular face: brown hair, thinning slightly, greying at the temples; good teeth, a warm smile.

Lisa nodded. The urge to rush out of the café was

10

subsiding. Aunt Grace had been right, she thought, in saying that the marriage wouldn't work out. But never once, when she knew about the divorce, had she said, "I told you so."

"You're looking better at any rate," the man said.

One good thing about glasses, Lisa thought, wiping them on her pocket handkerchief: they saved the embarrassment of tears rolling down one's chin. They simply lodged on the lower rims.

Lighting another cigarette, he said apologetically, "My wife says I smoke too much."

"She's probably right." She glanced across at him. What a miserable life he must lead, she considered. The poor devil must feel guilty every time he opens a cigarette packet or puts sugar in his tea.

"I must go now," she said. "Sorry for causing you so much trouble. You have been very kind. Really, most kind . . ."

"No, please don't go just yet. There's another cup of tea in the pot."

"You don't understand. I must get back with the bread. Mrs Fogarty will be waiting for it."

"Mrs Fogarty? A friend of yours?"

"Hardly. I happen to work for her."

"Oh? Fond of bread, is she?"

Lisa smiled. "You know what they say – 'Six loaves a day keeps the doctor away'."

The man returned her smile. "You have a good sense of humour."

"A warped sense of humour," she replied bitterly.

"Who told you that?"

"Someone. I forget who."

"What does this Mrs Fogarty do exactly?"

"She owns The Bay View Residential Hotel. Like The Windmill, we never close."

"Closed. Past tense," he said.

"Are you a – schoolmaster?"

He laughed. "Good God no! Why do you ask?"

"Your preoccupation with tenses, I suppose."

"Oh, that. I'm sorry." His laughter dried up at source. "I didn't mean to offend you. It's just that my wife, Pamela, has a thing about correctness of speech, and – well they do say that if you live with someone long enough you grow to be like them. How odd, I'd never really thought about it before."

"It's true," she said. "Live with someone long enough and their outlook on life become one's own. Their guilt, your guilt! I'm sorry, I shouldn't have said that."

"I'm rather glad you did." He paused reflectively to stub out his cigarette.

John and his wife would be on the beach now, Lisa thought. Their child, released from his push-chair, would be standing on unsteady legs, experimentally hitting the sand with his spade, needing attention; sitting down abruptly, puckering up his face and beginning to cry because he was tired and hungry . . .

"So you take in visitors all the year round?" the man asked.

"Not visitors, exactly. We let rooms to elderly people on a permanent basis."

"That can't be very exciting."

"It isn't, believe me."

She imagined John picking up his son, drying his tears. "I really must go now," she said abruptly, getting up from the table.

The man paid the bill, lifted her shopping bags and carried them to the pavement. "My car's parked just round the corner," he said, "I'll give you a lift home if you like, Mrs . . ."

"Hazell," she said, "Lisa Hazell. Thank you, but that won't be necessary. I can manage perfectly well on my own, Mr . . . ?"

"Miller," he reminded her. "Edward Miller."

"Oh yes, of course, how stupid of me. But I'm quite all right now. Thank you again for the tea and sympathy."

Sympathy for what? he wondered, as she walked away from him, shoulders squared, head held high, carrying her burden of bread. If only he knew the reason why she was so unhappy.

Alone in her basement room that night, Lisa remembered a piece of flotsam she had seen floating in the harbour one day: part of a herring-box, perhaps, tossed overboard from a trawler; jettisoned as rubbish because it had outlived its useful function in life; drifting helplessly with the tide.

At the same time, she wondered what had become of all the gumption and pride she'd possessed when she'd found out that John was having an affair.

The quality she most admired was courage. It had seemed courageous, at the time, to concede the victory to Linda – a much younger woman, capable of giving John the child he had set his heart on.

The consultant gynaecologist at the Northallerton Hospital she'd attended, had been very kind to her, understanding and sympathetic when he had told her, after all the tests and examinations she had undergone, that in his opinion it seemed highly unlikely she would ever bear a child. There was a slight malformation of the uterus, he'd explained. And, yes, of course, an operation to correct the malformation might prove successful in the case of a younger woman – a twenty or thirty-year-old. Even so, there could be no guarantee of success . . .

And yet her marriage had meant far more to Lisa Hazell than her inability to conceive. There were so many other aspects to life. The way she felt, for instance, waking up in the morning to draw back the curtains to the light of a new day. Hurrying down to the kitchen to cook breakfast, to permeate the air with the scent of freshly

13

ground coffee and crisply fried bacon; switching on the radio to hear the seven o'clock news-bulletin; awaiting the arrival of the postman's red van in the lane near the garden gate.

So many happy trivialities had been woven into the tapestry of that marriage that breaking those threads had seemed tantamount to the destruction of her own self and being.

Alone in her room, she remembered all the foolish, small things which had meant so much to her – burying her cat, Psyche, for instance, beneath a lilac tree in the garden; crying as if her heart would break because Psyche had been such a kind, well-mannered little cat.

How strange that she now remembered Psyche far more clearly than she recalled the mental agony she had endured when she had walked down the garden path from the cottage for the last time; had entered the waiting taxi, her head held high, not looking back. Not daring to look back at that arabesque of ivy above the front porch, the apple trees on the lawn . . .

Instead, she had sought refuge in the arms of her Aunt Grace, her one remaining source of strength and comfort in a shattering world of confusion and self-doubt in which she had needed, above all else, a shoulder to cry on, a wise and calming influence in her life.

Then, suddenly, appallingly, Lisa's beloved Aunt Grace had died early one morning of a brain haemorrhage, leaving her alone in the world; to face the future alone.

And so, she, Lisa, had come to Westsea with its happy memories of her youth and childhood, to make a fresh start, a new beginning.

Making ready for bed, divesting herself of her skirt, jumper and underwear, standing naked in front of the wardrobe mirror, staring critically at her reflection, Lisa saw herself as an undesirable middle-aged woman.

Taking off her glasses, her reflection narrowed to the slenderness of a young girl in the prime of life – a hopeful, eager girl with budding breasts and softly-rounded thighs – the girl she once was, long ago.

Chapter Two

"Men!" Mrs Hannersley the cook sounded off. "Two o'clock this morning when my old man rolled in from that Buffs' reunion dinner. I gave him Buffs' reunion, I can tell you!"

She had just come in to work, a stout lady with a pink face and fair fluffy hair covered with a fine net to keep it under control when steam from the pots and pans got at it.

"You want to think yourself lucky, Mrs Hazell, being on your own. Go where you please; do as you like. I wouldn't mind changing places with you, and that's a fact." Putting on the kettle for a cup of tea, she continued, "If you'll forgive me saying so, I have never understood what a nice woman like you is doing in a dump like this."

Lisa smiled. "Earning a living, the same as you."

"I know, but there's a bit of a difference, isn't there? You weren't cut out for the rough and tumble, that's obvious, and she's a bitch to you." She meant Mrs Fogarty. "How you put up with her I just don't know. And why should you? In my opinion, she's jealous because you're a lady and she isn't."

It wasn't often that the cook expressed her opinions so forcibly, especially when Mrs Fogarty might be within earshot.

She went on, "You don't look very well this morning. Why don't you take a holiday? You're due for one. Never mind what *she* says. You want to stand up to her a bit more, or she'll down you at every turn. She doesn't treat the domestics the way she treats you. Know why? They'd tell her to stuff her job and walk out of the front door!"

"I daresay, but they have homes to go to. I haven't."

"Hmmm, I see what you mean. But there are plenty of other live-in jobs, surely?"

"That's true," Lisa conceded, "but this is the best so far. I had a live-in job as companion-housekeeper to an old man before I came here. My room was scarcely big enough to swing a cat, and I dared not leave the door unlocked, if you see what I mean."

"What?" Mrs Hannersley bridled. "Why, the dirty old devil!" Making the tea, she went on, "Have you thought of renting a room somewhere? The papers are full of them at this time of year."

"I know. But I wouldn't want just one furnished room. I have my own furniture, you see. It's in store at the moment. If I did decide to make a change, I'd need a small unfurnished flat to rent. But that's like asking for the moon these days. I know, I've tried several estate agents. They look pained when they see me coming; either that or pretend they're not in."

"Is that what you want?" Mrs Hannersley poured the tea. "Well, I hadn't thought of that. I didn't know you had any furniture."

"Just a little." John had been quite fair when it came to the division of property, Lisa thought. But possibly Linda had wanted to rid the cottage of obvious reminders of the first Mrs Hazell.

Cook puckered her face. "Now, I wonder . . ."

"What, Mrs Hannersley?"

"Perhaps I shouldn't say. I don't want to build up your hopes too high, but my brother's got a house near the harbour. Now what was he saying about that flat on the top floor? He was on about it the other day, but I didn't take much notice. Was the girl having a baby and couldn't manage the stairs? Yes, that was it. The young couple who

17

rent it are moving into a council house. I mean, no way could they hump a push-chair up six flights of stairs, and where would they hang the nappies to dry in the cold weather?

"Mind you, I wouldn't care to live there me'self, an' that's a fact. I should cocoa! Stuck away at the top of a house, with no central heating and nothing to look at except the sea, isn't my idea of heaven, but I'll ask him about it again, if you like."

"Yes, please Mrs Hannersley. I'd be more than grateful if you would."

Sally and Alice, the domestics, entered the kitchen at that moment. Nothing more was said about the flat. The day was under way. Nothing out of the ordinary was going to happen, and yet, rolling butter, dropping the curled portions into cold water to keep their shape and consistency, Lisa's mind was busy with thoughts of the flat near the harbour.

The most miraculous thing of all would be privacy; a home to call her own; a door to close against the world. Behind that door, the core of her, the vital, living spark within, might just begin to flicker and burn again.

The dream firmly rooted, other dreams followed, bringing a sense of spiritual uplift. She began to think in terms of a sabbatical, living for one whole year on her meagre savings. A ridiculous notion of course, but she might just manage if she stopped having her hair permed and lived on bread, potatoes and porridge.

Washing the breakfast dishes, glancing out of the window now and then at the watercolour sky, smiling happily, she thought that if she got that flat, she would gather all her bits and pieces together again under one roof – albeit an attic roof.

Mrs Fogarty rustled into the still room like a thin wind blowing through a reed bed. "Mrs Pettifer complained that you did not put marmalade on her breakfast tray," she snapped. "Really, Mrs Hazell, that was most care- less of you. Mrs Pettifer is one of our higher bracket

18

guests. I will not tolerate having her upset in such a fashion."

"I'm sorry, Mrs Fogarty. It won't happen again."

"I should think not, indeed! There are times when your mind appears not to be on your work at all. Take Saturday afternoon, for example. I sent you on a simple errand, and what happened? The bread you brough back was totally insufficient. A French baton! What use, I ask you, is a baton of bread in a place like Bay View? Nor did you think to bring back a receipt, in which case I cannot possibly reimburse you, and that's final."

It was on the tip of Lisa's tongue to tell her employer that, had she ordered sufficient bread for the weekend in the first place, the situation would never have arisen, but what was the use? Mrs Fogarty had her cornered, and she knew it. They both knew it.

Peering into a cupboard, Mrs Fogarty ran a bony finger along the top shelf. "It's high time this cupboard was turned out," she grumbled. "Just look at the dust!"

Lisa looked. Saw nothing.

At that moment, Mrs Hannersley sang out, "Tea up!" from the kitchen. "Half-past ten. Break time!"

Ten minute's respite from the busy morning routine by grudging consent of the management. Mrs Fogarty stalked off to have her tea and biscuits in her private apartment. Sally, whose turn it was to carry the tray with its pristine cloth and Coalport china cup and saucer, sugar basin and milk jug, blurted, "Oh, God, I've forgotten her bloody teaspoon!"

"That's not all you've forgotten," Edith Hammersley reminded her. "What about the teapot?"

"Oh, lord," Sally wailed, "she just makes me so nervous, that's all! Her and her X-ray eyes! I'd forget my head if it was loose! Matter of fact, my hubby wants me to hand in my notice; says my working here is ruining his sex life with me being so nervous an' jumpy all the time!"

Drinking tea from a chipped kitchen cup, Lisa thought: when I take my sabbatical, I'll buy a cafetiere and treat myself to freshly ground coffee beans from that shop in the town centre. Continental blend. In that way she would derive the two-fold pleasure of buying the coffee and drinking it, and also, inhaling the aroma reminiscent of holidays to Austria and Switzerland in the early days of her marriage; Switzerland in particular, where she and John had breakfasted together on the balcony of their room, spreading freshly-baked croissants with butter and black cherry jam in the warm morning air.

John, she remembered, had leaned forward eagerly to entice a squirrel to take a crumb of croissant from his outstretched hand, calling quietly, *"Kommt Hansi. Hansi, kommt."*

Had his thoughts, even then, she wondered, been centred on a boy child who would squeal his delight at the antics of the squirrel holding up its paws in a gesture of supplication?

But that was all in the past. Now she must think of the future, however lonely and difficult that future might be.

Thinking about the flat near the harbour, how marvellous it would be to carry her coffee through to the sitting room and drink it slowly, savouring each mouthful, Lisa considered. Also, how wonderful to treat herself to a few pots of African violets and watch them grow; pink and parma – as shiny as sugared almonds.

She had left her pot-plants behind her at the cottage; the ivies and spider plants she had grown from cuttings, realising that one could not store living things in a furniture repository, not like tables, chairs, pictures and ornaments, bedding and carpets; Cornish kitchenware, cutlery and photograph albums . . .

After the lunchtime washing-up, Lisa half-expected Mrs

Fogarty's voice to call after her as she walked down the path to the back gate.

Safely away from Bay View, she paused on the promenade to look at the harbour, on which her thoughts were centred, and saw that the tide was out; that the wet sand near the sea's edge shone like mother-of-pearl.

The beach was crowded. Late summer visitors had formed an encampment close to the amusement arcades and the candy-floss stalls, the fish and chips restaurants and the ice-cream parlours, she noticed, as if their lives would fall apart and disintegrate if they were separated from their fellow human beings by a hair's-breadth; from food and entertainment.

How curious this herd instinct, she thought, walking near the water's edge; turning back occasionally to regard the implosion of her own footsteps in the sand which, for all the world resembled those of young girl in the prime of life. Who could possibly tell the difference except, perhaps, the perpetrator of the footprints? In any event, they would be washed away by the incoming tide a few hours hence: leaving no trace, by which time all the visitors would have gone back to their digs to delve into the food provided by their respective landladies.

This was the way of the world in an end-of-season seaside resort, Lisa reckoned, walking towards a cobbled slipway, her eyes glissading from the grey parish church overlooking the town, to the huddle of fishermen's cottages grouped about the harbour, plus a phalanx of taller houses crowning the hill, one of which might, conceivably, harbour her flat.

A carillon of bells rang suddenly from the parish church on the hill. Shaking the sand from her shoes, Lisa hurried up the slipway near the lifeboathouse, anxious to see the wedding.

The young bride and groom were standing together self-consciously, having their photographs taken. The bride, who looked about nineteen, wore a white satin dress, a veil secured with a headdress of mixed flowers, and carried a bouquet to match. She was pink-cheeked with happiness, smiling, clinging to her husband's arm. He, all of twenty, gazed down at her adoringly. A child stepped forward and handed her a silver horseshoe.

It wasn't a 'posh' wedding. The groom wore a dark lounge suit, and someone had pinned on his white carnation with the stalk showing. The guests were just nice, ordinary people wearing their best clothes, bought for the occasion, she imagined – the women's clothes at any rate – the brand new coats and hats, gloves, shoes and other accessories.

Standing on the edge of a group of sightseers, Lisa remembered her own wedding. Never had she admitted to Aunt Grace how much she had longed for a church wedding, however simple, knowing how much John would have hated it. And so she had compromised; agreed to a registry office wedding for his sake. But it had seemed so cold and formal, that functional office in which the ceremony had taken place.

Moving away from the small crowd of onlookers, Lisa re-traced her steps. Half-way down the hill to the foreshore, she came face to face with her ex-husband.

They stood stock still momentarily, staring at one another, not speaking, shocked at the encounter. Then John said hoarsely, "Lisa. What the hell are you doing here?"

"I live here."

"But I thought you were living in Wheatford with that aunt of yours!"

"Not any longer."

"Apparently not."

They faced each other warily, like duellists wearing masks. Lisa remained silent.

John said abruptly, "I'm going back to the hotel to fetch my camera," – as if that explained the world and everything in it.

"Of course," Lisa said quietly, keeping a tight rein on

her emotions. "You'll want to keep a record of your child's formative years."

"You *know?*" He stared at her uncertainly.

"That you have a son? Oh yes, I know."

"But how? I mean, there has been no communication between us since the divorce."

No, she thought, not so much as a Christmas or a birthday card. Nothing. John had cleared her out of his life as uncaringly as a road-sweeper might shovel away snow, autumn leaves, or convenience food cartons.

"I saw you, Linda and the child last weekend," she said. "You didn't see me."

"We're on holiday," he said defiantly.

"Of course. That thought had occurred to me, believe it or not."

"I never dreamt you'd be here."

"Why should you? I don't suppose it crossed your mind that I'd be anywhere in particular. I daresay you have never given my whereabouts a second thought. After all, you've had other things on your mind."

"That's not true, Lisa! It is grossly unfair of you to say that!" he exclaimed, beginning to bluster; to raise his voice.

"So you have thought about me?" She regarded him coolly, shoring up her defences against him, knowing that, suddenly, she had become the mistress of the situation; needing to say all the things she had never said before. "Tell me, John, I'd really like to know what you thought, how you felt that last day at the cottage, after I'd gone away."

"Oh, for God's sake, Lisa! Look, I can't stop to talk to you right now. Linda will be wondering what's happening. Why the delay with the camera!"

"You could tell her that you'd run out of film. You always were good at lying, remember?"

Turning away, she walked on down the hill to the foreshore; sensed that he was following her. Suddenly, she felt

23

his hand on her arm. Facing him once more, she asked coldly, "Well, what now?" denying the swift beating of her heart. "I thought you were in a hurry." Cruelty begat cruelty.

He said distractedly, running his fingers through his hair, "All this is bloody difficult for me. You must see that! I haven't the time right now! Where are you living?"

"At The Bay View Hotel. The number's in the phone book."

"I'll try to contact you later. Mind you, I can't promise."

"Of course not! As I recall, keeping a promise was never your strong point! Better not hold my breath, as the saying goes!"

As she walked on downhill, she knew he was watching her out of sight. But there could be no turning back, not now, not ever again. Not with Linda and their son awaiting his return to the beach to take photographs.

Chapter Three

Sunday morning seemed endless. This being Mrs Hannersley's day off, Lisa assumed command of the cooking. Not that she minded rumbling potatoes, scraping carrots, and making Yorkshire pudding batter, and Mrs Hannersley always pre-cooked the joint on Saturday to make sure it could be carved economically before re-heating.

No way could even the higher bracket guests at Bay View expect a cut from a freshly cooked roast, Cook would mutter darkly when upset, but then, Bay View wasn't the Savoy Hotel; nowt but an old folks' home with knobs on.

On this particular Sunday morning, disturbed by her meeting with her ex-husband the day before, Lisa's heart missed a beat every time the phone rang, thinking it might be John. But if he did ring, what would she say to him? He, to her? In any case, she was far too busy to break off in the middle of making the gravy, slicing the meat and worrying about the Yorkshire puddings and roast potatoes, to engage in an in-depth telephone conversation, when there was really nothing left to talk about.

He did not ring, of course. The Yorkshire puddings rose, thank God, and the potatoes emerged from the oven crisply done. Dishing up the food, her glasses became fogged up with steam and her latest perm turned frizzy. Ah well, just another day in the life of Lisa Hazell, general dogsbody, she thought philosophically.

At least she hadn't had 'The Fogarty' breathing down her neck all morning. Her employer had 'gorn orf' to visit friends of hers – a coven of witches, perhaps? The mind boggled.

When luncheon had been consumed, without complaint, thank heaven, the tables cleared and the washing up done, and after the afternoon staff had come on duty to re-set the tables for tea, Lisa went down to her room to put her feet up.

She noticed, staring at the window, that a blanket of grey mist, known locally as a 'sea-fret', was sweeping in from the sea, heralded by the booming of the fog-horn, and thought that John's child might well be fretful today, robbed of sunshine and the sands.

Picking up a magazine, Lisa flicked over the pages, wondering why she had bought the thing in the first place. Did she really need advice on skin-care for teenagers, or how to provide a romantic meal for two at under a tenner? Scarcely, since she had so often provided romantic meals for two for under a fiver, in the early days of her marriage, when she and John were as poor as church mice.

The trick, she had discovered, was to concentrate on the food. Never mind about the candles and flowers, because all men really cared about was the food . . .

Then, on another page:

'At the change of life', she read, 'above all else, a woman needs a loving understanding of her mid-life crisis.

The menopause heralds a natural slowing down of her physical and mental capabilities, added to the overwhelming realisation that her child-bearing days are over – although it is by no means uncommon for a woman to conceive during her menopause – and even when the menstrual flow has finally ceased, most women find that life has still much to offer by way of recompense.

The husband's role, at this stage, is all-important. It is up to him to convince his wife that the best is yet to come'.

26

Lisa frowned. But what about single women facing the mid-life crisis; the middle-aged spinsters caring for elderly parents? Divorced women whose husbands had swanned off with fecund girls half their age? Would they consider, for one moment, that the best was yet to come? Did she herself believe it? The answer came clear cut and simple. No, of course not. How could she?

She must have fallen asleep. When she awakened to the sound of a loud rapping on the door, the room was in darkness and the magazine had slipped to the floor.

"Yes, what is it?" she called out in alarm as the knocking continued.

"There's someone on the phone, wanting to speak to you." The voice belonged to Mrs Brazier, one of the afternoon helpers. "A man, in a phone-box by the sound of it, so you'd best hurry before his money runs out."

"Coming!" John, Lisa thought, galvanised into action, it must be John! Hurrying upstairs in her stockinged feet, her hair awry, she picked up the receiver. "Hello," she said breathlessly.

"Mrs Hazell?" The voice on the line seemed vaguely familiar, but it wasn't John's voice. Fighting back an intense feeling of disappointment, she said, "Yes, Lisa Hazell speaking, but who is this?"

"You may not remember me. Edward Miller?"

"*Edward Miller*? No, I'm afraid not."

"We had tea together a week ago yesterday," the voice reminded her. "You seemed a little – unwell – at the time, remember? I'm ringing to ask if you're feeling better now."

"Oh yes, of course," she said dully, "now I remember. And I'm fine, thank you. Perfectly all right." For the life of her she couldn't remember his face.

He said quietly, "I suppose you wouldn't care to have a drink with me this evening?"

He had put the question in the negative, she realised, not believing for one moment that she would say, yes.

27

"Well, I'm not sure," she prevaricated, touched by his concern. "That is, I had planned to wash my hair; have an early night."

"Let's say eight o'clock, shall we? Not to worry, I have no intention of making a nuisance of myself. I'd just like to talk to you, that's all."

"Oh, very well then, if you insist. But please don't ring the bell."

"Fair enough. I'll be the soul of discretion, I promise!" He laughed. "Tell me, Lisa, does your friend Mrs Fogarty peep from behind the net curtains?"

"Something like that." She warmed to his laughter. "The Colditz Story all over again!"

"In other words, a matter of escape?"

"That's one way of putting it."

"Eight o'clock, then? I'll park at the sea end of the street. I'll be wearing dark glasses, a down-turned trilby and a false moustache. The password is – escape."

Hanging up the receiver, Lisa knew she was making a mistake. Edward Miller was married to someone called Pamela. And presumably, he had not told his wife that he had invited another woman to have a drink with him.

So what should she have done? Slammed down the receiver, spent the evening alone in her room watching an old film on TV? She was still a woman, for heaven's sake, not a cipher, in need of companionship and laughter. Above all, laughter.

Even so, when the time came, she felt nervous at seeing him again, and sat with her spine pressed against the back of the passenger seat, having read somewhere that this was the best way to sit to reduce tension.

Thankfully, he seemed to realise that she was nervous, and made no attempt at lighthearted conversation, merely remarking what a lovely evening it was now the fog had cleared. His hands on the steering wheel were strong, she noticed, with impeccably manicured finger nails, and he was an excellent driver.

Gradually, she began to relax. Driving with John had been akin to a nightmare, especially on trips abroad when she had perched on the edge of her seat, afraid of missing a signpost; forever on the qui vive to spot their position on the road-map spread out on her lap, or delve into her shoulder-bag for their passports and so on, at border crossings; keenly aware of his impatience at her ineptitude if she failed to produce, in a matter of seconds, the required documentation. Then, "What the hell are you playing at?" he would demand irritably, effectively shattering her limited store of self-confidence.

She said, "You drive very well, Mr Miller."

"Do you really think so?" He seemed surprised.

"Don't you?"

"Far from. My wife says I'm a rotten driver."

Engaging second gear, signalling right, he turned off the main road into a country lane with high hedgerows on either side, and the interlaced branches of trees overhead forming a tunnel.

A little further on, Lisa asked, "Have you just told me, in a roundabout way, that your wife doesn't understand you?"

He laughed, genuinely amused. "On the contrary, she understands me only too well. I often feel like a pebble on the beach, scoured to its essential whiteness. Stripped. Bleached. I wonder if you understand what I mean?"

"Yes, I think so."

"I may be wrong, but I have the feeling that you, too, have been stripped, scoured and bleached, Mrs Hazell," he said wryly.

"What does your wife call you? Eddie? Ted?"

"No, she calls me Edward. Pamela doesn't believe in diminutives. By the same token, I always call her Pamela, never Pam."

The country lane had widened suddenly to disclose a

29

huddle of cottages clustered about a triangle of grass in the centre of which lay a dew-pond.

"This is a favourite place of mine," Edward explained; "the reason why I brought you here." He smiled, opening the car door for her. "The pub's a tad old-fashioned, but I thought you'd prefer it." Clasping her elbow, he added, "If you like coal fires and horse-brasses, that is."

"I do." She smiled up at him. "I adore old-fashioned pubs with coal fires and horse-brasses. That should bracket me perfectly, Mr Miller."

"It does, Mrs Hazell." He grinned happily as they entered the bar-parlour and he guided her towards a bank of moth-eaten red velvet seats facing a circular table of Victorian vintage. "So what would you like to drink, Lisa?"

"Whisky and American dry ginger, please."

"You should have said port and lemon to complete the bracketing," he said teasingly, crossing towards the bar.

Laying her gloves and handbag on the table, looking at the man objectively as he ordered their drinks, asked to describe, in one word, the way he appeared to her at that moment, the chosen word would have been 'respectable'.

When he came back with the drinks, they looked across the table at one another, forming opinions.

Lisa said, apropos of nothing, "Do you remember the film, *Brief Encounter*?"

"Yes, of course. Doesn't everyone? Every moment of it remains indelibly stamped in my memories of the 1950's: being sent away to boarding school on a steam train: waving goodbye to my mother. I must have been all of eight years old at the time. I didn't see the film till years later, at the Odeon Cinema in Leicester Square, as I recall. Ten years later, at a rough guess. Why do you ask?"

"I can't help wondering why Celia Johnson fell in love with Trevor Howard in the first place," Lisa said wistfully, cradling her glass, "when she had so much going for her at home."

"But surely," Edward said eagerly, "that was the whole point, wasn't it? They simply found qualities in each other which they had missed, or never even realised existed until they found one another in that station buffet? Possibly Celia Johnson saw that nice husband of hers as a frightful bore."

"Perhaps, but they did the decent thing in the end, didn't they?"

"If you are trying to point out to me that doing the right thing in the end makes for a less complicated way of life, possibly you're right," he admitted. "But life is never that easy or uncomplicated. So tell me, Lisa, what are you really driving at?"

"Perhaps I'm just feeling guilty," she confessed, "sitting here with another woman's husband."

"I thought that might be it," he said quietly. "So why, if you felt that way, did you accept my invitation?"

Dishonesty never paid dividends to Lisa's way of thinking. What had she to lose that had not been irretrievably lost anyway?

"If you must know, I was dozing in a chair when you rang, and wasn't sharp enough to think up an excuse not to. You know, something valid like being on duty. Besides, I felt flattered that someone wanted to take me out for a drink."

Edward stubbed out one cigarette, and immediately lit another.

"Your wife is right," she said. "You do smoke too much."

He smiled. "I know, but this is a special occasion. Tonight is escape night, remember? I'd have probably ordered champagne, if the landlord stocked such a thing, which I doubt. Besides which, I'm too much of a coward. Can you imagine the headlines in the local press? 'Tax Collector loses Driving Licence. Tells the Court, It was the bubbly what done it, your honour'."

"Tax collector? Is that what you are?" Laughter bubbled up in Lisa.

31

"Yes. Why? What's so funny?" He too was laughing.

"When you were standing at the bar just now, I tried to sum up your appearance in one word. The word that sprang to mind was 'respectable'. How right I was. What could be more respectable than a tax collector?"

"It's a job," he said, "something I do to keep a roof over my head. It has no bearing on the way I think and feel. Do you believe, Mrs Hazell, that tax collectors have no soul?"

"I've never thought about it before."

"What did you imagine my doing for a living?"

"Oh, I don't know. I didn't get that far. An estate agent, perhaps. That's a nice respectable job. Or a solicitor. A curator. A – taxidermist."

"Tell me, Lisa. After we'd had tea together that day, did you think about me afterwards?"

"No, I didn't." Her laughter faded. "I'm sorry, but you did ask."

"And yet I thought about you. I couldn't get you out of my mind."

"Hardly surprising, since I'd made such a spectacle of myself. What a fool you must have thought me, a middle-aged woman throwing a tantrum in a busy thoroughfare."

"Except that it wasn't a – tantrum. Far from. You were just standing there, crying as if your heart would break. There must have been a reason. Please, won't you tell me why? I'd really like to know."

"I'd rather not talk about it! This is a pub, not a confessional. In any case, it's none of your business."

Gathering her belongings, she said, "I'd like to go now, if you don't mind. I *am* rather tired, and I have to be up early in the morning." She rose to her feet.

"Oh, God, Lisa, I'm sorry, I didn't mean to upset you."

"All right. No need to make a song and dance about it. People are looking at us, in case you hadn't noticed. The landlord, and those men playing dominoes by the fire."

In the car-park, Edward Miller said quietly, "Has it

occurred to you, Lisa, that I might just need someone to be on my side, also?"

"Of course." Her anger was subsiding. "I'm sorry too. I over-reacted. It's just that – on the day in question – when we had tea together, I'd come up against something I couldn't cope with, and I still can't." Laying her hand on his sleeve, she said, gently, "It's not your fault. In any case, you have someone on your side, haven't you? Your wife? Pamela?"

They drove back to Bay View in comparative silence; bade each other a strained and formal good-night.

Later, in bed, tossing and turning, unable to sleep, Lisa recalled the country pub with its horse-brasses and roaring coal fire; the old men playing dominoes; the landlord polishing glasses; the red plush seats and Victorian tables, and – Edward Miller, a decent man who had been kind to her; whose kindness she had thrown back in his face; towards whom she had been both dismissive and cruel when she had said, "In any case, you have someone on your side, haven't you? Your wife? Pamela?"

She hadn't meant to be cruel, but she had sensed, at that moment, his withdrawal. Her fault, not his, because of John Hazell. Because she felt incapable of pinning her faith on one man ever again.

Chapter Four

Opening his eyes, stirring restlessly in his first moments of wakefulness, Edward Miller thought about Lisa; remembered every word they had spoken the night before; their laughter; the way she had looked in her grey two-piece suit and pink polo-neck sweater; softly plump and pretty, eyes accentuated with a trace of blue-grey eyeshadow, lipstick matching exactly the colour of her sweater.

Then, unforgivably, he had pried into her private life, and their evening together had ended on a sour note, which he deeply regretted. Why the hell hadn't he kept quiet?

Listening to his wife's regular breathing, feeling the soft weight of her sleeping body next to his, he lay rigid so as not to disturb her, knowing the moment she awoke the house would begin to crack smartly under her dominating influence.

He could visualise her, even now, sitting at the breakfast table making a list of all the things she must attend to during the day, and whatever went on to that list would be done with frightening efficiency.

Knowing Pamela, he would come home this evening after work to a house pervaded with the scent of well-cooked food, a tastefully appointed table with a crackling white tablecloth and polished silverware. There would be clean towels in the bathroom, a fresh tablet of soap, clean underwear in his dressing table drawers, a row of pristine, well-ironed shirts in his part of the wardrobe.

He wondered what her reaction would be if she knew he

had lied to her last night. And yet he felt no deep sense of guilt that he had spent the evening with another woman. He was not, by nature, a philanderer. He had simply wanted to see Lisa again; to feel warm and relaxed in her company.

Pamela seldom relaxed, nor did she allow him to do so. In her book, it was up to him to keep the fabric of the house in good repair; to mend what needed mending, paint what needed painting; fix loose tiles and clean out the gutters; mow the grass, weed the borders and stake up the flowers.

Maintenance of the car she lumped in with the house, so that he was kept constantly on his toes, at weekends and on fine summer evenings, fixing, tinkering, mowing and mending.

Never, during twenty-odd years of marriage, had he known a deep-seated feeling of peace within his own four walls. If only, just once in a while, he might come home from work to find the house in an uproar; dust on the furniture, flower petals strewn on the carpets, a heap of damp towels on the bathroom floor, and a smell of burning food from the kitchen.

Deep down, he envied at times his male colleagues' easy, affectionate relationships with their wives; couples who, in summertime, ate, alfresco, barbecued bangers and burgers, chops and chicken, washed down with wine, to the background accompaniment of the latest pop music beloved of their teenage sons and daughters.

In summertime, Ray Metcalf's, Rod Mead's and Barry Kean's wives, Maggie, Stella and Michelle, wore halter tops and shorts about the house and garden. Outgoing women, they flung clothes haphazardly into their washing-machines whatever the day of the week, Sundays included; stacked pots on the draining-board to dry; fed their respective husbands packaged meals from the local supermarket which they whizzed round, as per instructions, in their microwave ovens, to Pamela's disgust, who regarded such women as sluts.

35

"Really, Edward," she had said scornfully when he mentioned his colleagues' free and easy lifestyle, "I'd rather die than serve you a makeshift meal! Convenience food indeed! It's a woman's duty to provide her husband with well-balanced, home-cooked food rich in the essential vitamins!"

Now, lying flat on his back, staring up at the ceiling, Edward thought about his daughter, Judy, who had filled his life with love and laughter until she went away, six months ago, to a teacher-training college in Birmingham, and knew he was lost, just as surely as Lisa Hazell was lost in the whirlpool of life.

Lisa!

Last night, he had lied to his wife so convincingly, in order to meet Mrs Hazell, that Pamela, who thought she knew him so well, had swallowed that lie hook line and sinker. Not without grumbling, of course.

It wasn't right, she'd complained, that his office work should impinge on his time off. He wasn't an office boy to have his Sunday evening interfered with in such a mandatory fashion. Furthermore, if he organised his work better during the week, there would be no need for him to work overtime.

"I'm sorry, Pamela," he'd said placatingly, "it's just that a somewhat sticky tax-fiddle has come to light."

They'd been having lunch at the time – topside of beef and tureens of undercooked vegetables – when Pamela had asked him, point blank, what on earth was the matter with him – and so he'd lied to her deliberately – not even certain that Lisa would agree to go out with him that evening; simply hoping and praying that she would.

Having lied, he had watched, with a feeling of revulsion, the way Pamela's well-filled front teeth had bitten into the topside of beef, wondering why the hell she didn't have dentures instead of fillings? Why cling, at any cost, to what she deemed 'natural' even when Nature clamoured for assistance?

36

For the same reason, he imagined, that when Judy was born, she had pushed away the analgesic mask in order to suffer the full pain of their daughter's entry into the world – in order to make him suffer also, because he hadn't played the game according to the rules.

Suddenly, as though he had heard her eyelids click open, Edward knew that his wife was awake.

"Edward," she said, "what time is it?"

"Seven-thirty."

"Have you been awake long?"

"Twenty minutes or so."

"Then why aren't you up and doing?"

"There's time yet," he said.

Pamela sighed impatiently. "That is so typical of you, Edward," she reprimanded him. "You might have been up and doing ages ago; might have started the week with something in hand."

Something in hand! Thinking of Lisa, he longed suddenly to have her there beside him, smiling up at him, warm, loving and relaxed, to feel the touch of her lips on his.

His male instincts fully aroused, in urgent need of fulfilment, of release from his agony of desire, blindly he entered the body of his wife; heard her sharp intake of breath as he jerked rhythmically towards his climax.

"Really, Edward," Pamela said accusingly, "at this hour of the morning!" And he knew, turning away from her, that what he had just done to her was unforgivable, a desecration of her sleep-cleansed mind and spirit.

Now Pamela was in the bathroom, presumably ridding herself of all traces of his body fluid.

Sick at heart, pressing the palms of his hands against his eyes, Edward wished to God that Pamela had not awakened when she did; that Lisa, not his wife, had experienced the full tide of his passion.

*   *   *

"Still interested?" Mrs Hannersley asked Lisa, shaving parsnips.

"Interested?" Lisa's pulse quickened.

"In the flat. Had you forgotten?"

"No, I hadn't forgotten." Life had put a curb-rein on showing too much enthusiasm.

"Well, I saw my brother about the flat yesterday," the cook continued, "and I was right about the young couple moving to a council house." Plopping the parsnips into a pan of cold water, she continued, "It's not all that big, mind you. Only three rooms, a bed-sitting room, bathroom and kitchen." Adding salt to the water, she said, "Right up under the eaves. Personally, I don't care for sloping ceilings. Give me nice square rooms any day of the week."

"I like being high up in the world," Lisa said quickly. Dear God, she thought, remember me? Remember my confirmation? The girl in the white dress? If You do, Lord, then please let me get this flat.

Mrs Hannersley's soliloquy continued. "Happen you'll need an oxygen mask and a couple of sherpas. Seventy stairs! That's a lot of stairs. And it'll cost a bob or two to keep warm. Still, it could be made nice. Young folk haven't got much idea when it comes to furnishing. It's all flim-flam nowadays. Posters on the walls instead of pictures. 'Course there's bound to be a lot of folk after it, but Jake said he'd give you first refusal, if you're really interested, that is. Or have I put you off? Me and my big mouth!"

"No, you haven't put me off. I really am interested. Did your brother say when . . ."

"The young couple will be moving? No, he didn't. Not definitely. Shouldn't be all that long now, though. The lass is in her eighth month, with blood pressure, poor thing. Tell you what, I'll give you Jake's phone number. Best give him a ring. He'll be able to tell you more than I can."

"Yes, I'll do that. And thank you, Mrs Hannersley. You don't know how much this means to me."

"I just hope you won't be disappointed, that's all. What I mean is, I hope it will be good enough for you. Truth to tell, I always hated those attic rooms, even as a kid."

Later that day, Lisa telephoned Jake Colby.

"Yes?" The voice sounded laconic.

"My name is Lisa Hazell. I'm ringing about the flat."

"Oh yes. My sister said you'd be ringing. I expect you'd like to look at it."

"Yes. When? I mean, when would it be convenient?"

"Let's see now. Today's Monday. The young couple are moving out on Thursday. Shall we say Saturday?"

"That will suit me fine. What time?"

"Three o'clock?"

"Yes."

"Right, see you then."

"And the address?"

"Sand Place. Number 10. Do you know it?"

"No, but I'll find it. Thank you, Mr Colby. Thank you very much."

Gazing out of his office window, Edward saw heads bobbing along the main street; shop assistants on their way to work; visitors making the most of the early morning sunshine.

A seagull settled on a chimney-pot. Edward liked seagulls; envied their range and freedom. How marvellous it must be to rise up into a cloudless blue sky and drift, on silent air currents, over the shimmering herring-shoals far out at sea; to follow in the wake of some thumping-enginged trawler butting against the tide; to snigger contempt for the human race from a peach-coloured chimney-pot.

Sighing, he wondered what the hell had come over him; why this sudden affection for seagulls?

39

Pamela had served his bacon and eggs in complete silence, her lips grimly pursed. No need to ask why. He had not played the marriage game according to the rules. Sexual intercourse first thing on a Monday morning was not on, according to Pamela, nor, wishfully at any other day of the week, at *their* age!

He had deeply shocked her, and he was sorry. How she must have loathed the entire incident: the unloosening of his pyjama cord, the weight of his body on hers, his lack of self-control. And she was right. He had behaved abominably, and he knew it.

"Morning, Ted," Barry Kean poked his head round the door, "been here all night?"

Edward grinned. "How did you guess?"

"Had a good weekend?"

"Not bad. And you?"

"Great, just great! Michelle and I had friends over from Manchester. I've only just sobered up, truth to tell. Or have I? We had one helluva party on Saturday night, believe me. Well, you know Michelle. Any excuse for a rave-up!"

Edward's secretary arrived at that moment, very crisp and efficient, white-bloused and blooming. "Good-morning, Mr Miller," she said cheerfully, "isn't this a lovely day?"

"I walked to work this morning," Edward said proudly.

"My word. Feeling fit, were you?"

"No, but I thought I might if I walked."

Miss Smith uncovered her typewriter. She liked her boss, and this seemed like an especially good day, with the sun shining and everyone in a good humour.

"Letters," she announced briskly, when the postman had been.

"Anything important?" Edward looked up at her expectantly.

She smiled conspiratorially, knowing what he meant. "There's a personal letter with a Birmingham postmark. I've placed it on top of the pile."

"Thank you, Miss Smith."

When she had gone, he settled down to read the letter, savouring the opening words, '*My darling Daddy*,' . . . He could almost see his daughter's vivid, adorable face bending over the closely-written pages, her hair falling about her shoulders in a golden cloud.

Judy's official letters home always began: '*Dear Mummy and Dad,*' and went on, stiltedly, to explain about her forthcoming exams, which tutors she liked as opposed to those she did not, or her 'digs', meaning her rented room on the outskirts of Birmingham, not the archaeological variety.

"If she means lodgings, why on earth doesn't she say so?" Pamela would comment testily, clicking her tongue at her daughter's inexact terminology. "One would think she was living in the middle of a field surrounded by pot-shards and flint arrow-heads, not an ordinary room in a common-or-garden boarding house."

"Oh, for heaven's sake, Pamela, the girl's nineteen, not ninety: living in the present, not the past!"

"Oh, trust you to take her side! You always have done since the day she was born!" Then would come the usual period of silence, a sure and certain sign that he was in the 'dog-house' yet again.

But Judy's secret letters to her father revealed, to Edward's delight, all the things she had left unsaid in her letters home. The way she had felt, for instance, listening to a Chopin Recital on Radio Three – 'like a boiled sweet with a soft chewy centre', as the notes cascaded into her consciousness, making her want to cry because of its sheer perfection; followed by funny anecdotes about college life – all the things that made Judy what she was: a tender young woman poised on the brink of life, almost ready to spread her wings and fly . . .

In his return letter to his daughter, Edward would tell her about the seagull, but not about Lisa. How could a

41

father possibly tell his child that he had fallen in love with another woman?

No use pretending that it hadn't happened, because it *had*. Exactly why or when remained a mystery. All he knew was that he must ring her again as soon as possible; tell her how sorry he was that he had attempted to pry into her past life.

Picking up the telephone, he dialled the number of The Bay View Hotel.

A woman answered the call – Mrs Fogarty, at a rough guess. He said brusquely, "The Tax Office here. I wish to speak to a Mrs Hazell. Is she available?"

"Yes. Hang on just a minute."

When Lisa's voice came on the line, Edward said quietly, "I'm sorry about last night. I had no right whatever to pry into your past life the way I did. Please say you've forgiven me. It will never happen again, I promise. All I'm asking is a fair chance of survival; a chance to explain."

"I'm not sure." Mrs Fogarty was standing feet away from the phone, listening intently; pretending not to. Personal calls were frowned upon.

"Is someone listening?" Edward asked.

"Yes."

"Are you still angry with me?"

"No, I don't think so."

"I mustn't make things more difficult for you. I just wanted to apologise."

"Yes, I see. Well, thank you for ringing."

"What was all that about?" Mrs Fogarty wanted to know.

"Oh, just a query. Nothing important."

Chapter Five

"John! I wish you'd come in! Lunch has been ready over half an hour!"

"Oh, *blast*! All right, I'm coming!"

The trouble was, the garden was far too big, and he hadn't time to waste on it.

Eating lunch at one o'clock was a new fad of Linda's now their son was old enough to sit up and take notice. "It's all very well grown-ups eating when they feel like it," she'd said sanctimoniously, "but a child needs the security of a regular timetable."

Having stripped the borders of antirrhinums, straightening his back and wiping his neck with a towel, John marched indoors, irritably aware of all the school-work that needed seeing to; that he had only one clear day ahead of him in which to prepare lessons and atune his mind to the mental run-up of the new term.

Miles was already seated in his high-chair, banging expectantly with his spoon.

When John had washed his hands, Linda bustled the food on the table. "Why the hell you wear yourself to a frazzle pulling up flowers before they're dead, I can't understand," she grumbled. "Why plant the damn things in the first place? Besides, there'll be heaps more time to get the garden into shape before the end of October."

"There won't be any time at all when school starts."

"Don't talk so daft! Oh, what's the use? Let's eat. You

give Miles his mashed potatoes and gravy whilst I cut up his meat and carrots."

Watching solemnly, the child wangled his spoon on to his plate, and banged it down suddenly, splattering the gravy, scoring a direct hit on his father's face and sweater.

"*Blast*! Now look what he's done!"

The child crowed his delight.

Linda's sharp, pixie face flushed with annoyance. "For heaven's sake, John, a bit of gravy won't hurt! Here, let me!" She dabbed his face and sweater with a paper serviette. "I don't know what's come over you lately! Ever since we came back from Westsea, you've been like a bear with a sore head; cursing and blinding for no good reason! Well, I'm sick of it! So just shut up and let's get on with our meal, shall we?"

But anger never lasted long with Linda. Ruffling John's hair, winding her arms around his neck, she coaxed, "Come on, petty-pooh," in her 'baby' voice, "don't be cwoss. It's such a boo'full day."

Even so, John ate his lunch in aggrieved silence, conscious, not for the first time, of the age difference between them. Was it possible that he seemed – old – to her; as Lisa had seemed old to him?

Aware of a deep feeling of unrest, perhaps it had been a mistake to stay on in this damned cottage, he thought. But when he'd suggested moving to a modern house nearer the school, Linda had been up in arms at the very idea; as if the cottage possessed a deep-seated fascination for her which she had never explained to his satisfaction.

"But Johnny," she'd said excitedly, running her tongue over her lips, "the country air is so good for Miles, and I'd never know a moment's peace of mind if we moved. Think of all the town traffic. Besides, where would he play? In some grotty park or other?"

Some grotty park or other? The park, perhaps, in which their first clandestine meetings had taken place; in which,

44

uncaring of his wife, his job, his conscience, he had held Linda in his arms, rejoicing in her youth and charm; the way her dark, bobbed hair had swung about her cheeks; the way her pointed breasts had pushed against the fabric of the neat white blouses she had worn on those summer evenings – what seemed a lifetime ago. Wanting her so much, he could not have cared less about his wife, his career, or his conscience.

Now, the careless mistress had turned into a calculating wife and mother.

Having finished with his lamb, carrots and mash, Miles set up a wail, wanting something different. Immediately, Linda got up to remove his dish and spoon, crooning baby talk in the boy's ear, saying, "Who wants his 'nanas and custard, then?"

"You should make him wait," John said sourly.

"Don't be so petty! He's a child, not an elder statesman!"

"Even so, you're spoiling him to death, giving into him at every turn."

After lunch, John wandered through to the drawing room. Autumn sunshine slanted on the dust lying thickly on the furniture. Miles' toys were scattered in confusion on the carpet.

When challenged about the disorderly state of the cottage, Linda would say defensively that a home was meant to be lived in, not understanding that he could not work properly in a cluttered atmosphere.

"How come you are so faddy about mealtimes?" he had asked her. "So disorganised when it comes to keeping the house clean and tidy?"

"Because there are more important things in life than dusting and polishing all day long," she shot back at him.

"What, for instance?"

"Taking Miles to the clinic, for one thing; washing

45

and ironing your bloody shirts for another! Shopping and cooking. The trouble with you, Johnny, you think that things just – happen! Our son's quite a handful, or hadn't you noticed?"

Leaving his school work unattended, John delved in the garden until dusk, when Linda called him indoors for tea – a fireside meal of sandwiches, scones and shop-bought cake – after which, parking Miles on his lap, she went upstairs to run the child's bathwater.

It was then that John Hazell realised that his son's eyes, staring up at him, were Linda's eyes, not his; that the child was all hers, as if he had played little or no part whatsoever in the boy's conception.

"Come on then, darling." Picking up the child from his father's arms; cradling his head against her shoulder, she said, "Who's a tired boy, then? Never mind, nice warm bath all ready and waiting, then off to bed-i-byes."

Half an hour later, John went upstairs to say good-night to his son, but the child was already fast asleep, clutching his teddy bear, and Linda was busy gathering up the child's socks, vest and romper-suit; stuffing the next day's washing into the Ali-Baba basket in the bathroom.

When she had finished her tidying-up, standing beside John, she slipped her arm round his waist. Looking down at their sleeping child, she said huskily, "He's beautiful, isn't he?"

"Yes, he is."

Strangely moved, John imagined, for one fleeting moment, that he, Linda and their child were not alone; that someone else was there with them – a ghost from the past – watching them from the shadowy corners of the room. His common sense told him that it was merely an illusion; a whisper from the past invoked by the rising wind beyond the cottage windows; the rattling of the panes; a trick of moonlight shining on the glass.

"Darling." Linda paused, but he knew what she was about to say. "You know we agreed? Two children at least, and close together. I think we've waited long enough, don't you?"

In a blinding moment of despair, John Hazell knew that he was not cut out for fatherhood; never had been, never would be . . .

"Johnny darling," Linda whispered, "you know how much I want another child. Not next year or the year after, but *now*!"

Clinging to the sleeve of his sweater, she led him towards their bedroom . . .

Their lovemaking over, lying on his back, staring up at the ceiling, listening to the wind raking the cottage, the rustling of that arabesque of ivy above the front porch, he thought about Lisa; remembered that he had found nothing kind to say to her that day in Westsea; had not even bothered to call her on the telephone.

'And I have something to expiate –
A pettiness . . .'

The new phase of building at Railsford Comprehensive was underway.

Getting out of the car on the first morning of the new term, John regarded, with something akin to loathing, the pre-cast cement blocks and bubbled fascias; the contractors' lorries littering the driveway; remembered, with a deep sense of loss, the ancient stonework and soaring pinnacles of Oxford, pink blossom and mullioned windows, smooth green lawns; lilac blowing against a blue sky in Maytime; knowing that unforgettably lovely phase of his life would never come again.

"Morning, sir."

"Morning." Mechanically he returned the greetings of the older students, wishing this first day of term was over and

47

done with – assembly, the headmaster spouting on about effort and diligence; a new term, a new beginning.

Entering the old building, he wondered why this feeling of irritability seldom left him these days. Irritability linked to a sourness of spirit, a deep-seated sense of frustration akin to coming second in a race he could have won if he'd tried harder.

In the assembly hall, listening to the droning of the headmaster's voice, he experienced a feeling of wanting to run headlong towards some far-flung horizon, expending every ounce of his physical energy along the way, arriving exhausted yet exhilarated, to discover a different horizon ahead of him.

Making love to Linda in the first flush of their affair, when his body and emotions were at full stretch, he had achieved a peak of sexual fulfilment hitherto unknown. Afterwards had come an inescapable feeling of disappointment; the realisation that there were no other horizons ahead of him to conquer, that his glorious energy had been expended to no real purpose.

His feeling of unfulfilment, with Lisa, had stemmed from her inability to bear his child, or so he had thought at the time. Now he thought differently.

True enough, when Miles had been conceived, he had experienced, at first, a wild sensation of joy. Watching the thickening of Linda's body, feeling the child kicking lustily inside her had seemed the ultimate goal.

Then Linda had become involved in what he saw as the trivia of childbearing; preoccupied with the clearing out and decoration of the spare room as a nursery. Bitter arguments had ensued when he utterly refused to go shopping with her to choose the wallpaper and furniture.

"Oh for God's sake, Johnny, you've *got* to come with me," Linda had stormed at him. "No way am I going shopping on my own! Anyone would think you didn't care! Well, if you don't, *I* do! I care very much that our child has a proper place to sleep, with lots of pretty things to look at; mobiles, and that kind of thing. And what about the pram? If you think I'm going into Mothercare to choose the pram on my own, you have another think coming!"

The facile aspect of fatherhood had never even occurred to him. He had not given a passing thought to the fact that, once born, the embryo in his wife's womb would need to be fed, bathed, dressed, and wheeled about in a perambulator.

Obsessed with the child's conception, he had harboured a strange notion of wanting it born, gypsy fashion, in a ditch, beneath a night sky brilliant with stars; wrapped in a blanket and put to the breast beside a glowing campfire.

Meanwhile, Linda had started prenatal classes at the local clinic; swallowing vitamin pills, and sprawling on the settee reading endless magazines on baby care; prattling on about names for the infant; driving him mad with her plebeian attitudes to the miracle taking place inside her.

One night, when he had tried to explain to her his deep, secret desire to deliver the child himself; his love of the simple, Romany way of life, she had laughed herself hysterical.

"You mean that you want me to have my baby in some bloody ditch with you as the midwife? You're crackers! Plain bloody bonkers!" Then, knowing him as well as she thought she did, she had climbed aboard his lap, smothered his face with kisses, ruffled his hair, and exhorted him not to be "cwoss" with her, and he had been unable to equate the bloated figure of his wife with that of the slender girl who had once pressed her eager body against his in an agony of desire; wanting his love beneath the trees in the park.

Later, as her pregnancy progressed, came a dull, persistent feeling of jealousy that her finely-honed body was no longer his. The child he had given her had taken over, leaving no room for him; making him feel shut out, lost, rejected. Lonely.

He had seen his child born – not beneath the stars but

in the delivery room of the local hospital, with masked nurses in attendance, and he had felt as expendable as a spare bridegroom at a wedding, an interloper in a game that only women could play.

Next morning, visiting the hospital, bearing flowers, he had discovered his wife sitting up in bed, bright-eyed and bushy-tailed, surrounded with flowers and congratulation cards, apparently forgetful of her travail the night before, just as she had forgotten her mockery the night he shared with her his vision of a campfire beneath the stars.

A crazy idea, perhaps, not to be taken literally, simply his way of expressing his hatred of the obvious – the herding together of pregnant women in prenatal clinics; the choosing of wallpaper and furniture for a special room in the house, as far removed from the miracle of procreation as the sun from the moon.

Linda may have forgotten. He hadn't.

Assembly over, he walked seemingly endless corridors to his classroom, remembering Lisa, that, with her, he had never played second fiddle to another human being.

Linda loved parties; entertaining. Lisa had been protective of his privacy, so much so that he had, at times, resented their interdependence on one another; that gentle rhythm of life which had trapped him into feeling that death might claim him before he had even begun to live; his passage through the world leaving no footprints in the sand, no shadows on the grass.

Entering the classroom, he inhaled the familiar warm armpits smell of the girls, the curiously offensive scent of the randy young males seated at their desks, and knew, as he began calling the register, that their minds were closed against him as surely as Linda's had been ever since the day he had placed his weddingring on her finger.

Returning to the cottage after school, exhausted with all the heat, noise and frustration of the first day of term, he walked into the kitchen to find three young females, complete with offspring, drinking tea and nibbling chocolate biscuits; Linda dispensing tea with Miles on her lap, a fourth young mother, on a chair in the corner, blouse awry, breastfeeding her infant.

Humiliated beyond belief, he marched through to the drawing room without a word.

Half an hour later, Linda flung herself into the room in a towering rage. "Just who the hell do you think you are?" she demanded hoarsely. "How *dare* you treat my friends that way?"

"Friends?" he said bitterly. "Is that what you call them? More an overspill from the antenatal clinic if you ask me!"

"So what if they are? Look, John, I need to communicate with women of my own age!"

"You call that communicating? Filling my home with a lazy lot of hangers-on and their screaming brats? Is it really too much to ask that I should come home to a modicum of peace and quiet after a hard day's work?"

"So what do you suggest? Tell me, John, I'd really like to know. Should we put up a barbed wire fence with a 'Private. No Entry' notice in red paint? Or perhaps you'd rather I entered a nunnery?"

"Don't be so ridiculous!"

"Oh? Ridiculous now, am I? Yeah, well that figures! I must have been a croissant short of a continental breakfast to have married you in the first place! I'm beginning to wish now that I hadn't. And to think that I gave up a good job . . . Moreover, in case you've forgotten, Mr High and Mighty, this is my home too, so put that in the loo and pull the handle!"

An hour later, going through to the kitchen, he found her waltzing round the room with Miles in her arms, singing a snatch of 'Sur le pont d'Avignon', her anger forgotten, setting the table for tea.

Then, pushing the child's face close to his to be kissed, she taunted childishly, "Diddums have a cwoss-patch for a Daddy, then? And diddums Mummy have a cwoss-patch for a hubby?"

The meal over – fish fingers, mashed potatoes and frozen peas – standing alone in the garden, John Hazell knew that he was trapped by Linda's youth and energy, her refusal to take him seriously. Above all, by her physical demands on him; wanting love all the time. Another child; more children . . . The thought of Linda becoming pregnant with even a second child, dismayed him; the recurring ritual of the prenatal clinic; the magazines, the vitamin pills: the final horror of the delivery ward with all its blood, sweat and tears.

Walking a little way in the pellucid evening air, he came at last to the little plot of earth beneath a lilac tree, where Lisa had buried their cat, Psyche.

Such a charming, well-behaved little cat, he recalled, experiencing a soul-shattering tug of regret that he had let go of Lisa so easily, so unthinkingly, not understanding how much she had meant to him until – now.

Chapter Six

At three o'clock precisely, Lisa raised the heavy iron knocker of Number 10 Sand Place. She had waited until the church clock chimed the hour, experiencing a superstitious dread of being a minute early or late for her appointment.

A tall man opened the door. The first thing she noticed about him was his hair, grey and abundant, brushed back from his deeply tanned face. He was wearing an Arran sweater, the sleeves pushed up to his elbows, revealing his sinewy forearms. She smiled uncertainly. "I'm Lisa Hazell," she said.

He nodded briefly. "Jake Colby. Come in."

The passage was stone-flagged, much wider than she had expected, with a curving, iron-spindled staircase, the landing lit by a tall, uncurtained Georgian window.

"Oh, how lovely," she uttered breathlessly.

"The houses in this row were built for seafaring men; master mariners and the ship-building fraternity," Colby explained. "Men with plenty of money, and servants to look after them."

"The panelling's exquisite."

"Yes, but you'll notice it disappears after the second landing. Perhaps the architects thought servants didn't deserve panelling, only plaster. In any case, the poor devils wouldn't have cared much on their way to bed with their candles, I reckon."

Leading the way upstairs, "I should take a deep breath if I were you," he advised. "As you can see, this was no place for a pregnant young woman. In any case, the flat is only suitable for one person. Well, this is it."

Lisa looked at the white door, the one she had dreamed of. But what lay behind it? Mustn't get too excited. Dreams so seldom measured up to reality. Or was it the other way round? She wasn't thinking clearly.

Colby unlocked the door, opened it and stood aside for her to enter.

She was standing on the threshold of a long room with sloping ceilings; french windows opening on to a balcony at the far end of the apartment, and with bookshelves flanking a low, stone fireplace.

"Oh," she uttered bemusedly, "it's lovely! And a balcony! May I?"

"Sure, go ahead. It's built over a flat roof, and I put up the guard-rail myself, so it's as safe as houses. And the view's not bad, if you care for the sea, that is."

Standing with her hands on the guard-rail, Lisa saw the whole of Westsea Bay spread before her bedazzled eyes; the shimmering of sunlight on water, and heard the changeless beat of the waves on the shore.

Looking down, she saw the harbour, like a painted toy, far below, the raking masts of yachts in the outer marina pointing upward like a forest of leafless trees; the lighthouse on the fish-pier – for all the world like a white exclamation mark poised on its rocky peninsula.

With fast-beating heart, she noticed the red pantiled roofs of the fishermen's cottages tumbling in confusion about the narrow cobbled streets of the Old Town; a colourful chequer-board of gardens with washing strung out to dry; seagulls swooping about the decks of the fishing boats hawsered alongside the harbour walls.

Looking up, she saw the magnificent terrace of Victorian houses crowning the cliff tops overlooking the bay with its sweeping crescent of tawny sand; the lower promenade with its amusement arcades and ice-cream parlours.

"Well, what do you think of it?" Colby asked, watching her intently.

"I think . . ." But she couldn't speak coherently at that moment for the lump in her throat – as if she had swallowed a ping-pong ball. "It's very – nice," she managed eventually.

"This room isn't bad, I grant you," Colby said laconically, "but the kitchen isn't up to much; neither is the bathroom. A matter of trying to fit a quart into a pint pot. Want to take a look?"

She nodded.

He opened doors. "As you can see, they're both a bit narrow, with skylight windows, but there's a modern sink-unit in the kitchen, plenty of cupboard space, and a shower-unit in the bathroom, plus a hand-basin and so on."

"Yes, I see." Lisa cleared her throat, swallowed the ping-pong ball. "Er, how much?" she enquired nervously.

When he told her, her face fell, her lower lip quivered slightly. "I'll have to think about it," she said. "I'm sorry, Mr Colby, but I daren't bite off more than I can chew. You understand?"

Regarding her levelly, he said, "The sum I mentioned is inclusive of heating, rates and so on. So there would be no added extras."

"*Really*?" She looked at him in amazement. "But that means . . ."

"You'll take it?" he suggested quietly.

"Oh, *yes*, Mr Colby! You see – it's difficult to explain – but I've fallen in love with it! Everything about it – as if I somehow belong here!"

A private, taciturn man, he said gruffly, "Fair enough, then, if you want it, it's yours. Now, about furniture and so on. My sister tells me that you have your own belongings – carpets, curtains and so forth – in store for the time being. Am I right? In which case we'll need to set a firm date for the removal. Is your furniture stored locally, by the way?"

"No, in a place called Wheatford, a small country town

in the Midlands, where I lived once with my Aunt Grace who died recently. But that's a long story, I'm afraid. Most of my furniture belonged to her, but I have my own books, pictures and so on."

"Books?"

"Yes. You see, I was once a librarian, before I came to Westsea to live."

"Just as well, then, that I built those bookshelves in the sitting room," he said, as they walked down the curving staircase together.

At the front door, Lisa asked anxiously, "I'll let you know, shall I, when my furniture will arrive?" not quite believing her turn of fortune.

"Yes," Jake Colby said off-handedly, "give me a call when you know the removal date, and not to worry, I never go back on my word." He closed the door firmly behind her.

Walking downhill towards the seafront, lost in thought, she turned at the sound of her name. "Edward," she said, smiling, absurdly pleased to see him again, "what are you doing here?"

"I've been to that DIY shop near the market, buying paint. Have you time for a cup of tea?"

"Yes, it's my afternoon off."

"How's 'The Windmill' today? Still open?"

"Rather! Can-Can dancers in full bloom; red feather boas, sequins, the lot!"

"No burden of bread today?"

"I nipped out when Mrs Fogarty wasn't looking."

"You seem remarkably happy today, Mrs Hazell."

"I've just had the most amazing stroke of luck."

"Tell me about it," he said, steering her into a café.

"I've found an unfurnished flat to rent."

"But that's practically unheard of these days. Where is it? Tell me, what's it like?"

"It feels like home," she said simply. "Now I'm beginning to wonder what I've let myself in for. I didn't really stop to think."

"What is there to think about?"

"If the time I'll spend there will justify the expense."

"Assuming you remain at Bay View?" he said, ordering tea for two, and lighting a cigarette.

"I can't afford not to," she said, cupping her chin in her hands, gazing at the sea beyond the promenade railings. "It's a steady, permanent job. On the other hand . . ." She spoke haltingly of her dream of taking a sabbatical; living on lentils, potatoes and porridge.

Thinking how lovely she looked, studying her face, noticing the way her hair curved on to her forehead, her softly contoured cheekbones and sensitive mouth, "That's a marvellous idea," he said.

"No it isn't! It's a mad idea!"

"But isn't it nice to have – mad ideas now and then?" He smiled at her encouragingly.

"But the way things are going right now, with inflation and so on, I might land myself in an awful mess."

"You could always look for another job."

"Well yes, and I *have* tried, believe me, but librarians' jobs are thin on the ground right now. Besides, how to explain? I feel safe at Bay View. I like the old people, and I think they like me."

Pouring the tea when it arrived, and stubbing out his cigarette, he said, "Forgive my saying so, Lisa, but identifying too closely with old people may not be a wise thing to do."

"You don't understand; how could you? I lived with an older person most of my life, until . . . Well, never mind, it isn't important. Besides, I'm not young myself any more."

"That's nonsense, and you know it! From where I'm sitting, you are a lovely woman in the prime of life," Edward assured her. "As a matter of fact, you remind

57

me of my daughter, Judy, and she's not exactly long in the tooth."

"I didn't realise you had a – daughter." Lisa froze inwardly, unable to bear the thought that Edward was not only married, but a father.

"She's at a teacher training college in Birmingham at the moment," he said fondly, with pride in his voice – the kind of pride betrayed by most parents when they spoke of their offspring.

"I think you'd like Judy," he continued mistily. "She's very pretty, quick, bright, intelligent . . ."

Then, noticing Lisa's withdrawal, realising that he had hurt her in some way, "Or perhaps you're not interested in young people? Children?"

"I've never had any, so I'm scarcely qualified to say!" Sick at heart, recalling all those negative tests she had undergone in the early days of her marriage, the consultant's opinion that she was too old to ever bear a child, she picked up her handbag, rose to her feet, and said stiffly, "I have to leave now, if you don't mind! I've just remembered something I'd forgotten. Thanks for the tea!"

"Oh God," he said contritely, "I've upset you again, haven't I?" How or why, he had no more idea than the Man in the Moon. "Please wait, Lisa. I'll give you a lift."

"No thanks, I prefer to walk."

Hastily paying the bill for the tea, he hurried after her. "I'm giving you a lift whether you like it or not," he said sharply, marching her towards his car by her elbow. "God, but you're a difficult person to understand. I thought we were friends, not enemies!"

"Why try to understand me at all?" she countered hostilely. "You have your own life to live; I have mine!"

"In other words, 'East is east and West is west, and never the twain shall meet'? Is that it? But we *have* met, Lisa, and, for better or worse, I shall never regret, for one moment, that day you came into my life."

Parking the car round the corner from Bay View, he leaned forward to open the door for her.

Much calmer now, she noticed the colour of his eyes, a deep grey blue; the worried expression on his face. "I'm sorry, Edward," she apologised. "I behaved badly just now, and I really am sorry. Please forgive me."

He smiled. "Forget it," he said dismissively. "Everyone behaves badly now and then, for whatever reasons."

He thought briefly of Pamela. If taking a woman against her will in the early hours of a Monday morning did not come into the category of bad behaviour, what did?

He said wistfully, like a small boy in need of hope that his pet mouse had not fallen prey to the cat next door, "Please, Lisa, say you'll meet me tomorrow night. Same time, same place?"

"Very well then. If you can put up with me."

Resisting a strong impulse to kiss him, she hurried round the corner and up the front steps of the Bay View Hotel.

"Edward! You've been like a cat on hot bricks all day," Pamela reprimanded him. "Not that I'm entirely surprised you're so jumpy, having to work last Sunday evening and again tonight! Either they are piling too much work on to you, or you are not fit to do it!"

"I'm perfectly fit, Pamela. I admit there's a lot piling up, but we're short-staffed at the moment, with Miss Smith on holiday and Barry Kean down with the flu."

"If you mean influenza, why not say so?" Clearing the luncheon table, Pamela mulled over the injustice of her husband having to work overtime because another member of staff had not had the foresight to embark on a course of cod liver oil capsules at the end of the summer season.

Folding the tablecloth, she continued, "It has occurred to me, Edward, that you should relinquish your chairmanship of the school governors. There are, after all, younger men than you willing and able to step into your shoes."

"Heaven's above, Pamela, I'm fifty, not ninety," Edward reminded her.

"All right, Edward. No need to shout! I'm not hard of hearing!"

At that moment, the thought of having sexual intercourse with his wife ever again made Edward feel physically ill. Not that she would care one iota if he never so much as kissed her on the cheek; never made love to her ever again.

On the other hand, he knew precisely how she would react to his moving into the spare room to sleep. Married people occupying separate bedrooms was simply not on, in Pamela's opinion, no matter how deep her loathing of the marriage-bed might be. They had married for better or worse. The worse, so far as he was concerned . . .

Going upstairs to bathe and change after a long Sunday afternoon in the garden, weeding and hoeing the borders, creosoting the fence and cleaning the car, Edward wondered what had happened to the eager, hopeful young man who, twenty-odd years ago, had proposed marriage to his boss's daughter, Pamela Gainsford. He must have been mad at the time. The set-up had been so obvious, and he had gone into the trap with his eyes wide open. Rupert Gainsford had been on the lookout for a son-in-law, and he had been the obvious choice.

Visiting the Gainsford home, near Leicester, for the first time, he had been struck by the size of it – the kind of country residence appearing in the pages of quarterly glossy magazines – set in well-matured grounds, with stabling to the rear of the house. Not that they kept horses any longer, Gainsford, bluff, hearty, reminiscent of a country squire rather than a civil servant, had assured Edward, showing him round the estate before luncheon.

The front steps were flanked by sandstone pillars; the hall was spacious with a broad staircase to the upper landings; the drawing room contained the requisite number of deep settees and armchairs, shaded lamps, side-tables, oil-paintings, ornaments and flower arrangements, and yet there was an air of desolation about the place which Edward could not fathom – until he met Gainsford's wife.

She was a statuesque woman with a sad, pale face, iron-grey hair scraped back in a bun, and eyes which registered the dull, inert apathy of an old animal whose days are numbered. She neither spoke nor smiled when Gainsford made the introduction, as if looking beyond him at some object invisible to other people's eyes.

"And this is our daughter Pamela." Gainsford had stretched out a hand to the girl who had just entered the room, a slightly built young woman with fair hair and doll-like features, wearing a cotton dress and a hand-knitted cardigan, who smiled vaguely and uttered a primly polite, "How do you do?"

Had she done otherwise, the story might have had a different ending, Edward considered, sluicing himself beneath the shower. Had she betrayed by a word or a glance that she regarded him as a prospective husband, he would probably have turned tail and fled.

Probing his emotions of that time, he realised there had been a hint of a challenge in her aloofness. Frankly, she had piqued his curiosity. Moreover, she had aroused in him a sense of protectiveness not displeasing to his male ego. The impression imparted by her was that of extreme self-containment linked to – freshness – the only word to describe her coolness. Everything about her was fresh and dainty – her clothes, her hair, the fragrance of oatmeal soap and eau-de-Cologne. All these things combined had sharpened his desire to break down her barrier of reserve.

God, he thought, stepping from the shower, it must have been more than an ego trip. Whatever, six months later he had proposed marriage and been accepted. Not that the wedding took place immediately. Mrs Gainsford had become seriously ill around Christmas of that year, and died the following spring.

Supporting Pamela throughout the trauma of her mother's illness and funeral had added towards Edward's sense of protectiveness towards her, especially in view of Gainsford's strangely dismissive attitude towards his daughter on the day of the funeral, combined with an air of scarcely suppressed – excitement – for want of a better word, which hardly fitted his role as a stricken widower paying his last respects to his wife.

The ensuing scandal had been hushed up remarkably well. So well that Edward had no clear idea, even now, what exactly had happened. Pamela would not speak of it. The fact remained that Gainsford had disappeared like a thief in the night, his deputy had taken over as head of department, and, at Pamela's request, he, Edward, had applied for a transfer to another town – Westsea, as it happened.

Rumour had it that Gainsford had stolen a great deal of money, a theory disproved when it became clear that he had been the sole beneficiary of his wife's estate, and he had already placed a 'For Sale' notice – 'Fine, well-maintained Georgian residence. Spacious entrance hall. Six bedrooms, three reception. Servants' quarters. Stabling' – and so on, in the pages of several glossy county magazines.

Shortage of cash had never been a problem in the Gainsford household, Edward realised, and he had pooh-poohed the idea that his prospective father-in-law would stoop to larceny in any shape or form; had said as much to Pamela. "Do you really think so?" had been her reply.

Later, it had become abundantly clear that the hushed up scandal of Gainsford's disappearance involved the wife of a local magistrate. This, Edward was fully prepared to believe, also to understand, having met the late Mrs Gainsford.

It was Pamela he had felt sorry for at the time. It had beggared belief that any father could treat his only child in such a way, leaving her homeless and virtually penniless.

shadow of doubt, why his father-in-law had done what he did. It was really a matter of escape, the 'do or die' chance of a lifetime to design a new and better way of living for himself and the woman he loved.

He said, rising from the tea-table, "Well, I'd best be on my way!" Guilt gnawed at him as he pecked Pamela's cheek, and departed.

When he had gone, Pamela cleared the table and went through to the kitchen to begin the washing up, overwhelmed by a deep-seated sense of depression which had worried her a great deal of late, so that even her home, in which she had hitherto felt safe and secure, failed to provide solace.

From time to time, during the past weeks, she had found herself wandering aimlessly from room to room, duster in hand, straightening pictures that did not need straightening; opening drawers and closing them again for no reason; picking up ornaments, looking at them curiously, as if she had never seen them before.

To her credit, Edward had not noticed, and she would rather die than confess to him the struggle she had, at times, to carry out all the tasks she set herself so uncompromisingly – the daily rituals of washing and ironing; cleaning silver; shopping and cooking.

Swishing suds into the washing up water, she caught sight of herself in a mirror near the sink. Never a vain woman, she would have normally glanced away and got on with her work. Judith had hung the mirror there because the light was good, near the kitchen window, for applying make-up – a vanity of which her mother had strongly disapproved. Not that Judith had cared tuppence. She had simply laughed and said lightheartedly, "Oh, Mummy, don't be so old-fashioned! Every girl wears make-up nowadays!"

Now, against her will, Pamela stared into the mirror, seeing herself as a stranger. How pale she was; how drawn. She had never noticed before the faint network of worry lines beneath her eyes, the dry flakiness of her skin or the colour of her hair. How quickly, she thought, it had faded from blonde to ash grey.

Uttering a low cry, she jerked the mirror from wall and flung it into the rubbish bin near the sink.

Edward drove away from the house feeling Pamela's resentment as an arrow between his shoulder-blades, experienced an overwhelming feeling of relief as he swung the car on to the main road and saw the lights of Westsea in the distance, like jewels in a casket, clustered against a backdrop of indigo sky.

Touched almost to tears by the beauty of the night, a man craving affection, he pushed to the back of his mind that he had lied to his wife for a second time within a week to meet Mrs Hazell, his lovely Lisa. To what end or purpose, he was not entirely sure. Nor did he really care. All he knew, for certain, was that he was deeply in love with her.

Parking round the corner from Bay View, he switched on the car radio, noticing the way the lights of the promenade splintered between the branches of the trees. He lit a cigarette, listening to the closing movement of Beethoven's Ninth Symphony, and waited until, minutes later, Lisa hurried down the steps of the hotel, glancing over her shoulder to make certain she had not been observed.

When she got into the car, "You must get out of that damned place at once," he said angrily. "I hate the thought of a proud, intelligent woman like you scuttling out of that bloody building like a fugitive from justice!"

Lisa had had a bad day. Preparing lunch, she had been aware of Mrs Fogarty's shadow at her elbow, as if the woman was trying deliberately to unnerve her. If so, she had succeeded. Even the Yorkshire puddings hadn't risen properly, as if the old witch had ill-wished them in the making. The whole of the morning, Mrs Fogarty had been in and out of the kitchen like an ill wind blowing nobody any good, fault-finding, nit-picking, clock watching. Now this . . .

"Proud? Intelligent?" she said scornfully, fastening her seat-belt. "Quite the opposite, I'd say."

Edward knew what she meant – an assignation with a married man.

They went to the same pub, sat at the same table, yet everything seemed different tonight. The fire was not burning as brightly and the old men had not yet gathered for their game of dominoes.

"We're early," Edward remarked, bringing their drinks to the table.

"And you mustn't be late back."

"Don't spoil the evening before it's begun." He poured dry ginger into her whisky. "Don't—"

"Make you feel more guilty than you already are?"

"All right, Lisa, you win! There must be a strong sadistic streak in you. Or is it masochism?"

"Bound to be one or the other."

"Why the hell did you come, then?"

"I don't know. I'm beginning to wish I hadn't." She was punishing this man because of John. A hollow, unworthy act of attrition, because he was *not* John.

This couldn't go on, Edward thought despairingly, this fencing with words. He said, simply, "I love you, Lisa."

The sharp sword of resistance sheathed, she stared at him, momentarily robbed of speech.

"I love you," he repeated, experiencing a surge of relief that he had found the courage to tell her, and felt the ebbing of his pent-up anger and frustration on this simple tide of truth.

"How could you possibly? Love me, I mean? You don't know the first thing about me; my past life . . ."

"You did warn me not to pry, and I accepted that. In any case, what I feel for you has nothing to do with your

67

past, nothing to do with my present circumstances. It's something I can't explain; wouldn't even try to explain even if I knew how."

"You're wrong," she said slowly. "The past has made me what I am today – a not very lovable person; touchy, suspicious, bloody-minded, intolerant – the result of a broken marriage, the burnt-out embers of a love affair I thought would last forever."

"Please, don't tell me if you'd rather not," Edward said quietly.

"Why not? You have a right to know about this person you say you're in love with. The fact is, I don't believe in love any more. I believe in self-preservation; survival – call it what you will – certainly not love, a word so glibly uttered; so seldom meant."

"Not in this case, Lisa. I really do love you."

"More or less than you love your daughter? Judy, that's her name, isn't it?"

"Judy?" Edward frowned. "But a father's love for his child is a different thing entirely," he continued. "Surely you must see that?"

"And your wife? Pamela, what about her?"

"Let's just say that I married the wrong woman, you married the wrong man, and leave it at that, shall we?"

"That's just it," Lisa said dully. "I *didn't* marry the wrong man. I married the only man in the world for me."

The door opened at that moment, and three old men shuffled into the pub for their game of dominoes; country men, villagers, wearing flat caps and ancient tweed jackets hanging loosely about a variety of thick, hand-knitted jumpers.

The landlord busied himself with pulling pints of beer for the trio. One of the old men filled his pipe from a leather pouch in his jacket pocket, tamped down the tobacco, applied several matches, and when the pipe was lit to his satisfaction, settled back in his chair near the fire to scatter the dominoes on the tabletop.

Watching the proceedings, Lisa thought, how I wish I were a man; a very old man, all passion spent, smoking a pipe of tobacco; asking nothing more of life than a warm fire and a game of dominoes; going home afterwards to a bite of cold pie at suppertime. She imagined a cottage; a kindly wife; a feather bed.

"What are you thinking?" Edward asked.

When she told him, he burst out laughing.

"What's so funny?"

"Has it occurred to you that you may be entirely wrong?" Edward chuckled. "For all you know, the old man might go home to a nagging wife, a mouldy cheese sandwich, and a wire mattress in the spare room."

"I don't believe that. You've only to look at him to see he's a happy man."

"I wonder," Edward said musingly. "You see, we all wear masks, at times. In my view, there's no such thing as complete and utter happiness. Not all the time. Just little islands of happiness that float to the surface now and then." He paused. "Remember the first time we came here? You thought that doing the right thing made for a happy, uncomplicated life. I couldn't agree with you then, and I still can't. Tell me, can't you accept anything without a fight?"

"If you mean your saying you're in love with me, no, I'm sorry, Edward, I'm afraid not." She shivered suddenly. "Oh, for God's sake, let's get out of here. The atmosphere's all wrong tonight."

In the car-park, he pulled her close to him, and kissed her; not passionately, but gently. Then, without a word, he opened the car door for her, settled himself behind the wheel, and drove swiftly towards Westsea, towards a vantage point known as The Mount, from which the lights of the town below glimmered like fireflies in the dusky warmth of an Indian Summer night.

"Where are you taking me?" Lisa asked hoarsely.

"Somewhere we can be alone together."

"And what if I'd rather not be alone with you?"

"Lisa, we need to talk."

"What is there to talk about?"

"Us?"

"What about – *us*?"

"For heaven's sake, Lisa! I've told you I'm in love with you! Are you saying my love means nothing to you? I really can't accept that."

"Then you'd better try harder, hadn't you? Now, if you don't mind, please take me back to Bay View."

"But *why*?" he asked bleakly.

"Because I cannot bear the thought of this hole and corner affair; all the lies and subterfuge. You had no right to tell me you love me. None whatever! Can't you see that what we are doing right now makes a mockery of love?"

Turning the car roughly, bumping into a kerb, he drove her back to Bay View. He said bitterly, "The day you tell Mrs Fogarty to go to hell as succinctly as you have just told me, is the day you'll start to live again!"

"I'm sorry . . ."

"No apology necessary, I assure you! Goodbye, Lisa!"

Watching the car until it moved out of sight, then hurrying up the front steps, Lisa knew, by the sudden movement of a net curtain, that Mrs Fogarty had been there all along, peeping and prying from the dining room window.

When Edward walked into the drawing room, Pamela, who had been watching television, rose stiffly to her feet. "I'll make you some tea and sandwiches," she said.

"No, finish watching your programme, I'll do it myself."

"There's no need. *I'll* do it!"

His anger burst forth. "Oh, for Christ's sake, Pamela! Do you think me incapable of putting the kettle on to boil; shoving a bit of cold meat between two slices of bread?"

She sat down abruptly, as though he had struck her in the face.

In the kitchen, he clattered the kettle, slammed shut the door of the refrigerator, sawed the bread lopsidedly, made the tea and the sandwiches, and carried them through to the other room.

He had never seen such an expression of shocked disbelief on his wife's face before. The television programme continued unheeded. He knew all the signs. He had deeply offended her.

"I'm sorry I snapped at you," he said, putting down the tray, feeling sick at the thought of attempting a mouthful of food.

"You didn't *snap* at me, Edward," Pamela reminded him, close to tears, "you *swore* at me! *Blasphemed*! How could you have done such a thing? It was totally unneccessary. Unforgivable!"

"Yes, you are quite right, and I've said I'm sorry. What more can I say? I'm just a bit overtired, that's all."

"Very well, then, I'll say no more about it except that I was right all along about your working too hard."

At that moment, he felt a sudden urge to kneel at her feet, confess to her that he had fallen in love with another woman, to make her understand that he was neither saint nor sinner, just an ordinary man in the toils of a love affair he had never wanted to happen . . .

A 'love affair', he thought bitterly, going upstairs to bed – scarcely that. At most, a one-sided love affair, now over and done with before it had even begun.

When Pamela came upstairs and got into bed beside him, he lay sleepless beside her long after she had fallen fast asleep, staring up at the ceiling, wondering if he would ever see Lisa again.

Chapter Eight

Lisa had hit a snag with the Wheatford Repository. The receptionist was apologetic, but firm. Requests for long-haul removals must be made in writing. Company policy, she explained, as a precaution against fraud; which Lisa understood and accepted.

"No way could we risk letting go of your belongings on the strength of a phone-call," the woman went on, "so if you'll drop us a line, I'll make the necessary arrangements."

"Yes, of course. Thank you." And so she had written a letter requesting the delivery of her furniture the following Saturday afternoon, her half-day off.

Two days later came a reply. The firm did not engage in long distance haulage at weekends. Her belongings would therefore be delivered the following Monday, if convenient.

She rang Jake Colby to explain the nature of her dilemma; that she could not possibly take time off work on a Monday.

"Not to worry, Mrs Hazell," he said in that laconic way of his. "I'll take care of things at this end."

All well and good. Even so, Lisa felt that time was running away with her. Everything was happening too fast, and she had not yet plucked up the courage to tell Mrs Fogarty that, in future, she would not be spending her off-duty hours at Bay View. How her employer would react to that piece of information, she had no idea.

As for Edward Miller, no man would suffer the humiliation she had heaped upon him and come back for more. But why had she treated him so badly? Why hadn't she believed him when he told her he loved her?

Foregoing the mid-morning tea break, needing time to think, she went down to her room, worried sick about the future. What if Mrs Fogarty gave her the sack?

Suddenly there came a peremptory hammering on the door.

"Just a minute, I'm coming." Lisa opened the door.

Mrs Fogarty crossed the threshold. "Are you aware, Mrs Hazell, that you have extended your ten minute break to twenty?" she said accusingly. "And don't try to deny it because I've been timing you."

Lisa thought that she had never really seen the woman before; the way her lips folded together like a tightly closed purse; the glint of malice in her eyes; the angles of her body, no softness or roundness anywhere, for all the world like 'Jacob's Angel', but lacking Epstein's genius with mallet and chisel.

Lisa glanced at her watch. "Actually, I've been in my room exactly fifteen minutes," she said calmly. "I came downstairs at ten-thirty precisely. It is now a quarter to eleven."

Mrs Fogarty said triumphantly, "So you admit to over-staying your tea-break? Condemned from your own lips, Mrs Hazell!"

Lisa regarded the woman coolly despite the clamouring of her heart against her ribs. "*Condemned*, Mrs Fogarty?" she asked. "So just where do you propose my execution should take place? In the garden in front of a firing squad? Or on a gibbet on the esplanade?"

Mrs Fogarty's mouth sagged open. In that split-second, Lisa felt a surge of power, of elation, running up from the soles of her feet to the crown of her head, knowing that she was no longer afraid of 'Jacob's Angel'.

"How *dare* you speak to me like that?" The Fogarty had regained her power of speech.

Pondering the question, "I suppose it's a matter of how much one is willing to take, and for how long," Lisa said levelly. "You see, Mrs Fogarty, you have dared to speak to me in your unfortunate manner for some considerable time now, and I have been too gutless to tell you how deeply I've resented it – not to mention all the extra duties you have foisted on to me."

"Have you taken leave of your senses?" Mrs Fogarty stared at Lisa disbelievingly.

"On the contrary, I have just come to the realisation of how unfairly I've been treated here. What's more, you've enjoyed humiliating me in front of the staff and residents alike; stripping me of the right of every human being to be treated with respect, and I put up with it because I had nowhere else to go. But all that is changed now. I'm leaving here first thing Monday morning, so you'll get your money's worth out of me until then. All I hope and pray is that my successor, God help her, will be someone not bound by circumstance to accept your dictates as I have done.

"In other words, Mrs Fogarty," Lisa concluded happily, "you can go to hell!"

"Eh, I never thought I'd live to see the day," Mrs Hannersley said admiringly. "We couldn't help overhearing, could we, girls? Seeing as how your door was open."

Sally and Alice, goggle-eyed, nodded their assent. Sally broke in excitedly, "That bit about the firing squad in the garden got me! I'd never have *dared*. Truth to tell, Mrs Hazell, I didn't think you had it in you, and when you told her to go to hell – well, I wish it had been me, that's all! And serve her damn well right!"

"Have you really got someplace else to go?" Alice asked eagerly.

"Oh yes." Lisa glanced at Mrs Hannersley. "Thanks to a very good friend of mine, I've found a flat in the Old Town. I'm moving in on Monday."

"Well, all I can say is, good luck, Mrs Hazell," Sally said mistily. "It's been a pleasure working with you, an' we'll miss you, won't we, Alice?"

"Yeah, we sure will." Alice had a fondness for American soap operas on television. "Like Sal said, all the best Mrs H. They don't come any better than you!"

"So it's all fixed, is it?" Edith Hannersley asked, when they had gone, her hands in a bowl of flour, rubbing in lard to make dumplings.

"Yes, it's all fixed, thanks to you – and your brother." Lisa smiled. "He's been goodness itself."

"Aye, well Jake's a good sort at heart," the cook commented, "though he isn't everyone's cup of tea – far from, and he doesn't suffer fools gladly, believe me. But he never goes back on his word, I'll say that for him."

Adding a smidgin of water to the dumpling mixture, she continued, "He's always been a loner has Jake. Even as a kid, he would wander off on his own along the shore, poking into rock-pools, gathering sea shells or whatever; wool-gathering most of the time, I shouldn't wonder. The other kids would laugh at him until . . ." Edith chuckled, "he grew so tall they mended their manners all of a sudden. Not that *he* noticed. He couldn't have cared less what they thought of him in the first place."

The butcher's lad came to the back door at that moment. "What have you brought up this weekend?" Mrs Hannersley wanted to know.

"Brisket." The lad was fifteen, and shy.

"Oh? Well I hope it's not too fatty. Here, let's be having it. The sooner I get it in the oven, the better, an' here's a shilling for yourself. A shilling? Hark at me, I'm still thinking in old money!"

The lad grinned, and departed, whistling. Lisa had made a start on the vegetables in the sink; carrots and parsnips to accompany the neck of mutton casserole and dumplings for today's lunch.

"Have you thought," Mrs Hannersley asked, "this brisket'll be the last Sunday meal you'll be serving in this – joint?" She sighed. "I'll miss you too, and so will 'Madame Defarge'." Mrs Hannersley retained fond memories of *A Tale of Two Cities*, seen from the back row of the Odeon Cinema in her courting days. "Where's she got to, by the way?"

"Mrs Fogarty? I think she's gone out," Lisa said.

"Ah well, if you can't stand the heat, keep out of the kitchen, as the saying goes. You certainly gave her a roasting. She's probably nipped down to the pub for a shot of brandy." She paused. "So all's set for Monday, is it? I thought you had next Saturday in mind."

"So I had, but the removal firm sent a letter explaining they don't work long distance at weekends. I can see why; the men would probably have to put up somewhere overnight."

"And demand overtime," the cook pointed out. "So what will you do when you've got yourself settled in? Look for another job?"

"Oh, yes. I'd hate to remain idle." She had really burned her boats this time, Lisa thought, but it had been worth it. She remembered Edward's words; "The day you tell Mrs Fogarty to go to hell as succinctly as you have just told me, is the day you'll start to live again."

Pamela said primly, "Really, Edward, it is high time you consulted Dr Soames."

"Why, for heaven's sake?"

"For one thing, you are not eating properly, just picking at your food. Besides which, you are still smoking like a chimney, despite the health warnings on the cigarette packets."

"Not in the house," he said wearily.

"But you are not always in the house, are you?" she continued, sanitising a work surface with Dettol. "I dread to think how many cigarettes you smoke behind my back.

But I can always tell by the smell of smoke hanging about your hair and clothes when you come home from work. It really is a disgusting habit, and totally unnecessary, in my view, that a man of your age and standing in the community should resort to what, after all, is nothing short of drug usage."

"*Drug usage?* Oh, come off it, Pamela! I'm smoking tobacco, not cannabis!"

"That is beside the point. Totally irrelevant to this conversation. You are obviously not yourself, which is why you should consult the doctor. Take last Sunday evening, for example. Never, in all the years we've been married had you spoken to me in such a fashion before."

"I know, and I did apologise, if you remember."

"Yes, and I accepted your apology. It is the reason why you exploded in such a way that concerns me. After all, I do try my best to provide a diet rich in the essential minerals . . ."

Oh lord, here we go again, he thought bleakly – now it would be bran flakes and vitamin pills for breakfast; more iceberg lettuce and tomatoes and low-fat mayonnaise at tea-time – when he'd give his soul for a good plateful of grease-sodden fish and chips from the take-away chippie in the shopping precinct.

"Or perhaps you are not getting enough exercise?" Pamela suggested.

"You mean on top of gardening, cleaning the car, painting the conservatory, creosoting the fence, and fixing the gutters?"

"No need of sarcasm, Edward," Pamela said huffily, "they are jobs that every self-respecting married man tackles as a matter of course."

"Very well then, what say we go for a walk this afternoon, as far as the harbour and back?"

"Don't be ridiculous," Pamela sniffed her contempt at the suggestion, "you know perfectly well that I spend my Saturday afternoons in church, arranging flowers for the Sunday morning service."

"Oh yes. Sorry, I'd forgotten."

"But there is nothing to prevent you from taking a good long walk in the fresh air if you feel like it. You can clean the car when you get back."

When Pamela had finished her work in the kitchen, she put on her hat and coat, collected the church flowers from a bucket of water in the conservatory, and marched down the garden path, her thoughts fully occupied with the task in hand – the cleaning of the church brasses and the arrangement of the flowers, knowing exactly where she would put them – the white chrysanthemums near the altar, the bronze and lemon near the lectern, the mauve and pink ones in the baptistry. This, seemed to Pamela, a reason for living.

When she had gone, Edward thought about Lisa, wondering what the hell had possessed him to tell her he loved her. She had not believed him, and why should she? No wonder he couldn't eat or sleep properly. She was in his thoughts every waking moment of every day.

He had been half joking about walking as far as the harbour and back. This was the kind of thing he always meant to do, though never got around to. But why not?

Hurrying upstairs, he changed quickly into a roll-neck sweater and slipped on a pair of walking shoes, thick-soled, with tie-up laces, in which, in his youth, he had once completed the Lyke Wake Walk, to his parents' delight. . . . His parents, nice, ordinary uncomplicated people whose lives had been snuffed out in a motorway pile-up, in thick fog, shortly after his nineteenth birthday celebrations.

Crossing the road towards the cliff path leading down to the beach, he felt compelled to look back at the house. There it stood, a detached brick box surrounded with neatly-mown grass and freshly creosoted larch fencing.

And the better part of his life, he thought, plunging down

the cliff path to the beach, had been devoted to buying furniture to fill that brick box; decorating its walls; clearing its gutters of fallen leaves, stopping leaks, and sweating hard to keep abreast of the garden lest the bindweed and couch-grass gained the upper hand when he wasn't looking.

Marry, buy a house, raise a family, work hard, and you'll be happy my son, had been the format when he was a boy, drummed into him by his father.

On this gold and blue autumn afternoon, with seagulls drifting lazily overhead, Edward Miller knew that happiness had passed him by. He scarcely knew the meaning of the word; had never even begun to live.

Breathing in the salt air, he felt better when the rough path gave way to shingle, and his shoes bit deeply into the firm wet sand near the sea's edge. Savouring this new-found sense of freedom, he thought how much he hated the po-faced, bowler-hatted image with which his job as a civil servant had saddled him.

No wonder Lisa had laughed when she knew what he did for a living.

Lisa! He would, in all probability, never see her again, and yet he would think of her over and over again, in the secret corners of the mind, hoping and praying she would find the courage to make a fresh start one day, away from Bay View.

He could see, in the distance, people strolling along the promenade near the amusement arcades on this mild, bright autumn afternoon, and remembered a favourite tune which conjured up Saturday night dances of his youth, long before he had met Pamela. 'Indian Summer'. How did the song go?

'You're the ghost of a romance in bloom,
Going astray; ending too soon . . .'

Strange how people herded together. Only one other person

was walking on this deserted stretch of beach – a woman, coming towards him. A fair-haired woman walking proudly upright. *Lisa*!

Hurrying towards her, he experienced a sudden feeling of relief, an uprush of tenderness, a soaring of the spirit. The sky tilted crazily as he started to run, hands outstretched to greet her, calling her name, the sand crunching beneath his shoes; the words of an old song running through his brain, not caring a damn who saw him, a middle-aged man behaving like a teenager running towards the girl he loved, calling her name as he ran, calling out, "Lisa! *Lisa*!"

Catching her name on the breeze, she stopped walking. Then, seeing him, smiling, she ran to meet him, and suddenly she was in his arms, her face buried against his shoulder, half-laughing, half-crying.

"Lisa," he began.

"No, don't say anything. Let me tell you!" Looking up at him, "I've done it! I've actually *done* it!

"What have you done, my darling?"

"Mrs Fogarty. I told her to go to hell!"

"Just like that?"

"Exactly like that! In those very words!"

He held on to her shoulders, feeling the trembling of her body, scarcely believing that all this was happening; that she was really there, his lovely Lisa, laughing in the wine-sweet sunshine of an Indian Summer day.

"What made you do it? Tell me, darling, I want to know."

"I stopped being afraid," she said. "It's as simple as that. I stopped being afraid."

"Come on," he said, "let's walk to the promenade. I'll buy you a knickerbocker glory to celebrate."

They walked, holding hands. The afternoon was theirs. Nothing else mattered. He had escaped down that path to the beach, leaving his prison-house behind him.

"I'm leaving Bay View on Monday morning," Lisa said

eagerly. "The removal people are bringing my furniture to the flat about midday. Can you imagine the muddle? You know what it's like? First you find the tea-caddy then discover you haven't any tea, so you dash out to buy some; then you can't find the kettle."

"Our removal wasn't like that," he sighed. "I wish it had been. Pamela had everything organised to the nth degree; the packing cases labelled, carpets laid, curtains hung well in advance. A place for everything and everything in its place. I missed the fun of searching for the kettle."

They had reached the promenade and found an ice-cream parlour. "I'd rather just have tea, if you don't mind," Lisa said. "I don't think I could tackle a knickerbocker glory after neck of mutton and dumplings. Or don't they serve tea in ice-cream parlours? Funny, isn't it?"

"What is?"

"Why they're called ice-cream parlours, not ice-cream cafés." Tears welled up in her eyes.

"Lisa, what is it? What's wrong?"

"It's called whistling in the dark," she said, finding her hanky. "To be honest, I'm a bit scared. At least Bay View gave me a feeling of security; a wage-packet at the end of the week."

"If you need money, darling . . ."

"Oh no! Please, I didn't mean it like that. I'll manage somehow."

"But I don't want you to worry, to feel in any way insecure. I want you to be happy; to be a part of that happiness, if you'll let me."

He reached for her hand across the table. "Everyone needs someone, Lisa. I need *you*. My life is empty without you. I am stating a simple truth, and it doesn't matter if our only contact is across a marble-topped table in an ice-cream parlour. It's knowing someone shares that need that really matters."

"Do you ever read poetry, Edward?"

"Not now. Not any longer. I used to when I was at university. I did a lot of things then that I don't do any more, but I still remember some of the lines. One poem in particular: 'How do I love thee? Let me count the ways . . .' Oh, lord, I've forgotten how it goes on."

"'I love thee to the depth and breadth and height my soul can reach, when feeling out of sight for the ends of Being and Ideal Grace,'" Lisa reminded him, and smiled, knowing that she loved him.

Chapter Nine

Awaiting the arrival of a taxi, Lisa stood in the hall of Bay View, her personal belongings, suitcases and carrier bags, at her feet, looking her last at the house which had been home to her since she came to work there almost eight months ago.

It was a spacious Victorian building with a broad, red-carpeted staircase, the dining room to the left of the entrance, the residents' lounge on the right, next to Mrs Fogarty's private apartment; the kitchen and still-room at the far end of the hall, at the head of the basement stairs.

Now the time had come to leave, Lisa remembered all the good things about it: her bay-windowed room overlooking the garden; the fun and laughter she'd shared with her fellow workers when 'Jacob's Angel' was out of earshot; the residents, mainly elderly widows or spinsters in need of care and attention in their twilight years, all of whom she had come to know well in her role as general assistant-cum-dogsbody, when she had been called upon to sort out and distribute their laundry, empty their electricity meters, change light bulbs, bring back their prescriptions from the chemist, along with bottles of Lucozade, boxes of Kleenex tissues, or whatever.

Mrs Fogarty had been the fly in the ointment, not the staff or the old folk themselves. Mrs Fogarty, greedy, imperious and self-centred, with her penny-pinching ways, who treated the residents as guests rather than human beings in need of love and understanding.

Well, all that was over and done with now. The Fogarty had handed Lisa her final pay-packet moments ago, with the sour remark, "I hope you realise, Mrs Hazell, that your days here were numbered in any case; and I shall certainly not hesitate to tell a prospective employer of yours of your reprehensible behaviour, your untrustworthiness; the way you have left me in the lurch."

Lisa made no reply. It would have been nice to make the grand gesture of handing back the pay-packet, but she needed the money.

Mrs Hannersley, who usually met her brother on Sunday evenings, had promised to tell him that Lisa would be free to help with the removal after all.

She had ordered the taxi for eight o'clock, to be away from Bay View before the old people came down to breakfast. She was alone in the hall. Sally, Alice and Mrs Hannersley would be here soon, but they had already said their goodbyes, and so far as she knew the residents had not been told of her departure. She was wrong.

To her amazement, a delegation of ladies came downstairs at five minutes to eight to present her with a bunch of yellow chrysanthemums and a Good Luck card. Their spokeswoman, Mrs Pettifer, said mistily, "It has been a pleasure knowing you, Mrs Hazell. Bay View won't be the same without you. We've all signed the card, so you'll have something to remember us by."

The removal men had off-loaded her furniture and humped it to the top floor, puffing and panting. "Rather you than me, missis," the gaffer said when they had finished, "climbing those stairs every day. Mind you, it's a nice little place you've got here."

"Thank you. I'm more than grateful. You've been very quick, very efficient." She handed him a ten pound note from her pay-packet.

"Oh, thanks very much, missis. Mind you, that bloke on

84

the ground floor done his fair share. He hefted that roll of carpet upstairs like it was a havana cigar."

"Yes, I know." Jake Colby had been magnificent, Lisa thought, lending the men a hand; providing them with mugs of tea and sandwiches.

Alone in the flat when the men had departed, she ran her hand over a small octagonal table which had belonged to Aunt Grace, and remembered that she·used to polish it religiously on Sunday mornings in the old days.

Now, smoothing away the dust, Lisa discerned a trace of the old lustre, and it seemed that Aunt Grace was here with her, a living part of her life once more.

Standing near the balcony window, reliving old memories, she noticed a change in the weather. The early morning sunshine had faded, the wind had risen, bringing with it a scattering of raindrops.

Inevitably, memory drew her back to the day she and John had moved into the cottage; how she had wandered from room to room, making discoveries; buttering the cat's paws; scenting spring in the air . . .

Turning away from the window, putting aside memories, she looked at her new home; this room with its sloping ceilings, stone fireplace and empty shelves, the tea-chests and cardboard cartons which needed emptying, the pliofilm bags of bedding, the single divan, the sofa and armchairs and various other items of furniture which would form the nucleus of her home.

The larger pieces, Aunt Grace's bedroom furniture of Victorian vintage, the dining room table and chairs and sideboard, had been sold at auction after her aunt's death, along with the spare room bedroom suite and the cane furniture from the conservatory, which Grace had fondly referred to as "The Studio".

Sadly, her aunt's house in Wheatford had been rented property which the owner had been anxious to sell, otherwise Lisa might have remained there after the divorce. But life was never that simple, that easy. Circumstances had forced her to move away from Wheatford, to make a new life for herself. Now here she was in a rented flat in Westsea, feeling cold and – lonely.

She was on her knees, cleaning the skirting boards, when Jake Colby came upstairs with a flask of hot chicken soup and a plate of ham sandwiches.

"I thought you might be feeling hungry," he said off-handedly.

"Yes, as a matter of fact, though I hadn't really thought about it. The soup's delicious. Did your wife make it?"

"No, I made it myself. Now, about this carpet. It will need cutting to make it fit. I'll see to it first thing tomorrow morning, if that's all right. You'll never get straight, otherwise."

"I suppose not," Lisa conceded. "You are quite right, of course, but I'm sorry to cause you so much trouble."

"No trouble," he said laconically, "that's what I'm here for."

Gathering up the empty flask, soup dish and plate, he departed as silently as he had arrived.

Lisa's feeling of loneliness intensified as darkness fell. Rain was falling steadily now, blurring the glass of the balcony window. She heard the slam of a door on the lower landing, the sound of voices as the occupants of another flat went downstairs. Strangers.

It was then Edward came to her.

Answering the rap on her door, she stared at him in disbelief, then clung to him, her loneliness dispelled.

Holding her, "Some people were on their way out," he said, "so I came in. Now I'm taking you to a hotel in town. The Victoria, opposite the station. You'll have dinner there and, hopefully, a good night's sleep."

"But . . ."

"No buts!" He smiled. "For one thing, that bed will need

airing before you sleep in it; for another, you must be tired out. Believe me, darling, you'll feel much better after a night's sleep and a full English breakfast."

"But I . . ."

"What a woman for argument. Do you trust me or don't you?" He ruffled her hair.

"Of course I do. It's just that . . ."

"The room is booked and paid for, if that's what's worrying you," he said lightly. "All you have to do is stop arguing, pack an overnight case, and come with me."

"But Mr Colby's coming first thing in the morning to lay the carpet!"

"So what? I take it he has a spare key? Lisa, my love, I thought you told me you had stopped being afraid. In any case, all you have to do is order early breakfast in your room. Now, are you coming with me, or not?"

"Yes, of course, and thank you, Edward. Just give me a moment to find my nightdress and toothbrush."

At the Victoria, a commercial hotel in the town square, Lisa signed the register; the receptionist handed her the key to her room, told her that the dining room would open in half an hour, then Lisa and Edward, walked upstairs together, not bothering to wait for the lift.

In a neat, impersonal room on the third floor, Edward drew the curtains against the neon glow of the square below, and the beating of the rain on the windowpanes.

From a distance came the time signal of the six o'clock news on Radio Four; the hooter of the six o'clock train to York, about to leave the station across the road.

The world beyond the window pulsed an early evening heartbeat. Inside the room, time had ceased to exist. Not a word was spoken. No need of words.

Holding Lisa in his arms, gently and carefully Edward traced the outline of her body with his fingertips, whispering that he loved her, knowing that what he said was true;

87

wanting her more than he had ever wanted anything or anyone in his life before. And Lisa had never meant this to happen, the shedding of her garments, her inhibitions; had never thought it could happen, ever again, this overwhelming need of love in the arms of a man other than her husband's.

Lying close together, naked, on the narrow single bed, Edward thought briefly of Pamela; that thrusting against the hard core of her resistance which had somehow made a mockery of love. Love? No, with Pamela it was not and never had been love, merely marital intercourse.

With John, Lisa thought, what she had most feared was not becoming pregnant. Now nothing mattered except giving herself to the man she loved without let or hindrance; joyously, with no regrets . . .

Their lovemaking over, "I love you, Lisa," Edward said tenderly, caressing her hair, her face, her mouth.

"And I love you, Edward."

She had wept then, overcome by the simplicity and rightness of it all. And then they lay quietly in each other's arms for a while, listening to the beating of the rain on the windowpanes, to each other's heartbeats; the whirr of the lift on the landing outside the room; the click of the metal gates, until, switching on the bedside lamp to look at his watch, Edward said resignedly, "I'm sorry, my darling. It's eight o'clock . . ."

This was the moment she had dreaded. He said gently, "You knew I'd have to leave sooner or later."

"You'd better get dressed, then, hadn't you?"

"How do you think I feel," he said wearily, "leaving you alone like this? Do you imagine I want to go home after what has happened between us?"

Not speaking, she noticed the tired lines about his eyes, the strands of greying hair at his temples.

Getting up, he strode jerkily to the window and back. Watching him, Lisa wondered what he would say to his wife when he arrived home; how he would account for his lateness; if lying would come easily; how he would spend the rest of the evening; if, to salve his conscience, he would feel it necessary to make love to Pamela tonight?

She covered her face with her hands. Holding her wrists, he forced her to look at him. As if he knew what she was thinking, he said angrily, "If it was up to me, I'd drag you out of that bed, throw a couple of suitcases in the car and get the hell out of this town and everyone in it! How do you think I'll feel, sitting at home, watching television, eating a meal I don't want; lying through my teeth? Do you imagine, do you honestly believe that my life can ever be the same again after tonight? Can *yours*, Lisa? Can yours?"

She shook her head, blinded by tears. "No, Edward. Nothing will ever be the same for me again."

"Then hang on to this love of ours," he said tautly. "Hold on to it even when I'm gone."

He dressed, kissed her, and went away without another word.

Lying there, staring at the door, she wanted to cry out, "Don't go! Don't leave me!"

Pulling on her dressing gown, she hurried to the window, parted the curtains and stared down at the street below, hoping to catch a glimpse of him. All she could see were people hurrying along beneath opened umbrellas, street lights shining on wet pavements; garish neon signs emblazoned against the darkness; passengers getting into taxis in the station forecourt.

Cold and lonely, standing there in the slip of a room where their love had come to fruition, she thought of Edward hurrying towards his car, slamming the door, driving away from her on that long road out of town.

Chapter Ten

Linda waltzed into the cottage humming a tune she had heard on the radio that morning – 'That's the Story of Love' – which had haunted her ever since. Not because she liked it particularly, but because it was catchy and suited her mood.

Miles was with Annette Dawson who lived in the village, a particular crony of hers who, when Linda had explained about wanting the child off her hands for a few hours, had suggested keeping him overnight.

"He might fret," Linda had said dubiously. "He's never been away from home before."

"He'll be all right with my brood," Annette, the strong-minded mother of three assured her. "In any case, I can always nip him back to you if he won't settle."

And so Linda had packed the necessities and parked Miles with her friend, who understood the need for a husband and wife to be alone together on special occasions.

The Indian Summer days continued, spinning out like a spider's thread. September had slipped beautifully into October, the pale warm sunshine lighting up the shorn fields of corn now that the harvest had been gathered in; the acrid smell of burning stubble drifting, like incense, on the warm air.

This autumn had seemed an especially significant time for the new Mrs Hazell. Passing through the hall on her way to the kitchen, she paused awhile to glance at her reflection in the long mirror near the drawing room door. Smiling, smoothing her hands over her belly, she imagined the way her reflection would appear come next spring.

Late October sunshine showed up the dust on the dining room table, not that that worried her unduly. Johnny wouldn't even notice the dust when the table was spread with the embroidered cloth someone had given them as a wedding present; when she had placed on it a centrepiece of roses from the garden.

The fun lay in planning the special meal for their tête-à-tête; deciding what to wear . . .

Truth to tell, she felt a bit guilty about foisting Miles on to Annette, but John had been so on edge lately that it had seemed politic to tell him about the new baby in a relaxed atmosphere. She didn't want any table mishaps, Miles splattering gravy, for instance.

Making herself a mug of coffee, sitting in the porch to drink it, looking out at the garden, the apple trees, the line of hills in the distance; feeling as contented, sleepy and warm as a young, pregnant animal, Linda knew that nothing on earth could persuade her to leave this place.

She had wanted this cottage from the moment she saw it. John Hazell, too, come to think of it, because of the height of him, the looks of him, the challenge of him − knowing that he was already spoken for − married to a much older woman as plain as a pikestaff; as dull as ditchwater.

She had been working at Railton Comprehensive at the time, as the headmaster's secretary; living in digs with Anne Terry, the domestic-science teacher, who had told her all about John Hazell and his wife . . . Poor, plain, elderly Lisa Hazell who, one gathered, could not get pregnant.

Later, much later, had come a cheese and wine wing-ding at the cottage, hosted by John Hazell and his wife in aid of Amnesty International − an event promoted by the headmaster who had a been in his bonnet about 'prisoners of conscience'.

Entering the cottage that evening, entranced by the spaciousness of the rooms, the diamond-paned windows, the fairy-lit apple trees on the lawn beyond the windows, Linda had known, beyond a shadow of doubt, it was here she belonged, as the mistress of the house; that, if she so willed it, nothing on earth could prevent her from separating John Hazell from his wife. And she *had* so willed it! So now, here she was, the new Mrs Hazell, the mother of one child; another on the way.

Linda smiled, remembering the night of that Amnesty International party. How, glancing across the crowded drawing room, she had caught and held Johnnie's attention by the simple expedient of appearing all coy and innocent; slightly confused, when he looked her way; drooping her eyelids to draw attention to her bodice; her black-lace brassiere just visible above the low-cut tank-top she just happened to be wearing at the time . . .

Now the shining autumn day was fast edging towards four o'clock. Linda hadn't bothered with lunch. Pointless, really, when she had planned *coq au vin* for dinner; had spent the entire morning peeling and preparing the vegetables, dusting spasmodically, sipping wine from one of the two bottles of *vin rosé* in the refrigerator.

Housework did not delight her. She derived no particular pleasure from seeing things neat and polished; tended to start one job then drifted on to something else, so that nothing got done thoroughly, except lovemaking. She was very thorough, in bed.

Conscious of her body, the shapeliness and strength of it, its power as a weapon, she pottered happily, humming the tune running through her head, slopping more wine into the casserole, thinking about John.

Her mother always maintained that no matter how well you thought you knew a man, you didn't know him at all until you were married to him, and although she had shrugged aside such a sweeping generalisation, Linda had to admit that her mother was right.

There were times nowadays when she scarcely recognised, in John, the passionate lover of their early days. He had been so reckless then, and determined, not caring a damn what might happen if a whiff of scandal reached the headmaster's ears.

It had never occurred to either of them how much they owed to Lisa's discretion when she had found out about the affair. Linda saw Lisa's discretion as gutlessness. A woman unwilling to fight tooth and claw for her husband did not deserve to have one, in Linda's opinion.

All was ready now. She had cluttered Miles's toys from the drawing room carpet into a cardboard box, which she had kicked out of sight behind the settee. The dining room table was set with red candles, and the centrepiece of roses on the slightly crumpled cloth which she had not bothered to iron. The casserole smelt good, and she had ditched one of the wine bottles – the one she had emptied into herself and the *coq au vin* in more or less equal quantities – in the swing-top rubbish bin near the sink.

Upstairs, she had showered, washed and blow-dried her hair, then put on the new dress she had bought specially for this intimate dinner for two – a stunning dress: bright red, with a short circular skirt and a low-cut bodice. Laughing tipsily, she twirled in front of the bedroom mirror; keeping an ear open for the sound of the car in the lane.

At last! There it was. Racing downstairs, she ran to the front door. John was coming up the path with his bag full of school books, looking tired as usual, which irritated Linda. Why the hell did he appear so exhausted? That fortnight in Westsea had been marvellous; the beach every day, the weather holding, Miles revelling in the sand-pies she had made for him; the donkey rides, the ice-cream cornets . . .

Hurrying to meet John, standing on tiptoe, she threw her

arms about his neck, and kissed him. "Where's Miles?" he asked sourly.

"Ah well, that's a secret for the time being." She smiled teasingly. "Aren't you going to tell me I look nice?"

"I asked you a question."

"He's with Annette Dawson, if you must know."

"Yes. The whereabouts of my son is rather important to me."

Angered by his lack of response, that he had not even noticed her new dress, Linda turned on him. "Why? Did you imagine I'd given him away to a gypsy beggar?" Her voice was heavy with sarcasm. "Or maybe you'd like that? After all, you did want him born in a ditch!"

"Shut your bloody mouth!"

Staring at him as if he had struck her in the face, she turned and ran into the house; raced upstairs to the bedroom and locked the door behind her; heard his footsteps pounding on the stairs, the rattling of the handle, his voice calling to her to let him in.

"Go away! Leave me alone, you – bastard!"

"I'm sorry, I didn't mean to upset you!"

"And I said go away! Just who do you think you are, telling me to shut my bloody mouth?"

Tearing off her new dress, she kicked it across the room. He didn't deserve a woman to dress up for him, to cook and slave for him; did not deserve this new baby she'd conceived for him. Well, she wouldn't have the bloody kid, she'd have an abortion.

Hoisting a suitcase from the wardrobe, opening the lid, she threw clothes into it haphazardly. Sweeping up an armful of dresses, skirts, blouses and underwear, she flung them into the case, sobbing hysterically, uncaring that the case still bore traces of sand from Westsea which she hadn't bothered to remove; thinking tipsily that she would pick up Miles from Annette's then go to Anne Terry's flat; stay there until she had decided what to do next.

Anne would welcome her with open arms, she felt sure. Meanwhile, John was still on the landing, rattling the door-knob, calling to her to let him in, saying he wanted to talk to her.

"Well I don't bloody well want to talk to you!"

"I've seen the table, the flowers. I realise that this was meant to be something special . . ."

"Oh, you've seen the table, have you? You've probably seen the chicken as well! So eat it yourself, and I hope it bloody well chokes you!"

Suddenly all the fight went out of her. The room was spinning round. Sinking to her knees, whimpering, she crawled to the door, unlocked it, and knelt there on the floor; tears streaming down her face.

Then John was beside her, rocking her like a child, saying over and over, "I'm sorry, darling, I'm sorry, I'm sorry."

A feeling of triumph welled up in Linda. She had John exactly where she wanted him now, at her feet, guilt-ridden and penitent. So much for a tame dinner, a manufactured setting. This was ten times better.

Thank God she had rid herself of the red dress, had stripped down to her bra and panties. Keeping her eyes closed, she continued to sob wildly, but her reactions were carefully calculated now, her sense of domination was absolute. "Take me to bed, Johnny," she whispered brokenly, "I'm so tired, so – confused."

Lifting her up in his arms, he laid her gently on the bed, kissing her cheeks, her eyelids, her mouth; unhooking her bra. Now he was undressing, tearing off his clothes with reckless haste; wanting her as he had done in the early days of their marriage.

But she had not yet quite extracted her full quota of revenge for his cruelty towards her as she lay there impassively for a while, pretending not to care tuppence about the state he was in; making him wait until she was good and ready to allow him to make love to her.

Afterwards, when he was sated with lovemaking, when she knew that he was sublimely and utterly hers to do with as she liked, Linda told him she was pregnant.

He awoke suddenly in the darkness, sweating with the reality of his nightmare.

In his dream, he had been back in his childhood home in the West Riding of Yorkshire – a two-up, two-down terrace house near Wakefield, and his father had just come home from the pub one Sunday lunchtime, the worse for drink.

In his nightmare, John Hazell had relived his patient mother's anxiety that the food she had provided would be dried-up by the time her lord and master sat down at the table to eat it; not meeting with his approval.

Nor had it. In his dream, in the way of nightmares, his father's dinner had turned to mush on his plate, and he had started banging down his spoon, splattering the gravy . . .

And, in his dream, his mother had said, "Take no notice of your father, my son. He's a good provider. I just worry, at times, how he'll manage on his own when I'm gone. Soon, very soon, now . . ."

Then, in his nightmare, John had been at his mother's graveside, scattering soil on her coffin, his father beside him – a hungry toad snatching at a dragon-fly with his tongue . . .

Fully awake, John Hazell stared into the darkness, trembling and sweating, until he remembered that he was at home in the cottage, his wife lying naked beside him; remembered that she was pregnant with a second child.

Linda stirred in her sleep as he got up, put on his dressing-gown, and went downstairs.

In the drawing room, he switched on a table-lamp, and saw, with an upsurge of guilt, that his bag of school-books was still on the carpet where he had dropped it – the essays unread.

Glancing at the carriage clock on the mantelpiece, he saw

that the time was three-thirty. Sniffing the air, catching a whiff of burning, he hurried through to the kitchen to switch off the cooker.

Taking the casserole from the oven, lifting the lid, he saw that the chicken pieces within were burned black, like coal cinders, or anthracite.

Glancing into the dining room, he saw that the centrepiece of roses had drooped and faded – for the simple reason that Linda had neglected to add water to the vase.

Returning to the drawing room, which Linda referred to as "the lounge", sitting down in an armchair, John Hazell lit a cigarette, conscious of his own erratic heartbeats in the quiet room, remembering Lisa – a poem he had once read to her . . .

'Oh just beyond the fairest thoughts that throng,
The thought of thee waits, hidden yet bright,
But it must never, never come in sight,
I must stop short of thee the whole day long'.

Now, John Hazell knew that he had stopped short of Lisa every hour of every day since the break up of their marriage.

And now, the memory of her love came back to haunt him in this quiet room, this cottage, this home of which she had once been the mistress – if that tide of peace running between them in the early days of their marriage could be construed as love. And if it could not? Then he had himself to blame for wanting more – excitement, passionate physical fulfilment. And so he had treated Lisa badly, and he knew it, as a whipping boy – especially on those trips abroad when he had derived a masochistic pleasure from making her appear foolishly incompetent, totally inadequate when it came to map-reading and border crossings, for the simple reason that she was so easily intimidated by his far stronger, more dominant personality; that gentle, highly intelligent wife of his whose sole defect lay in her inability to conceive, to give him the child he had so desperately wanted at the time.

Deep in thought, John Hazell remembered that last morning at the cottage, when Lisa had walked down the garden path, for the last time, to enter the awaiting taxi at the garden gate; that he had not even deigned to help with her luggage or even to kiss her goodbye – because of Linda – the new, exciting love of his life.

And so he and Lisa had parted as strangers, which probably explained his present desolation and sourness of spirit.

Chapter Eleven

He had walked into her life, and there was no way of leaving it without hurting her. Equally, he stood to hurt her just as much by staying in it, if the affair was discovered.

And yet Edward went to Lisa as often as possible, pushing thoughts of discovery to the back of his mind, convincing himself that life owed him this first love affair which had, miraculously, lifted him to a higher plane of awareness, threading his days with joy whenever he saw her.

Music, colours, the sun, the sea – even his work meant more to him now than they had ever done before, because of Lisa. And so, Edward Miller reasoned that something so beautiful could not be wrong.

At night he would lie awake thinking of her alone in the flat, and imagined an umbilical cord of love stretching between them; wanting her with him always, knowing this would mean asking Pamela to release him from a marriage which had brought little happiness into either one of their lives.

Now that she had left Bay View and its petty restrictions behind her, Lisa had begun to relish her new-found independence, deriving pleasure from making ends meet; living as frugally as possible on porridge, boiled eggs and toast; shopping at the weekends for cheap cuts of meat and inexpensive vegetables for a hot-pot or casserole which, eked out with dumplings – á la Mrs Hannersley

– and mashed potatoes, would suffice for two or three days.

To her delight, she had begun to lose weight, due partially to her enforced diet and the fact that she was taking more exercise; exploring the many twisting streets and alleyways of the Old Town which she had never really seen before, or walking on the beach, whatever the weather; now that November was here, wearing slacks, a thick-knit sweater, and her old green anorak.

Cancelling her fortnightly hairdressing appointments, she was letting her hair grow, pinning it back from her face with kirbigrips until it was long enough to sweep into a french pleat.

Now, pleasantly, little by little, she was coming to terms with her new home. Not merely her own flat, but the house as a whole; the occupants of the other flats. The young couple on the landing below, for instance, who worked hard during the week and played hard at weekends – the Lassiters, Paul and Marilyn, who had proffered a careless invitation to come down any weekend for a glass of wine and a bite to eat, if she felt lonely.

More in her league was the elderly lady, Miss Pargeter, who occupied the front flat further along the third landing, who had invited Lisa in for coffee one morning to show her photographs of her fiancé who had been killed in Italy during the war.

In descending order of stairs, the first and second floor flats were inhabited by fairly mundane middle-aged couples who kept themselves to themselves, although they would smile and comment on the weather whenever Lisa passed them on her way in or out of the building, on their various landings, if, perchance, they happened to be going out or coming in at the same time.

The only door that had remained, so far, closed against her, was that of her landlord, Jake Colby – a white-painted door at the far end of the stone-flagged hallway . . . What lay beyond that door, Lisa had not the remotest idea. But then, according to his sister, Edith Hammersley, Jake Colby had always been a 'Loner', and she should know.

Edward had observed, with admiration and tenderness combined, the way in which Lisa had set about putting her flat to rights. In the words of John Donne, 'To make one little room an everywhere'.

Her divan bed, near the balcony window, was now covered with a tobacco-brown, hand-sewn spread and a scattering of cushions in muted shades of green and gold, made from material picked up for a song at a closing down sale.

The carpet was moss green, and she had arranged her three-seater settee and matching armchairs in front of the fireplace. There were side-tables with softly-shaded lamps; books, African violets and ornaments on the fireplace shelves; a carved oak chest beneath a long, gilt-framed mirror, a Victorian chest-of-drawers and a single wardrobe in which she kept her clothes. Her bedding lived in drawers beneath the divan bed. She had hung moss green velvet curtains at the french window, beside which stood Aunt Grace's octagonal table.

Whenever Edward came to her, he would find her moving items of furniture from place to place, trying to establish the correct balance, not wanting the room to appear too overcrowded, too 'bedroomy', and she hadn't yet finished unpacking – a tea-chest remained unopened – a chest containing many of her aunt's personal belongings, she explained, which she felt reluctant to delve into for the time being.

She had told him, then, something of her past life in Wheatford in the home she had shared with Aunt Grace, and a picture had emerged of a strong-minded, charismatic, slightly eccentric lady who had devoted the greater part of her life to her niece's welfare, following the death of Lisa's parents during an Asian flu epidemic when the girl was only seven years old.

Later, over a space of time between Edward's fleeting visits to the flat, Lisa had told him about her marriage to John Hazell; her inability to bear his child; about the cottage, and John's affair with Linda Trentham which had brought about the end of their marriage. And, listening, came the terrible thought that he, Edward Miller, might well destroy Lisa's happiness just as surely as John Hazell had done.

Strangely, he found it impossible to discuss aspects of his marriage to Pamela. Lisa's marriage was over and done with, a thing of the past; his was not.

He might have felt differently, less guilty, had he been able to tell Lisa that he no longer shared a bed with his wife. Sensitivity prevented his disclosure that he wished this was not so; that he did not sleep with Pamela in the accepted sense of the word. He was not in love with Pamela who held the trump cards of Marriage and Respectability, but he did still retain a sense of loyalty towards her – the mother of his child.

All he could possibly do was tell Lisa, over and over again, how much he loved her, that she was the most important person in his life, realising, at the same time, how empty and meaningless the words must seem to her whenever he glanced at his watch, kissed her goodbye, and left her alone in her room.

The offer of a job in a different department came as a godsend to Edward. He accepted with alacrity when he was told this would entail working away from the office when necessary, possibly after office hours.

Pamela had been coldly angry. "And I suppose it never even occurred to you to ask my opinion?"

"No, not really," he confessed. "I'm sorry, but it seemed politic not to hesitate unduly. After all, I was next in line for promotion; a commensurate increase in salary."

The argument made sense to Pamela. "Just as long as they do not expect you to work on Sundays," she said.

"Why not? What's so special about Sundays?" The moment afterwards, he could have bitten his tongue. How boorish, how insensitive to have asked such a question.

Pamela's lips trembled. "Sundays have always been special to me, as I hoped they might be to you. There's the morning church service for one thing . . . Oh, I realise that you consider church-going a bore; that you have never shown much interest in doing the things most married couples do on Sundays."

He knew what she meant; pottering in the garden before lunch; going out for a drive afterwards if the weather was fine, stopping off somewhere for tea and scones – or, if the weather was wet, doing the *Observer* crossword; working out anagrams; sitting in the drawing room opposite his wife, hearing the click, click clicking of her knitting needles, watching the endless unwinding of the ball of wool from the work-bag suspended from the handle of her chair near the simulated coal-effect of the electric fire.

He was not, never had been, a godless man. Far from, and Pamela was wrong in thinking that he considered church-going a bore. After all, one day, who knew when or how, a miracle might happen – a sudden, blinding light on his private and personal Road to Damascus.

Now that miracle had happened. He had met Lisa, and his new job would mean spending more time with her.

What he could not bear was the endless stretches of time, at weekends, when he could not get in touch with her, even from the phone-box in the village, for the simple reason that Lisa was not on the phone. But this was ridiculous . . .

At their next meeting, he said forcefully, "Listen, darling, call me selfish, but a telephone is essential! No argument, *please!* I'll pay for the installation." Not stopping to consider that a telephone might tie Lisa indoors awaiting his calls.

103

Truth to tell, that possibility had not occurred to her either until after the phone, with Jake Colby's permission, had been installed, she found herself pinned down in the flat at weekends, constantly on the qui vive awaiting the phone to ring, worrying about the affair which had taken over her life; knowing that her love for Edward had strengthened her in some ways; weakened her in others.

She now knew that right and wrong did not enter into it when two people became involved in a love affair of this intensity. She had at least gained some inkling of the guilt feelings John must have suffered over his affair with Linda. Now she, God help her, was in the same boat.

Waking early one Sunday morning, her mind filled with thoughts of Edward, Lisa tried to envisage her life without him; imagined her days unlit by the hope that he would come to her, however briefly, to hold her in his arms and tell her he loved her.

Staring up at the ceiling, she tried all the usual tacks: . . . we are not really hurting anyone . . . I am not attempting to take Edward away from his wife . . . I am content to remain in the background . . . But she knew, deep down, that this was not so. Every time Edward glanced at his watch, each time he left her alone in the flat, she felt expendable, shut out of his life. Nothing more than his 'bit on the side'; his mistress – the 'Other Woman'.

Worse still, she was fast becoming obsessed with Pamela. How did she look? Was she short, tall, fat, thin, pretty or ugly?

Common sense warned her that Edward would not have married an ugly woman. Relationships changed and altered with the years, she well knew, but surely Edward must have loved Pamela once upon a time? – enough to impregnate her with his daughter, Judith.

If only Edward would set her mind at rest concerning his present relationship with his wife. Did he still make love to her, Lisa wondered? If so, how did he feel afterwards? If only she *knew*.

It was then she remembered Aunt Grace; something she had said to her long ago: "Men are not like women, my dear. Always bear in mind that Mother Nature blotted her copybook in that respect; the reason why I have never married. The thought of living with a polygamous male was more than I could stomach."

Getting out of bed one grey November Sunday morning, Lisa slipped into a kaftan made from the same length of material as her divan cover. Tying the thick, tasselled cord, glancing in the long mirror above the carved oak chest, she saw herself as a stranger, a much slimmer woman with straight, almost shoulder-length hair, and thought of the long hours she used to spend at the hairdressers, and worrying about her latest perm turning frizzy in the rain; the times she had emerged from the salon looking like Harpo Marx in his tightly curled wig.

Mrs Hannersley was right about the flat being cold. Shivering, she plugged in the electric fire, feeling guilty at using Jake Colby's electricity, afraid of using too much, wishing she had a slot-meter. She would mention this the next time she went down to his office to pay her rent.

Going through to the kitchen, she measured coffee – Continental blend – into the percolator, and set it to blurp. Deciding not to make porridge this morning, she wandered back to the living room to look at her African violets in their copper container, and realised, by their shrivelled leaves that they were dying from lack of warmth.

That they should die on her was unthinkable. Hurrying back to the kitchen, rummaging through a drawer, she found what she was looking for – a roll of pliofilm bags.

"If you think I'm letting you die without a struggle," she told the violets severely, tucking them up in pliofilm, "you've got another think coming."

The carriage-clock on the mantelpiece chimed eleven, by which time she had drunk two cups of coffee, prepared the vegetables, carrots, onions and potatoes for the scrag-end of mutton casserole she had planned for her evening meal, had made her bed and smoothed the cover, and still the phone had not rung, which meant that Edward had gone to church with Pamela.

Had he simply driven her to morning service and made some excuse or other not to accompany her into church, he would have rung by this time. Or perhaps he had been delayed for some reason, had stopped off at a garage to buy petrol, for instance, and the phone would ring any minute now.

The tension of waiting strung her nerves to concert pitch. Opening the french window, she stood on the balcony and looked down at the harbour; saw the reassuring bulk of a timber boat hawsered alongside the quay, heard a snatch of song as a galleyman threw overboard a handful of scraps; heard the screaming of the gulls as they fought over the food.

And still the phone had not rung.

Knowing she must do something positive, she began unpacking the tea-chest containing Aunt Grace's personal possessions, and suddenly the room seemed filled with her presence.

Flicking over the pages of old photograph albums, memories ploughed long furrows in Lisa's mind: memories of a dog called Rover, a daft-as-a-brush collie who had been her constant childhood companion. Memories of her parents smiling at the camera: sandwiched between them a plump little girl in a cotton dress and ankle-socks, in the garden of their home in Walthamstow, grouped together beneath the branches of an apple tree in full bloom.

There were other photographs too, of long-forgotten great uncles and aunts, and pictures of unknown men who had been killed in the 1914–18 War, whose names she would never know. Men who had, perhaps, once paid court to her Aunt Grace at the height of her youth and beauty. And Aunt Grace had been very beautiful, Lisa thought fondly looking at a photograph of a fair-haired girl wearing a fur-trimmed robe and a diamanté crown, inscribed with the words: 'Rose Queen. Wheatford Carnival'.

Gently laying aside the photograph albums, Lisa lifted from the chest the pictures that her aunt had painted long ago, and remembered how she would stand for hours on end in her conservatory studio, in her younger days, daubing colours on to canvas, breaking off now and then to explain about light and shade and perspective over a cup of coffee and a Gauloises cigarette or, better still, a Gauloises cigarette and a glass of pale, dry Portofino sherry.

The paintings were good, Lisa realised. Aunt Grace had used her brush with imagination. One picture in particular, that of a clump of dianthus near the garden gate, breathed the scent of a long gone summer day in their exact shades of pink and purple.

Unearthing her aunt's palette from the chest, Lisa remembered the day the old lady had cleaned it for the last time, and laid aside her brushes, when her hands became too stiff with arthritis to paint any more.

Opening her aunt's paint-box, Lisa caught the lingering smell of turpentine. The paint-tubes were rock solid now, dried up with age.

Finally, to her delight, Lisa rediscovered, at the bottom of the chest, a small table-easel and a virgin canvas. Carrying the easel to the octagonal table near the window and propping up the canvas; picking up the palette and a brush experimentally, she wondered if she also might take up art as a hobby; as a means of filling in her lonely, wasteful hours awaiting the telephone to ring.

The phone rang.

Dropping the palette and brush, Lisa hurried to answer the call.

107

"I'm sorry, darling," Edward said apologetically, sounding a long way off, obviously ringing from a phone-box. "I meant to ring earlier."

"Where are you?"

"At a garage, buying petrol."

"Have you been to church?"

"Yes. Pamela insisted. She seemed – upset."

"I see."

"Tell me, darling, what are you doing right now?"

"Painting."

"Painting? You mean – decorating?"

"No, I mean painting. The kind of thing that Monet and Manet, Caraveggio and Constable used to do in the dim and distant past." She was deeply angry, and he knew it.

He said, "Please, Lisa, don't be angry with me. Things are difficult for me too, remember."

"Yes," she said dully, "I suppose they must be, with a wife on one hand, a mistress on the other, both complaining bitterly that they don't see enough of you these days. A bit like walking a tightrope without a safety-net, I imagine."

"Listen, Lisa," he said hurriedly, "I'll be with you tomorrow evening, around eight. We'll talk then. Sorry, I must go now. 'Bye, darling, and remember, I love you!"

The phone went dead. His money had run out.

Replacing the hand-set, Lisa stared about the room, her thoughts centred on tomorrow evening at eight.

Seeing him again seemed a reason for living.

Chapter Twelve

Coming in from the cold, Lisa's softly-lit room seemed a haven to Edward. "I'm sorry about yesterday," he said urgently, "sorry I made you angry. It was a difficult situation; a special service to mark the visit of the rural dean; a matter of 'showing the flag', of not upsetting the apple cart . . ." He meant Pamela's apple cart.

"It really doesn't matter. I'm sorry too," Lisa said. "I shouldn't have said what I did about, well, you know. That was petty of me."

"It wasn't your fault." He kissed her.

"The sabbatical idea isn't working very well," she admitted. "I have too much time on my hands. Now the flat is more or less shipshape, I'm thinking of finding a part-time job over the Christmas period."

"Look, darling," he said impatiently, "I've told you before, if it's money you need, I'll help you."

Lisa shook her head. "No, it isn't just money, I need to be busy." She drew him down beside her on the settee. "I miss having something definite to do; a purpose in life."

"Yes, I can see that. But I wouldn't want you to take another menial job."

"That depends what's on offer. Perhaps I could find a temporary job as an assistant in one of the department stores. I think I'd enjoy selling perfume, lingerie or whatever; being part of the Christmas rush . . ."

"Being cooped up in some overheated atmosphere day in, day out," he interrupted, "listening to piped Muzac:

109

'Jingle Bells' and 'Hark, the Herald Angels'. Coming home tired out."

He felt bedevilled with guilt that he had nothing to offer her apart from body; that intangible thing called love which possessed the power, at times, to wound more deeply than it healed.

"At least I have a home to come back to," she said quietly, sensing his weariness, and something far deeper, a hint of disapproval, of withdrawal. "What I'm trying to say is, I love this place, every angle and corner of it so much that I couldn't bear the thought of losing it."

"Oh, for God's sake, Lisa! Do you imagine for one moment I would stand by and watch you lose your home? If it came to that, I'd make you accept my help whether you wanted it or not!"

"That's impossible, and you know it! I take it your wife knows how many beans make five? Besides, keeping my head above water is my own affair. I have my pride, Edward, no intention of becoming a kept woman!"

"I see," he said bitterly, "so that's what all this is about, is it? You really know how to put the knife in, don't you?" He rose to his feet. "I shouldn't have come tonight," he said, picking up his outdoor coat. "I'd better leave before we both say things we'll regret later."

"As you wish."

"I'll phone you," he said briefly.

Oh yes, she thought, that bloody telephone. And he had not even kissed her goodbye.

Later, in bed, staring up at the ceiling, noticing the way the glow of her bedside lamp illuminated the tiny flaws and imperfections, how could she possibly have told Edward what it felt like to be the 'other woman'? There came a time when playing second fiddle undermined the foundations of every unorthodox relationship, she imagined.

Restless, unable to sleep, she got up to look out of the window. Leaning her head against the glass, she saw the street lights winking along the shore, the sea fluorescent by starlight; heard the sound of the waves sucking against the harbour wall.

The phone rang at midnight. Edward's voice came on the line. Speaking very quietly, he said, "I'm sorry, darling. See you soon?"

She realised he was ringing from home. He must have waited until Pamela was asleep, wanting to make up for his abrupt departure, needing to put things right between them.

"Yes," she said softly, "it's all right. See you soon. Goodnight, darling," and imagined him going back to bed, absolved, ready for sleep, moving quietly so as not to disturb his wife.

The woman at the employment agency was pleasantly efficient. "A few personal details first, please, if you don't mind, Mrs Hazell," she said. "Full name, date of birth, marital status, children, that kind of thing, for our records."

"Yes, of course."

"Now, Mrs Hazell," the woman continued, when the initial details had been written down, "what kind of work are you looking for? Secretarial, shop-work, domestic?"

"I'd prefer a full-time job as a librarian," Lisa said hopefully.

The woman shook her head. "Sorry, no chance of that, I'm afraid. Full-time specialised jobs are rarer than hen's teeth these days. We deal mainly in part-time employment. Stop-gaps for want of a better description. Our clients are largely women – and men of course – willing to step in as temps when staff holidays and so on create short-term vacancies."

At least stop-gap sounded better than dogsbody, Lisa thought.

"Have you secretarial skills?" the interviewer enquired. "Shorthand, typing? Office work crops up occasionally." She smiled expectantly. "No? Well, not to worry. Let me

111

see." She flicked through a card-index on the desk. "Ah, here's something. There's a vacancy for a general assistant at The Bay View Residential Hotel. Board and lodging provided, if required."

"Thank you, but no," Lisa said hastily, trying hard not to laugh. "I have my own home, and I don't particularly want hotel work."

"Hm, well, that narrows the field somewhat," the woman said sharply. "What about shop work?"

"Yes, I think I could manage that," Lisa replied quiescently, not wanting to try the woman's patience more than she had already done so. "I enjoy – selling; persuading people to buy something they had no intention of buying."

"Oh?" The woman perked up a little. "Well, that's splendid. I had no idea you were an experienced saleslady." Back she went to the card-index. "Here's something that might interest you. There's a vacancy for an experienced salesperson in the fancy goods department at Dogberries, over the Christmas period. Hours nine to five-thirty, apart from late-opening hours in the run-up to Christmas. Well, what do you think?"

"I'll take it," Lisa said gratefully.

"Fine, that's settled then. I'll give you a letter of introduction to the store-manager, Mr Whiteley. The sooner you see him, the better. Today, if possible."

"By all means. I'll go right away, if that's convenient."

"Good! Here's your letter of intro, and I'll ring him to expect you within the next half-hour or so." The interviewer added, unnecessarily from Lisa's viewpoint, "The poor man is really quite desperate to find someone capable of taking charge of the department."

Taking charge of the department? Lisa's mind boggled. But the die was cast. No way was she prepared to admit to the lady behind the desk that her 'salesperson' experience amounted to nothing more spectacular than standing behind a stall in the Wheatford Village Hall, at various Christmas bazaars, persuading elderly ladies to purchase bottles of bath-salts, hand-knitted teacosies, and bed-jackets, and rattling the money into a tin box behind the counter when the bargaining had been completed.

Well, serve her right, she thought, if Mr Whiteley was not quite desperate enough to take on an imposter.

Even so, an hour later, after treating herself to a cup of coffee and a lukewarm sausage-roll along the way, she entered Dogberries' departmental store, smiling bravely; presented her letter of introduction to a worried-looking assistant, and, within minutes, came face-to-face with an even more worried-looking store-manager, who asked her, distractedly, how soon she could start.

"Now, if you like," Lisa said gently, feeling intensely sorry for the man.

"You could? Oh, wonderful!" He was a very tall, thin man. "There's a bit of a crisis at the moment. Miss Prior, the manageress of the fancy good department has met with an accident. I really need someone – er, mature and dependable to take charge of the younger staff until Miss Prior is fit to return to work."

"How long will that be?" Lisa asked.

"A week or a fortnight, I imagine. Now, if you'd care to come with me, I'll show you round and explain things to you."

Dogberries occupied a corner site in a busy street off the main thoroughfare. It was well-established, and retained an aura of the past. The name was synonymous with good value for money. There was no piped Muzac, and the atmosphere was not overpoweringly hot, to Lisa's relief.

The fancy goods on show consisted mainly of purses, key-rings, personalised pens and door-plates, wallets and shopping bags, baubles, bangles and beads; notepaper and compendiums, cottonwool and tissue containers, belts and leather bookmarkers, telephone pads and racks of greeting cards.

There were two junior assistants, slender girls with long hair in pony-tails, named Tara and Jenny, doing the dusting. All the goods were clearly marked, Mr Whiteley explained, and there was a staff restaurant on the top floor where coffee, snacks and hot food were available if required. "Our cook does a very nice shepherd's pie," he said pleasantly, "and a really excellent hot-pot."

"Before we go any further," Lisa said quietly, "I should explain that I am not really qualified to work here. I'm sorry. It's all my fault. I'm afraid I misled the interviewer."

"You'd better come through to my office," he said, leading the way.

"Now, Mrs Hazell," he began, when they were seated. "Perhaps you'd care to explain."

"It's the old story," Lisa smiled ruefully. "I need a job, but not at any price. I think I'd make a fairly good assistant, but running a department is beyond my scope, and I know it. It simply wouldn't be fair to you to attempt such a thing. I might land you in one hell of a mess."

Mr Whiteley regarded her coolly across his desk. "Know what I think, Mrs Hazell?" he said appraisingly. "That you could run the fancy goods department with one hand tied behind your back!"

"I'm sorry? I don't understand." She looked at him as if he had taken leave of his senses. "What makes you think so?"

"Let me put it this way. Because you had the guts to tell me the truth. Dogberries is an old-fashioned store with old-fashioned principles; the reason why you are welcome to work here, if you wish to do so, during the Christmas period." He smiled boyishly. "Well, what do you say?"

"What could I possibly say except – yes, and thank you, Mr Whiteley. Thank you very much indeed!"

*　　　*　　　*

114

Edward came to her that evening, contritely, in need of love and understanding; his need as great as hers.

Later, lying warm and relaxed in his arms, utterly fulfilled; overwhelmed by the tenderness and passion of their lovemaking, Lisa wondered how long this subterfuge could last; how long they could stand the strain of their illicit relationship.

The time had come when she wanted the whole meal, not just the starter; to make plans for their future together; to hear him say that he could not go on living without her. At the same time, common sense warned her that no person on earth had the right to own another human being.

She also knew that, when the time came, glancing at his watch, he would leave her; drive on that long road out of town, back to Pamela.

Driving home, Edward understood the situation far better than Lisa realised. Contrary to what she might think, he felt an ever deepening love for her; far deeper than mere physical love or desire.

Lisa occupied a unique place in his life – that other dimension to living which he had always hoped might exist – to 'the ends of being and ideal grace'.

As the tyres sped over the road, taking him away from Lisa, back to Pamela, Edward experienced an overpowering sense of guilt, laced with longing.

How strange, he thought, that in an affair of this complexity, women assumed that the man suffered least – or not at all. But here he was, a man fighting a titanic battle of conscience. A man who had assumed, against his will, his better judgement, a cloak of respectability totally at odds with his dreams of escape from his marital treadmill.

So why not pack in this absurd charade? His role as a model husband?

Telling Pamela about Lisa would prove difficult, but not impossible, he considered, and Judy was now old enough to understand that the marriage of parents, often enough, nowadays, did not work out right in the end.

Above all, he knew what this underhand affair was doing to Lisa.

Leaving Pamela, he would make sure that she was well provided for, he told himself on that long drive out of town. She would have the house, and a regular income from his salary, plus whatever else he could offer her by way of recompense for his infidelity. And when the break had been made, Pamela would certainly have the sympathy of her friends – those admirable women who served with her on the church social committee.

But what about Lisa? Would she mind being poor? Because they would be comparatively poor when he left Pamela. And what were the chances of his finding another well-paid job at his age?

He and Lisa were not, after all, twenty-year-olds, agog with life and hope, and the years ahead might well prove difficult for them, robbed of the wild expectations of youth.

In time to come, in the way of things, physical desire would diminish as they grew older, and they would have to face the pressure of knowing that the new life they had built up together was based on the ruins of the old, at the expense of Pamela's happiness, and Judy's.

Arriving home, he turned the car into the driveway with accustomed ease and practice, knowing the exact moment to angle the bonnet to avoid hitting the gateposts.

And this, he thought, was what his life was all about: gauging distances; knowing how far to advance, and when to stop, within a confined space, to avoid a collision.

Lisa had not told Edward about the job. It had seemed expedient not to re-tread dangerous ground. It seemed scarcely worthwhile causing an upset over something as trivial as a few weeks at Dogberries – six at the most.

Thinking positively, the experience, the change, would

do her good and the money would come in handy. She liked the shop enormously for its unpretentiousness and its air of solid respectability, the feeling of safety and security about it, that it had not succumbed entirely to modernisation.

Some of the old oak counters were still in situ in the lingerie department, and so were the original display cabinets in the china department. Nearer Christmas, Mr Whiteley had told her on their tour of inspection, there would be a Santa's Grotto in the toy department, and an eight foot Christmas tree in the foyer. And she mustn't worry in the least about running the fancy goods department pro tem. The stock had already been ordered, delivered and priced, so it was simply a matter of replenishment of the goods on display on a day to day basis.

The staff, he explained, were allowed a quarter-hour break morning and afternoons; an hour and a quarter for lunch, and ten per cent discount personal on items purchased from the various departments, at which moment Lisa's thoughts had turned to the replenishment of her wardrobe: a new dress, perhaps; a couple of sweaters; a lace-trimmed nightie and matching négligé . . . A new anorak?

Meanwhile, she had decided to have a word with her landlord about having an electricity meter installed in her room.

With this uppermost in her mind, she went down early the following Monday morning to his office near the front door, to pay her rent and explain her reasons for wanting a meter.

Entering the office, she found Jake Colby seated at his desk, in receipt of custom.

"My word, Mrs Hazell," he said in that 'Come day, go day, God send pay-day' way of his, "you're up early."

"Yes, well I'm on my way to work." Handing him her rent-book and cheque, she continued, "The thing is, I'd like an electricity meter in my room."

117

"You would? May one ask why?" He leaned back in his chair, one eyebrow raised slightly.

Irritated by his sang-froid, she replied, "Because, Mr Colby, I hate feeling guilty every time I switch on the fire or boil a kettle. The fact is, it's freezing cold up there, especially now, at this time of year, and I'd rather pay for my own heating, if you don't mind."

"I see. Very well then, it shall be so. A pearl above price is an independent woman with her mind of her own."

"It's the way I was brought up," she said tartly, picking up her rent-book.

"Blessed is she that expecteth nothing, is that it?" he suggested coolly.

"Not at all, Mr Colby. More a case of 'blessed is she that expecteth nothing she can't afford to pay for herself.' Now, if you'll excuse me." She closed the front door with unnecessary force.

From her first wage-packet, she treated herself to a green tweed skirt and a matching sweater; from the second, a portable Dimplex heater, by which time Santa Claus had taken up residence in his grotto at Dogberries, the Christmas tree had been erected in the foyer, and a slot-meter had been installed in her flat.

There was still no sign of the accident-prone Miss Prior, who had suffered a broken wrist and ankle in a fall from a stepladder, Lisa had gleaned from Tara and Jenny, the young sales' assistants, during brief moments of conversation between customers. Not that they appeared to mind very much being in charge of herself, a newcomer to Dogberries.

"She'll be spinning out the anguish, I daresay," Tara surmised, "wanting Tim Whiteley to dance attendance on her, the silly cow! And her old enough to be his mother!"

"Yeah, but she *is* well preserved for her age," Jenny argued, "and it's high time he was married, a nice bloke like him. Truth to tell," she added wistfully, "I've given him the 'glad-eye' myself more than once, but no go! He's a real 'mother's boy', and no mistake."

"Either that, or 'queer'," Tara interrupted. "Have you noticed the way he quirks up his little finger drinking coffee in the canteen?"

"I couldn't care less if he's as queer as 'Dick's hatband'," Jenny retorted, "I think he's a real nice bloke. What do *you* think, Mrs Hazell?"

"I think it's high time you two stopped gossiping and got on with your work! You, Tara, had better go down to the stockroom and bring up a fresh consignment of purses. Here's the docket, and you, Jenny, had better start refilling the greeting cards display. OK?"

And, "Yes, Mrs Hazell," they said obediently, accepting her authority. A feather in her cap; evidence that she had succeeded in this new challenge of hers. She thought, 'My cup runneth over', and knew that seldom in her life before, had she been happier than she was right now, with money in her purse to spend on a few small luxuries of living – a Sunday roast, for example, instead of scrag end of mutton; a brand new anorak; fresh tubes of paint to replace those she had discovered, rock-hard, in Aunt Grace's tea-chest; the purchase of a cashmere sweater as her Christmas present to Edward.

Christmas!

Chapter Thirteen

She had told Edward quietly, guiltily, about her job at Dogberries, fearing another explosion, another quarrel. But nothing of the kind had occurred.

He had simply said, when she mentioned that this was a temporary job over the Christmas period, "Oh yes, Christmas. I'd half-forgotten how close it is now. Too close for comfort."

"You mean you don't like Christmas?"

"Like it? Not now; not any more. I used to once upon a time, of course, as a child, when I believed in Santa Claus. Have you thought, Lisa, the shocking discovery, in the mind of a child, when it finds out that no such person exists? It's the first, possibly the ultimate betrayal. The first lie uttered by those closest to that child; the shattering of the child's faith in its parents."

"Please, darling, try not to look at things in that light. I don't remember feeling more than vaguely disappointed when I knew there wasn't a Father Christmas, but then I had suffered the loss of my parents, so I hadn't much else to lose," Lisa said gently, holding his hand.

"Oh, darling, I'm sorry. It's just that . . . Well, what's really bugging me is you being on your own at a time of — celebration, so called. You see, love, Judy is coming home for Christmas. I had a letter from her this morning. She'll arrive on Christmas Eve. I had thought she might spend Christmas in Birmingham, with her latest boyfriend, but apparently not."

Lisa said brightly, "No need to worry about me. I shan't mind being on my own. Honestly, I mean it! I'll let my hair down; relax. Read, listen to the radio, go to Communion on Christmas morning, come home and cook dinner; treat myself to a bottle of Bell's; go for a walk along the beach. The possibilities are endless! I'll probably spend the whole of Christmas in an alcoholic haze!" She laughed unconvincingly.

"I'll keep in touch if at all possible," Edward promised, "and I'll see you on Christmas Eve, on my way to the station to meet Judy. Her train's not due till nine-thirty."

"And you don't mind about my job at Dogberries?" Lisa asked wistfully.

"No, darling, I don't mind in the least, just as long as you're happy."

Rescuing Judy's mirror from the rubbish bin where she had thrown it, and replacing it on the hook near the kitchen window, had been for Pamela, an act of conscience. Looking into it was a different matter entirely. Vanity was a sin, her mother had drilled into her, tantamount to greed, lust and impurity of spirit; the decrees of the devil; the fallen angel Lucifer, to be fought against with all one's might and main, through prayer, fasting and self-abnegation.

Pamela had fought the battle – and won. Her lustless, pure, unvain mode of living had been achieved after many a long and lonely struggle, countless hours spent in prayer – had yielded little by way of recompense. Certainly not happiness. Not even peace of mind.

A sudden swirl of laughter invaded the room. Helga! More often of late, the memory of her dead sister had returned to haunt her, a ghostly figure flitting through the corridors of her mind, bringing with her memories of their childhood home, the house by the river; of Sunday luncheon, their father carving the Sunday roast, the maid bringing in the tureens of vegetables.

Staring into the mirror, Pamela saw not her own pale image reflected there, but the sparkling face of Helga, her twin sister, who had possessed all the beauty and vitality lacking in herself. Twins were supposed to look alike, but she and Helga might have been born years apart, of different parents.

How strange, she thought, that she had never told Edward about Helga, that she had never felt close enough to share with him the bitterest, most terrible experience of her life so far; the tragedy which had tainted not only her life, but others, and particularly that of her mother.

Turning away from the mirror, Pamela remembered her wedding night, her fear of what lay ahead, seeing herself as Helga; Edward the destroyer of innocence.

If only she had felt close enough to voice her fears, to tell Edward about Helga, but there had been no words to bridge the gulf between them. Her father had forced her into a loveless marriage, stripping her of the security of home and money, leaving her no choice other than to marry the man he had picked out for her.

The tragedy had happened when she and Helga were seven years old. Memory drew Pamela back to that lovely spring day when she and her sister had run across the fields to the river to play hide-and-seek among the willows. There had been daisies and cowslips, she remembered, and lambs trotting after their ewes, white clouds sailing the sky like galleons, their mother waving to them from the open drawing room windows.

She had been so happy then, held fast in a net of security and love, with Helga, her constant companion, tripping along beside her.

The memory of that last morning with her sister was fixed in Pamela's mind like a clip from a motion picture. She had no clear recollection of what had happened immediately afterwards. Presumably they had raced back to the house for lunch. No matter how hard she tried, she could not clearly remember what she and Helga had done that afternoon. Perhaps they had gone to Sunday school, afterwards to drawing room tea, as they had usually done on Sundays.

What she did clearly remember was standing at the foot of the stairs much later, hearing the sound of her mother's weeping, her words, uttered on a wail of anguish: "If only I had known! If only I had gone with her!"

Then had come her father's angry retort: "You should have made it your business to go with her! You knew she wanted to see the lambs before bedtime! I hold you entirely responsible for what has happened!"

"No, Rupert, I beg of you! Please don't go! Don't leave me! I can't bear it!"

Then had come the sound of a slammed door on the landing above, the heavy tread of her father's footsteps on the stairs as he came down to the hall from his wife's room, not even noticing herself, a frightened child, standing in the shadowy hall near the foot of the staircase, whimpering because she knew that something terrible had happened to Helga.

What followed had seemed like a nightmare of endless comings and goings. Even worse was being sent away, without explanation, to stay with distant relations in Wiltshire, and the whispering that went on there; conversations that stopped abruptly whenever she entered a room.

Listening at doors, she had learned the awful truth, that Helga was dead; that she had been attacked in a field near their home and left in a ditch to die.

A month later, she had returned home to a changed household, a father who could scarcely bear the sight of her, a mother who had donned the armour of religious fervour against the unspeakable horror of Helga's death.

Soon afterwards, they had moved away from the area, to the Georgian house near Leicester, where she had met Edward, but nobody had taken her aside and told her what had happened that spring evening when Helga had disappeared from her life forever. How could they have done? How to explain to a child that her formerly happy life had been swept away because a tramp, who lusted after children, had raped Helga to death?

I should never have married, Pamela told herself, plunging her hands into the washing up water. No matter what my father said, however much he tried to push me into marrying Edward, I should have refused, feeling the way I did about men. He must have known by that time that I had found out the truth about Helga. Did he hate me so much that he wanted rid of me too, because I reminded him of her, and he wished to punish me because I was not her?

By the same token, had he turned to other women to punish his wife whom he had held responsible for Helga's death? There must have been other women apart from the magistrate's wife, she surmised. And even before the death of her mother, had he planned exactly what he would do afterwards – to sell the family home, scoop the inheritance in full – her own as well as his – and simply disappear like a thief in the night?

Oh yes, she thought bitterly, knowing her father, he would have planned everything down to the last detail; persuaded her mentally sick mother to will everything to him; the house, the furniture, her money, her jewellery. *Everything!*

Fighting against old, unhappy memories, Pamela put on a pan of milk to warm, and made herself a cup of coffee, resisting the knowledge that drinking coffee, mid-morning, was a sign of weakness, remembering the times her mother had warned her against the dangers of self-indulgence. Her mother, shrivelled to dust these many years, who nevertheless remained an integral part of her life, her way of thinking; who had whispered to her, on her deathbed, to shut out the wickedness of the world in work and prayer.

Measuring a spoonful of instant coffee into a cup and pouring into it the hot milk, Pamela realised that all the distressing physical symptoms she had experienced lately, the depression, her inability to concentrate fully, the ringing in her ears, her uneven monthly cycles, the pins and needles sensation in her fingers, were all part and parcel of the menopause.

Sipping the coffee, it seemed a shameful thing that a woman of her age should still be capable of child-bearing, and recalled not merely the disgust, but the terror she had experienced when Edward had made love to her that Monday morning, without precaution, thinking of no one but himself; his own physical satisfaction.

Edward!

Seated at the kitchen table, drinking her coffee, Pamela remembered the day he had carried their baby daughter home from the hospital; the way she had turned her head away as he cradled the child in his arms, knowing the harmful effects of jealousy on the human spirit.

But every day of her life, since Judith was born, had been tainted with feelings of relegation and neglect, the kind of feelings she had experienced the day Helga died, when she had cowered, alone and forgotten at the foot of the stairs.

She loved the girl, of course she did, even knowing that Judith thought far more of her father than she ever had done of herself. But Edward had not understood her natural concern when Judith had announced joyously that she had won a place at a teacher-training college in Birmingham. Birmingham, of all places; a sprawling city in which a young girl might be easily led astray.

When she had voiced her fears concerning their daughter's welfare away from home, Edward had said angrily, "For heaven's sake, Pamela, why can't you ever let go? Why not encourage the girl?"

She had wanted to scream back at him, "Because of Helga! Because my sister was raped to death not a stone's throw away from safety. If such a thing could happen to an innocent child within sight of home, what chance of survival for an innocent young girl far away in a strange place?"

Instead, she had tightened her lips and gone into another room, closing the door behind her so that he should not follow her; witness the tears she shed. Not that he had attempted to follow her, and she had known why not. Habit! That habitual barrier of non-communication which had grown up between them over the years.

Finishing her coffee, getting up to rinse the cup, she was engulfed by a sudden wave of nausea. She grabbed hold of the draining-board for support, and spewed her stomach contents into the sink; stared in disbelief at the horrid mess, then turned on the taps to flush away the vomit.

In a little while, when she felt better, she walked unsteadily to the hall telephone and dialled a number. When the receptionist replied, she said, "Hello, this is Mrs Edward Miller. I wish to make an appointment to consult Dr Soames as soon as possible."

Chapter Fourteen

Lisa had seldom felt happier, more relaxed or more hopeful than she had done in the run-up to Christmas, at Dogberries. She loved the feeling of being useful once more, the cheerful crowds of shoppers wanting cards, purses, belts and compendiums; children counting out the coins they had saved to buy their mums a present; popping their purchases into paper-bags printed with the words: 'The Season's Greetings to One and All. Come Back Soon to Shop at Dogberries, The Store With a Soul'.

And this was true, Lisa thought joyfully, looking forward to the staff party in the restaurant on the twenty-second of December, when they would all exchange Christmas cards, and tuck into turkey sandwiches and hot mince-pies. Her one and only deep regret was that, when the store closed on Christmas Eve, she would no longer be a part of 'The Store With a Soul'.

Even so, she had made friends along the way, saved a little money in her Post Office account, and come to terms with the fact that she would spend Christmas alone in her flat. So what? With books to read, good food to eat, the view of the sea from her sitting room window, how could she possibly feel lonely or unhappy? Or so she chose to believe, thrusting to the back of her mind that Edward would spend Christmas with his family; with Pamela and his beloved daughter, Judy.

He had, at least, promised to visit her on Christmas Eve, on his way to the station to meet the 9.30 train, and he had reiterated that promise this evening, when, after lovemaking, he had told her how much he needed her – to 'the ends of being and ideal grace . . .'

He had then left her alone to drive home to – Pamela.

Turning the car into the driveway with accustomed ease and precision, braking at exactly the right moment to admit the car to the garage, Edward entered the house by the back door, praying to heaven that Pamela had gone to bed early; that she would not be in the drawing-room, querying his late arrival, grumbling about his having to work overtime.

There, on the kitchen table, he discovered a plate of neatly-cut sandwiches and a flask of coffee, and he experienced a sudden stab of remorse that his wife had taken the trouble to provide sustenance for a husband she cared for so little, or not at all.

Suddenly, there came to him the gut-feeling that something was wrong. Apart from the kitchen, the rest of the house was in darkness. Normally, when he arrived home, Pamela would be in the drawing room, knitting, sewing, or watching television. But not tonight.

At the foot of the stairs, he called out to her: "Pamela?" No reply. It was then he heard the sound of retching from their room on the landing.

Taking the stairs two at time, he flung open the bedroom door. "Pamela, what's wrong? Are you ill?" he cried out in alarm.

The room was in darkness. Switching on the light, he saw his wife lying supine on the bed, her face buried in a towel, and smelt the sour smell of vomit in the air.

Deeply shocked, he demanded hoarsely, "My God! How long have you been like this?" hurrying to her side.

Unable to answer, she retched feebly into the towel, and he thought how thin, bleached and insipid she looked, as

128

though illness had drained away the essential life-force from her body, leaving a dried up skeleton; a pale, emaciated ghost of a woman.

"Come along." He lifted her as he would have done Judy, gently and with infinite compassion. For the first time ever she appeared to need his strength and support. "I'm taking you to Judy's room."

She moaned, her sides heaved, but nothing came. Wrapping her in a thick blanket from the chest at the foot of the bed, he carried her along the landing to their daughter's room. Her teeth had begun to chatter, her body temperature had dropped alarmingly.

Making sure that she had a couple of clean towels, he tucked her up in bed, hurried down to the kitchen, plugged in the kettle, found a hot-water bottle, filled it, then, going through to the drawing room, he poured a stiff tot of brandy, and sped back upstairs.

She had not been sick again, but her chalk-white face resembled a death-mask.

Pushing the hot-water bottle beneath the bedclothes, putting his arm beneath her shoulders, lifting her into a semi-sitting position, "Here, drink this," he said.

"What is it?"

"Brandy."

"No, I . . ."

"I insist! It will do you good!" He held the glass to her lips. She drank, then spluttered. "That's good. Are you feeling any warmer?"

She nodded. A tinge of colour stained her cheeks. He sat beside her; realised, with a jolt, that she had been weeping. But Pamela never wept. Throughout the years he had known her, he had never once seen her cry. Not even at her mother's funeral.

"I'm going to call Dr Soames," he said firmly.

"*No!*"

"For heaven's sake, Pamela, be sensible," he persisted.

129

"There must be a reason for this. Perhaps you've eaten something . . ."

"*No*!" She looked at Edward directly, her face a mask of hatred and disgust. "I do not want you to call Dr Soames. He has no remedy for what ails me. No cure for the kind of nausea I feel at this moment."

"What do you mean?" But he knew exactly what she meant.

"I rang your office earlier this evening," she said coldly. "I spoke to a colleague of yours who told me, as I had suspected, that at no time during the past few weeks have you worked overtime."

"I see."

"You don't deny it?"

"No, Pamela, I don't deny it." A curious feeling of relief washed over him at that moment. "All I can say is, I'm sorry."

"*Sorry?*" Her face contorted with anger. "Tell me, Edward, *why* are you sorry? Sorry that you lied to me so convincingly, or sorry that I found out? Tell me, Edward, what kind of a man are you?"

"Please, Pamela, try to understand . . ."

"*Understand*? Tell me, Edward, what am I supposed to understand? That you have made a mockery of our marriage? That you have been meeting another woman behind my back? That's the truth of the matter, isn't it? Well, frankly, Edward, you disgust me! You are no better than that filthy beast who raped my sister to death!"

"My God, Pam, what are you saying? What – sister? What are you talking about?" He gripped her arm.

Wincing, "That's right," she hissed, "add physical pain into the bargain! What more could I expect of you – a womaniser, a liar, a whited sepulchre? Or perhaps this whore of yours enjoys physical pain? Tell me, Edward, does she enjoy being whipped? Some women do, you know!"

"For God's sake, Pamela, you don't know what you are saying." Edward buried his face in his hands.

Pamela continued hysterically, "I shall find out, of course, who she is. I'll make it my business to find out her name and where she lives . . ."

"I'm going to call the doctor," Edward said briefly, lifting his head from his hands.

Pamela uttered a bitter, unmirthful laugh. "There's no need," she responded. "I consulted Dr Soames some time ago. I know exactly what is wrong with me! I am pregnant! Pregnant by a man involved in an affair with another woman! The reason I asked, what kind of man *are* you?"

Overwhelmed by a searing feeling of despair, Edward went downstairs to the drawing room.

Pouring himself a stiff drink, he slumped in a chair near the fire, staring at the monotonously flickering coal effect, unable to grasp the awful implications of his wife's pregnancy. She could not possibly have the child, he thought; she must not. The doctor would make her see sense. Pamela must realise the sheer impossibility of going ahead with the pregnancy. On the other hand, he knew only too well her capacity for self-inflicted stoicism, her stubborness and stiff-necked pride in doing what she saw as her duty. *Duty!*

He was still sitting there when, an hour later, Pamela came into the room, wearing a blue dressing gown, clutching at chair backs to steady herself.

"For God's sake, Pam!" He stared at her disbelievingly. "You shouldn't have come down. I thought you'd be asleep. Here, let me help you!" He half rose to his feet.

"Sit down, Edward! I don't want your help. I came down because I have something to say. Now. Tonight!"

"What's the point? We are both too tired and upset to talk to any purpose," he said wearily.

131

"You misunderstand. *I* am going to talk, you are going to listen. What I have to say concerns – Judith."

"Judith? What about her? What has she to do with – all this?" The hastily gulped brandy, the first glass followed by a second and third, had gone to his head. He couldn't think clearly.

Sitting down in the chair opposite, her usual chair, the knitting-bag on the arm of which spilled forth a tangled skein of wool, knitting needles, and a bed-jacket pattern, Pamela said coldly, decisively, "Judith must be told about my condition, and that you have been carrying on a sordid affair behind my back. And you must be the one to tell her."

"For God's sake, Pamela! She's only a girl! What has happened between us has nothing to do with her!"

"You think not?" Pamela smiled grimly. "I think differently. It seems entirely relevant to me that our daughter should know that her mother is expecting a child; that her father has been consorting with the lowest of the low – a common-or-garden whore!"

"Stop it!" Rising strongly to his feet, Edward confronted his wife. "You have no right to refer to a fine, decent person as a whore! You know nothing whatever about Lisa, nor could you begin to understand her even if you did."

"I believe you, Edward," Pamela flung back at him. "An adulteress is beyond my comprehension. I know now, of course, that you substituted my body for hers that Monday morning when you used me so shamefully. Tell me, had you quarrelled the night before? I take it that you had been with her the night before? You had, after all, lied to me in order to stay out late that night, remember?"

"Yes. But I scarcely knew her then. We'd had a drink together, that's all! You must believe me!"

"Believe you? My dear Edward, I wouldn't believe you if you told me tomorrow's date! The truth is, you substituted my body for hers! Thinking about *her*, you abused *me*! Well, deny it if you can!"

132

"I can't," he said quietly. "You are perfectly right as usual, Pamela. You said you hated me, but I had never dreamt how much. All I can possibly say is this, the woman I love is a fine, decent human being, capable of all the warmth and understanding I have longed for so desperately all the days of my life."

"I wondered how long it would be before you managed to put the blame on me," Pamela said bitterly. "You are a coward, Edward. When have you ever given me the chance to understand you? It has always been Judith you turned to, Judith you confided in, treating me as a stranger – a housekeeper! In which case, it should not prove too difficult for you to tell Judith the whole sordid story from beginning to end; to confide in her about this woman, this – Lisa – you are 'in love' with."

Rising stiffly to her feet, she continued, "A word of warning, Edward: you will put an end to your affair, or suffer the consequences. Make no mistake, I shall find out the name of your whore, confront her, if necessary, tell her I am pregnant! I wonder what she will think of you then?"

"Just a moment, before you go: you said something about a sister; some filthy beast who had raped her to death. I'd like an explanation. Why have you never mentioned this before? You spoke of understanding, or the lack of it. The boot's on the other foot, isn't it?"

Grasping the back of a chair, she said icily, "I do not propose to discuss that now or ever. Take it as an indication that never, throughout all the years we've been married, have I felt able to confide in you." She added bleakly, "I am going back to bed now. From now on, you will occupy the spare room."

"Just a minute, Pamela. You've had your say, now it's my turn. Hurt me if you like, but not Judy and – Lisa."

"You dare to ask that of me? To spare that – woman!"

"What happened was all my fault," he said wearily. "*I* did the pursuing. Whether or not you believe me, that is the truth! Please, I beg of you, Pamela, don't destroy her life, as you have destroyed your own."

"I don't know what you mean!"

Gripping his wife's shoulders, he said, "Then I suggest you think about it. Tell me, Pam, throughout the years we've been together, was there ever a moment when you felt more than a sense of duty towards me? It beggars belief that never once, until tonight, have you mentioned your sister. Are you incapable of love? That sister of yours, did you hate her too?"

Pamela covered her face with her hands. Sobs racked her thin body. Relaxing his grip, Edward walked to the window; saw that it was beginning to snow outside, that the grass beyond the window was filmed white by the steadily falling snow. "I'm sorry, Pam," he said tiredly, "just go back to bed now. So far as I'm concerned, we have nothing more of importance, to say to one another . . ."

"No, Edward, you are wrong if that is what you think," Pamela interrupted. "I loved Helga with all my heart! She was my twin. I loved her more than anyone else on earth!"

Turning away from the window, Edward experienced a feeling of shock at the fanatical expression of joy on his wife's face – the face of a martyr tied to a stake, awaiting, with a kind of religious fervour, the thrusting of the torch into the pile of kindling at her feet.

Twisting a handkerchief between shaking fingers, she cried, "We were inseparable! She was so full of life. I could always tell when Helga was near me by the sound of her laughter. The sun shone wherever she went. I worshipped the ground she walked on, and it was such a lovely house, with willow trees near the river. I remember every inch of it; the feeling of spaciousness and grace; the dining room overlooking the shrubbery; the scent of lilacs drifting in through the open windows . . . The dinner service was green with a gold-leaf border. On Sundays, Father would carve the roast and hand round the plates. Helga never stopped

134

chattering; trying to make Bessie laugh. Bessie was the maid who brought in the tureens of vegetables, and one day, Helga made her laugh so much that she dropped the tureen she was carrying and the carrots and peas rolled on to the carpet. Father was furious at first, but no one could be cross with Helga for very long."

Pamela drew in a shuddering breath of despair. "Then everything changed. Helga went out one evening alone, to look at the lambs. I must have been in bed. I – I can't quite remember why I didn't go with her. All I remember is waking up to find her bed was empty. I got up and went downstairs to look for her. It was late. I heard voices, from my parents' room. My father was saying terrible things; my mother was weeping."

"I'm sorry, Pamela," Edward said quietly, "please, don't tell me any more if you'd rather not." But the floodgates had opened. He doubted if she had even heard what he said.

"I was sent away to stay with people I had never seen before. If only someone had told me what had happened to Helga, that she had died and gone to heaven – the lie that parents usually feed to a child to explain the inexplicable. No one did. Nobody cared about me enough to comfort me, especially not my father, and my mother's door was closed against me. I know now that she was too ill, too shocked to see anyone. My father blamed her, you see, for Helga's death.

"Some time later, we moved to Leicester. I hated the new house. It seemed so cold, so empty without Helga. My parents seemed like strangers. They no longer shared a room; seldom even spoke to one another, much less to me. I grew to hate my father, and the feeling was mutual. He wanted rid of me. I grew up knowing that. Then you came along."

Pamela's face contorted. "Oh, I knew why you had been invited to luncheon that day. There had been others before you who had run a mile when they realised the set-up. My father never gave up. He wanted me off his hands. Knowing that I did not want to marry added fuel to his determination to make me do so against my will. And he succeeded in the long run. My one prayer, throughout the years; that he has been made to suffer as he made others suffer, especially my mother."

"Oh, Pamela, I'm so sorry." Overwhelmed with a feeling of pity, Edward moved towards her, wanting to hold her, to smooth her hair, dry her tears.

Staring up at him, "I don't want your pity," she said dully. Moving away from him like an old woman, she closed the door in his face and went back to bed.

Next morning, Edward rang the office to explain that he wouldn't be in to work until after the holidays. Not that his absence would matter. This was Christmas Eve. Nobody would be working much anyway, simply clearing their desks in readiness for the four day break; looking forward to the office party in the staff-room later that afternoon.

"Anything wrong? Not ill, are you?" Barry Kean had asked concernedly, answering the call.

"No, I'm fine. It's Pamela," Edward replied. "She's not at all well. A touch of – food poisoning, I suspect – or a flu bug."

"Oh, bad luck! At Christmas of all times! Sorry you'll miss the office party, old chap." Hesitantly, he said, "By the way, Pam rang up last night, wanting to get in touch with you. I answered the call; she asked if you were working overtime again. Hope I didn't put my foot in it?"

"Of course not. She was feeling ill at the time. In any case, I was on my way home."

"Oh, that's all right then. Well, Merry Christmas, old son! Don't do anything I wouldn't do!"

Hanging up the receiver, Edward knew that Barry had guessed exactly what he had been up to when Pamela had rung the office the night before; also that he could trust

Barry not to say a word to anyone else. A friend in a million, Barry Kean.

Going upstairs to his wife's room, carrying a tray of tea and toast, he found Pamela half lying down, half sitting up, propped up with pillows, her eyes wide open.

"I'm not going in to work today," he said, setting down the tray on the bedside table, "I thought there might be some last minute shopping you would want me to do."

"How thoughtful," she uttered sarcastically, "what a perfect excuse."

"I don't understand. A perfect excuse for – what?"

"Oh come now, Edward, don't tell me you haven't planned everything down to the last detail? Why make shopping an excuse? You'll be seeing – *her* – of course!"

"Please don't, Pamela," he said wearily.

"Don't – *what*?" She laughed mirthlessly. "But surely I have the right to surmise? Tell me, Edward, is this whore of yours available at any time of the day or night? In the back seat of the car, for example? Or has she some seedy little bed-sitting room in a back street somewhere in Westsea?"

Sick at heart, he moved towards the door.

Pamela continued hysterically, "What have you bought your whore for Christmas, Edward? Perfume? Black silk stockings? A see-through négligé? A new whip?"

Deeply shaken, he walked out of the bedroom, closing the door behind him.

Chapter Fifteen

It seemed odd, shopping for a Christmas she would spend alone, Lisa thought. Even so, the effort must be made. Life must go on.

Pushing round the covered market, buying fruit and vegetables, she wondered if one of the women standing at the greengrocer's stall was Pamela. Perhaps they had already rubbed shoulders without knowing. Was Pamela the woman in the smart red trouser-suit and cream raincoat, with newly-coiffed hair? The drab-looking woman with a heavily-laden shopping trolley, or perhaps Edward's wife had visited Dogberries fancy goods department during the past weeks, and she, Lisa, had served her unwittingly?

Hardly likely. Common sense told Lisa that Edward's wife would be more inclined to shop in her own neighbourhood, three miles out of town – an upper-crust area by all accounts – rejoicing in the name 'Higher Westsea': "Where the 'nobs' lived", according to Tara and Jenny, including Mr Whiteley and his mother. A kind of village with its own lending library and shopping precinct, lots of trees and detached houses, neatly mown grass verges and 'Keep Off the Grass' notices.

In which case, Lisa surmised, Pamela would be scarcely likely to come into Westsea to buy her fruit and vegetables, nor enter the portals of 'The Store With a Soul' to purchase her Christmas presents.

The picture of Pamela she had painted in her mind, was that of a slim, elegant middle-aged woman, as pernickety about her personal appearance as she was about her dislike of diminutives; a pillar of the local church; a carping woman with a mind of her own, whose word was law in the Miller household, and she was very nearly right in every particular apart from Pamela's looks. Never once had Lisa visualised Pamela as a dried out shell of a woman with rapidly greying hair; prematurely lined skin, and a body as thin and underdeveloped as that of a skinny teenage child.

Leaving the market, turning up her coat collar against the biting wind raking in from the sea, Lisa recalled, with joy, the weeks she had spent at Dogberries; the staff party in the canteen two night's ago; the turkey sandwiches, canapés and hot mince pies; the laughter, the non-alcoholic fruit cup, the exchange of Christmas cards; the colourful balloons and streamers decorating the room, swiftly followed by the sadness of bidding goodbye to Tara, Jenny, Mr Whiteley, and all the other friends she had garnered along the way, when the store had finally closed its doors on this Christmas Eve.

Humping her shopping bags containing potatoes, carrots, onions, a small chicken, a dozen clementines and a bunch of grapes, Lisa realised that there was something of importance she had forgotten to buy. But what?

Pausing momentarily on her way to the bus stop, she remembered the cottage; the low-beamed rooms she had loved so much; the way the firelight had danced on the baubled Christmas tree in the drawing room.

Standing stock still on a greasy, ice-filmed pavement, she remembered a neat kitchen redolent with the scent of newly-baked mince pies; a marmalade cat asleep in her basket beside the Aga; John bringing in a basket of logs from the garden shed. Above all, the Christmas tree!

On a sudden impulse, she turned and hurried back to the market.

Alone in her flat, awaiting Edward's arrival, this was it, Lisa thought. No use regretting all the things one wished for which remained unbought. The shops would all be closed now; the streets deserted. A sudden quietude had descended on the world outside, a sense of holiness and peace.

When Edward came to her, she said, drawing him into the room, "Look, I've bought a Christmas tree. The first since the cottage. Do you suppose that it will be visible out at sea? Wouldn't it be marvellous if some passing ship noticed the lights winking through the darkness?"

"It's beautiful, darling," Edward said bleakly, holding her close, dreading his moment of truth; wondering how he could possibly extinguish her childlike joy in a small fir tree hung with coloured lights.

"What is it, darling?" she asked sharply. "You're shaking. You look – ill! Sit down. I'll pour you a drink!"

Sinking down on the divan, he covered his face with his hands. Lisa stared at him in dismay. "Edward, you *are* ill! What is it? What's wrong? Is it – Judy? Has something happened to Judy?"

He shook his head. "No, not Judy. It's – Pamela. She knows about – *us*!"

"Oh, I see." Relief flooded through her. "Perhaps it's just as well." Kneeling beside him, taking his hand in hers, she said, "It hasn't been easy, has it? All the lies and pretence? Poor Pamela. Was she very upset when you told her?"

"It didn't happen quite like that," he said slowly, feeling for the right words. "Pamela rang the office; found out I'd been lying."

"Go on." She had never seen him like this before. His skin looked grey, the colour of putty. "Please, darling, you must tell me what has happened to upset you like this."

"Oh God, Lisa, it's worse than you could possibly imagine. There's something else, you see. Something you'll have to know sooner or later."

"You'd better tell me then, hadn't you?"

He said huskily, "Pamela – Pamela is expecting a child."

Lisa got up and walked to the window. She saw, through

a mist of tears, the lights along the shore, far-off lights of Christmas trees in the seaward facing windows of the houses on the upper promenade, the colours blurred as if by rain.

Edward hurried towards her. "Please, darling, I . . . Don't turn away from me. Lisa, I need your help, your understanding . . ."

"No. Don't touch me! Please don't touch me ever again!"

"I know what you must be thinking, feeling. It simply isn't true. Lisa, darling, you must listen to me, let me explain . . ."

She turned then to face him. "Explain? What is there to explain? You had better leave now. If you only knew how tired I am of trusting, believing – caring. My own fault entirely. I should have known better." Her eyes were those of a stranger.

He said hoarsely, "Nothing has changed. I still love you Lisa. I always will."

"*Everything* has changed," she uttered bleakly. "It's over, Edward, this so-called love affair of ours! I never want to see you or hear from you ever again!"

"I can't accept that, after all we have been to one another," he said desperately. You're being unfair, Lisa: condemning me without a hearing."

"Has it occurred to you," she said dully, "that had you been fair with me in the first place, if you had told me that you still loved your wife, none of this would have happened? Now, please go. Get on with your own life and leave me alone to get on with mine!"

"Very well then." He knew it would be pointless to stay any longer. "By the way, I brought these for you." He lay two small parcels on the octagonal table. "Please open them, and remember that what I told you is true. It's you I love. You and only you."

Closing the door behind him, he hurried downstairs to his car; saw, by the dashboard clock, that Judy's train was due in ten minutes.

*　　*　　*

141

She looked very small and vulnerable, coming towards him along the platform, carrying a holdall, the hood of her grey anorak framing her face.

"Hello, Daddy." She lifted her face to be kissed, and yet there was a lack of enthusiasm, a sense of withdrawal. For the first time ever, Edward felt ill-at-ease with his daughter.

Carrying her holdall, walking towards the car parked in the station forecourt, he asked, "Was the train very crowded?"

"Not really, just stuffy. Terribly hot and stuffy." She spoke impatiently.

Sitting beside him in the car, she shook off the hood of her anorak. He noticed, with a deep feeling of shock, that she had cut her hair. All the bright, flying gold was gone, in its place a kind of helmet of hair moulded to her head, cropped short at the back and sides, with a spikily-cut fringe on her forehead.

"Why didn't you tell me?" he asked hoarsely.

"Tell you what?"

"About your hair."

"Oh that!" She shrugged her shoulders dismissively. "I had it cut ages ago, didn't I tell you? I thought I had. Why? Don't you like it?"

"No, Judy, I don't like it at all. You look – different somehow. Much older."

"The reason why I had it cut in the first place. I *wanted* to look older: to be like the other girls." She laughed briefly, "I don't suppose Mother will like it either! But what the hell? It's only hair, for God's sake!"

Switching on the ignition, on the long road out of town Edward said carefully, "Don't be too hard on her, darling, she isn't very well at the moment."

"Mother not well? Why? What's wrong with her?" Opening her shoulder-bag, Judy lit a cigarette, inhaled deeply and blew out the smoke. "Has it to do with her age?"

"You've started smoking," Edward said disbelievingly.

"Yeah, so what? You can't disapprove of that, surely? You, a forty-a-day man!"

His little girl seemed like a stranger to him now. His little girl? But no, she was not a little girl any longer, not really. Just a girl pretending to be a grown woman.

Sick at heart, he said heavily, "Your mother is – pregnant."

He heard his daughter's sharp intake of breath. "Mummy? But she can't possibly be pregnant, not at her age!" Judy crushed out her cigarette with trembling fingers. "But she can't possibly go through with it, can she? Well, *can* she? Not Mummy, not at her age? She might die! What does the doctor say?"

"I haven't spoken to the doctor," Edward confessed uneasily, concentrating on the road ahead.

"You *haven't*? Why the hell not?"

"It's a long story," Edward said despairingly. "You are bound to find out sooner or later. The fact is, there's someone else in my life now. Someone I am deeply in love with. Her name is Lisa. She is a fine, decent human being."

"And I suppose Mummy isn't? Is that it? So what are you really saying? That this fine, decent woman friend of yours didn't want to know about – sex – so you lumbered Mother, not her, with the fruit of your loins?"

"*Judy*!"

"The truth hurts, doesn't it?" Judith riposted sharply. "Well, what did you expect me to say? 'Oh, how nice, Daddy, that you have started acting like a schoolboy'? I always assumed that you and Mummy were like the Rock of Gibraltar. Apparently I was wrong!"

Tears filled her eyes. "It has come as a bit of a shock to know that *you*, of all people, betrayed our trust in such a way!"

"Look, Judy, we have to talk!"

"I thought we were – talking." She was sitting with her

143

spine pressed hard against the seat, staring unblinkingly through the windscreen, trying hard not to cry.

"Not here. Not like this. There's a pub just ahead. I'll stop there."

"So that you can get in your two-cent's worth first?" Judith said bitterly as the car ground to a halt in a pebbled driveway.

"More importantly," Edward said quietly, "because you have the right to know what happened, and why."

"And what if I don't want to listen to your tuppenny-ha'penny excuses? About this – Lisa – you say you are in love with? *Love*? I doubt if you know the meaning of the word!"

"And *you* do? Is that it?"

"I don't know what you mean!"

Edward said gently, "I think you do, Judy. I think you know exactly what I mean!"

"Oh very well then," she flung back at him. "So I've been living with someone! Oh, not to worry, it's all over and done with now!"

"Darling, why didn't you tell me?"

"How could I? I sensed your withdrawal. Your letters weren't the same any more!"

"Neither were yours," he reminded her gently. "Tell me, Judy, this man you mentioned, is he the reason for your new hairstyle; the cigarettes?"

"What if he is? He – Kit – prefers girls with short hair; the gamine look. Funny, isn't it? He said he loved me then set about changing me. What I'm saying is, if he wanted a sophisticated girl with spiky hair, why choose me in the first place?"

The pub was brightly-lit, crowded, far different from the village pub with its coal fire and Victorian fittings, on the other side of town. Edward ordered the drinks, and found a table for two as far away from the bar as possible.

"Not exactly conducive to quiet conversation, is it?" Judy

144

said bitterly. "We'd have been better off in the car. Frankly, Dad, I'm surprised you told me about this woman you've been messing about with behind Mum's back. Oh, I get it! She told *you* to tell me or *she* would. Poor old Dad. Talk about the devil and the deep blue sea." Lighting a cigarette, she continued, "Well, you'd best get on with it, hadn't you? Just spare me the violins."

Edward shook his head. "No, Judith, I'm sorry, I've already told you that Lisa is a fine, decent person. What happened between us was my fault entirely. You are not a child any longer, experience must have taught you that these things happen, born of need, I imagine; a kind of inner loneliness bordering on despair." He smiled ruefully. "That's all I'm prepared to say on the subject. I've obeyed instructions, told you about Lisa; now you must draw your own conclusions.

"Just one thing more before we go; I am not ashamed of my relationship with Lisa, nor ever shall be. She brought a new dimension into my life; a warmth and sweetness I had known only once before, when you were a little girl. Now, if you've finished your drink . . . Mother will be wondering what has happened to us."

In the car, Judy said quietly, "Thanks, Daddy, for not telling me the ins and outs of your affair. I couldn't have borne that; couldn't have borne it if you'd piled the blame on Mother. I'm not blind, you know. I know there's more to life than a spotless house and clean clothes; that love has a way of sneaking up on you when you're not looking, and that's all *I'm* prepared to say on the subject. So let's go home, shall we, and face the music together?"

Chapter Sixteen

Lisa stood by the window for a long time, looking at the world beyond the glass, feeling as if she was no longer a part of that world; as if she were imprisoned in this room she had loved so much; in solitary confinement.

The house was still. Her downstairs neighbours had gone away for the Christmas holidays; the only sound she could hear was the buffeting of the wind against the panes, the roaring sound of the sea racing in on the shore, the dull crump of the tide washing against the lighthouse pier.

Turning away from the window, she saw the room as a setting for a play by Terence Rattigan or J.B. Priestley; the furniture and fittings, the shaded lamps, the books, ornaments, the tray of drinks and glasses and the fruit-bowl on the carved oak chest, the fairy-lit Christmas tree as meaningless props on the stage of life; a kind of One Act Play at the end of which the audience had gone away complaining at its brief, unsatisfactory conclusion.

Staring at the packages Edward had lain on the octagonal table intensified her feelings of loneliness and loss. She felt the way she had done the day she knew that Aunt Grace had died, when she had wandered about the house like a lost soul, unable to accept that someone she had loved so intensely was no longer a part of her life, and never would be again – except in memory.

Now Edward had gone away from her because she had willed it so. But what else could she have done? She had reacted in the same way when she knew that John was having an affair, had conceded the victory to the victor. In this case, Pamela Miller – the woman who was carrying Edward's child. She had quit the field yet again, as a matter of pride and self-respect; of conscience; knowing when she was beaten.

Picking up the packages, she crossed to the divan and knelt beside it to open them.

The first package contained a slim volume of poems by Elizabeth Barrett Browning, inscribed with the words: 'For Lisa, to the level of every day's most quiet need, by sun and candle-light.'

Fingering the soft tooled-leather binding, turning the pages, there came a scent of age, of pot-pourri; faded lavender and rose petals reminiscent of long-gone summertimes when the book was new, not old and shabby as it now was, and she thought of Edward, searching second-hand bookshops to discover exactly the right gift at the right time.

The second package revealed a small morocco box containing a garnet and seed-pearl ring of Victorian vintage. The accompanying note read: 'For Lisa, the love of my life. Edward'.

Holding Edward's gifts in her hands, Lisa wept as if her heart would break, remembering all that he had meant to her: that day on the beach when he had called her name and she had run into the shelter of his arms; that night in the Victoria Hotel when she had given herself to him so trustingly, and everything about him she had learned to love so much – his strength, his self-deprecating sense of humour; the way in which he had taken control of her at their first meeting; his caring concern for her welfare . . . All over and done with now.

In urgent need of escape from this room; this powerhouse of memories too painful to recall, not stopping to change her indoor shoes or to put on a coat or mackintosh, she hurried down the curving staircase to the hall below and into the night, unaware of Jake Colby's presence in his office; the spillage of light into the passageway beyond; the turning of his head as he heard her stumbling footsteps on the stairs. Nor did she hear him call out to her, "Is that you, Mrs Hazell?" as she blundered down the front steps and on to the lighthouse pier, her eyes blurred with tears, the wind tearing at her hair, with no other thought in mind than to become as one with the night; the sea pounding on the rocks at the end of the pier.

Her breath catching in her throat as she ran towards an effulgent circle of light at the end of the pier, a lamppost haloed about with all the colours of the rainbow, Lisa remembered a cottage garden; fairy-lights strung among the branches of an apple tree long ago; the scent of a warm kitchen at dusk; an old lady daubing colours on canvas; a little cat buried beneath a lilac bush: all the things that had meant so much to her during her lifetime – books, music – life itself, and saw, with a sweet feeling of relief, the great void of darkness, of forgetfulness, awaiting her beyond the riding light at the end of the jetty . . .

The hand on her arm was gently restraining. The voice, too, was gentle. "Don't you think you'd be better off at home, Mrs Hazell?" Jake Colby said kindly. "Come on, lass. Come home, before you catch your death of cold."

Seated in a high-backed chair near Colby's fire, Lisa recalled vaguely having her feet put into a pair of men's slippers, a plaid rug wrapped round her shoulders, and swallowing a sizeable tot of brandy from a glass held by Jake Colby, who kept on saying, "Another sip. Take another sip. That's right, now another," in the manner of a mother persuading a child to take its medicine.

Her teeth were chattering so much that the first sips had run from the corners of her mouth. Still, Colby persevered, dabbing away the overspill with a Kleenex tissue, telling her not to worry; that she would soon be feeling much warmer, and he was right. The raw spirit gradually restored sensation to her frozen limbs, although she could not remember clearly at first why she was here in Colby's private apartment, being treated as an invalid. At that point, her stumbling walk along the jetty, the confusion of the night, the biting sea wind tearing at her hair and clothing, the haloed light at the pier-end she had struggled so hard to reach, seemed akin to a dream sequence in an avant-garde movie.

The fire drew her eyes like a magnet, a richly roaring edifice of pine logs shooting flames up a smoke-blackened chimney. The high mantelpiece, she noticed, was crowded with ornaments, sprigs of holly, and Christmas cards – including the one she had sent him.

Alone in the room momentarily, she noticed that the walls were half-panelled; the space above the panelling decorated with pictures of sailing ships in full rig; old original oil paintings, gilt-framed, of wind-jammers, merchantmen, clippers, barques, and brigantines sailing to glory on wave-capped seas . . .

In a little while, Jake came through from the kitchen with a tray of tea and sandwiches. Curiously, Lisa felt no sense of embarrassment that she was wearing his slippers, that her hair was hanging loose and straight about her shoulders. It seemed the most natural thing in the world to be here in this quiet room – a kind of haven of peace from the buffeting wind beyond the circumference of this firelit parlour with its shadowy nooks and corners, its rug-strewn floor and solid antique furniture: Victorian tall-boys, Georgian armchairs, Regency display cabinets, and the book-filled shelves flanking the fireplace.

"Here," Colby said levelly, pouring the tea from a common-or-garden Mason-ware teapot, and handing Lisa a cup. "Drink this whilst it's hot. It will do you good."

Lisa said huskily, "I'm sorry to have caused you so much trouble."

"No trouble. I saw you go out. It occurred to me that you hadn't realised how cold it was outdoors."

"You followed me deliberately?"

Taking a pipe from the rack near his chair, dipping a spill into the fire, he lit, with due care and consideration, the tobacco in the bowl of the pipe. Blowing out a cloud of blue-grey smoke, he said, "Just as well I did, don't you think? Otherwise, you might have been dead and gone right now! Or was that what you intended? God dammit, woman, does life mean so little to you that you could throw it aside like a – worn-out shoe?"

Lisa buried her face in her hands.

Colby regarded her thoughtfully. He said, "Tell me to mind my own business if you like, but I noticed your 'friend' leaving earlier on this evening. He left in a devil of a hurry to my way of thinking. Oh, I'm not shocked, believe me! What my tenants do behind closed doors is largely their own business. What does concern me is that you, Mrs Hazell, whom I believed to be a responsible, sensible human being, should rush out of my house, inadequately dressed, in the middle of winter, to commit suicide!

"Of course I bloody well followed you! Think of the alternative! A damn fine Christmas, I must say, spent at the local police station answering questions about the 'deceased's' state of mind! Or perhaps you couldn't have cared less about the people left behind to shoulder your own responsibilities?"

Overwhelmed by a feeling of shame that Colby had guessed the relationship between herself and Edward; that he saw her, perhaps, as a futile, middle-aged whore, she said wearily, "I'm sorry, Mr Colby, but you needn't worry. My 'friend', so called, will never set foot in this house again. And, quite honestly, the thought of committing suicide had never crossed my mind. I just needed to be alone for a little while, to come to terms with my life. Now, if you don't mind, I'd like to go upstairs to my flat. I am rather – tired."

"What are you doing tomorrow?" Jake asked abruptly, at the door of his apartment.

"Nothing of importance. Why do you ask?"

"It simply occurred to me," Jake said levelly, "that a couple of misfits in the scheme of things entire might as well spend Christmas Day together."

"And 'mould them nearer to our heart's desire'?"

"Well, yes, Mrs Hazell, though I'm not all that hot on quotations. I am, on the other hand, a fairly adequate cook!"

She said wistfully, "I thought you'd be spending Christmas Day with your family."

"My sister, you mean? No, I go to Edith's on Boxing Day. She knows that I prefer to spend Christmas Day here in my own surroundings. In any case, she'll be working: cooking Christmas dinner for the old folk at Bay View."

Bay View, Lisa thought, wishing herself back there, filling marmalade dishes, rumbling potatoes, scraping carrots, or whatever, before Edward Miller had entered her life to destroy, so abruptly, so cruelly, her belief in the enduring nature of their love affair . . . To 'the ends of being and ideal grace'.

"You haven't answered my question," Jake said. "Of course, if you don't want to come . . ."

"I'm not sure what I want at the moment."

"Fair enough. Sleep on it. The invitation stands. Come down if you feel like it. Just one thing, no more nocturnal wanderings along that blasted jetty, all right?"

"You could always lock the front door and throw away the key."

Colby smiled grimly. "If that's what it takes."

She heard the telephone ringing as she went upstairs to the flat. Edward, she thought; it would be Edward in some phonebox, wanting to talk to her. To say – what? Sorry? "Please, Lisa, I must see you again. You must let me explain . . ."

As if talking or explanation could mend something broken beyond repair.

The phone kept on ringing as she undressed and got into bed. When it finally stopped, she lay staring at the ceiling. Had she really meant to throw away her life like a worn-out shoe? What madness had possessed her to rush out into the wind-wracked night wearing a jumper and skirt, not even a coat or a headscarf?

It was as if her brain had stopped functioning when Edward told her that his wife was expecting a child. Incapable of coherent thought, she had withdrawn into herself, overwhelmed by a feeling of betrayal so intense that even now she dare not plumb the depths of her emotion. Not yet. But the pain was there, dormant for the time being, beyond this strange sensation of numbness, awaiting release, the moment when a tidal wave of regret would wash over her, when she would ask herself, "What next? Where shall I go from here?"

And this, she knew, was the reason why she had rushed away from the house and along the lighthouse jetty. "A matter of escape," Edward had said that night on the phone, at Bay View. "The password is escape." Then he had said jokingly that he would wear dark glasses, a down-turned trilby and a false moustache.

Oh, Edward, she thought bleakly. *Edward*.

She had placed the photograph of Aunt Grace in her carnival robes, along with the one of herself sandwiched between her parents, on her bedside table. Turning on her side to look at them, deriving comfort from memories of happier times, she recalled the excitement of Aunt Grace alighting from a taxi-cab at the front gate of the house in Walthamstow to spend Christmas – a bizarre figure in an ankle-length sealskin coat with a nutria collar, a violet bedecked toque perched on her head; bringing with her a mountain of luggage – two heavy cases and several hat-boxes – one containing the creation she would wear to church on

Christmas Day, the rest stuffed with the brightly-wrapped presents she would place under the tree on Christmas Eve, labelled, 'With Love from Father Christmas'.

Such exciting presents: beribboned boxes of chocolates, dainty lace-trimmed underwear and cashmere shawls for her mother, boxes of Du Maurier cigarettes, silk ties and leather stud-boxes for Father; Russian dolls, pop-up books and pencil-boxes for herself, plus paints and crayons and inexpensive items of jewellery – fake pearl necklaces and slender charm bracelets, tins of toffees; ribbons for her hair . . .

How simple and lovely life had been then, in that Victorian villa in Walthamstow, especially at Christmas. Even Rover, the dog, had not been forgotten. There would always be a new ball or a rubber bone for him to play with, plus a massive helping of turkey giblets and dog-biscuits for his Christmas dinner.

At least she had those happy days to look back on, Lisa thought. Then, switching off her bedside lamp, she heard above the buffeting of the wind, the muffled sound of bells from the church on the hill; remembered hazily she had told Edward that she would attend Midnight Mass. Too late now. Too late now!

Seated in his chair near the dying embers of the fire, Jake Colby heard the peal of bells from the church on the hill.

Smoking a last pipe of tobacco before bedtime, he thought about Lisa Hazell; in particular, the morning she had come down to his office to pay her rent and request the installation of an electricity meter.

He'd been in a pragmatic mood that morning, he remembered; out of sorts, tetchy for some reason or other; in what his sister termed one of his 'Clever Dick' moods. But Mrs Hazell had cut him down to size right enough on that occasion. His "Blessed is she that expecteth nothing" remark had more than warranted her pithy reply, of, "Not at all, Mr Colby. More a case of 'blessed is she that expecteth nothing she can't afford to pay for herself'!" And he had relished that quick retort of hers ever since.

He had quickly established the fact that she had a gentleman friend, an 'admirer'. Strictly speaking, none of his business until tonight, when he had made it very much his business to hurry after her along the lighthouse jetty, heart-in-mouth, quickening his footsteps when it had seemed likely she would keep on walking into oblivion.

Had she meant to commit suicide? He hoped not, but he couldn't be sure. One thing *was* for sure: she had touched the deep inner core of him the day she had come to look at the flat, when she had said, "It's difficult to explain, but I've fallen in love with it, as if I somehow belong here." That was after he had lied to her about the rent being inclusive of heating and so on, for the simple reason that he had wanted her to take the apartment, to feel secure, settled, and happy.

Would he have reacted differently, he wondered, knocking the ash from his pipe, if he had known then about the man in her life? Possibly, but he couldn't be sure.

Getting ready for bed, switching off lights, placing a guard round the hearth; easing his considerable length between the sheets, resting his head on the pillows; it occurred to Colby that there was a hell of a lot he wasn't sure of any more since Lisa Hazell had moved into the top flat of No. 10 Sand Place.

Lisa went downstairs to Colby's apartment at ten-thirty next day, uncertain of welcome, half-wishing she had possessed the strength of mind to spend Christmas Day alone. But she needed companionship as a dry summer garden needs rain; just to be with someone – another human being capable of speech – to break the agony of introspection.

"Oh," Colby said off-handedly, "so you decided to come after all. In which case you might as well make yourself useful in the kitchen. This way, and mind the steps."

Colby's kitchen, two steps down from the living room, overlooked a long, walled garden seen through a glassed-in verandah containing a clutter of fishing rods, wellington boots, garden tools, and oil-skin capes.

The table was scrubbed to the cleanliness of a butcher's block at closing time. Cooking utensils, saucepans, skillets and colanders hung from a row of hooks near a floor to ceiling dresser, the shelves of which displayed ribbed stone jars containing wooden spoons and spatulas, Victorian egg-holders, covered cheese-dishes, and the kind of kitchen scales Lisa's mother had once used, with a metal scoop and a pyramid of brass weights.

"Those meat dishes and dinner plates belonged to my grandmother," Colby said.

"They're Coalport, aren't they?"

"Fancy knowing that." Raising a quizzical eyebrow, "Are you interested in antiques?"

"Very." Lisa smiled reflectively. "I like to imagine the people who handled such things long before we were born or thought of, to whom they were a part of everyday life in what I think of in a more civilised era. Or am I being fanciful? Is the past so precious to me because it is over and done with, like old love letters tied with ribbon; neatly laid away and forgotten?"

"All passion spent, you mean?"

"Yes, that's exactly what I meant."

"You have some nice pieces of your own," Colby commented, refuelling the Aga, "especially that octagonal table, the oak chest and those ornaments on your fireside shelves."

"They belonged to my Aunt Grace, who was knowledge-able about antiques."

Putting the kettle on to boil, "Which would you prefer, tea or coffee?" Colby asked.

155

"Coffee, please. But I thought I was here to make myself useful?"

"There's time enough yet," Colby reminded her in that clipped, off-hand way of his which appeared to be second nature to him; a kind of defence-barrier against the world, born of shyness or a deep-seated feeling of insecurity, Lisa realised, remembering his sister's description of him as a 'loner'; wondering why this was so. And yet, he was by no means a cold uncaring human being beneath his brusque exterior. Quite the reverse.

He said, making the coffee, "There's a capon in the pantry; sprouts, potatoes and carrots. Nothing fancy; frozen beans and broccoli in the deep freeze if you don't care for sprouts and carrots; smoked salmon in the refrigerator for starters. The choice is yours. We'll eat at one o'clock, if that's all right?"

Glancing at the wall-clock above the door, "It's time the bird went into the oven," he said, disappearing into the pantry, emerging seconds later with the capon, pale and plump, on a Coalport meat dish. "Well, what do you think, Mrs Hazell? Will three hours be enough cooking time?"

"Just about right, I would think," Lisa conceded as Colby unearthed a roasting tin from a cupboard under the sink and placed into it the 'corpus delicti' which he had stuffed beforehand with sage and onion stuffing and sausage meat. "Now, if you'll tell me where the knives are kept, I'll make a start on the potatoes etc."

"Fair enough. They're in the top left hand drawer of the dresser. The vegetables are in the pantry."

Lisa had almost forgotten that such things as pantries existed nowadays. This one smelt cool and fresh. The shelves were stacked with tinned foods; pots of pickles and home-made jam; bottled peaches and raspberries, plums and apricots; the vegetables were stored in white plastic racks. Beneath one of the higher shelves hummed a small refrigerator with a deep-freeze compartment in which reposed the string beans and broccoli. Lower down were the smoked salmon fillets, covered with cling-film, several bottles of milk, and a cling-film protected trifle smothered in whipped cream and decorated with flaked almonds and glacé cherries.

For some unfathomable reason, tears sprang to Lisa's eyes. Then, drying her eyes with the back of her hand, she chose the vegetables, squared her shoulders, and marched to the sink to begin peeling and paring the carrots, sprouts and potatoes for their Christmas dinner; hers and Colby's.

Standing with her back to him, she asked brightly, "How is Mrs Hannersley, by the way?"

"Edith? Oh, she's all right. She misses you, though," Colby replied briskly, sliding the capon into the Aga. "There have been a few non-starters since you left Bay View, apparently. The first applicant lasted a week; the second a fortnight."

Lisa laughed, scraping carrots. "Would you believe it? When I signed on at the employment agency, I was offered the job of general assistant at Bay View! Thankfully, the interviewer pointed me in the direction of Dogberries – The Store With a Soul – just a temporary job, of course, over the Christmas period, but I loved every minute of it. I'm just so sorry it didn't last longer. But that's life, isn't it? Here today, gone tomorrow!"

Colby said quietly, "Are you thinking of going back there to work?"

"I really don't know." She explained about Miss Prior whose job she had filled on a temporary basis. "Hardly likely, I'd say, unless she manages to fall off another ladder."

"In that case, would you consider working for me?" Jake asked the question diffidently, uncertain of her reaction.

"For *you*?" She turned away from the detritus of carrot scrapings, potato peel and sprout leaves in the sink to face Colby. "Doing *what*?" she enquired in surprise, drying her hands on a tea-towel, wondering if he needed a cook-housekeeper, a secretary or whatever.

"The fact is," he said slowly, "I own a small antiques shop in Silver Street, scarcely a stone's throw away from here, and I need someone capable to take charge of it. You, Mrs Hazell, would be the ideal person, I reckon; if you are interested, that is."

"*Interested*? Of course I am! Please tell me more!"

"Well, I open up most weekends, even during the off-season months; full-time from May to October when business is brisk; that's when I buy in the stock from country-house sales, and so on – house clearance and the like; for which I pay fair prices, I might add, and sell quickly at a low profit margin. You see, Mrs Hazell, I am not and never have been a – 'get rich quick merchant' – I just happen to like dealing in antiques. You understand?"

"Oh yes, Mr Colby, I understand perfectly," Lisa said happily, "and I accept your offer."

Regarding her thoughtfully, it occurred to him that most women would have wanted to know how many hours per week, and for how much money. But not Lisa Hazell.

With an uplifting of the heart, he knew that he had been right about her all along, from the first moment he'd set eyes on her; when crossing the threshold of No. 10 Sand Place, she had looked up at the uncurtained Georgian window on the landing, and had uttered breathlessly, "Oh, how lovely!"

All he said now was, "Good, that's settled then. We'll discuss the details later, shall we?"

"Yes, whenever," she agreed, turning back to the sink to give the vegetables a final rinse in cold water. "By the way, are you going to parboil the potatoes first, before roasting? Or would you prefer them mashed?" She sniffed the air. "Just a sec," she reminded him with an upsurge of her keen sense of humour, "if you don't want that capon to emerge as a burnt offering on a funeral pyre, you'd best

158

relegate it to a lower shelf or turn down the temperature of oven somewhat. Unless, of course, you have a penchant for overcooked capon and raw sage and onion stuffing!"

"So what if I have, Mrs Hazell?"

"What indeed, Mr Colby?"

"Call me Jake," he muttered darkly.

"Call me Lisa," she responded warmly.

Chapter Seventeen

John Hazell felt trapped by Christmas, as he used to as a schoolboy, when he would sit upstairs in his bedroom rather than venture downstairs to greet his Aunt Flo and Uncle Fred who came for Christmas dinner every year, bringing with them their pallid, acned son Wilfrid and his sister Mary, all of whom he had hated as much as he hated his pot-bellied, beer-swilling father.

"Oh, do come down, John." His patient mother would come up to his room, wringing her hands despairingly, her face puckered with worry-lines. "Dinner's almost ready. Your dad and Uncle Fred will be back from the pub any minute, and Auntie Flo keeps on asking if you're poorly. I don't know what to say to her, I'm sure, and you know what your dad's like when he comes in from the pub with a few pints inside him? He'll go mad if he finds you up here with your head stuck in a book, then *I'll* be the one to suffer! What's wrong with you anyway? Surely it's not too much to ask to keep the peace? After all, it *is* Christmas!"

And so he had been coerced to take his seat at the festive board, so called, to watch his father slicing into the goose, digging into its innards for tablespoons of greasy stuffing; slopping gravy over the mashed potatoes; smattering his plate of Christmas pudding with dollops of rum sauce.

Hardest of all to bear had been sitting in the front room, after dinner, listening to Aunt Flo going on about her latest operation for what she termed discreetly, her 'waterworks'

– 'gasworks' more like, he'd thought disgustedly, knowing that soon would come the horror of a tea-time return to the dining room to face wedges of boiled bacon, cold and fatty, served with pickles; followed by lukewarm mince-pies, sherry trifle, and slices of moist Christmas cake crowned with marzipan stuck on with apricot jam.

This Christmas might have been endurable had not Linda insisted on inviting her parents to stay at the cottage, John thought mutinously, dreading the prospect of making conversation with Linda's father, and listening to her mother going on and on about last summer's package tour of France, accompanied by the boring photographs she had taken *en route*. Above all, he felt incapable of answering puerile questions about his job, Miles, and the new baby. This, he dreaded most of all.

Inevitably, Linda had made motherhood the excuse for this invasion of his privacy: Miles, the innocent peg on which she had hung her demand for a good old-fashioned Family Christmas.

He'd rebelled. "But Johnny," she'd argued, "it's only fair that Miles should grow up knowing his grandparents. We owe it to him to give him that kind of stability. As a matter of fact, I'd thought of inviting your father too. The poor soul must be feeling pretty lonely since the death of your mother. But it's still not too late, is it? I could easily drop him a line . . ."

"For God's sake, Linda!" The very idea of inviting his father to the cottage was the last straw. "I don't want him here, do you understand?"

"No, Johnny, quite frankly I don't. After all, he *is* your father; Miles' grandfather. It seems all wrong to me, turning your back on your own flesh and blood the way you have done! Oh, very well then, have it your own way. Perhaps I'll invite him to the christening instead!"

*　　*　　*

161

On Christmas Eve, Linda chivvied him out of the cottage an hour before time, to fetch her parents from the station.

"Why all the rush?" he demanded angrily. "Do you imagine I don't know how long it takes to drive into town? Ten minutes at the most!"

"I know, Johnny, but the roads are bad, and I don't want Mummy and Daddy standing about in the cold waiting for you to arrive."

"What about me having to stand about in the cold waiting for them?"

"That's different," Linda reminded him. "You're much younger than they are. Oh, for heaven's sake, John, just *go* and stop arguing. I have a hundred and one things to see to right now!"

Hurrying out to the car, he'd felt aggrieved by Linda's idiotic preparations for Christmas: dotting the windowpanes with stuck-on cottonwool; decorating the Christmas tree she had planted lopsidedly in a plastic bucket of soil with coloured baubles and fairy-lights; looping up Christmas cards round the drawing room walls; thrusting flowers haphazardly into cut-glass vases . . .

A pale wintry sun gilded the hills on Christmas morning.

Mrs Trentham, Linda's mother, wearing a red trouser-suit and a bright green nylon overall to indicate that she was 'helping', her hair tinted the colour of ripe blackberries in an autumn hedgerow, ogled John over her third glass of sweet sherry. "So you've got my little girl pregnant again, have you?" she enquired archly. "Well, that's only to be expected. I mean, two healthy young people in love. I'm just so relieved to know she's *secure*. You wouldn't believe how scared Daddy and I were that she would marry one of those penniless young students who used to hang about our house before – oh, long before she met you, of course, dear."

162

She held out her glass for a refill. "But trust Lin to know which side her bread is buttered! I'm glad she had the commonsense to wait until the right man came along. Someone old enough to take care of her."

She giggled coyly, "Not that anyone would guess the age difference between you. I mean to say, you haven't lost your hair yet, Johnny, which is such a relief. Neither has Daddy, I'm thankful to say! I don't think I'd fancy a bald man, though I daresay it doesn't matter all that much with the lights out. Like they say, what does it matter if there's snow on the roof as long as there's a fire in the hearth?"

"I say, steady on, old girl!" Archie Trentham, standing with his back to the fire, advised John not to fill his wife's glass to the brim. "She always gets a bit skittish after the third glass," he said bluffly.

Linda entered the room at that moment with Miles in her arms, wearing a cotton overall smocked above the breasts. Was it John's imagination, or was she pushing her belly forward deliberately to give the impression of a more advanced pregnancy?

"What has Mummy been saying?" she asked carelessly.

John got up quickly from his chair, pushing past Linda, goaded beyond endurance by his mother-in-law's mindless chatter. "I'm going for a walk," he said grimly, rummaging in the cluttered hall cupboard to find the thick-soled boots he had bought in Switzerland, what seemed a lifetime ago, from a specialist shoe-shop in Davros, when he and Lisa had gone there on holiday together.

Standing at his elbow, Linda said furiously, "Listen, John, if you set foot outside the door, you're to ask my father to go with you. Mummy too. Is that clear?"

Finding the boots, knotting the laces, intent on escape, he thrust aside Linda's restraining hand on his arm, and, shrugging on his anorak, he opened the front door.

At that moment, Linda called out defiantly, "Daddy,

John's going out for a walk. He wants you to go with him!"

Archie appeared from the drawing room, grinning foolishly. "Oh, fine," he said. "Yes, I'd like a breather before lunch. I'll just go upstairs and get my hat and coat."

"You too, Mummy," Linda sang out in a high-pitched voice.

"No, I don't think so, darling, if you don't mind," Gloria Trentham demurred, "I'd rather stay here and help with the cooking." She swayed a little, giggling, her cheeks as red as her trousers. "Oh, it's all so *thrilling*," she enthused, "a real country Christmas in the bosom of my family." Then, as Archie came downstairs wearing a mackintosh and a deer-stalker hat, she clasped his arm, saying, "Now, don't you two stay out too long. Lunch is at one o'clock, remember? Well, give or take half an hour. Now, off you go, and enjoy your walk!"

Ignoring his father-in-law, John set off down the path ahead of him.

Half-way down the lane to the village, Archie caught up with him, puffing and panting, keeping an eye open for the nearest pub. God dammit, he thought hopefully, there must be a pub somewhere close at hand? Every frigging village must have a pub. If not, stuff country life. He'd just as soon keep on his dry-cleaning business in Harrogate for the time being, thank you very much. Moreover, he wasn't all that keen on his daughter's husband; a surly brute, in his opinion. But what the hell? In for a penny in for a pound; as long as Linda was happy . . . "Nothing like a drop of good country air," he bellowed unconvincingly.

The menfolk out of sight, Linda turned on her mother in a fury. "Don't you think you've had enough of that?" she snapped, as Gloria poured herself another glass of sherry. Having had her way in the matter of the walk, forcing John to do her bidding, disgruntled that the day had started badly,

164

and feeling that this was the fault of everyone except herself, she made her mother the whipping boy. "What did you say to upset John?"

"Say? I didn't say anything! I didn't have to. That husband of yours was in a foul mood last night when he drove Daddy and me from the station. Ask Daddy if you don't believe me. We discussed it in bed last night."

"Oh, so that's what all the whispering was about." Flopping into a chair, Linda dumped Miles on the floor. He started whimpering. "Oh for heaven's sake play with your toys, child," she said crossly.

"No need to take it out on my grandson," Gloria retorted, holding out her arms. "There, there, darling, come to Grammie."

"For God's sake, Mummy, leave him where he is!" Linda took a cigarette from a box on the table, lit it and inhaled deeply.

Gloria started to cry into a lace-edged hanky. "I'm beginning to wish we'd never come. In fact, I'll go up and pack. We'll go home on the first available train."

"You'll have a damn long wait then. There aren't any trains on Christmas Day, so just shut up and stop talking through the top of your head!"

Gloria began to wail like a banshee. Miles joined in. "Now see what you've done," Linda burst forth. "Oh do be *quiet*!" Then, with a typical change of mood, she tried to make amends. Patching up quarrels came as easily to Linda Hazell as cobbling holes in a cot blanket. "Of course you're not going home. You're going to stay here and we're all going to have a simply marvellous Christmas. You mustn't take any notice of Johnny; he's tired that's all, after the strain of last term."

"That's all very well, but other people get tired, too. I do; so does Daddy, but we don't go about being actively unpleasant." Gloria dabbed her eyes. "No, it's more than that. I think there's something wrong with John."

"Wrong?" Linda's temper flared once more. "What the hell do you mean?"

"Since you ask, he seems to have a chip on his shoulder about something. Daddy has noticed it too. You know, darling, I often wonder if you did a wise thing marrying a man so much older than yourself; divorced into the bargain. And how you can bear to go on living in this cottage, I really don't know."

"That's enough!" Stubbing out the cigarette, Linda jumped to her feet. "You'll be telling me next that he hasn't got over his first wife. Well, if that's what you think, you are bloody well wrong!"

Confused by the amount of sherry she had drunk, not understanding exactly how or why the row had erupted, Gloria said tipsily, "Don't forget that I am your mother. I only want what is best for you. Of course I didn't mean that John is hankering after his first wife. I mean to say, Lisa – or whatever her name is – must be forty-five now, if she's a day. He must have been mad to marry her in the first place. Of course one feels sorry for the woman, but John did right to get rid of her when he did. It's just that Daddy and I agreed, when you got married, that it might have been wiser to move into a new house. This is a lovely cottage, of course," she glanced round nervously, "but don't you ever feel . . . ?"

"Feel – *what*?" Linda demanded.

"Uneasy," Gloria said unexpectedly.

"As I said to Lin's mother only the other day," Archie Trentham gasped breathlessly, "I wouldn't mind living in the country when I retire. Nice little cottage, a bit of garden to potter about in; visits to the local; join the golf club, that kind of thing!" His breath whirled away like cigarette smoke; his face was reddish purple with the cold. He was a man who normally took little exercise other than walking to his car.

Loping along, John experienced a grim satisfaction in

166

making the man step it out, wondering how soon he would make an excuse to stop. He might have guessed.

When the Crossed Keys came into view, Archie's relief was evident. "Ah, that's what I call a pretty sight," he said fervently. "What say we stop for a noggin? After all, there's plenty of time. Lunch won't be ready for ages yet, if I know my wife."

Damn the man, John thought. Damn his insensitivity, his plebeian attitudes, his pomposity. The last thing he wanted was to sit in some fuggy bar-parlour supping beer. He hated the stuff.

The road ahead led through the village, past a row of neat stone cottages, and branched, when the village ran out, at a signpost pointing the way to the main road and a Pedestrians Only footpath leading up to the Hambleton hills. It was there that John Hazell wanted to be, high up in the world among those silent, winterbound hills, to feel the wind in his face, his boots biting into the frost-rimmed grass.

His capitulation to Archie's desire for warmth and camaraderie seemed a betrayal of self. Aware of a searing sense of despair, of failure, he crossed the threshold of the pub.

"Uneasy? You have the nerve to suggest that I feel uneasy in my own home?" Linda's voice was like ice.

"No, darling, I didn't mean that exactly. Oh my God, why all this? Why pounce on every word I utter? I'm not on trial, you know." Gloria's lips quivered. "I have a right to my opinion, and you *did* ask!"

Linda capitulated. Scooping Miles into her arms, she dried his tears with a piece of kitchen roll. "Don't cry, Mummy," she said. "I'm sorry. Let's get on with the cooking, shall we?" She added hesitantly, "The fact is . . ."

"What, darling?"

Linda shrugged her shoulders dismissively. "I have felt a bit – uneasy, lately."

"Go on, darling, you can tell me." Gloria fiddled in her simulated crocodile handbag for a fresh hanky.

"I know, but it isn't all that easy to explain. It's just that Johnny has been so awkward and irritable lately, so hard to handle."

"Sexually, you mean?" Gloria's eagerness bordered on the disgusting.

"No, of course not! I'm pregnant, aren't I?"

"Then John wanted another child?"

"Yes." But Linda's answer came a shade too quickly.

Catching the uncertainty of her daughter's reply, Gloria asked, "Are you sure about that?" slopping more sherry into her glass.

"No, if you really must know. I'd been on about another baby for ages. We'd agreed, you see, two babies close together, but he kept on making excuses so, in the end, I took the initiative. I *had* to. Well, you know how it is?"

"But why didn't he want a second child, if that's what you'd agreed?" Gloria's lips folded eagerly over the rim of her glass.

"I don't honestly know. We don't discuss things any more; we simply quarrel. There's something else, Mummy, about this cottage . . ."

"Tell me."

"Well, in the beginning, I wanted it more than I wanted John, if that makes sense. The first time I ever came here . . . I knew Johnny was married, of course. I suppose I was curious about his wife. I'd got it into my head she'd be a dumpy, matronly little woman, but she wasn't. She was young-looking for her age; rather pretty."

"Go on."

"I thought, why should she have all the luck? She had it all: Johnny, the cottage, security; everything except a child, that is . . . It seemed all wrong, somehow, and she was far too old for him anyway, so I went for the jackpot! The trouble was, Lisa made the victory too easy. I thought she'd fight tooth and nail to hang on to what belonged to her, but she didn't. I've never forgiven her for that!"

"Lin, darling, what are you saying?"

"I'm not entirely sure. It's hard to explain. It started as a kind of game, I suppose. Winner take all! Well, I won, but I didn't take all; not by a long chalk. Oh, I might have done if the bloody woman had kicked up a fuss, turned Johnny against her; if he had stopped feeling guilty about her; if she had stopped playing the martyr.

"Now I have the strangest feeling that a part of John still belongs to her – to Lisa. Don't ask me how I know, I just do. Not that he ever talks about her, but she's here all the time. Oh yes, she's here right enough, and I can't get rid of her! I often have the feeling she's watching us from the shadows. So now you know!"

Archie's laughter brayed inanely against the cacophony of the pub parlour. In his element, he was buying drinks for complete strangers, saying, "God bless, my dear old pals! Bottom's up! Christmas comes but once a year, more's the pity!" becoming drunker by the minute.

If this meaningless charade typified the way so-called Christians celebrated the birth of Jesus Christ, John thought disgustedly, he was glad that he was agnostic; a disbeliever in the Lord and Saviour of mankind.

"Darling, we must get on with lunch. They'll be back soon," Gloria reminded her daughter, swaying through to the kitchen, sherry glass in one hand, the bottle in the other, having reached that stage of inebriation in which everything seemed much clearer all of a sudden.

The turkey was sizzling alarmingly in the oven. Heaving the bird from its covering of foil, she basted it lavishly with hot fat, and tipped into the roasting tin a panful of raw potatoes which Linda are pared earlier.

"Whoops, in they go," she chortled merrily, shoving the

bird and the potatoes back in the oven, after which she placed a pan of sprouts on a back burner of the Aga to boil. "Now for the pudding! I think that's the lot, isn't it, apart from the rum sauce and the gravy? Have you set the table, by the way?"

An hour and a half later, Gloria was standing near the drawing room window staring anxiously at the driveway. The time was now two-thirty.

Miles, having wailed incessantly since one o'clock, had been fed a sliver of turkey breast, a dish of ice-cream from the deep-freeze, and put to sleep in his cot. No way could he have eaten blackened potatoes and stewed sprouts; boiled-dry Christmas pudding; lumpy rum sauce and even lumpier gravy.

Surveying the ruins of the Christmas dinner, "It's too bad!" Linda exploded, forgetting that it was her fault entirely for sending her father on a pre-luncheon walk to an inevitable destination.

"They're coming!" Gloria's vigil was rewarded by the sight of the two men walking up the path to the front door. "Now, Lin," she said warningly, "no use being cross. We've had enough, traumas for one day!"

"Hello, there! Why, whassamatter? Why the black looks, Lin love?" Archie enquired foolishly, crossing the threshold. "Where's my grandson?"

"In bed," Linda snapped.

"In bed? At this time of day?"

"The time," Linda pointed out coldly, "is very nearly a quarter to three. My son could not wait for his food, even if you could!"

Inured to this kind of crisis, Gloria saw nothing untoward in serving badly cooked food which no one was in a fit state to enjoy anyway. Making light of the contretemps, "Go upstairs and wash your hands, you two," she said brightly. "Lunch will be on the table when you come down."

When John and Archie had gone upstairs, Linda turned on her mother in a fury, to no avail.

"Now you listen to me, my girl. They're both a bit plastered; so what?" Full of Dutch courage, Gloria continued smartly, "Just be thankful they're here at all." Assuming that John also was inebriated, she advised, "In my experience, men are much more managable when they've had a skinful, especially when they know they're in the wrong."

This was true, Linda realised, recalling the evening she had told John about the new baby; not that he had been 'plastered' at the time, indeed she had never known him to drink too much before. It might be infinitely rewarding to find out how he'd react physically, robbed of his inhibitions.

Archie brayed incessantly throughout the meal, pulled crackers with abandon; wore his paper crown pulled down over his eyebrows, told several *risqué* jokes; said he'd never tasted a finer bit of turkey in his life before, all to the accompaniment of several glasses of Madeira, until even Gloria realised he'd had enough booze for the time being.

"Come on, love," she said eventually, helping him up from his chair, "time for a nap."

When they had gone upstairs, Linda said lazily, to hide her excitement, "Shall we follow suite? It's still quite safe, you know."

Cracking a Brazil nut, John dropped the shell into the remains of the Christmas pudding, knowing she was hell-bent on getting him into bed; the reason why she had kept topping up his glass of wine; that she wanted him drunk, stupid, helpless and between the sheets. "What is?" he asked coldly. "What is still quite safe?"

"For heaven's sake, Johnny, you know damn well what I mean." She smiled at him coquettishly over the rim of her glass, so sure of her power over him. The poor, silly,

171

pathetic bitch, he thought bleakly, remembering the pathway to the hill where a man might walk as a man, not a puppet; feeling the wind in his face; where the massed battalions of clouds overhead resembled the unconquered mountain ranges of some unknown land far removed from this place; this home, this cottage which he had once loved and now hated with every fibre of his being.

No, he was wrong; it was not the cottage he hated, but its present inhabitants; his ghastly in-laws and their as common-as-dirt daughter whose libido resembled that of a female rabbit.

Rising to his feet, he strode from the dining room to the drawing room, which his wife called 'the lounge', with its looped-up Christmas cards, lopsided tree, and his son's latest batch of toys strewn across the carpet.

Following closely in his wake, angry beyond belief that he had left the dining table so abruptly, Linda demanded hoarsely, "Just what the hell do you think you are doing?" as he picked up the telephone.

"Ringing Directory Enquiries," he said brusquely, remembering that Lisa had told him she was living in Westsea, at The Bay View Hotel.

Chapter Eighteen

"I'm warning you, John," Linda cried wildly, "if you ring that bloody woman I'll leave here right away! I mean what I say! I'll go home with my parents; take Miles with me – have an abortion! Do you take me for an absolute fool? Now I know why you've been acting so strangely ever since we left Westsea! You'd been seeing her all along, hadn't you? Making love to her, I daresay!"

"That is not true!"

"Of course it's bloody well true! You *did* meet her there, didn't you?"

"Yes, just once, briefly, in the street," he acknowledged.

"Just once, briefly, in the street," Linda mimicked savagely, "and you really expect me to believe that? More likely you were having it off with her in some shelter or other whilst I was in the hotel taking care of our son! Or perhaps she has a nice little flat tucked away somewhere, with a king-size bed and lots of nice soft pillows! You – *bastard!* Well, pick up that telephone again if you dare!"

Gloria appeared on the threshold at that moment, hair awry, wearing a padded dressing-gown, a puzzled expression on her face. "What on earth's going on?" she demanded. "Daddy and I could hear you screaming upstairs!"

Linda burst into tears. "Ask *him!*" she sobbed. "Ask John! It's all his fault!"

"I don't understand," Gloria said vacuously, in the throes

of a sherry-induced hangover. "John? What have you done to upset her?"

Linda burst forth, "*Done*? I'll tell you what he's done! He's been seeing that bloody ex-wife of his behind my back! But he won't get away with it! No way! We're leaving right now! Tell Daddy! Start packing!"

Gloria said bemusedly, "But we *can't*! You said yourself there are no trains on Christmas Day!"

"Then we'll hire a taxi, or bloody well walk, if necessary!"

Linda rushed headlong upstairs. The sound of her footsteps could be heard in the room above, then came the wailing of a child disturbed from his sleep.

"John, I really think you owe me an explanation," Gloria said aggressively. "I've never seen Lin in such a state before. It can't be good for her, not in her condition. Is it true what she said, that you've been seeing your ex-wife behind her back?"

"Keep your nose out of it," John muttered savagely. "It's none of your business!"

"Well, I must say!" Deeply affronted, Gloria stared after him as, pushing past her, he took the stairs two at a time.

Linda was in Miles' nursery, holding the sobbing child in her arms.

"Put my son back in his cot," John said coldly.

"Go to hell!" Linda's tears were over now. "You've gone too far this time. I can see it all now. You've wanted her back all along, haven't you, that gutless first wife of yours! Not that she ever left this bloody cottage. She's been here all the time, hasn't she?"

"I don't know what you mean."

"Then think about it! No wonder I couldn't do anything right for you. You and your bloody books and – poetry. What you need is a plaster saint, not a flesh and blood woman; someone to sit at your feet and gaze up at you adoringly,

174

the way she used to, I daresay – a mother figure, not a wife. What a pity she couldn't have had an – immaculate conception!"

"That's enough, Linda!"

"Not for me, it isn't! I haven't even begun to say what I'm thinking! You disgust me, John, if you really want to know! All those high-flown ideas of yours about gypsies and camp-fires! Ha, well, your precious Lisa would probably have gone along with that had the occasion arisen! *If*. But it never did, because she was too bloody old!"

John struck Linda across the face with the flat of his hand, then, turning abruptly, he walked downstairs, brushing past Archie who had emerged from his bedroom, minus dentures, to hover on the landing mumbling bemusedly, "Eh? What's going on?"

Seconds later, marching on to the landing with Miles in her arms, Linda called out in a light, clear voice, "Come up and help me pack, Mummy. The party's over! We're leaving!"

"But, darling . . ."

"Just do it!"

John recognised the challenging note of excitement in his wife's voice, and knew, even now, that she was playing a game of truth or dare; willing him to go up to her; to grovel, to say he was sorry that he had struck her; a frantic appeal not to leave him; the inevitable capitulation and copulation. But not this time. Never again . . .

In the drawing room, he stared out of the window. The Christmas Day he had dreaded was almost over now.

From where he was standing, he could see the line of fir trees, at the garden's edge, silhouetted against the glow of a gas-lamp in the lane beyond the grey stone wall, and knew that what Linda said was true. Lisa had been here all the time, treading softly, making no sound.

From overhead came the sound of hurrying footsteps, of voices, the thumping and bumping of suitcases from

175

cupboards. Finally came the clatter of feet on the stairs as Archie and Gloria descended with their luggage.

Gloria entered the drawing room alone, pink with indignation; a mink jacket slung about her shoulders; a flowered silk turban covering her blackberry-coloured coiffure. "Now look here, John," she said stiffly, "you cannot simply stand there doing nothing! You must tell Linda you're sorry. She's in the hall, ringing up for a taxi. Everything would settle down if you would just go to her and admit you were in the wrong. And you *were*, you know. I mean, attempting to ring your first wife was a bit much, with Linda in her condition!"

Turning his head away, John stared into the fire, thinking of Lisa's cat buried out there in the garden; the way she had wept over the grave; had laid on it a bunch of white lilac.

"Oh, so that's your attitude, is it?" Gloria bridled. "The silent treatment? Ignorant swine! I knew it all along! 'No breeding there,' I said to Daddy. Ask him if you don't believe me. No feelings either, apparently. But what about your son? What about the new baby?

"Huh, you really don't care, do you? Skulking in here with that supercilious smirk on your face! Well let me assure you, John Hazell, you'll smile on the other side of your face when our solicitor hears about this! Acutally striking a pregnant woman! Oh yes, Linda told me all about it! Great drunken brute! Just think yourself damned lucky that my husband didn't punch you on the nose when you struck our daughter! It would have served you damn well right, if you ask me!"

The diatribe ended abruptly. Gloria stood there uncertainly, nonplussed that her tirade had fallen on deaf ears. Turning on her heels, she fired her parting shot. "But don't think for one minute you've heard the last of this, because you haven't! You'll be hearing from our solicitor in due course, you know. Oh yes, Daddy and I can afford to hire the best, and we'll make you pay dearly for what you have done to our daughter, believe you me!"

John believed her.

When she had stormed out of the room, slamming the door behind her, he felt no sense of regret that Linda was leaving him.

Staring into the fire, he heard the arrival of the taxi, the chugging of its engine, and when it had driven away carrying Linda, Miles, and her parents, plus a vast assortment of luggage, he experienced a deep, sweet feeling of relief that the charade was over and done with at last.

Later, he walked slowly about the cottage surveying the wreckage they had left behind them; noticed, with a sense of loathing, the lipstick-daubed tissues, spilt powder and forgotten kirby-grips on his mother-in-law's dressing table; the sticky glasses in the washbasin.

Entering the bathroom, he saw, with disgust, the crumpled towels on the floor; the rim of dirt round the bath, which Linda had never bothered to clean away properly; the soiled clothing spilling over from the Ali-Baba basket. Systematically, he began the clearing-up process.

Working his way down from the bedrooms, armed with cleaning materials and bin-liners, uppermost in his mind came the fervent desire to have everything clean and unsullied once more; sweet-smelling and fragrant; uncluttered, as it had been in the beginning.

Stripping the beds, he carried the crumpled sheets and pillowcases, along with the contents of the Ali-Baba basket and the damp bathroom towels, to the washing machine in the utility room, to which he added the requisite amount of soap powder before switching on the wash-cycle.

This done, he cleared up the mess in the dining room, crumpling Archie's paper crown disdainfully in the palm of his hand, before shovelling the Brazil nut shells, the mucous remains of the rum sauce, and the red paper serviettes into a bin-liner, after which, when the table had been cleared, he went through to the kitchen to begin washing the stacked-up mounds of dirty plates, pans and dishes on the draining-board; filling the sink over and over again with scalding hot soapy water; tackling the burned remainders of a meal he would never forget with a Brillo pad and a scouring brush, and jamming the remains of the turkey, along with the rock-hard remnants of the Christmas pudding into another bag which, in due course, he dumped into the nearest dustbin.

When the dining room and the kitchen had been cleared to his satisfaction, going through to the drawing room, unlooping the Christmas cards from the walls, he threw them on the fire and watched them burn. He then humped outdoors the Christmas tree; patiently picked the stuck-on cotton wool 'snow' from the windows; gathered up Miles' toys from the carpet and put them away in the cupboard under the stairs, with no deep-seated sense of regret that the boy might, from now on, no longer be a part of his life. He felt, simply, an overwhelming feeling of relief that the house was silent once more; a sense of blessedness that he was free, now, to live his own life in his own way; hopefully, one day with the woman he really loved beside him. *Lisa*.

To the accompaniment of his favourite recording of Elgar's 'Enigma Variations', he picked up the telephone, and dialled the number of The Bay View Hotel.

Chapter Nineteen

Judy's brief love affair with Kit Chalmers had left her feeling – soiled for the want of a better description.

She had known from the beginning his reputation as a womaniser; even so, she had gone like a lamb to the slaughter. Stubbornly, she had refused to listen to the gossiping tongues of her fellow students, prefering to draw her own conclusions.

Tasting freedom for the first time, away from the restrictive influence of her mother, it had seemed important to make her own decisions – the reason why she had chosen to rent a bed-sitting room away from the college precincts. Even this had become a bone of contention between herself and Pamela. Her mother had made abundantly clear, in a prissily-worded letter, that she, Judith, would be better off in one of the students' hostels within the campus confines. What on earth had possessed her to waste money on rented accommodation, she could not begin to imagine; a young girl with no experience of looking after herself whatsoever. How would she manage to feed herself properly, for one thing? And was she sure the room was absolutely *clean*? The bedding in particular.

Replying to that letter, Judith had assured her mother that the room she had rented was perfectly clean; light and airy, the windows overlooking a small but well-maintained garden belonging to the house-owners who lived on the ground floor, and large enough to include a kitchenette in which she could cook for herself, if necessary, simple meals such as poached eggs or baked beans on toast. So really, there was no need to worry, since she lunched adequately in the college refectory during the hour-long break between lectures.

She had thought it politic not to mention that, most evenings, she and a few of her special cronies would sally forth to the local pub to drink half-pints of shandy and scoff the landlady's *spécialitiés de la maison* – Lancashire hot-pots, Chicken Maryland and chips, and rare roast-beef sandwiches served with a side-salad of thinly-sliced raw onions, green peppers and cos lettuce smothered in home-made mayonnaise.

It was in this pub, one Saturday evening, that Judy had first set eyes on Kit Chalmers. He had been standing near the bar; a tall, attractive figure of a man, casually dressed in a shabby leather jacket, tight-fitting jeans and a polo-neck sweater, laughing with a group of his fellow students, tossing back his mane of tawny hair, displaying a set of teeth that would have done credit to a TV toothpaste commercial.

Then suddenly, unaccountably, their eyes had met across the crowded bar-parlour, and the man had smiled in her direction.

With a fast-beating heart, "Who is that man at the bar?" Judith asked her companions.

"Oh, you mean Kit Chalmers?" Althea Gardiner, a slim brunette with blue eyes, sniffed audibly. "A wolf in sheep's clothing, if you ask me! Just say the word and he's yours, the bastard!"

"Althea's right," June Jackson, a chunky redhead, broke in, "the man's a menace, and I should know! He led me one hell of a dance before I saw sense and told him to get lost! He's a womaniser pure and simple; after only one thing. Well, you know what I mean? I'd give him a wide berth if I were you!"

Their warnings had fallen on deaf ears.

That Kit Chalmers had noticed her at all had seemed like

a miracle to Judy. She was pretty enough, she supposed, in a fair, fluffy, unformed kind of way, with still much of the child about her. Romantically inclined yet strongly opposed to sex without love, she had gained, unbeknown to herself, a reputation for untouchability – so far and no further – according to the male students she had been out with occasionally.

Money had been wagered that even Chalmers – the old smoothie himself – would be unable to storm this particular citadel. He had been given a fortnight in which to accomplish her deflowering. The wager had included persuading Judith to have her hair cut short and to take up smoking.

"Easy as falling off a log," Chalmers had assured them, smiling broadly. "Like taking candy from a baby!"

She had demurred, initially, when after a visit to the cinema, he had invited her to his flat for coffee, making the excuse that she didn't want to be home late.

"Of course, I understand," he said charmingly, "another time, perhaps?" And she had fallen for the ploy hook line and sinker. Fearing that there might not be another time, she had changed her mind and accepted his invitation.

His flat, so called, consisted of a small sitting room, a bedroom and a kitchenette, on the top floor of a far from well-maintained three storey house in a cul-de-sac near a shop-lined thoroughfare.

The bathroom and lavatory were on the second floor, he explained, preceding her up a narrow staircase and pressing the time-switches as he went, which was a bit of a darned nuisance at times, but then, beggars could not be choosers and, thankfully, the house-owners, a Pakistani couple, did not live on the premises. They simply called once a week to collect the rent.

Entering Kit's sitting room, Judith had stared in bewilderment at the untidy clutter of his personal belongings:

the bizarre wall-posters depicting bull-fights and toreadors; Can-Can dancers at the *Folies Bergère* in Paris; Toulouse Lautrec smoking a thick black cigar, and Vincent Van Gogh seated at a bistro table beneath a heaven thick with stars.

And this, Judith thought, was a world far removed from any she had known before; a liberated world of freedom of movement, just as Kit Chalmers was unlike anyone she had met before – a free spirit; certainly intelligent and well-read by the amount of books over-spilling the shelves flanking the fireplace with its ancient gas fire and cigarette-littered hearth.

Emerging from the kitchenette with two mugs of steaming hot coffee, Kit had apologised for the state of the room. "I'd have tidied up a bit first had I known you were coming," he said boyishly. "Frankly, I still can't quite believe that you are here, Judy. After all, why should a nice girl like you be bothered with a – drop-out – like me?"

"You, a drop-out? Oh no, surely not?"

"Well, maybe I'm not as black as I'm painted," he confessed. "Do you mind if I smoke, by the way?"

"No, of course not. Why should I?"

"Oh, I don't know. Put it this way, I'd feel happier if you joined me." Offering her his cigarette packet, he urged, "Please, Judy, at least try one for my sake. Who knows, you might quite enjoy it!"

"Oh, very well then, if you insist!" And so she had taken her first tentative puff on a cigarette . . . and that was the first step in the right direction so far as Kit Chalmers was concerned. Obviously, the poor silly little bitch was already head-over-heels in love with him. It was simply a matter of time before he pocketed the fifty-quid wager-money. Now all he had to do was state his preference for short-haired women, very subtly of course, and get her into bed with him. No problem. The fifty quid was as good as his.

Their first lovemaking had left her feeling weak, shaken and

182

somehow inadequate. Something was missing, she realised afterwards. That something was tenderness.

When it was over, he had lain on his back against the pillows and lit a cigarette, and she had not been able to understand why such a soul-searing experience had made so little impression on him.

Finishing his cigarette, he had pulled on his jeans and padded to the kitchenette to make coffee. Returning, he found her in tears.

"Hey, what's wrong? Wasn't it good for you?"

"I don't know. I mean, I – this was my first time."

"Nothing to get upset about. All you need is a little more practice."

If only he had held her in his arms and told her he loved her. She felt shut out, expendable, as he dressed more fully, saying that if they hurried they might just be in time for a drink before the pub closed, not realising that she couldn't hurry, the state she was in – in dire need of the bathroom. He might have known her predicament had he been more sensitive, more understanding. Or perhaps he had never made love to a virgin before?

It was then she had begun slowly and painfully to realise that he was not in love with her as she was with him, and yet during the tenure of their brief, one-sided 'love affair', she had done her best to please him physically; had even cut her hair to please him; unable to bear the thought of losing him. But how could one lose something that one had never owned in the first place?

Even when they were closest, in the physical sense, she knew that she had not touched him at all, except with her hands, lips, and body.

She had, at least, possessed enough gumption and common-sense to end the affair with dignity towards the end of the autumn semester, before the commencement of the Christmas vacation; clearing his flat of her belongings with a closed expression, holding back her tears, knowing he did not care tuppence that she was leaving him for good.

At the station, he had carried her case to the barrier, kissed her briefly on the cheek, wished her a Merry Christmas, and then he was gone. Looking back, she saw him pushing impatiently through the crowds cluttering the concourse.

Seated in the train, she had pictured him striding into the nearest pub, lounging against the bar, chatting up some girl with cropped blonde hair, screwing up his eyes from the rising smoke of a cigarette, carefully weighing up the girl's potential before inviting her back to his flat.

Closing her eyes had not helped. Images flickered through her mind like a magic-lantern show. She could almost see him opening the door of his flat, peeling off his leather jacket, putting a match to the gas fire; telling the girl to make herself comfortable; fetching coffee or cans of Budweiser beer from the kitchen; putting on a Roberta Flack record – 'The First Time Ever I Saw Your Face' – sitting beside the girl on the sofa . . .

She knew, from bitter experience, exactly how the seduction scene would begin, because this was the way it had started with her. Nothing hurried about it initially; just talk and music, the hypnotic plopping of the ancient gas fire; the slow smile, the touching of hands, the eventual meeting of lips; those meaningless words of his: "Know what? I think I'm falling in love with you."

As the train jogged on towards Westsea, suddenly, quite desperately, Judith longed for a return of innocence, of childhood; to be home once more; to sleep in her own bed; to turn back the pages of time to the beginning.

And yet, she had known, deep down, as she walked towards the station barrier at Westsea, that there could be no return to the past. The child and the laughing, carefree girl who had once inhabited her skin, were gone forever. She had been hurt, ultimately rejected.

Meeting her father at the barrier, she knew that he, too, had changed. Difficult to say why. She had simply known that she no longer felt as close to him as she used to, as if a barrier of thorns had suddenly sprung up between them.

Then, when he had thrust at her the fact of her mother's pregnancy, and admitted that he was having an affair with another woman, angry and humiliated, she had felt as soiled by her father as she had been by her lover; totally on her mother's side for once, because Pamela had also been rejected.

Then had come a kind of balancing act between the parents she loved; the scales of which had tipped for a while in favour of her father, until . . .

Entering the drawing room, shocked at the sight of her mother huddled in a chair by the fire, for all the world like a woman twice her age, Judith knelt beside her. "Mummy, you're ill, you should be in bed," she said hoarsely.

"*No*! Leave me alone! I am quite all right! Just go away and leave me alone!"

Judith turned on her father in a fury. "Well don't just stand there doing nothing," she flung at him. "Can't you see Mummy is on the verge of collapse? We must get her upstairs at once; send for the doctor."

"Your mother refuses to see the doctor," Edward said wearily.

"To hell with that! If you won't call him, I will!"

"All right, Judy, I'll do it."

"And don't let him shilly-shally or try to put you off until after the holiday. Tell him this is an emergency. My God, if I could lay hands on that woman you told me about, I'd shake her till her teeth rattled! This is all her fault!"

"Stop it, Judy! I'm the one to blame." He dialled the number. "Hello, Dr Soames? Sorry to call you at this late hour . . ."

*   *   *

Edward had carried Pamela upstairs to bed, and Judith was sitting beside her when he hurried downstairs to answer the doorbell.

Dr Soames, tall and thin, slightly irritable at being called away from a dinner party, arrived wearing evening dress. These so-called emergencies were usually in the minds of the patients' nearest and dearest, he thought, entering the bedroom. He had agreed to this visit in view of Mrs Miller's pregnancy at an advanced age – all the more unusual in respect of her somewhat frigid personality; an unlikely candidate for pregnancy at any age, in his opinion.

Assuming his bedside manner, he said, "Now, Mrs Miller, what appears to be the trouble?"

Twisting and turning, with tears streaming down her sunken cheeks, Pamela moaned, "Don't let her go out to see the lambs."

"Lambs?" Soames looked sharply at Edward. "What is she talking about?"

"Something that happened a long time ago."

Shaking his thermometer, he turned back to his patient. "All right, Mrs Miller, try to keep calm, I'm just going to take your temperature."

"What *did* Mummy mean about the lambs?" Judy asked her father in a low voice.

Edward shook his head. "It's a long story. I'll tell you later."

Reading the thermometer, Soames looked worried. "How long has she been like this?"

"I'm not sure. I went to the station to meet my daughter. My wife seemed much as usual when I left her." But that was over two hours ago, Edward thought dully, with an upsurge of guilt. "She was sitting in her chair by the drawing room fire . . ."

"I could see at once that my mother was ill," Judith broke in nervously, clenching her hands. "It was my idea to send for you."

186

The doctor brushed aside further explanation with a peremptory wave of his hand. "Rightly so," he muttered, "her temperature is sky-high, the reason why your mother is hallucinating . . ."

Suddenly, Pamela uttered a low cry of pain as the initial drop of blood staining the bed-cover quickly spread and deepened in colour.

"Where's the phone?" Soames demanded hoarsely.

"In the hall," Edward told him. "Why? What's happening?"

"Your wife's aborting! We must get her into hospital as quickly as possible!"

In the ambulance, Judith said bleakly, "Funny, isn't it? Mummy didn't even notice my hair."

Until his child was lost, Edward had not thought of that embryo as a potential person, an individual human being. In his despair, its very existence had appalled him as a threat to his peace of mind; a source of torment to Pamela. Never once, until now, had he regarded it as his own creation; a vital, living part of his own body.

Now that the embryo was gone; carried away on great gouts of blood, he felt frozen, numb with shock, filled with an intense, inconsolable grief.

In the early hours of next morning – Christmas Day – when Pamela was out of danger, Judith had phoned for a taxi to take them home. Leading her father by the hand, she deeply regretted her former hostility towards him.

Making tea and sandwiches, she carried the tray to the drawing room where her father was sitting, his head buried in his hands. "Please, Daddy," she said gently, "try to eat. *Please*, for your own sake as well as mine. You must be famished. I know I am."

He shook his head. "I'm not hungry."

Kneeling beside him, she laid her head on his lap. "Oh

God," she said wearily, "I'm so dreadfully unhappy. Daddy, please help me. I *need* you."

Absently ruffling her hair, he thought how small her skull felt, shorn of its silky golden cloud, and experienced a surge of hatred towards the man who had robbed his child of her innocence. He said bitterly, "The man you told me about – are you still in love with him?"

Looking up at her father, her eyes bright with tears, "Yes," she said quietly. "I've tried not to be, and he doesn't know how I feel. Not that he would care tuppence if he did. He never loved me; I know that now. It was all my fault. I wanted him more than he wanted me. But I had never met anyone like him before – had never wanted anyone to touch me before. Do you understand?"

"Yes, I understand." Edward thought of the importance of touch conveyed through loving hands and soft, welcoming flesh. More importantly, that intangible touching of mind and spirit without which real love and understanding were impossible. He had never touched Pamela in any of these ways.

Judith said, "I always took it for granted that you and Mummy were happy together. That's the way all children see their parents, I imagine. Perhaps I was blind. I'd never really thought about it before – the differences between you. I never thought of you as individuals, just two people who lived together under the same roof. That's why I was shocked when you told me about – Lisa. It never occurred to me that you might need someone else. I was jealous that Lisa had come between us."

Sitting back on her heels, staring at the fire-glow, "Strange, isn't it," she continued, "that when it came to something tremendously important in both our lives, we couldn't communicate at all? You wrote to me about a seagull on a chimney-pot, I wrote to you about a Chopin recital on Radio Three. As for Mummy – I wonder what she would have thought about those secret letters of ours? How cruel we were, shutting her out of our lives the way we did. I shall never forgive myself for that; for poking fun at her behind her back . . ."

"Please, don't go on," Edward said brokenly. "In any case, it is simply not true. Your mother could have read any one of those letters, in which her name was never even mentioned, much less made fun of."

"Yes, but I was awful to her at times, trying deliberately to shock her, accusing her of being stuffy and old-fashioned. I had the feeling that she was trying to hold me back in some way. You encouraged me to be independent; with Mummy it was always don't do this and don't do that, as if she was trying to wrap me in cotton wool, and I hated it."

"She had her reasons." Edward knew the time had come to tell her about Helga. Getting up from his chair, he crossed to the window and looked out. It had started to snow, the flakes driven by a keening wind reminiscent of the spirits of all the lonely, lost children of the world crying out for love.

He thought, staring into the darkness, that he had failed everyone – his wife, Judith, his unborn child, and Lisa. His selfish stab at happiness had destroyed all their lives; a fabric so delicately interwoven that no one person had the right to tear it to shreds, as he had done. Nor could he hope to mend what he had destroyed. Too late for that. And yet . . .

Returning to the fireside, taking Judy's hands in his, it seemed to him that telling her about Helga might, at least, bring about a closer understanding between his daughter and her mother in time to come.

Chapter Twenty

The Christmas dinner had been served and eaten at a gate-legged table drawn up in front of the sitting room fire. First the smoked salmon fillets, then the capon, stuffing and vegetables, followed by the sumptuous-looking trifle Lisa had seen in the pantry.

"Sorry, forgot the Christmas pudding," Jake said, placing the trifle on the polished tabletop, having removed the remains of the capon, the vegetable tureens and the gravy-boat to the kitchen along with the soiled Coalport dinner-plates and the silverware cutlery and condiments. "Good job Edie brought round one of her specials." In point of fact, they had both eaten relatively little; had said even less, each busy with their own thoughts in this firelit room, with dusk falling gently on the world beyond the tall Georgian windows overlooking the walled garden, with the sound of the sea in the distance and the solemn ticking of a grandfather clock close at hand.

When the meal was over, Lisa had insisted on helping with the washing up. "You must remember I'm by way of being a professional washer-upper," she reminded him, running hot water into the sink and adding the washing-up liquid. "I'll wash, you dry."

"In which case, you'll need an apron," he said off-handedly, opening a drawer. "Here, try this for size!" adding brusquely, "It belonged to my wife, Isabel. She forgot to take it with her when she left me. Not surprising, really. Isabel hated washing up!"

"Oh, Jake, I'm sorry," Lisa faltered, "I had no idea . . ."

"That I'd been married?" Jake said grimly, handing Lisa the apron. "But why on earth should you? It was just another mistake that happens along life's way. Frankly, we were both too young to shoulder the responsibilities of a lifelong commitment to one another. Now, let's get on with the washing up, shall we?"

When the kitchen had been tidied and the dishes put back on the dresser, Jake made coffee and carried it through to the other room. Lisa wondered if he had meant to tell her about Isabel, or if the snippet of information had been unintentional. Certainly he had seemed unwilling to pursue the matter. His abrupt, "Now, let's get on with the washing up, shall we?" had effectively put paid to the subject of Isabel and the break-up of their marriage.

Sipping her coffee, staring into the fire, Lisa thought about the break-up of her own marriage; that last Christmas at the cottage when she had sensed John's restlessness and need of escape, not realising at the time that it was herself he wished to escape from.

"A penny for your thoughts," Jake said, unexpectedly, from his chair opposite to hers, drawn up close to the fire, within the circumference of the glow of the crackling logs on the hearth.

It was then, in an atmosphere conducive to confession, that Lisa told him quietly about John's affair with a younger woman, and the cottage she had loved so much; the age difference between herself and John, which had seemed unimportant at first; which had mattered a great deal in the long run, when she had failed to bear him the child he had set his heart on.

"So you set him free to marry the younger woman? Is that it?" Jake asked gently, thinking how lovely Lisa looked by firelight.

"Well, yes, I suppose so," she assented, with a brief shrug

of her shoulders. "You see, I couldn't 'fight City Hall', as the saying goes. I knew when I was beaten, and I wanted John to be happy . . . Letting go of him seemed the only solution to the problem at the time. In any case, our marriage was virtually over and done with anyway, and I wanted to quit the field with some kind of grace and dignity still left to me, if that makes sense."

"Yes, of course it does," Jake admitted, leaning forward to place another log on the fire. "The truth is, I let go of Isabel for the self same reason, when she told me she was expecting a child by another man – a friend of mine, as it happened. Not that I was as forebearing as you were – not by a long chalk! I just told her to go to her fancy-man; to go to the devil for all I cared . . ."

"And then what?" Lisa asked.

Staring into the fire, Jake said bleakly, "Isabel died in childbirth, and I shall never forgive myself for casting her aside the way I did. If only I had been less aggressive, more understanding. But what's the use of talking? What's done is done. The trouble is, having to live with the past for the rest of one's life."

"At least you've learned to take care of yourself," Lisa said, "and you have this house, and your antiques business."

"Which reminds me," Jake said, filling his pipe and lighting it, "if you have nothing planned for tomorrow, perhaps you'd like to have a look at the shop in the morning before going on to Edie's for lunch?"

"Well yes, I'd love to look round the shop, but I can't very well turn up for lunch uninvited."

Jake laughed. "No need to worry, it's open house at Edie's on Boxing Day – a free for all; nothing in the least formal, I assure you. Edie provides a running buffet, so folk just help themselves, and everyone's welcome. In fact, Edie's so-called lunches have been known to continue till midnight."

* * *

Later, he went through to the kitchen to make tea and sandwiches which he placed on the gate-legged table, along with a small shop-bought Christmas cake, and Lisa thought, what a kind and caring human being he was, deep down, beneath his brusque exterior; pleased that she now understood, to some small degree, the reasons why he had built up a barrier between himself and most other human beings; why his sister, Edie Hannersley, had referred to him as a 'loner'.

And this was something they had in common, Lisa thought, in dusky room in which she and Jake Colby had somehow drawn closer together across a firelit hearth, because she too was a 'loner' at heart.

When the sandwiches had been eaten, the tea drunk, and the trifle and the Christmas cake sampled, Lisa thanked Jake for his hospitality and went upstairs to her flat, tired and emotionally drained yet curiously happy at the thought of their next meeting at eleven o'clock on Boxing Day morning.

Crossing the threshold, she heard the insistent ringing of the telephone, and stared at it uncertainly, wondering whether or not to pick up the receiver. This, after all, was Christmas Day, a supreme time of forgiveness. But what could she possibly say to Edward that had not already been said? What was the point or purpose of relighting, however briefly, the embers of a burnt-out love affair?

She had no way of knowing that it was not Edward on the other end of the line.

"Well, this is it." Unlocking the door of his shop, Jake stood aside to allow Lisa to enter first. "It isn't very big, I'm afraid – the reason why I stock mainly small items; the kind of bric-à-brac that tourists want to take home with them."

Pausing on the threshold of what appeared to be an

193

Aladdin's Cave of treasures, "Oh, it's lovely," Lisa said ecstatically, as Jake switched on the lights, and she moved forward to examine more closely the wealth of goods on display, as if she had suddenly entered a time-warp; as if the modern, workaday world beyond the shop door had ceased to exist.

There were Victorian dressing-table sets, ring-holders, powder bowls, candlesticks; silver-backed brushes and hand-mirrors; Georgian tea-caddies, cut-glass decanters; porcelain cups and saucers; silver spoons and snuff-boxes; items of Victorian jewellery, Mizpah brooches, diamanté-studded combs, dog-collar necklaces, jet mourning rings, lockets and brooches and ivory fans, in the display cabinets.

The walls were hung with texts and samplers, prints and oil-paintings. One print in particular caught her eye; that of a young girl, barefoot on some unknown beach, arms flung wide to embrace the sea – a picture she knew and loved, a facsimile of which had once hung on her bedroom wall in the old house in Walthamstow, entitled 'Dream Ships', from an original painting by Margaret Tarrant.

"That picture," Lisa said, explaining how much it meant to her, and that it had somehow disappeared after the death of her parents, when the house had been sold and the furniture had gone to the saleroom. "Is it for sale? If so, I'd like to buy it."

"Sorry, afraid not," Jake said off-handedly, "it's already spoken for."

Hiding her disappointment, she turned to look at a Victorian powder bowl. Lifting the lid, she saw that the bowl contained a swansdown powder puff, smelling faintly of attar of roses. "I wonder who this belonged to?" she said wistfully, imagining some slender Victorian lady seated at her dressing table, getting ready for a dance or a dinner-party perhaps. "Wouldn't it be wonderful if we could look into the past, to see things as they really were, not as we imagine them to be?"

"Perhaps," Jake conceded, "but maybe it's best not to know. Some things are better left to the imagination. For all we know, that powder bowl might have belonged to some old harridan who made her servants' lives a misery. Well, shall we press on? You'll have noticed that all the items are priced, and there's no question of bargaining. It happens all the time in this kind of shop; people wanting a pound or two knocked off the stated selling price. Forewarned is forearmed. In any case, there's a notice to that effect near the till."

"Yes, I see." Lisa read the notice: 'The price of goods on sale in this shop are not negotiable'. Clear, succinct and to the point, she thought, and lacking sentimentality, a bit like the owner of the shop.

"There's a little private room through here," he went on, opening a door behind the counter, "with tea-making facilities and so on."

Standing on the threshold, Lisa noticed a small sink in one corner; next to it a laminated unit with an enamel tray, an electric kettle, mugs and spoons, and a basket containing tea-bags and a jar of instant coffee.

On the far side of the room stood a small desk stacked with box-files and folders, a pocket calculator and a telephone. The office-cum-refreshment room contained also a metal filing cabinet, a swivel chair, and slatted shelves bearing an assortment of paper bags in varying sizes; wrapping and tissue paper and empty boxes, rolls of sellotape and balls of string.

Obviously, Jake Colby was a man who meant business, Lisa thought, realising that she had not even begun to understand or come to grips with so complex a human being. In any case, did it really matter whether or not she understood him? He had offered her a job, she had accepted that offer, and that effectually, was that. So long as she continued to pay her rent on time, and did not, when the time came, negotiate deals with the customers, she should manage quite well on the whole.

He said gruffly, "Well, we'd best be going now. Almost lunch time. Edie will be expecting us."

Mrs Hannersley welcomed Lisa with open arms. "Why, Mrs Hazell," she cried delightedly, "I'm real pleased to see you again! Well, don't just stand there, Jake, take her coat and give her something to eat!"

The food was set out, buffet fashion, on a long table covered with a pristine, lace-edged tablecloth. There were plates of home-made sausage rolls, mushroom vol-au-vents, platters of cold turkey, chicken and ham, slabs of veal and ham pie, bowls of salad, mounds of bread rolls, vases of celery; jars of pickled onions and beetroot, sherry trifles, and a nobly proportioned Christmas cake.

The room was filled with laughing, chattering people, some of whom had spilled over into the hall where a sprig of mistletoe had been affixed to the light shade. Children, wearing paper hats and clutching colourful balloons, were running amok, getting in everyone's way.

Lisa laughed, glad of the warmth and hospitality, the smiling people about her – nice, ordinary uncomplicated people talking about ordinary, everyday things – what they had been given for Christmas; New Year Resolutions; next year's summer holidays; the Christmas Day television programmes; the inevitability of the James Bond and Walt Disney films they had seen a dozen times before . . .

Some couples had started to dance to the background recording of a James Last tape, smiling into each other's eyes; pausing to kiss beneath the mistletoe.

Drinks were being served in the kitchen where the older men had gathered together to discuss football; England's chances in the World Cup; the present plight of the fishing industry, or whatever, at the same time moistening their throats with long pulls of canned beer or lager; growing mellower by the minute.

When Jake asked her what she wanted to drink, "Whisky

and American dry ginger," she replied, remembering Edward's teasing words: "You should have said port and lemon to complete the bracketing."

"Lisa, is anything the matter?" Jake placed a sustaining hand beneath her elbow.

"No, of course not. I'm just a bit – overwhelmed – that's all, by all this excitement."

"We can leave whenever you want to," he reminded her. "No one will notice."

"No, I don't want to leave! I'm enjoying myself enormously, though I am rather hungry, and it would seem a pity to let all that lovely food go to waste!"

When he had returned from the kitchen with her whisky and ginger, and a glass of lager for himself, he led her towards the buffet, to pick and choose between the dishes on offer, and yet, deep down, Jake knew that Lisa was not as happy as she pretended to be.

Pushing her way through the crowd gathered about the buffet, her husband in tow, Edith Hannersley said brightly, "Mrs Hazell, I'd like you to meet Bert. The 'Buffs' Reunion, remember?"

"Indeed I do! How could I ever forget?"

"Pleased ter meetcha, I'm sure," Bert responded amiably, clasping Lisa's hand in what resembled a chain-mail gauntlet, "an' yer every bit as nice an' good-lookin' as she told me you was!"

"Oh, take no notice of him," Mrs Hannersley said dismissively, "he's as high as a kite already! No, what I really wanted to say is how much I miss you up at Bay View, and so do the old folk. I was up there yesterday, cooking their Christmas Dinner, and I thought to myself how lonely they must feel, being alone at Christmas, I mean."

Lisa thought, if it hadn't been for Jake Colby, she too would have been alone on Christmas Day. Alone and unhappy.

* * *

Daylight was fast fading when Lisa walked back, with Jake, to Sand Place. The wind had dropped, but it was still bitterly cold.

Turning the corner, she half-noticed a car drawn up outside No. 10. Holding her arm, Jake said quietly, "You had a dicey moment or two, back there, didn't you? I knew! I could tell!"

"Well, yes, but I'm fine now, thanks to you. I really can't begin to tell you . . ."

"What, Lisa?"

But the question remained unanswered.

The door of the parked car opened suddenly. A tall man emerged from the driver's seat. "Lisa," he called out impatiently, "I've been waiting for ages. Where the hell have you been?"

In disbelief, she stared at him, the man hurrying towards her across the ice-filmed pavement.

Chapter Twenty-One

Restless and frustrated by the lack of response to his repeated phonecalls, John Hazell had decided to take action. Might as well drive up to Westsea instead of pacing endlessly about the cottage. There was a great deal to discuss, to settle between himself and Lisa.

Driving quickly and confidently, his restlessness had given way to a feeling of euphoria. He had no doubt that Lisa would come back to him when he told her that Linda had left him.

The ritual cleansing of the cottage had been the final act of attrition against the Trenthams – mother, father and daughter – who had fouled the atmosphere with their plebeian attitudes, just as they had fouled the cottage with their sticky glasses, unmade beds, tide-marks round the bath, littered waste-paper baskets, and the disgusting mess they had made at the dining table and in the kitchen.

Only with Lisa could he regain his lost peace of mind; slip back into his own skin once more. It had not occurred to him that Lisa might feel differently. Why should she? He knew her so well; or thought he did. How did the saying go? 'Whistle, and I'll come, my lad'? In this case, 'Whistle, and you'll come, my lass'.

John was the last person in the world Lisa had expected to see. Their last meeting had left a sour taste in her mouth. The shock of seeing him hurrying towards her had stunned her into a feeling of unreality. She wished that

Jake had not gone indoors, leaving her alone to cope with the reappearance of her ex-husband. But what else *could* he have done? Presumably, he thought that she would be overjoyed to see John again, and who could blame him? He must have assumed, albeit mistakenly, that she would welcome his visit with open arms. Except, of course, that Jake hadn't a clue that the man was John.

Startled, she said primly, "Well, since you're here, you'd best come upstairs." Leading the way, she wondered *why* he had come. Had he decided to visit his parents in the West Riding, and made a detour? The idea struck her as ludicrous. But then, the whole situation was ludicrous.

Showing him into her flat, she said, "You'd better take your coat off, and sit down. I'll make you some coffee. You look half-frozen."

Entering the apartment, staring about him, obviously perplexed, "This is rather more than a bed-sitting room, isn't it?" he said accusingly, in that dogmatic way of his she remembered so well.

Stung by his attitude, she said coldly, "Just a minute, John, the last time we met – I don't recall having said I lived in a bed-sit. How could I have done? I was working at The Bay View Hotel at the time. I had a room there, true enough, but it went with the job. That day we met in the street, I hadn't even seen this flat. In any case, I might have been living in a rabbit-hutch for all you cared!"

"Someone at Bay View told me you had a bed-sitting room in the Old Town," he said edgily.

"You mean – you've been there?"

"No, I rang up on Christmas Day. The woman who answered the phone told me she'd sacked you some time ago; that you had rented a furnished bed-sit in Sand Place – a bit of a dump by all accounts. You wouldn't believe the trouble I've taken to find you . . ."

"So it would seem. But *why*" she demanded, nearing the end of her tether. "Oh, for God's sake, John," she snapped impatiently, "stop hovering and sit down!" She switched on the electric fire. "Do you want coffee or not? Because *I* do even if you don't!"

Still he continued to hover. Suspiciously, he asked, "Who is that man you came home with?"

"He's a friend of mine, if it's any of your concern!"

"Living under the same roof, apparently!"

"Well yes, since he happens to own the roof; the entire house, as a matter of fact!"

"You'd been out together?"

"Yes, to a Boxing Day party! It was great fun! I enjoyed myself enormously!" If John imagined that he could simply walk in from the cold and start his bullying tactics all over again, he had another think coming.

She said levelly, despite the pounding of her heart against her ribs, hating every moment of this curious encounter, "Look, John, you came here of your own accord, for what possible reason I can't imagine. Now, I think it's time you realised that I have my own life to live, just as you have yours! It was *your* decision, remember, to – get rid of me!" With a twisted smile of regret for a past long over and done with, she continued, "Now all I want is to live my own life in my own way, and what I choose to do with my life, from now on, is none of your business!"

"That's where you are wrong, Lisa," John said wearily, sinking down on the settee in front of the fire. "I came here for one purpose only: to take you home with me, back to the cottage, where you really belong."

She sat down abruptly in the chair opposite; legs shaking, staring at John in bewilderment. "*What* did you say?" she demanded hoarsely. "Are you out of your mind? But what about Linda? Your son? Have you been drinking? Is that it?"

He said heavily, "Marrying Linda was a mistake, I can see that quite clearly now. She never gave me a moment's peace of mind; never understood that I couldn't work in the kind

201

of muddle she created. Well, that's all over and done with now. The fact is, Linda has left me. Now I want you to come home again, Lisa, to make a fresh start, a new beginning."

"As *what*?" Lisa demanded. "Your housekeeper, your 'minder', your 'whipping boy'?"

The last thing he had expected was bitterness; sarcasm. Lisa had always been so compliant, so eager to smooth his path. Nettled, he said sharply, "Don't put up barriers between us! This is bloody difficult for me, and you are not making it any easier!"

"My God," she said in amazement, "it was you who erected the barriers. Insurmountable barriers, I'd have thought. Think about it, John. Did you honestly imagine that all you had to do was walk back into my life to undo all the misery of the past few years?"

He stared at her disbelievingly. "I don't understand your hostility towards me. I came in good faith, not to listen to a diabtribe about the past, but to put forward proposals for the future. I can't believe that you've grown such a hard shell."

"I had to," she said, "as a matter of survival. I found myself very much alone in the world after the death of my aunt. I had no home, no job, not much money. I moved away from Wheatford to make a new life for myself. It hasn't been easy, believe me."

"I didn't know about your aunt," he said dismissively, "but her death can't have come as a very great shock to you, surely? She was pretty old . . ." He added awkwardly, "I'm sorry, I . . ."

"*Sorry*? Why? You never liked her and you know it!" Tears were close to the surface. But she must not cry; must not allow John's stronger personality to dominate her now as it had done in the past.

He said, apropos of Aunt Grace, "With good reason, we were scarcely compatible. She was autocratic, domineering, dogmatic . . ."

Lisa laughed briefly, scornfully, "All the things that you are not? Or did you dislike her so much because she saw through you?"

Getting up, pacing the room, he said, "Look, Lisa, I didn't come here to quarrel about your aunt." Things were not working out as he had planned. He tried another tack: "I still love you, Lisa. I always have."

"Really? Is that why you did your best to shatter my self-confidence? You rapped it into me so hard and so often that I was your intellectual inferior that I began to believe it. I should read Kafka and Proust, you told me. Or was that just part of the softening-up process, so that when the time came I wouldn't have the strength of mind to put up a fight for what was mine by right – my home and my husband?"

Pacing angrily, "Why rake up the past this way?" he demanded harshly.

"Because I need to say now what I should have said a long time ago," Lisa thrust back at him, springing to her feet to face him. "I really didn't stand a cat in hell's chance, did I? I couldn't give you the child you wanted, so what happened as a result? You traded me in for someone who wouldn't know Keats from a hole in the head; who probably thinks that Kafka is some kind of cheese spread!"

"For Christ's sake, Lisa!"

"Ah, so now you are taking The Lord's name in vain? Tell me, John, why has Linda left you? Has she found another man, is that it? Is that why you are here, your begging-bowl at the ready?"

He ran his fingers through his hair in a well-remembered gesture of irritation. "There is no other man involved," he said tersely. "The truth is, Linda and I are poles apart in every way possible. She gave me no rest; no peace of mind."

Lisa said scornfully, "But it wasn't peace of mind you wanted. What you craved was sexual titillation; the excitement of secret meetings in the park; someone to fulfil your desire to procreate! Linda, on the other hand, wanted everything that belonged to me – and you handed her all the things I most valued in life on the proverbial plate!"

"If you mean the cottage," John said, subdued by Lisa's outburst, "Linda never cared for it the way you did. That is why I am asking you to come home with me."

He had found her Achille's heel at last.

The cottage, Lisa thought, remembering once again that low, rambling house she had loved so much – the ivy-framed windows; the fir trees at the garden's edge; deep blue shadows etched against the first snow of winter; the daffodils that came when the snowdrops and the gold and mauve crocuses had finished blooming; the apple trees, pink-starred in springtime; white lilac scenting the air with its unbearably sweet perfume. The crooked staircase leading up to the bedroom; the drawing room fireplace ablaze with logs in winter. The warm and friendly Aga in the kitchen. In autumn, the scent of bonfires drifting in through the open windows. All the scents of home, so long denied her.

In her mind's eye, she saw once more the lane beyond the cottage, ditches ablaze, in summertime, with campion and dog-roses, with meadowsweet and purple clover – in autumn, rich with ripening blackberries; green with newly fallen horsechestnuts. The woods at Gatford Hollow where, in springtime, the spaces between the trees were thick with bluebells, the air filled with the bitter-sweet scent of that magical carpet of flowers permeated with underlying richness of the soft, moist earth from which they had sprung. Earth wet with the soft rains of early spring mornings; the latent snow of the passing winter.

Suddenly, Lisa covered her face with her hands, overwhelmed by the memories of all that had been lost – beyond recall.

At that moment, John said quietly, persuasively, "We were happy once, and we could be again. At least come back to me for a little while. A month or two, perhaps. We'll take it from there."

Forcing back her tears, she replied, "But that's impossible! Don't you see? You cannot really believe that Linda will not come back to you?"

"I don't want her back," John said sullenly. "You don't understand, how could you, the way things have been between us of late? Her carelessness, her . . ."

Facing him squarely, "No, *don't* John! I don't want to know the details!" Lisa said hoarsely. "What has happened between you and Linda is none of my business. But what about your son? You cannot abandon your marriage with a child's future at stake!"

"Not even a child is capable of binding the wrong people together," he said bitterly.

"But this isn't just '*a* child' we're talking about," she reminded him, "this is *your* child! Your own flesh and blood!" It occurred to Lisa, at that moment, how utterly ludicrous that here she was, the barren ex-wife, battling for the rights of the current wife's son.

Closing her eyes, feeling inclined to laugh at the sheer awfulness of the situation, not laughing inside; close to tears, she said weakly, "What a waste of time it has all been. What a sheer, bloody awful waste of life!"

"But it needn't be; not if you'll come back to me," John reiterated, speaking forcefully, determined to have his own way. "My son will be well taken care of, I promise you. Things will be different, if only you'll come back to me. I really do love you, you know."

"I don't know! I honestly don't know! How can I be sure that you mean what you say?" Too tired and confused to think clearly for the time being, "I want you to leave me alone now, John," she said distractedly, opening the door of her flat to hasten his departure.

"Very well, then," he said, on the threshold, "but please, Lisa, promise you'll consider my offer. Ring me any time, at the cottage, and remember all that is left to us to enjoy together – books, music, poetry. Have you forgotten 'Snake'?" He quoted softly:

> "A snake came to my water trough
> And I, in pyjamas for the heat,
> To drink there . . ."

"No, I hadn't forgotten," Lisa said quietly, "I thought that you had. 'And I have something to expiate – a pettiness', remember?"

"*Touché!*" He smiled briefly, and when he was gone, she remembered their wedding day: the crowd of early-morning shoppers outside the register office, gathered there to await the emergence of the bride and groom; the way she had felt then, in her blue dress and jacket, fingering the shiny new wedding ring on her finger, smiling up at John, so certain of her future happiness with the man she loved at her side, clutching her posy of pink rosebuds.

And now, if what John had told her was really true, that he still loved her, all she had to do was to take a retrograde step in time; to forget the present and return to the past; to the cottage. Above all, the cottage . . .

Chapter Twenty-Two

Edward and Judith went to visit Pamela in hospital on Christmas Day afternoon, taking with them a case containing clean night-gowns, a lacey, hand-knitted bed-jacket, a lightweight dressing-gown, soap, toothbrush and toothpaste, a fresh cake of unscented oatmeal soap, a face flannel, a hairbrush and comb and, at Judy's insistence, a bottle of 4711 eau-de-cologne.

"You know how particular Mum is about personal freshness," Judith said. "She's bound to feel dreadful in one of those awful hospital nightshirts, and being washed with hospital soap and someone else's flannel. I just wish we had something else to take her to remind her that this *is* Christmas. I know! Let's take her our Christmas presents, shall we?"

"If you say so, darling," Edward agreed, too tired to think clearly, overwhelmed by his daughter's youth and energy, dreading the visit; wondering what he would find to say to a sick woman whose life he had ruined beyond redemption.

"Oh, come on, Daddy," Judith adjured him sharply, "this isn't the end of the world, you know, unless . . . You did remember to buy her a present, didn't you?"

"Of course. It's under the Christmas tree in the drawing room. Something she asked for especially before . . ."

"Before she found out about – Lisa, you mean?"

"Yes, before she found out about Lisa. Now she hates the sight of me. She told me so at the time. Oh, Judy, what the hell am I to do?"

"There's only one thing you can do now, I imagine. Prove to her that you still care for her a great deal, because you *do*, don't you? I knew that in the early hours of this morning when you told me about Helga. You were crying, Daddy, actually weeping. And Helga was Mummy's twin sister, remember?"

Edward nodded briefly.

"That's all right, then. What *did* she ask for, by the way?"

"A vegetarian cookery book," he admitted. "Of all things, a vegetarian cook book!"

Judith laughed. "Trust Mum to think of the inner man! My present is far less prosaic, I'm afraid. I bought her a rather expensive basket of bathtime preparations: bath-oil, shower-gel, body-lotion, and so on – discreetly perfumed, of course." She paused. "There, Daddy, I've made you smile."

"It feels a bit like whistling in the dark."

"For me, too. But we have to be strong for Mummy's sake."

"I'll try," he said.

"It's – Lisa, isn't it?" Judith said sympathetically. "You're missing her."

"I'll have to go on missing her," he said. "She made it quite clear that she never wants to see me again. It all happened so quickly. It was like – being stabbed and left to bleed to death slowly." He smiled ruefully. "Sorry, I'm being over-dramatic."

"I know what you mean," she said softly, "I felt the same way when I realised it was all over between Kit and me, the difference being that ours was a one-sided love affair."

"I'm sorry, darling, I've handed you a pretty raw deal, haven't I? You, Mother, and – Lisa. I shall never forgive myself for the harm I've done."

She thought how worn and old he looked, as if the life-force had drained away from him, leaving behind the

208

pale shadow of the man he used to be. She said, "Perhaps you should try to see Lisa again; talk things over calmly and quietly. Has it occurred to you that she too might be – bleeding to death slowly? The fine, decent person you've described to me would surely want an end to all the pain and unhappiness between you?"

"Thanks, Judy, but no. I have tried to phone her, but there was no reply. I think she'd have hung up on me anyway."

"But you can't go on like this, Dad, with nothing solved or settled between you. You'll make yourself ill with worry. I mean, much worse than you already are, and then what?"

"Don't worry, love, I'll manage somehow."

But Judith thought differently. Her father was on the verge of a nervous breakdown, she realised, and she must do something about it. She *must*, and she *would*!

"Mrs Hazell?"

"Yes. Can I help you?"

Perhaps the pretty, anxious-looking teenager on the doorstep was collecting for charity, or had mislaid her key, Lisa thought. Or possibly she was a friend of the gregarious couple on the floor below, not knowing they had gone away for the holidays, and she had rung her doorbell by mistake, or even deliberately to find out when they'd be back.

The girl, wearing slacks and a grey anorak, said briefly, "May I come in, please? I – I need to talk to you. My name is Judith Miller."

"*Judy!*"

"Well, yes, my father always calls me that, and I'm sorry to bother you. Perhaps I shouldn't have come. I'm beginning to wish that I hadn't. I've been outside for ages, trying to pluck up my courage."

"Come in, Judy. My flat's on the top floor – a rather stiff climb, I'm afraid."

Entering the flat, glancing about her, taking in the neatness of the sitting room, the appearance of her hostess, plainly dressed in a moss-green sweater and tweed skirt, her fair hair caught back in french pleat, "You're not at all what I expected," Judith said frankly.

What *had* she expected, Lisa wondered, a *femme fatale* wearing a chiffon négligé, reclining on a feather mattress? She smiled faintly. John yesterday. Edward's daughter today. The world appeared to be beating a path to her doorstep. "Please sit down," she said. "Would you care for coffee, by the way? You must be cold from all that standing about outside."

"Yes, coffee would be fine," Judith said nervously. "Do you mind if I smoke?"

"No, of course not. There's an ashtray on the coffee table near the armchair. Shan't be a sec!"

Returning with the coffee things, the cafetiere, the mugs, spoons, milk jug and sugar basin on a tray, Lisa discovered Judith enveloped in a haze of cigarette smoke, sitting nervously on the edge of the chair. "Hunched up like a monkey on a bonfire," Aunt Grace would have said in that dry, humorous way of hers.

"Milk and sugar?" Lisa asked, pouring the coffee.

"No, just black please. I'm trying to lose weight."

"So am I. Not easy, is it, at this time of the year?"

"No, I suppose not," Judith conceded, wishing herself far away. "This is very good coffee by the way. Oh, I'm sorry, would you care for a cigarette?"

Lisa smiled, "Thank you, yes. Not that I smoke very often, only when I'm nervous – an alternative to biting one's nails, I'm told." Leaning forward for the lighter, she continued, "And I am feeling somewhat nervous at the moment since you have obviously come to discuss a subject I'd rather not talk about anyway."

Judith frowned uncertainly. "My father didn't send me, if that's what you're thinking. He'd be horrified if he knew, but I just *had* to come, for his sake. You see, Mrs Hazell, he's taken all that has happened so badly that I couldn't simply stand by and do nothing to help him.

"Oh, I'm not denying that I hated your guts when he told me about you. I felt so upset, so angry at first, but we've talked a lot over Christmas, and I think we've grown closer as a result."

"I thought you were always close," Lisa said. "At least that's the impression I gained."

"Well yes, we were, until . . ."

"Until he told you about me? Is that it?" Lisa stubbed out the cigarette she had not wanted to smoke at all. "When did he tell you about me?" she asked gently, liking the girl enormously; wondering why she had felt jealous of her in the first place, that day in the café on the foreshore when Edward had spoken so lovingly of his daughter. But of course she knew why; had known why all along. Jealousy, the green-eyed monster waiting in the wings to inject its subtle poison into the lives of ordinary people acting out their roles on the stage of life.

"He told me about you on Christmas Eve," Judith said wistfully, "when he came to the station to meet me. I knew that something was wrong. Then he told me that Mummy was not very well . . ."

"Please, go on."

"It came as a shock, that's all, Mummy getting pregnant at her age. The two things coming on top of each other the way they did. I felt sick at heart. I still do! Common sense told me that Mum couldn't possibly go through having a baby at her age, but to lose it the way she did seemed so – undignified, so *unfair*!"

"Your mother lost the baby?" Lisa closed her eyes momentarily to hold back her tears. Poor Edward, she thought. Poor, dear Edward. If only she had been more forebearing, more understanding, less selfish, less bigoted.

Rising to her feet, she walked to the window and leaned her forehead against the ice-cold glass. Staring out to sea,

211

she saw the outline of a timber-boat on the horizon; thought bleakly that if only she had been less vulnerable, more decisive that evening when Edward had rung The Bay View Hotel to invite her out for a drink, none of this would have happened.

Judith continued forlornly, "We very nearly lost Mummy, too. Until that happened, I hadn't realised how much she meant to me; how cruelly I had treated her, mocking her for her silly, old-fashioned ways. I could never get through to her, you see. She was always so critical, so self-righteous."

Turning away from the window, "Please don't tell me any more, Judy," Lisa said hoarsely, "I can't bear it!"

"I'm sorry," Judith said contritely, "it was horrid of me; disloyal to Mummy. I just wanted you to understand the way things were between us before all this happened, and not to think too badly of my father, because he really does need help, and you are the only one who can help him right now."

Judith's lips trembled. "The truth is, I don't think he's strong enough to face up to the future without your forgiveness. You see, Mother is going to need all the strength and support he has to give her from now on. But he has no strength left to give to anyone, not even himself, without your help. Please, Mrs Hazell, I came here to beg you to help him. I love him so much, that I can't bear to see him so – lost and unhappy!"

"What do you want me to do?" Lisa asked.

Judith said urgently, "Just see him once more; make things right between you. He has suffered so much! Please! He said you were a fine, decent person! I didn't believe that at first; how could I? I just couldn't bring myself to believe that a decent person would have an affair with a married man, but now that I've met you, I can understand why it happened, why my father fell in love with you."

Lisa said quietly, "Believe me, Judy, we never meant it

to happen; never meant to hurt anyone. Neither of us knew what was happening until it was too late."

Memories flooded back to her, as fleeting as rain against a windowpane – music heard on a car radio; the clicking of dominoes in an olde-world pub; the feel of the sand in her shoes that day on the beach when she saw Edward coming towards her; the crying of the seagulls overhead; a narrow hotel bedroom opposite the station; the background noises of the six o'clock new bulletin on Radio Four and the whistle of the six o'clock train drawing away from the platform. Memories encapsulated within a few precious moments in time which belonged to herself and Edward, and to no one else in the world.

Judith said quietly, "You might be happier, too, if you saw my father just once more. He can't live with his feeling of failure, you see? Could anyone? Could you?"

"No, I suppose not," Lisa said.

And so the time had come for quietness and truth between herself and Edward.

The day was cold and bright. Dressing warmly, she walked downhill to the seafront, and saw Edward's car parked near the ice-cream parlour where she had first realised that she loved him.

All the promenade shops and cafés were closed now, along with the amusement arcades and bingo halls, and there were few people about apart from a group of children playing beach football, and a solitary man walking his dog. She could not have borne Edward to come to the flat, and wondered, nearing the car, if Judy was right in thinking that this meeting would make him feel happier, and yet the love she had shared with Edward deserved a kindly burial.

Petty jealousy and anger, seen in retrospect, somehow detracted from all that had gone before, demeaning their brief, passionate love affair. Now that the jealousy and anger had all been spent, it was not the physical side of their relationship she remembered so much as quiet conversation by fireglow, shared laughter; the tenderness they had known together.

Opening the door for her, he said, "Judy shouldn't have come to see you. I'm afraid I was angry with her for arranging this meeting. How could I be sure that you wanted it?"

"I'm glad she did. It couldn't have been easy for her." She could tell by his words, his manner of speech, that he was under a great deal of pressure. He looked grey with worry. Her heart went out to him.

Sitting beside him, she saw as if for the first time the face she had grown to love so well. It was just an ordinary face that one would pass by in a crowd without a second glance, and she remembered the first time he had rung her at Bay View when she could not recall his name, let alone his face. She had thought of him then as a masculine shape with a pleasant voice and a kind manner. How could she have known, then, that his face, the way his hair grew, the shape of his head, his eyes, his mouth, would become infinitely dear to her.

He said wearily, "You know what keeps on running through my mind? If I hadn't told you about Pamela, none of this would have happened. I shall never forgive myself for blurting it out to you the way I did."

"It had to be said."

"I should have been more sensitive. I should have told you how things really were between Pamela and me; that the baby was a mistake. She didn't want it any more than I did. To my everlasting shame, it was you I was thinking of at the time . . ."

"Please, don't! Your marriage is your own affair; yours and Pamela's. It always has been. It still is. The past is over and done with, all that matters now is the future – yours and hers."

"I can't tell you how much I'll miss just talking to you,

214

my darling. Waking up each morning in the hope of seeing you. Lisa, must it really be like this? Couldn't we meet just once in a while?"

"No, Edward. I'm sorry. It wouldn't be fair to Pamela or to me. Not to Judy, or yourself. There can be no going back." She smiled sadly. "Do you remember that night in the pub?"

"The Seabird?" he said. "Of course I remember. Why do you ask?"

"We talked about *Brief Encounter*, and you argued with me when I said that doing the right thing makes for an uncomplicated life. Do you still hold to that point of view?"

"If you mean do I regret having met you, the answer is no. Until you came into my life, I had never begun to live. The days came and went in a precise pattern; no surprises, nothing to fire the imagination. I saw my life as a – seismograph; the needle moving over the paper in an unwavering line. Then, at last came the earthquake! Until I met you, my darling, I never realised, never knew the full meaning of life; the way it felt to love and to be loved in return."

"Please, Edward, don't say any more. I don't want to listen!"

"But you *must* listen! I am not denigrating Pamela, believe me. She has been a good wife to me – a splendid housekeeper. No reason to delve into the past too deeply; sufficient to say that she had been through a difficult time and needed someone to take care of her. Not the ideal basis for marriage, I admit, but I went into it with my eyes wide open and have only myself to blame for the outcome.

"You see, Lisa, I had never been in love before until I met you. Now I can't bear the thought of that seismograph needle moving on and on across the blank pages of my life – until . . ." He covered his face with his hands. "Oh, God! What a bloody mess I've made of things!"

Deeply shaken, Lisa said quietly, "But it need not be like that at all now, darling. Pamela needs you now more than ever."

Uncovering his face, he said, "But what about you, Lisa? What about *your* needs?"

She replied slowly, "John came to see me on Boxing Day. He wants me to go back to him. Back to the cottage." She lay her hand on his. "I *had* to tell you, Edward, I felt you had the right to know."

"But you *can't* go back to him," Edward said vehemently, "you mustn't! It would be madness to even think of it!" Clasping her hands tightly in his, he said, "For God's sake, Lisa, think what it would mean. You said yourself, a moment ago, there could be no going back! Promise me you won't go back to that man!"

"I'm sorry, Edward, I'll make up my own mind when the time comes. I haven't thought it through yet."

"But what about his wife and child?"

"Linda? She has left him; taking the child with her."

"But why? For what reason? What kind of security would you have under those circumstances?"

The car felt hot and stuffy. "Let's walk for a little while, shall we?" Lisa suggested.

They walked along the beach to the sea's edge where the sand was ribbed like purl and plain knitting. The children playing football had all gone home now, and the man walking his dog had disappeared from view.

Picking up a sea-shell; "Bleached to its essential whiteness," Lisa said softly. "Remember?"

"Remember? Of course I remember. I shall remember everything about you; every word we have spoken to one another, until the day I die," Edward said tenderly, knowing the end was near.

Lisa said tautly, her eyes filling with tears, "Do you remember telling me to cling on to this love of ours, even when we're apart?"

"Then you do still love me, Lisa? Oh, thank God! Thank God!"

"Yes, Edward, I still love you, for all that you have meant to me. Nothing can ever change that. Now it's time for us to say goodbye."

Cupping her face in his hands, he kissed her, tasting her tears on his lips. "So this is really it? The end of the affair?" he asked gently. "Oh, my love, what do you want me to say?"

Drawing away from him, she replied, "Oh, I don't know. Something lighthearted and trivial. No, please don't kiss me again!" Lisa closed her eyes momentarily against the pain of this, their final leave-taking.

Rallying for her sake, smiling, squaring his shoulders, "I know," he said bravely. "Remember the film, *This Happy Breed*, when Robert Newton and Stanley Holloway came home drunk after a Buffs' reunion?"

"Yes."

"How's this, then? 'Steady the Buffs'!"

Smiling up at him, "'Steady the Buffs' my darling," she replied.

Saluting smartly, he walked away from her.

Watching him go, Lisa knew that the final chapter of a love affair had been written; that the book was now closed.

At last Mrs Hazell was alone on the beach. Quite alone. But not in the way she had envisaged when the autumn leaves were drifting down from the trees.

Never again would come that magical feeling of youth, the vision of herself as a girl in blue denims, walking barefoot by the water's edge, letting the sea wash over her feet.

The beach was littered with driftwood, pitted with stones and shells, bubbled with bladderwrack washed in by the tide. Walking head bent, she noticed a white feathered wing among the debris, a gracefully curved thing, useless now denied the power of flight.

The brightness of the day was fading, the tide receding, her footprints biting deeply into the wet sand near the water's edge. Storm clouds were massing on the horizon. Seagulls, driven inland to look for food, wheeled and screamed overhead as Lisa made her way homeward.

Now that Edward was gone; no longer a physical presence in her life; the pain of their parting washed over in a tide of longing and regret.

Moving restlessly about the flat, she picked up the book of Elizabeth Barrett Browning poems, but could not bear to open it; nor could she have borne to look at the ring he had given her.

Looking out of the window, she stared at the sea. Lights were springing up along the shore and the upper promenade near The Bay View Hotel, in windows, and the gardens winding up from the seafront; pricking the darkness like fireflies.

Coming to Westsea to live, she had not envisaged the beginning and end of a love affair which would change her life, her way of thinking, highlighting the flaws and weaknesses in her character, revealing the darker side of her nature, and she thought how differently she had reacted to the break-up of her marriage to John.

When Linda had appeared on the scene, she had behaved with a dignity and restraint totally lacking when Edward had told her of his wife's pregnancy. But why? She had far less claim on Edward than John, and yet Edward's betrayal had hurt her more deeply than John's ever had. So what was the answer?

In any case, the end result had been the same. She had lost the two men in her life she had loved, for whatever reasons.

And yet, in curiously similiar situations, her underlying

218

common sense had warned her that no good could come of clinging to the spars of a sinking ship in a stormy sea.

She had let go of John knowing that she could not begin to fight the much younger woman he had fallen in love with; a fecund girl with youth and vitality on her side, capable of giving him the child he had wanted so much.

She now knew, with a deep inner certainty, that she could not, with a clear conscience, have continued her affair with Edward Miller, and he would never know what it had cost her to say goodbye to him; how strong the impulse to call after him: "Edward! Don't leave me! Please don't leave me!" And if she had yielded to that impulse, what then? How could they have built a future together on the foundations of other people's unhappiness?

Closing her eyes against the pain of the present, suddenly she remembered the bluebell wood at Gatford Hollow; the wind-rippled hills beyond the cottage. She imagined herself lying in the long grass near the ancient, humped burial mounds on Gatford Hill, her eyes closed against the sunshine of a warm summer day, hearing a soft breeze sighing and whispering about the resting places of the forgotten people of a bygone age, buried there with their spears and earthenware vessels about them; comforting artefacts betokening their brief time on earth.

Chapter Twenty-Three

The journey had been a nightmare from beginning to end. Miles had wailed incessantly from the back seat of the taxi, whilst Archie, in the front seat beside the driver had watched, with a kind of horrified fascination, the amount being clocked up on the meter – akin to sitting in the cupboard under the stairs watching the disc of the electricity meter spinning round like a roulette wheel gone crazy.

Still befuddled from the amount of liquor he'd imbibed earlier, he wasn't entirely sure why the sudden exodus from the cottage had happened. One minute he'd been tucked up in bed, asleep and snoring; seconds later he'd been on the landing, minus his dentures, with all hell let loose about him, his grandson screaming his head off and his daughter and son-in-law engaged in a slanging match which had made his head spin faster than the final cycle of a washing machine programme in one of his own launderettes.

Now here they were: Gloria, Linda, his grandson and himself, on their way back to Harrogate in a money-gobbling taxi, their Christmas ruined beyond repair, and with nothing to look forward to except a chilly homecoming, a wailing child to placate, and nothing to eat worth considering. Not to mention the continual bickering of his wife and daughter about whose fault it was that they had been landed in this situation.

They were still going at it hammer and tongs when, dismounting from the taxi at its destination, they had entered the house, leaving him in the driveway to fork out the contents of his wallet to the driver, plus a cheque backed up by his Access card number; thereafter to hump indoors the many hurriedly-packed cases and carrier-bags that his wife and daughter had brought with them on the journey, not caring tuppence that he was left out in the cold to part with the thick end of a hundred quid. Now his stomach felt like a flag at half-mast after that bloody awful Christmas dinner of dried-up turkey, stewed sprouts and burnt black roast potatoes he'd been served. Not that he had really noticed at the time, but he was far less inebriated now than then. As the master of the house, with his dentures firmly in place once more, he felt it his right to have his say: "Now, you just listen to me," he began pontifically, "you Gloria and you too, Linda. All this could have waited until after the holidays! I mean to say, what's a bit of a squabble between a man and his wife? But no, Linda, you went over the top as usual, and you, Gloria, hadn't the sense to stay out of the argument, so we've all been robbed of a pleasant Christmas in the country."

"Oh, shut up, Daddy," Linda interrupted rudely. "For your information, John not only struck me, but he has also been trying to contact his ex-wife! Now do you understand why I couldn't bear to stay in the cottage a moment longer? Well, Mummy understands if you don't!" Daring Gloria to disagree with her by a wicked glance in her direction, she continued, "Well, go on, Mummy, you saw what happened, didn't you? You saw Johnny strike me, didn't you?"

"Well yes, darling, if you say so, I must have done." Gloria wavered uncertainly, "In which case, perhaps John should have been the one to leave, not us?" Puckering her forehead, she said, "I still can't understand why . . ."

"Look, just let's have something to eat first. Miles is starving, aren't you my lambykins? What's in the fridge?"

"Nothing," Gloria confessed weepily, "I defrosted it before we left for the cottage. Well, how was I to know?"

"You mean there's no milk or bread in the house?" Linda

started banging open cupboard doors. "My God, baked beans, soup, corned beef! Is that all there is? What's in the deep-freeze? Don't tell me you defrosted that too?"

"No, there's lamb chops, chicken – all kinds of stuff. Oh dear, why all this? Anyone would think this is my fault. Whatever I say or do seems to be wrong lately."

"I'll tell you whose fault it is," Linda said grimly. "It's *her* fault. John's ex! That's whose fault it is! Well she needn't think she's going to get away with it! I'll nail that bitch if it's the last thing I do. First thing tomorrow morning I'm off to Westsea to have it out with her! I'll make her wish she'd never been born, playing fast and loose with my husband!"

"But you can't just fly off at a tangent. Besides, there won't be any trains . . ." Clutching at straws, Gloria said the first thing that came into her head.

"Trains? Who said anything about trains? I'll take Daddy's car!"

"Eh?" Archie's head shot up at the mention of his car; his Daimler, his pride and joy. "Oh no you won't, my girl! I had it through the carwash the day before yesterday. It's in the garage now, and that's where it's staying. The way you drive, it would probably end up wrapped round a lamppost!" Turning pale at the thought, "I need a drink," he said hoarsely, "a large whisky and soda. I'll be in the front room if you want me."

"I'm coming with you," Gloria announced. "I need a drink too. A brandy and dry ginger to settle my nerves!"

"Oh that's right, leave me to cope on my own as usual," Linda called after them, blaming everyone but herself for a predicament of her own making; above all, Lisa Hazell who had started the chain of events. Well, she'd soon settle *her* hash. Then it would be Johnny's turn to come to heel, and that would be the sweetest form of revenge; making him crawl back to beg her forgiveness for having struck her.

Not that she would forgive him right away. Oh no, she'd

222

keep him dangling for a while; make him sweat, tell him she had decided to have an abortion; threaten him with divorce proceedings. Ah yes, she would enjoy that enormously, she thought, opening a tin of tomato soup and tipping the contents into a saucepan to heat for her son's supper, the poor, wet, weeping little sod.

"There, there, my precious," she whispered, as the soup boiled over, "you'll soon be tucked up nice and warm in bed-i-byes."

'The best laid schemes of mice and men gang aft aglae' . . .

Next day, Boxing Day morning, Miles had developed a runny cold and a higher than normal temperature, necessitating the postponement of Linda's trip to Westsea until the child showed signs of improvement – to Gloria and Archie's relief, although they were worried sick about their grandchild.

In the event, Archie set forth in his car to scour the district in search of bread and milk for the boy. Meanwhile, Gloria had unearthed a chicken, sprouts, sausages and fish-fingers from the deep-freeze, pausing momentarily to sip sweet sherry from a glass, via the bottle she had placed on the kitchen table, reminding herself, as she did so, that this was *still* Christmas, so why not enjoy it?

When Archie returned triumphant with a quart of milk, two large sliced loaves of bread and a dozen eggs, purchased from a Pakistani store on the outskirts of town, she threw her arms about him in a transport of delight and told him what a clever boy he was, and assured him that Linda would have forgotten, by this time, her potty idea of driving to Westsea to confront John's ex-wife.

But she was wrong.

Three days later, when Miles was better, despite the hand-wringing of her mother and Archie's dismay that his beloved Daimler might end up in a ditch, the mood his daughter was in, Linda began her journey to Westsea, an expression of grim determination on her face as, with a clashing of gears, she backed the car out of the garage, missing one of the gateposts by inches.

The car sped out of sight. "Why didn't you stop her, Archie?" Gloria wailed, holding her grandson in her arms.

Archie sighed deeply, his breath whirling away in the cold morning air. "Stop her?" he pondered, shaking his head. "Know what, love? I can't help feeling sorry for — what's-her-name? Lisa? I wouldn't be in her shoes now for all the tea in China!"

Lisa was busy about the flat when the knock came at her door. It would be her downstair neighbours, she assumed, come to tell her they were home, since the front doorbell hadn't rung.

Opening the door, smiling, expecting to see Paul or Marilyn on the landing, Lisa's words of welcome died on her lips when she saw Linda standing there, her sharp, pointed face stung with the cold, wearing navy slacks and a red anorak, her dark eyes glittering with malice, lips upturned in a travesty of a smile.

"Surprised to see me?" she asked insolently. "Silly question! Well, aren't you going to ask me in, or does it give you a kick to see a pregnant woman half-fainting on her feet after all those stairs?"

"Pregnant?" Lisa stared at Linda disbelievingly.

"Oh, didn't Johnny tell you? How remiss of him. But I guess he forgot to mention that unimportant little detail when he rang you on Christmas Eve. But I am well and truly 'preggers' I assure you."

Pushing past Lisa, she stared offensively about the room. "Oh, so this is your little love-nest, is it? And to think that I accused Johnny of having it off with you in a public shelter! Common sense should have told me that a nicely brought-up lady like you would want it lying down with a couple of pillows under your bum! Tell me, did you burn incense and put on a record of 'Ave Maria' to get him in the mood for his bit on the side?"

Lisa remained silent as Linda wandered about the room, picking up ornaments, pretending to examine them closely, enjoying Lisa's discomfiture; glancing at her sideways, smiling wickedly all the time until finally, lying down full length on the divan and bunching the scatter cushions beneath her head, Linda said lazily, maliciously, "Know what I think? That husband of mine should be castrated! What a man! Never satisfied until his wife has a bun in the oven!

"Oh, sorry, old girl! No offence meant; none taken, I hope. Of course Johnny never put a bun in your oven, did he? Perhaps you should have tried standing on your head once in a while!"

"You disgust me," Lisa said quietly.

"Do I really?" Linda laughed. "That's rich coming from you." But Lisa's coolly uttered remark had found its target. She felt disadvantaged suddenly, sprawled on the divan, looking up at John's ex-wife, reading not shame, but pity in those clear blue eyes of hers.

"Perhaps you'd care to explain why you felt it necessary to come here? What it is that you want from me?" Lisa said patiently.

"*Want*?" Linda stopped laughing. Rising quickly from the divan, facing her protagonist, she said, "I want you out of my life, and John's, once and for all! Do I make myself clear?"

"Perfectly clear, though you appear to have forgotten that I've been out of your lives for some considerable time now."

"Oh, don't come the holier than thou act with me, my lady! You know damn well what I mean! Johnny has rung you, hasn't he? Well, go on, deny it if you can!" Linda's temper was getting the better of her now.

At that moment, Lisa experienced the kind of elation she had done the day she told Mrs Fogarty to go to hell. She said calmly, "More importantly, Linda, John came to see me on Boxing Day. Strange, isn't it, the importance that a barren ex-wife has suddenly assumed in the scheme of things? As a matter of interest, John has asked me to go back to him. Listening to you, Linda, I can understand why."

Linda's anger exploded in a torrent of verbal abuse. "*What*? You really expect me to believe that? I don't believe a word of it, you lying cow you!"

Lisa smiled faintly. "Scarcely that, surely? A cow, after all is a breeding animal. Now, would you mind leaving? I am rather particular with whom I share my – byre."

Blustering, on the defensive now, Linda said savagely, "I'm warning you, my lady, set foot in that cottage and I'll make life a living hell for the pair of you, and you'd better believe it!"

"I *do* believe it. Why not? Making life a living hell for others appears to be your forte, your supreme talent, your mission in life."

"Oh lah-di-bloody-dah! Aren't you the clever one? But no way will you and Johnny be happy together. Don't kid yourself he still loves you; he doesn't. What he wants is someone to stand up to him, to fight him every inch of the way. You gave in to him at every turn and he despised you for it.

"Why do you think it was me he turned to? I'll tell you why. He was sick of the sight of you. He needed a woman not a plaster saint; a wife who could give him what he really wanted, and we both know what that is, don't we? Well he got what he wanted from *me*, and don't you forget it. So what have you to say to that, my lady?"

"I'm sure you're right. The surprising thing is that, despite your youth, vitality and breeding capacity, your failure to hold on to your husband is more remarkable than my own, wouldn't you say?"

226

Linda was beaten, and she knew it. Deep down, she knew that coming here to confront Lisa had been a mistake. She had come expecting a slanging-match; a quarrel from which she would have emerged the clear winner. The last thing she had expected was an opponent whose unruffled calm would take the wind from her sails; an attractive woman to boot, not at all like the Mrs Hazell she had met briefly at that party at the cottage the night she had decided to relieve Lisa of her home and her husband.

Even so, it was not in Linda's nature to quit the battlefield without a parting shot or two.

Heading towards the door, standing on the threshold, she said in a high-pitched tone of voice, drawing on the last of her battle resources, "If you think you've got the better of me, my lady, you are very much mistaken! Like it or not, Johnny is the father of *my* children; responsible for their welfare and mine from now on, and I meant what I said. If you so much as set foot in that cottage, I'll not only sting him for every ha'penny he has, but ruin his career into the bargain. Is that perfectly clear?"

"Abundantly clear," Lisa said calmly, "except that, if you ruin his career, possibly even a ha'penny would prove too large a sum by way of maintenance for yourself and your children."

Receiving the final *coup de grâce*, slamming the door behind her, Linda hurried downstairs to her father's car, first switching on the headlights then the windscreen wipers instead of the ignition, so rattled that she scarcely knew what she was doing or where she was going.

Watching from his office window, Jake Colby saw the car jerk forward in a series of kangaroo hops, mount the pavement, reverse, then disappear from view at a rate of knots – as if the Devil was driving.

The woman had been to see Lisa Hazell; this he knew because he had let her into the house a half-hour ago when he had come back from Silver Street to find her on the doorstep examining the names on the bell-pushes near the front door. Not that she had bothered to thank him; she had merely pushed past him and hurried upstairs to the top landing.

He returned to his desk. Lisa had received a number of callers recently, he pondered. Apart from the man he thought of as her lover, who had turned up at regular intervals since the early days of her tenancy, there had been that tall, sour-looking individual who had called out her name on Boxing Day night, after Edie's party, whom she had taken upstairs with her; and a rather nice-looking, fair-haired teenager who had spent a good hour and a half in her company, yesterday or the day before.

So who were all these strangers who appeared to be beating a path to Mrs Hazell's front door? And what business was it of his anyway, just as long as her rent was paid on time? He was, after all, a man of the world, not a moralist, well-inured to the vagaries of human nature, and yet . . .

Seated at his desk, Colby knew exactly what was bugging him. He had fallen in love with Mrs Hazell. No use fudging or denying what he knew in his heart was true. He had fallen in love with her the day she came to look at the flat, God help him. Why else would he have hurried after her on Christmas Eve; brought her home with him and taken care of her the way he had? Not that she cared a brass farthing for him, and who could blame her − an abrupt, secretive individual, incapable of expressing his innermost feelings; lacking in charm and sentimentality, as his late wife Isabel, had discovered to her cost.

Isabel!

Chapter Twenty-Four

No. 10. Sand Place had belonged latterly to Jake's grand-father; had been handed down to his own father, in the fullness of time.

When Jake, his elder brother Billy, and their sister Edie were children, this office had been the family parlour or 'best' room, in use mainly at Christmas or on other special occasions such as birthday parties and wedding receptions.

The house had been full to overflowing in those days, when his ageing grandparents had occupied rooms on the first landing, alongside a maiden aunt on his mother's side, who had once come for a week's holiday and stayed seventeen years.

Things were vastly different now. Jake's grandparents and his Aunt Cecily had died during the last war, and his father, who had joined the Merchant Navy as a Chief Petty Officer in the spring of 1940, had lost his life on convoy duty in the North Atlantic in the winter of 1944, leaving his grieving widow, Beatrice Colby, to bring up their children alone. Jake had been ten years old at the time, Edie twelve, and Billy fourteen.

Eight years later, Billy had emigrated to Australia, Edie had married Bert Hannersley, and Jake had fallen in love with a girl called Isabel Matthews whom he had met at a church social.

In retrospect, Jake knew that his mother had harboured misgivings about the suitability of the match. Not that she had disliked Isabel. She had simply thought her too young, at seventeen, to undertake the responsibilites of marriage, and, as things had turned out, she was right, especially since Jake had elected to bring his bride to Sand Place to live after the honeymoon.

The suggestion had been made from the unselfish motive of not wanting his mother to be left alone in the house, and Isabel had raised no objections to the plan; indeed she had welcomed the idea of living in such a fine old mansion.

Trouble had stemmed initially from the fact that Isabel had shown no inclination for housework; even less for shopping and learning how to cook.

What was the point in dusting and cleaning all those big, unoccupied rooms? she grumbled, besides which, she hated cooking and washing up; being told what and what not to do by her mother-in-law who treated her as a servant, not the mistress of the house.

"For the good and sufficient reason that you are *not* the mistress of the house," Jake had reminded her. "This is my mother's house, and you'd do well to remember that."

"Yes, but it will be *ours* when she dies," Isabel flung back at him, and he had been appalled by her insensitivity. "Well, that's right, isn't it?" she'd pursued relentlessly. "Then you'll be well off enough to afford a cook and someone to do the scrubbing and cleaning."

He had known then, in his heart of hearts, that he had married the wrong girl. Admitting it, even to himself, had been a different matter entirely. But she was so young and innocent, so enchantingly pretty with her long fair hair and forget-me-not blue eyes; so eager to respond to his lovemaking when they were alone together, that he could not be too hard on her.

Even so, he could not help noticing, from that day on, that his mother seemed far from well, which he ascribed to the fact that she was missing Billy, now on the far side of the world, and married to an Australian girl who had recently

230

given birth to their first child, a boy named Ruben after his grandfather Colby, Jake's father.

One day, Jake said quietly, "Look, Mother, why not take a trip to Australia to visit Billy? He's begged you to go often enough, so what's stopping you?"

Smiling faintly, Beatrice said quietly, "This is stopping me," laying a hand on her heart, "this silly old 'ticker' of mine. Frankly, I couldn't face the journey, the excitement. I asked the doctor and he said no. I'm sorry, Jake, but you had to know sooner or later: I've been given a year to live; eighteen months at the most, if I take things easy."

"Oh no, Ma, I can't believe it! I won't believe it!"

"Now listen to me, son, when I am gone this house will be yours entirely to live in or to get rid of as you please, plus a certain sum of money to keep yourself and Isabel well provided for in the future.

"Billy and Edie will benefit equally, from a financial point of view, by way of a trust fund instituted by your Grandpa Colby in the year preceding his death. He was not a poor man, as you well know. But this house is a different matter entirely. Your father willed it to me, God rest him, and I have willed it to you, knowing how much it means to you; has always meant to you. Now, having settled all that, let's get on with the rest of our lives, shall we?"

His brave, humorous, great-hearted mother had died a year later. After her funeral, Jake had decided, to Isabel's scarcely concealed anger, to convert the house into a series of self-contained flats; the front parlour into an office, the rear premises, including the old family living room, the kitchen and a series of smaller rooms overlooking the garden, into a self-contained apartment for himself and his wife.

"If you think I'm going to live in this 'poke-hole', to cook and clean for you like a common-or-garden servant, you have another think coming, Jake Colby," she'd reminded him bitterly. "I thought you loved me, but you don't, not really, and after all I've been through, taking care of your mother these past few months! I'm a young woman for God's sake, in need of fun and excitment; money to spend on nice clothes, make-up and jewellery as the mistress of the house is entitled to do, not poked away in a few crumby rooms on the ground floor, peeling carrots and potatoes all day long, or up to my elbows in washing up water!"

And that, Jake thought, had been the beginning of the end of their marriage, when Isabel, intent on having a good time, had turned to another man for solace; had conceived a child by him, and when he, Jake, had told her to go to hell for all he cared.

Events of that time seemed telescoped in retrospect, or perhaps he had chosen to block out of his mind all those things too painful to remember – the harsh words spoken in the heat of the moment; the quarrels, the lies, the deceit of which his wife was capable to cover up the fact that she was seeing another man behind his back.

He had been too preoccupied with the house, too shattered by his mother's death to notice what Isabel was up to at first. When she said she had been to the cinema with a girlfriend; to her friend's house for supper afterwards, he had believed her, and when she came home from shopping with more new clothes than groceries, he had bitten his tongue at her extravagance, telling himself it was only natural that a pretty lass like Isabel should want to look as smart and attractive as possible for her husband. After all, the poor kid had been through a rough time during his mother's illness, and it could not have been easy for her taking charge of the cooking, fetching and carrying trays to her mother-in-law's room when Beatrice had been confined to her bed during the last few days of her time on earth.

Edie had been a tower of strength at the time, coming in daily to do the washing and ironing, to change the bed-linen and give their mother bed-baths night and morning, often staying with her till well past midnight, knowing it would have broken Beatrice's heart to die anywhere other than in her own home, in her own bed.

To Jake's everlasting gratitude and relief, Billy had flown home from Australia in time to say goodbye to his mother before she had died, very quietly, in her sleep – as if she could not have borne to let go of life until her children were all safely gathered together once more.

Edie's husband, Bert Hannersley, had been on the landing outside the sickroom, hovering on the threshold, not wanting to intrude, yet there if needed, Jake recalled. The person that he had most needed and wanted near him that night, his wife Isabel, had gone to bed at nine o'clock, complaining peevishly of a sick headache.

He had never felt so lost and lonely in his life before as he had done then, when, going downstairs to their room, he had found her fast asleep, neither knowing nor caring that this was now a house of mourning.

Thereafter, from that night on, he had stopped loving Isabel as he used to. Not that it was as cut and dried as all that at the time, simply a deep-seated feeling of disappointment that she had not been there for him in his hour of need; a kind of coldness in place of old warmth and happiness he had known on their wedding day, akin to the fading of a summer sky in September before the onset of winter. The feeling was irreversible, he had discovered as time went by, as their harsh words and quarrels had gained in intensity and she had begun to brag that if *he* didn't care about her, someone else did.

Deeply jealous, when he had demanded to know the name of the other man, she had laughed and told him she was teasing, that she had made up the story to add a bit of spice to her life. This time he hadn't believed her tale of a cinema visit with a girlfriend and a bite of supper afterwards at her friend's house – for the good and sufficient reason that he followed her, one evening, down Sand Place to the foreshore; had seen her get into a parked car – a car with a number-plate he knew by heart – a car belonging to a man, a member of the Westsea fishing fraternity, a trawlerman who had been a groomsman at their wedding.

Sick at heart, Jake had awaited Isabel's homecoming, at midnight. It was then, entering the house in a state of euphoria, that she had laughed in his face and told him she was two month's pregnant by her current admirer, and asked what, if anything, he intended to do about it? Not that she really cared one way or the other since her lover, Ted Berry, could offer her a far better life than he, Jake, ever had, and the sooner he divorced her, the better, so that she could marry the father of her child; because Ted really loved her, which was more than *he* had ever done, her selfish bastard of a husband.

Inflamed with self-righteous anger, Jake had told Isabel to pack her belongings and get the hell out of his life; to go to the Devil so far as he was concerned; that he wanted nothing more to do with her now, or at any time in the future. "You've made your bed, now lie in it," had been his parting shot as he slammed shut the front door behind her.

The last time he'd seen her, she had been lying in a narrow hospital bed, eyes closed against the pain of living – the loss of her child and her lover. Ted Berry had not wanted to marry her after all.

Jake had seen, with tear-filled eyes, how limply her hair hung about her pale, pinched little face. Holding her hand, he had whispered her name in the vain hope that she would open her eyes to see him there beside her, to hear him say he was sorry for having treated her so badly, and wanted her home once again when she was well enough, but she had slipped into the sleep of death without regaining consciousness.

Leaving the hospital, Jake felt as if a part of himself had died also, that day. From then on he had withdrawn into a lonely world of his own making, living vicariously on the fringes of other people's lives; those of his tenants and his

234

family; throwing himself into his work, the maintenance of his property; learning how to cook for himself; collecting antiques, opening his shop in Silver Street; tending his garden; reading, listening to music – to fill up the void of his life.

He had been startled, at first, by the number of unattached women who had attempted to 'console' him on the death of his wife; the number of invitations he had received from members of the church-going community to which he had belonged at that time, to supper and tea-parties, none of which he had accepted, until, at last, as a matter of self-preservation, he had stopped going to church at all, apart from early communion.

His uncommunicative lifestyle had suited him well enough, devoid of emotional entanglement until the day Lisa Hazell had turned up on his doorstep, a somewhat nervous, fair-haired woman who, according to his sister Edie, had also experienced a bumpy passage through life.

Leaning back in his chair, he turned his mind to thoughts of the New Year, and wondered what, if anything, Lisa had planned for New Year's Eve. Perhaps she would care to have dinner with him prior to the advent of the year 1982; to drink a toast to the future at the last stroke of midnight?

Then, if the time seemed right, and if he could pluck up enough courage, he would give her the small present he had chosen for her earlier, and gift-wrapped, not in common-or-garden Christmas paper, but in a copy of a 1952 newspaper tied with string. And if she understood the message on the card attached to the string, she would also understand his depth of feeling towards her.

'Of mice and men' . . .

Linda's visit had upset Lisa more deeply than she had realised at the time. Fencing with words had been comparatively easy compared with the problem of what to do about John; where she should go from here.

235

She had not rung John at the cottage for the simple reason that she had not yet made up her mind whether or not to go back to him. How could she be sure that her return to the past would be to her advantage? And yet she needed, above all things, to feel – not only secure, but necessary once more to another human being, and she could not forget how necessary she had once been to John in the early days of their marriage.

'Nothing in earth or heaven comes as it came before'. This she knew and accepted, but her heart yearned for the old familiar sights and sounds of home, the upthrusting of the first snowdrops near a grey garden wall, the twitter of nesting birds in that arabesque of ivy over the front porch.

On this, New Year's Eve, a kind of crossroads with an invisible signpost looming in front of her, she knew she must reach her decision very soon now.

Lisa wanted to repay Jake for his many acts of kindness towards her; the way he had helped on the day of her removal, had taken the trouble to fit her carpet afterwards, and had taken care of her that fraught Christmas Eve when her stupidity may well have cost her her life. On her way to the shops to buy in food for the New Year, she slipped a note under his door, inviting him to supper that evening, around eight.

New Year's Eve had always been a very special celebration when Aunt Grace was alive. Refusing to succumb to the underlying sadness of the occasion, the loss of dear ones, family and friends close to her heart, Grace had said, in that funny, quirky way of hers, "No use looking back with regret. Far better to look forward with hope to a better future." Then she would set about baking sausage rolls, mince-pies, and making sandwiches for the buffet-supper she had planned for the friends still left to her.

On her way to the town-centre, this New Year's Eve, Lisa

wondered what Aunt Grace would have said if she knew she was contemplating a return to the cottage; the gathering together of the threads of her past in the hope of weaving a new pattern for the future. But Aunt Grace was nothing more than a memory now. It was up to herself and herself alone to decide her future role in life.

The shopping-precinct was thronged with people intent on making last minute purchases of food and wine, as if the coming of the New Year might herald a famine in the land; ill-fortune if they had forgotten to buy in enough bread, milk, meat and vegetables to last over the weekend.

Joining a long queue at a supermarket check-out, Lisa paid for the contents of her wire shopping-basket – a cooked chicken, roast ham, a selection of cheeses, a pack of frozen sausage rolls, a bottle of Chateau-Neuf-du-Pape.

Crossing the road to a bakery to buy bread, a French baton, a small sliced wholemeal loaf, a dozen bridge rolls and a portion of Black Forest Gateau, she thought of her first meeting with Edward; remembered the way he had steered towards that café where he had offered her tea and sympathy; had, unwittingly, altered the course of her life, bringing her to her present state of indecision regarding the future.

She was deep in thought, memories running through her mind like a series of clips from the film *Brief Encounter*; scarcely aware of the crowds of people around her, the coloured fairy-lights strung between the branches of the trees in the shopping precinct, the weight of her shopping bags, the aching of her shoulder-muscles, her deep, innate longing for the peace of mind so long denied her. An end to the misery of indecision . . . "Oh, I'm so sorry," she murmured, as she bumped into a frail-looking woman with silver-grey hair, wearing a putty-coloured mackintosh, and clinging tightly to the arm of the much younger woman at her side. *Judy*! Judy Miller!

How she had kept from speaking Judy's name aloud; saying, "Oh, hello, Judy," Lisa would never know. A warning glance, perhaps? Judy's obvious fear that a word of greeting, however innocent, would require some explanation, some lie, perhaps, to the woman at her side, who must be her mother, Pamela Miller – Edward's lawfully wedded wife.

Never would Lisa forget the expression of gratitude in Judy's eyes as she, Lisa, walked on, humping her shopping bags, her mind in a turmoil, having met Edward's wife face to face at last. Not at all the smart, dominant, well-dressed woman she had imagined her to be in the wakeful moments of many a long and sleepless night, when she had visualised Pamela as a desirable blonde with immaculately manicured fingernails; very much the mistress of any given situation, including her home and her husband.

How wrong she had been. But then, she had been wrong about so many things in her life before. Practically everything, come to think of it, apart from her love of Aunt Grace, the cottage, and John Hazell in the early days of their marriage. And Edward. Of course, Edward, who was not and never could be a part of her life ever again. Her brief encounter with Pamela Miller had convinced her of that once and for all: that pale, anxious-looking wreck of a woman.

Walking homeward in the deepening dusk of a winter afternoon, despite her high-flown altruism and their final words of farewell, hers and Edward's, uttered at a time of intense emotion, missing him so much, Lisa had held to her heart the faintest possibility that their love affair would blossom again one day. Not now. Not any more.

She now knew, now realised that Pamela's need of Edward was far greater than her own had ever been or ever could be – the need of an unhappy wife desperately in search of the happiness so long denied her.

Returning home, picking up the telephone, Lisa rang John, at the cottage, to tell him that she had reached her decision.

And now the die was cast, there could be no turning back from that hard-won decision to give her first love a second chance of success.

Chapter Twenty-Five

"Come in, Jake."

She was wearing a blue woollen dress and jacket. The buffet supper she had prepared was set on the oak chest. The room was warm and welcoming. He noticed the lighted Christmas tree on the octagonal table, the vase of daffodils on the mantelshelf.

There was background music, soft and low – 'Nocturnes' by Chopin – wine-glasses on the coffee table near the fire. This woman was, by nature, a homemaker, he realised, handing her the present he had brought her, wondering if she would understand the significance of the unorthodox packaging, the newspaper and string; the message on the gift-tag. 'Bright is the Ring of Words . . .'

"It's by way of a house-warming present," he said diffidently.

Turning the parcel in her hands, looking curiously at the wrapping paper, reading the message, she flushed slightly. "How exciting! What is it?"

"Why not open it and find out?"

Untying the string, she uttered a cry of delight. "'Dream Ships'! So that's what you meant when you said it was spoken for? Oh, Jake, I can't thank you enough! It's – priceless! And the newspaper and string. How clever of you to remind me of the old times when life seemed so much simpler than it does today."

Holding the picture in her hands, suddenly she felt the hot rush of tears to her eyes, tears beyond her power to hold in check as she remembered her bedroom in the old house at Walthamstow; 'Dream Ships' hanging above the narrow, white-painted fireplace opposite her bed; recalled the sound of her mother's footsteps on the stairs, the way she had leant over to kiss her good-night.

"I didn't mean to upset you," Jake said, feeling awkward, ill at ease.

"You haven't, believe me, at least not in the way you imagine. It's hard to explain, this longing of mine to turn back the clock, to go back in time, to re-live the past – as if everything in between had never happened."

Now the time had come, Lisa scarcely knew how to frame the words. "I'm sorry, Jake, but the fact is I shall not be here for very much longer."

Startled beyond belief, "Why not, for God's sake?" he exclaimed. "I thought you liked the flat. I thought you were happy here, I thought . . ."

"I know, Jake, and you were right. I *have* been happy here. This flat has been a haven for me, a caravanserai, a resting place; but things have changed now. Please sit down, let me try to explain."

She continued quietly, "Remember when we came home from Edie's party? The man who got out of his car?"

"Yes, of course I remember," Jake said grimly.

"That man was John Hazell, my ex-husband," Lisa explained, deeply aware of Jake's hostility towards her, evident by his body-language, hunched forward shoulders and tightly clenched hands. "Please don't be angry with me. John has asked me to go back to him and, rightly or wrongly, I've agreed to give our marriage a second chance. Can you blame me for wanting a second stab at happiness?"

"That all depends on what you think of as – happiness."

"What do *you* think of as happiness, Jake?"

"That's a hard question to answer."

"Even so . . ."

"Very well then, a place to call home; peace of mind,

241

the putting down of roots; music, good books to read at bedtime; decent food to eat; keeping faith with the past yet moving into the future with no regrets for all the mistakes that one has made along with way. No deep emotional entanglements . . ."

Lisa said quietly, "The man who came here to visit me quite often when I first moved into the flat; I loved him very much, I still do, but that's over and done with now that he has gone back to his wife, with my blessing."

"You amaze me, Lisa," Jake said bluntly. "Off with the new, on with the old? Is that your creed? In other words, are you so weak-minded, so spiritually depleted that you would rather return to John Hazell than stand up on your own two feet and tell that two-timing bastard to go to hell and pump thunder?"

"Well yes, I suppose I must be, since that is precisely what I intend doing," Lisa flared back at him, "but you said yourself that happiness is a place to call home, the putting down of roots; keeping faith with the past yet moving into the future with no regrets for all the mistakes that one has made along the way."

"I take it, then, that you are no longer interested in taking on board the management of the Silver Street shop? Well, not to worry unduly, Mrs Hazell, someone else is sure to turn up sooner or later. That's the way of the world, isn't it? There's always someone willing to step into someone else's shoes."

"Please, Jake," Lisa said quietly, "I never meant any of this to happen. It just has, that's all! For all I know, I may be on the verge of making the second greatest mistake of my life in going back to John. The truth is, this is something that I alone can solve in the long run. Now, please, since you are here and so am I, why not enjoy the time left to us? Why not open the bottle of wine in the fridge and drink a toast to the New Year?"

"As you wish," Jake said heavily, uncorking the bottle of

Chateau-Neuf-du-Pape as the midnight bells from the church on the hill rang out the old year; heralding the new.

Now she will never know how I feel about her, Colby thought wistfully, charging their glasses; proposing a toast to the future. Just as well, perhaps. After all, Silence was Golden, and he had lived long enough in the silent world of his own creation to come to terms with that particular adage. So be it.

But ah, how much he would miss his Mrs Hazell, his beloved Lisa, when she had gone away from him, her departure from his life adding a further crust to his veneer of loneliness so that soon, in time to come, his fellow human beings would regard him as an eccentric; a vacant fool of a man, wandering the beach alone at midnight, in search of some lost kingdom of the soul, some simple happiness of the heart forever denied him.

"When are you thinking of leaving?" he asked.

"Quite soon. Tomorrow or the day after. As soon as I've made certain arrangements. My furniture will have to go in store until I decide what to do about it."

"Back to square one, in other words?" Jake suggested, putting down his glass. "Well, anything I can do to help . . ."

"I can't begin to tell you how much your friendship has meant to me." The words sounded trite but they came from the heart.

Friendship, Colby thought on his way downstairs, what he wanted was not friendship but – love.

243

Chapter Twenty-Six

Lisa wished the train would start moving. She had arrived at the station far too early, and so she had only herself to blame for the hiatus. Jake had offered to drive her, but she had preferred to call a taxi. Even so, he had carried her case downstairs; had made her sandwiches and a flask of coffee for the journey.

The past three days had been spent clearing up the flat, getting rid of the Christmas tree, emptying and defrosting the refrigerator, feeding leftover bread to the gulls; washing and ironing, deciding which clothes to take with her, which to leave behind. She would, in any event, have to return to Westsea in a few weeks' time to pack her pictures and ornaments and so on in readiness for the respository, but it was too soon to make clear-cut arrangements until she had discussed things with John.

Turning on the threshold at the last minute, she had felt a tug of regret for all the flat had meant to her during her brief tenancy of these three rooms with their poignant memories of good times, and bad, as if she was leaving behind an integral part of herself; her hopes, dreams and ambitions. Above all, perhaps, the view of the sea from the balcony window.

"I'll be in touch," she had promised Colby, entering the taxi.

The train was freezing cold at this hour of the morning. Hopefully the main line train from York would be much warmer. Her feet felt like blocks of ice despite her fur-lined boots.

Sitting there, tensed up with a cold and the nervous feeling in the pit of her stomach, she noticed the ingrained dirt round the carriage windows, the vandalised upholstery, the stench of urine from a nearby toilet.

Then other passengers began to filter through the barrier, to board the train, and there came a quivering and shaking as the diesel engine sprang to life; a sense of urgency as latecomers hustled to occupy unclaimed seats, to pacify crying children with gob-stopping dummies, packets of crisps and bottles of pop; young mothers and harassed fathers who had, most probably, spent the New Year with their childrens' doting grandparents.

Who knew? Who could tell? Lisa wondered, thinking how little one really knew or understood the intricate patterns of human behaviour. Take herself for example. Would any of her fellow passengers, supposing they were interested enough to cast a glance in her direction, see her as anything more than a po-faced, middle-aged woman about to visit relatives who, likely as not would be glad to see the back of her when the visit was over?

Looking out of the window as the train moved forward at last, Lisa noticed that the early morning sky above Westsea, was stained blood-red with the dawning of a new day, holding the promise of brief intervals of sunshine on the sea before the inevitable gathering of rain-clouds on the horizon.

As the train gathered momentum, Lisa garnered together her memories of the town she had grown to love so much during her fleeting acquaintance with its streets, its ships, its shore, as if an important, unforgettable part of her life would remain forever encapsulated against a backdrop of a small, insignificant seaside town in which she had discovered the full meaning of life – and love.

Sitting upright, her spine pressed against the upholstery in an attempt at relaxation, Lisa wished that memories might be dusted away as easily as chalk from a blackboard. But memories, like luggage, must be picked up and carried, on even the shortest journey, from the lumbered attics of the mind.

Attics! Sloping ceilings seamed with cracks. But one seldom noticed the imperfections of a ceiling when sunlight filtered into a room at early morning, glinting on china and cut-glass, books and pictures – the painting of a clump of dianthus near a garden gate, for instance. Dianthus. Flowers. . . . Her African violets! She had forgotten to ask Jake to keep an eye on her African violets . . . How could she have been so stupid?

Jake, to whom she owed so much by way of his unde-manding friendship. Jake, a private, dignified man, impos-sibly tetchy and irritable at times, but a friend worth having.

As the train jogged on, Lisa considered that, possibly, she had best leave her carpets in situ for the next occupant of her flat. Yes, she decided, that would be the best, the easiest thing to do.

Turning her mind to the cottage, she remembered that the rug in the hall had a way of bunching up in the middle; a source of irritation to John, who had never got around to buying some kind of carpet backing to anchor it securely to the floor. Or perhaps Linda had got rid of that rug because of the child? Because a toddler might fall down and hurt himself on a rug that rucked up like a switchback at the merest footfall?

The cottage!

At her return, Lisa wondered, would she feel entirely at ease there? Or would she discover reminders of Linda in, say, the odd pen or pencil which had slipped down between the cushions of a chair; a forgotten jar of cold cream in the bathroom cabinet; a pair of tights in the Ali-Baba basket? A hanky reeking of Estee Lauder's 'Youth Dew' – Linda's favourite perfume?

More importantly, would John expect her to sleep with him on her return to the cottage? And what would be his reaction if she refused? Would he even begin to understand that she must, for the time being at least, occupy her own room, her own space; must be allowed to sink back gradually into their former relationship as man and wife?

Oh God, if only she knew the answers to all these self-imposed questions. And now the train was charging onward towards York, where, in a matter of minutes, she must change platforms to catch the mainline train to Edinburgh.

Crossing the iron bridge, at York, humping her heavy case and the carrier-bag containing Jake Colby's sandwiches and flask of coffee, she felt like Sydney Carton mounting the steps of the guillotine, uttering his final speech – 'It is a far, far better thing . . .' and all that jazz from Dickens' *A Tale of Two Cities*.

Aunt Grace's spine-stiffening saying at times of stress sprang to mind: "I am Captain of my Soul, Master of my Fate". Twenty minutes to wait. Silly, perhaps, to buy a cup of coffee when she had a flask in her carrier bag, but the platform was freezing cold. Might just as well wait in the refreshment room. The girl behind the counter was singing along to the latest pop record on the juke-box.

She sat at a table near the window. Coffee. Continental blend, she thought, remembering the day Mrs Hannersley had told her about the flat; how she had made up her mind that, if she were lucky enough to get it, she would start to live again. This she had done, but not in the way she'd imagined.

Life had taken her by the scruff of the neck, changing her preconceived idea of a sabbatical, flinging her into a brief but passionate love affair, leaving her shaken by the squandering of so much emotion, destroying her peace of mind. And yet, despite the emotional upheaval, she had known moments of deep joy and contentment in that room overlooking the harbour.

Now she might never again know the simple joy of being alone, of making her own decisions. John had a way of eating up peace. Even when she had wandered alone in the bluebell wood at Gatford Hollow, or lain on the hill near the burial mounds, breathing in the scent of the long grass and listening to joyous songs of larks ascending, she had kept an eye on her watch because of the time factor involved in getting back to the cottage in time to cook the evening meal. Later had come the catechism – where had she been, what had she been doing all day?

The announcer's voice intoned the arrival of the Edinburgh train at platform nine, stopping at Darlington, Thirsk and Newcastle.

Collecting her belongings, she watched the train pulling into the station. It was more crowded than she had imagined it would be. Carriage doors swung open. Someone behind her said testily, "What are you hanging back for? Why don't you get in?"

"Sorry."

The man pushed past her, a big, angry looking individual with a mountain of luggage who obviously thought she was crazy, a simple-minded middle-aged woman dithering about getting into a train.

Doors banged shut. The guard signalled the driver – a hand signal – they didn't wave a green flag any more. She felt like crying as the train slid away from the platform. Turning away, she walked back over the iron bridge. 'It is a far, far better thing that I do . . .' Dear Sydney Carton.

She would have to ring John, of course, before he set off for Thirsk Station. He would be terribly angry and upset. Not that it mattered: she wouldn't be there to bear the brunt of his anger. In any case, she could always hang up the receiver. One click, then silence. Blessed silence. Linda would go back to him eventually, of course.

No need to worry about that rucked-up hall carpet, finding

248

stray kirbigrips, tights or pots of face-cream in the bathroom. The cottage was Linda's province now, as it had been ever since she, Lisa, had walked down the garden path for the last time.

There could be no going back to a past best put aside and – not forgotten – but laid to rest. There were other apple trees in other gardens, other snowdrops pushing up through the snow of winter. Other daffodils, other bluebells, other woods, other hills to climb.

Gripped by a strange, exhilarating feeling of excitement, she asked a porter the time of the next train to Westsea.

"Due to depart in ten minutes from Platform seven," he told her, grinning at her enthusiasm. "The ticket office's over yonder. Not to worry, Miss, you've plenty of time."

"Thank you. Thank you very much." She could have kissed him.

Ticket in hand, she ran along the platform, not giving a damn that her suitcase was bumping awkwardly against her legs. She was going Home.

Opening the front door with her latchkey, leaving her suitcase in the hall, she saw, with infinite joy and relief, the graceful staircase curving up to the special place awaiting her return.

Crossing the threshold of her flat, everything seemed clean and fresh to her; free of ghosts and unhappy memories.

Opening the balcony window, she stepped outside to feel the wind on her face, to taste the salt air of home on her lips.

The tide was on the turn, the sky lightening with straggling rays of sunshine streaming through the tattered clouds. And soon, she thought, Springtime, not Autumn would come to Mrs Hazell; new challenges, a whole fresh new future to look forward to.

Closing the window, she saw, with delight, Aunt Grace's

painting of dianthus above the mantelshelf; 'Dream Ships' on the wall near her special armchair; remembered that she had never made use of that virgin canvas among her aunt's belongings, but there was all the time in the world now to learn how to paint. Perhaps she would join an Art club? The possibilities were endless now she was home once more, and at peace with herself at last.

Removing the pliofilm bags from her African violets, she saw, with tear-filled eyes, that tiny leaves were springing up from the roots, and thread-like filaments from which, in time, new flowers would grow – pink and purple, sheened like sugar almonds.

Suddenly she heard the pounding of footsteps on the stairs, and turned as Jake entered the room, his face grim with worry.

"I saw your case in the hall," he said breathlessly. "Are you all right? What happened? An accident?"

> 'Bright is the ring of words
> When the right man rings them . . .'

"No accident." She smiled up at him. "I decided to come home, that's all."

Jake drew in a deep breath of relief. It might take months, even years, he thought, to convince Mrs Hazell that they belonged together. But he was a patient man: he could wait.

VIEW FROM A BALCONY

Part One

One

S tepping down from the train, making her way to the station
forecourt in search of a taxi, Kate thought at least three things
about Scarborough had not changed: the sea fog, the moaning of the
foghorn, and the crying of seabirds overhead. But what had happened
to the "Brief Encounter" buffet, the wooden ticket hut near the barrier,
the newspapers and magazines kiosk on platform Number One and the
Nestlé's chocolate machine?

"Where to, Miss?" the taxi driver asked offhandedly, stowing her
luggage in the boot of his car.

"The Crown Hotel," she said, glad of the mist, the distant sound of
the foghorn, the plaintive clamour of the gulls, as familiar to her as
breathing: thankful to be home again, albeit against her better judgement.

Even so, this place, this town had always been at the back of her
mind, lovingly remembered, never revisited – until today.

They say we shouldn't look back, much less return to the
scene of remembered happiness in search of old familiar landmarks, and people who may no longer exist. But what alternative was possible in her situation? A woman in desperate need
of a fresh begining, the creation of a new life from the ruins of
the old.

At least the prestigious Crown Hotel, built in the Victorian era and
reminiscent of "Tara" in *Gone With the Wind*, had not changed
outwardly in appearance, Kate thought, walking up the front steps
to the reception area and signing the register of new arrivals, "Mrs Kate
Ford"; her address, from force of habit: "April Cottage, Woodley,
Devizes, Wiltshire".

The ironwork felt cold and wet beneath her outspread hands. The sea
was invisible but she knew it was there from the relentless ebb and flow

3

of the tide on the shore and the intermittent booming of the foghorn on the lighthouse pier.

Lamplights on the promenade beneath the balcony of her room, diffused by the fog, glimmered softly like pale primroses in a springtime wood.

But this was autumn, not springtime. Now her wood, silent and still, adrift with the fallen leaves of summertime, would have settled down to its long winter sleep.

Rain would soon rot the leaves to compost. The tractor road between the trees, dry and rutted in summer, would become a sea of mud until the frosts of winter stiffened its resolve. Then fitful gleams of wintry sunlight, without warmth, would sparkle momentarily on ice, and there would be icicles, not catkins, on the hazel branches.

Re-entering the warmth of her room, closing the balcony window and drawing the curtains, Kate wondered if it would always be like this, this preoccupation with the past, allowing her no peace of mind.

Even the smallest things possessed the power to unleash a chain of memories best put aside and forgotten. Roses in a florist's window, for instance, reminiscent of her wedding bouquet. Dance tunes of the 50s: "When I Fall in Love", "Tammy", "Witchcraft". Romantic black-and-white movies on late night television; the scent of newly mown grass on summer afternoons. A baby fast asleep in its pushchair – the most poignant reminder of everything she had lost when her husband of twenty years had admitted to having an affair with a younger woman, and asked her to divorce him.

They were in the kitchen at the time, Kate recalled. She cooking spaghetti bolognese, he nursing a glass of Bordeaux. A familiar ritual. Don always drank wine on his return to the cottage after a working day in London as a freelance tabloid journalist – what he termed his "bread and butter" earnings, supporting his output of radio and TV plays, documentaries and short stories for various women's magazines, written in his private sanctum – a refurbished and insulated shed at the far end of the garden.

She had sensed something was wrong. Impossible not to have reached that conclusion with someone she knew almost as intimately as she knew herself. Even so, she had been totally unprepared for the bombshell, the shattering of her life and happiness when he'd told her about the other woman – Lucia Keane, a newspaper colleague, with whom he had fallen deeply in love.

"I'm so sorry," he said. "I never meant this to happen. Never meant to hurt you."

She faced him disbelievingly. "Never meant it to happen? Then why did you let it happen? A man of your age and a girl young enough to be your daughter. What the hell were you thinking of? As for hurting me, you must have known every time you met this – other woman – the risks you were running, what it would do to me if I found out. Or didn't you care? Now *this*!"

"I've said I'm sorry. What more can I say?"

"A great deal more! You can't just turn your back on your responsibilities and walk away from them as if they never existed! I'm your wife, for God's sake! This is your home! Have you so little respect for me to tell me, in the kitchen of all places, that you want a divorce?"

"I know you're angry. Upset. Can't we at least discuss this in a civilised way? I've told you I'm in love with Lucia, that I want my freedom to marry her. I've been entirely honest with you. What's wrong with that?"

The truth had dawned on Kate slowly, inevitably. She said, "Lucia's pregnant, isn't she?" and knew by his face that she had hit the nail on the head.

She had relived this sequence of events time and time again since the break up of her marriage. Now, in desperate need of escape from haunting memories of the past, Kate hurried down a curving Victorian staircase, through the reception lounge and crossed the road towards the railings bordering the steep descent of woods and paths to the Spa Grand Hall and the seashore below.

Silver flecks blurred her vision. Straining her eyes, all she could see was the fog-bound esplanade fronting the hotel. Then, miraculously, there came the smell of seaweed borne inland from the shore. Familiar yet half forgotten, as many things had been forgotten in her transition from child to woman: the bitter-sweetness of a first and only love affair, still linked in her mind to the loss of her parents; leaving home to begin a new life with a comparative stranger – an act of blind faith centred on the belief that the love of two people, herself and Don, would last till the end of time.

Walking alone in the foggy darkness, following the curve of the esplanade by the diffused light of the lamp-standards spaced out like beads on a rosary, she recalled the kindness of her brother Greg and his wife Cynthia's invitation to stay with them indefinitely after the divorce and the sale of April Cottage.

But there were no springtime woods bordering their neatly maintained garden in the Greater Manchester area, and the sprawl of streets and houses, to someone accustomed to space and freedom, had resembled a straitjacket.

She and Greg had always been close to one another, even as children, when they had played together on the sands in summertime, making sand-pies and building castles, soon to be swept away by the incoming tide. He, the older of the two, keeping a watchful eye on his kid sister; holding her by the hand when they paddled together in the rock pools near the Children's Corner.

Recently, deeply aware of her unhappy state of mind, he said gently, "Look, Kate, you're a free agent now. Don treated you shabbily, I know. At least he had the decency to hand over the deeds of the cottage, to grant you a modicum of financial security. Now, isn't it time you stopped fretting over the past and looked to the future?"

"What *future*? I haven't got a future."

"That's nonsense, and you know it! Everyone has a future! I know you're not happy here in Manchester, and I can't blame you for that! I wouldn't be here myself if it weren't for my job and my mortgage repayments!"

He smiled ruefully. "Given half a chance, I'd give up teaching, go back to Scarborough and open a fish and chip shop!"

"I see." Returning his smile, she added, "So that's the future you have mapped out for me, is it? As the proprietress of a 'chish and fip' shop?"

"No, Kate. Far from. All I'm saying is, why not go back to your roots? At least give yourself a fair chance of happiness in a place you love. A new start, a new beginning in life."

She couldn't afford to stay at the Crown indefinitely, Kate realised. Coming here had been in the nature of a "thumb to nose" gesture to bolster her flagging ego. Coming home, she had wanted to splash out on the best that money could buy – a balcony room in the town's oldest and most prestigious hotel, rather than sidle, unnoticed, into a boarding house in the town centre. Well, now she was here, and she couldn't see a damn thing, much less the view from her balcony, for the blasted sea fog blanketing the lights of home.

Regarding the future: she had never had a paid job in her life, so far.

After leaving school, she had been called upon to nurse her mother and keep house for her father. Greg had been at Durham University at the time, coming home at weekends to offer his help and support.

Their mother's illness was something they had never dreamt possible. The sudden death of a beloved person had been their first brush with the harsh reality of life. Worse was to come. Devastated by the death of his wife, their father had taken ill and died a year later. In retrospect, it seemed to Kate that he had simply lost the will to live.

At that rock-bottom stage of her life, when she'd been alone in a rented house far too big for just one person, wandering about the rooms like a lost soul, not knowing what to do for the best, trying to sort out her parents' belongings, to decide what to keep and what to sell when the time came to move out, an old schoolfriend of hers had badgered her into making up a foursome for a trip to the pictures.

Jenny Laird, fun-loving, bubbly and curvaceous, explained the reason for the blind date. Her current boyfriend, a young reporter, sharing digs with a newcomer to the *Evening News*, felt duty-bound to show the chap a good time.

When Kate demurred, "Oh, come on, love," Jenny insisted. "It'll do you good to go out for a change. What I mean is, you needn't see him again if you don't like him. Just sit next to him in the cinema, have a bite to eat and a couple of drinks afterwards. What's wrong with that? His name's Don Ford, by the way."

But she had liked Don Ford a great deal. This was no impecunious cub reporter but a seasoned newspaperman, ambitious, clever and charming. Despite the six year difference in their ages, she'd found him easy to talk to, and sympathetic and understanding when she'd told him briefly about the loss of her parents, not wanting to burden him with her troubles. They were, after all, meant to be having a jolly evening, not a wake.

To her surprise and pleasure, when the evening ended, he had invited her out to a meal the following weekend – "tête-a-tête, next time". Soon they had started seeing a great deal of one another: walking together, hand-in-hand, beneath a harvest moon as summertime drifted into autumn. She falling more deeply in love with him every passing day, every precious hour they spent together; hoping and praying that he too was falling in love.

But how could she be sure? Don had made it clear to her that his stay in Scarborough was of a temporary nature; had stated his intention of moving on when a suitable opportunity occurred – an editor's job, for instance, offering better prospects, a sizeable salary increase. More importantly, the cachet of becoming the man in charge of policy and editorial comment.

Kate's heart had sunk to her shoes when, in the early spring of the following year, Don told her he'd been offered, and had accepted the editorship of *The Wiltshire Herald*. She'd dreaded their forthcoming separation, the absence from her life of the man she loved – until . . .

"I want you to come with me to Wiltshire," Don said, matter-of-factly, planting a kiss on her forehead. "How long will it take you to fix up our wedding? If you want to marry me, that is? Just don't make it a big affair, with a posse of bridesmaids and all that jazz! It's you I want, not the world and his wife!"

And so they had been married, very quietly, early one morning, in St Mary's Church, overlooking the "Old Town" of Scarborough – that maze of streets and alleyways glissading down to the harbour, each of which Kate had known as intimately as the back of her hand during her carefree childhood with her brother Greg by her side. Greg who had given her in marriage to a handsome stranger, against his own better judgement.

On the eve of the wedding, he asked, "Are you sure you're doing the right thing, Kate? How long have you known Don? Six months? Is that really long enough to know your own mind?"

"I love Don, and he loves me."

"I know, and I'm glad you're happy. I just don't want you to get hurt."

"You think Don will hurt me? Why should he? He loves me!"

"He's much older than you are; far more experienced." Greg paused momentarily. "I'm sorry, I shouldn't have said that." He added ruefully, "I'm just saying what Mum and Dad might have said if they were still here. Everything's happened so fast, I guess I haven't come to terms with losing you as well. After all, Wiltshire's a long way from home. I'll miss you, Kate."

Returning to the hotel, Kate wondered if Don would have asked her to marry him had it not been for that editor's job he'd been offered in the early stages of their blossoming love affair.

She preferred to think so, but she couldn't be sure. Losing Don to another woman had planted seeds of doubt in her mind. Raking over the embers of a burnt-out marriage, she asked herself if there had been other affairs of his of which she had known nothing. Had she been too trusting, too complacent, to notice the warning signs? Had her complacency, her preoccupation with housework, cooking and gardening, been to blame for Don's affair with Lucia?

In bed with his mistress, had he told her tales of that boring, predictable wife of his? Her own fault if he had. Kate knew that now. What had she done with her time apart from cleaning house, mowing grass, pulling up weeds, trimming hedges, planning menus and cooking traditional Sunday lunches – prodigious amounts of food which neither of them had really wanted or enjoyed?

Seldom, if ever, had she picked up a book and read it from cover to cover. Never had she evinced the slightest interest in political or social issues. She'd been far too busy making jam and chutney, pickling onions and beetroot, to bother her head about what was happening in the world beyond the four walls of April Cottage; or too busy walking alone in her wood, especially in springtime when the ground beneath the trees was misted over with bluebells, and in autumn when the earth lay thick with fallen leaves, richly patterned in shades of crimson, brown and gold.

Seated at the dressing table, brushing her fair, shoulder-length hair into the semblance of a French pleat, Kate thought that if the future was to hold any meaning at all, she must expand her horizons. Join the human race, find herself a job and a place to live, a furnished flat or a bed-sit.

What kind of job she had no idea. Stacking supermarket shelves or cleaning hotel bedrooms, at a rough guess. Hardly likely that anyone would jump at the chance of employing a middle-aged woman without a hygiene certificate to her name, her only qualification being housekeeping within the parameters of a failed marriage.

Frustrated by her inability to cope with her hair, worn long to please Don, at the first opportunity, Kate decided, she would have it cut short – to please herself.

On the threshold of the dining room, glancing nervously about her at the many occupied tables – busy waiters and waitresses serving the food and wine, feeling intensely lonely and vulnerable, somewhat dowdy in her blue wool dress, more suited to a vicarage tea-party than dinner in a five star hotel, she felt there was no way she could she run the gauntlet of curious glances or walk across the room to a table for one near the window. In which case, the sooner she went back to her room, the better.

A smiling young waiter spared her the humiliation of a full-scale retreat. "A table for one, madam?" he asked pleasantly. Kate nodded. Leading the way, pulling back a chair and handing her the menu, he said, "Would madam care for anything to drink? A carafe of wine, perhaps?"

"No, thanks. Just Perrier water, with ice and a twist of lemon."

Glancing up from the menu, Kate's eyes met those of the man at the next table, also dining alone, informally dressed in a tweed suit, a Paisley scarf tucked into an open-neck shirt, and with a copy of *The Times* propped up against the cruet. He advised her cheerfully to plump for the chicken supreme.

"Thanks, but I'd prefer the grilled plaice," she replied nonchalantly.

Afterwards, in bed, wide awake, Kate heard the faint whirring of the lift, the metallic clang of its gates as they opened and closed on the first floor landing, then a drift of dance music from a function room somewhere inside the hotel – comforting sounds of life going on around her, expelling momentarily her deep-seated sense of isolation.

After falling fast asleep, emotionally and physically exhausted by the events of the day – saying goodbye to Greg and Cindy at Manchester Station, clinging to her brother at the last moment, afraid of the future, Kate awoke in the early hours of the next morning to the sound of silence, apart from the faint murmur of the sea washing in on the shore.

Getting up, swiftly crossing the room, drawing back the curtains, stepping on to the balcony, she saw that the fog had lifted at last.

Looking down, she saw the lights of home shining through the dark. A necklace of lamp lights outlining the sweeping curve of the South Bay. Pinpricks of light twinkling from the "Old Town" of Scarborough, nestled about the harbour, rising in tiers to a vast rocky promontory crowned with the sombre ruins of a floodlit Norman fortress.

Looking up, blinking back tears, she saw, high above her, a black velvet sky littered with a myriad crystal-clear stars shining down on her, and knew, in one blinding moment of revelation, that this homecoming

10

of hers had been no mistake. It was here she truly belonged, and here she would stay, come hell or high water.

Contemplating the stars, Kate uttered a fervent prayer for courage enough to march, unafraid, into the unknown future ahead of her.

Two

T here was no sign of the man Kate thought of as "the Loner" at breakfast next morning. He must have eaten earlier and left the hotel. Not that it mattered. "Ships that pass in the night, and speak each other in passing"!

Fallen leaves littered the steeply plunging paths of the Spa gardens. The air was threaded with the scents of autumn: of scythed meadow-sweet and those brown-tipped grasses she thought of as "bows and arrows"; the pungent smoke of a bonfire on which council workmen were burning the detritus of summertime.

Pausing awhile, she gazed at well-remembered landmarks: the parish church of St Mary near Castle Hill, standing guard over the Old Town; the lighthouse on the west pier. Nothing had changed much outwardly, Kate thought. But appearances could be deceptive, as she knew to her cost.

Changes were bound to have taken place in the twenty-odd years of her absence. Time moved on relentlessly, sweeping all before it. Gone forever were the happy, carefree days of her youth and childhood lived in anticipation of only the good things in life: school holidays, birthday parties, picnics and Punch and Judy. At Christmas, building snowmen, not sandcastles.

This was a day of latent warmth and sunshine prior to the onset of winter. Soon, children would be lighting bonfires on the beach, burning effigies of Guy Fawkes, letting off fireworks in the cold night air. Then would come Remembrance Sunday, that depressing Cenotaph Cere-mony in Whitehall. No warmth, no joy – November . . .

They say we shouldn't look back. It would be tantamount to madness, Kate realised, to revisit St Mary's Church, to dredge up memories best laid aside and forgotten. But what hope for the future unless she came to terms with the past?

The street called Paradise, curving up from Sandside to the parish

12

church was much steeper than she recalled. Gone were the days when she had run up it, not pausing for breath. Inside the church all was silent. No organ music. No echo of a young bride's nervous footsteps on stone flags. No wintry scent of daffodils in the air, just the autumnal smell of chrysanthemums from the altar vases.

Yet how clearly she remembered that cold spring morning long ago. Don turning his head to smile at her as she stood beside him holding her bouquet of red roses. "O, Perfect Love".

All over and done with now – that brief early-morning wedding ceremony, the hastily arranged reception afterwards in the Albion Hotel across the road from the church – salmon sandwiches and sausage rolls, the obligatory speeches, the bridesmaid flirting with every man in sight. Having to keep an eye on the time because the London train was due to leave the station at eleven thirty.

This the first leg of their journey. Arriving at King's Cross, they'd have to cross London to Paddington to catch a connection to the West Country, Don had explained beforehand.

It had been a long, tiring journey. Kate now recalled, as if it were yesterday, her acute feeling of disorientation during that seemingly endless passage through unfamiliar scenery, far from home.

If only Don had suggested breaking their journey – an overnight stay in London, a hotel room somewhere, a decent meal, a continuation of their journey to Wiltshire the following day. Instead of which, she'd been subjected to a mad dash, by tube trains, to Paddington; then, a couple of damp ham sandwiches and a cup of bitter-tasting coffee in a station buffet, before haring along the platform, in Don's wake, to board the mainline train to Exeter. By which time, almost too exhausted to stand up straight, all she had really wanted was a good night's sleep in a comfortable bed. Alone, for preference.

She'd realised afterwards that this had been the culmination of too many emotional upheavals for a girl of her age: the deaths of her parents; falling in love with a man she scarcely knew. Everything happening far too fast – bereavement, grief, uncertainty, the stress of leaving the house that had been her home for as far back as she could remember.

All these things led up to her wedding day nerves and that strange feeling of disorientation on the long journey into an unknown future, wanting nothing more than the benison of hot water, food and an uninterrupted night's sleep – of the kind she had known as a child

Louise Brindley

after a long day on the beach, donkey riding and building sandcastles . . .

Closing the church door quietly behind her, Kate walked down Castle Road to the town centre in search of a hairdressing salon, one of those "Appointments Not Always Necessary" places with assistants at a loose end now the holiday season was over.

"Promise me you'll never cut your hair," Don had said once, long ago. "It's so pretty the way it is." And so she had promised. But promises were made to be broken, weren't they? Especially promises to love and to cherish till death us do part.

When the young male assistant who'd cut her hair suggested having her hair highlighted, Kate told him to go ahead. Anything would be preferable to struggling with that darned French pleat of hers, ending up looking like the archetypal "maiden aunt" in an old Bette Davis movie, mousey and faded.

Seeing her face in the salon mirror as the assistant hooked strands of hair through a kind of bathing cap, lathered on the bleach and applied the strips of foil, Kate thought how drained she looked. Recent events had taken their toll: the divorce trauma, selling April Cottage, leaving behind her all that she and Don had created together during twenty years of marriage.

Would things have been different if their first child had survived the fifth month of her pregnancy? A child they had wanted so much. The bitterest pill to swallow was that the other woman in Don's life was carrying his baby. And that one inescapable truth had meant far more to him than she ever had. Kate saw that quite clearly now, the sexual urge of a dominant male intent on the procreation of his own image, letting his seed fall where it may . . .

"Well, is madam pleased with the result?" the assistant hair-stylist asked eagerly, holding a hand-mirror reflecting the rear view of her shorn head. "Yes," Kate replied, feeling half-naked, yet admiring the highlights and the short, bouffant fringe just clearing her eyebrows. "You've done wonders! Made me feel much younger all of a sudden!"

The thought occurred to her, as she left the salon, that she was not old. She had begun thinking old after her first miscarriage, when a consultant gynaecologist had warned her of the improbability of her ever carrying a child full term. And so she had turned to housekeeping, gardening and cooking as panacea against the pain of regret that she could not give her husband the children he desperately wanted.

14

After her third miscarriage, she had given up all hope of mother-hood. She had, at least, given Don a pin-clean home, glowing, colourful flowerbeds and well-cooked food, none of which he had really wanted or appreciated.

By nature creative and untidy, he had begun spending more and more time in his so-called studio at the end of the garden, and often disappeared for hours at a time to the village pub to play darts and dominoes with the locals, drinking far more than was good for him, returning home when he felt like it, to make love to her – if he felt so inclined.

All over and done with now, Kate thought, walking down Westborough, Scarborough's main thoroughfare. But what had happened to the magnificent Pavilion Hotel opposite the station? What had become of The Londesborough Cinema, where, as a child, she had laughed at the antics of Laurel and Hardy, and thrilled to the love duet "Ah, Sweet Mystery of Life", sung by Jeanette MacDonald and Nelson Eddy, her father in the seat beside her feeding her chocolate drops from a white paper bag.

She and her father had often gone out together to the "first house" of the pictures, Kate recalled, whilst Mum was busy in the kitchen preparing their supper, and her brother Greg was doing his homework.

With infinite pleasure she recalled the thrill of homecoming to that old, draughty Victorian villa in Albemarle Crescent, close to the town centre, and those simple meals of bangers and mash, shepherd's pie or rissoles. They'd never been well-off financially; just rich beyond measure in other, more important ways.

Had her parents lived, she might well have never met Don Ford. In the natural course of events, leaving school, she would have gone out to work like other girls of her generation, as a shop assistant, most likely, in one of the department stores, Marshall and Snelgrove, Tonks or Rowntrees, selling lingerie, lampshades or make-up, paying Mum so much a week from her wages, eventually meeting some nice ordinary young man with whom she'd walk out on Sunday afternoons, subject to her parents' approval. She knew, deep down, that they would not have taken to Don as a prospective son-in-law – a "fly-by-night" newspaper reporter, far too old for a tender, starry-eyed young girl on the threshold of life.

Tired and hungry, Kate had coffee and a sandwich in a snack bar overlooking the main street. Exhausted by memories, the changes wrought by time in this home town of hers, the passing of an old familiar way of life, realising the validity of the words "Nothing in earth or heaven comes as it came before", she knew her future depended on finding herself a place to live, employment of some kind, however menial or uncongenial – not in squandering money recklessly, as she had done so far, on expensive hotel accommodation and an attractive but unnecessary new hairstyle – not in making inroads on her capital from the sale of April Cottage, which was invested in a building society account, but in standing on her own two feet. She must prove to Don and his new wife, Lucia, now living in New York with their offspring, Tobias, that she did not need her ex-husband's maintenance cheques paid quarterly into her Lloyd's bank account.

Above all, she loathed her feeling of dependence on her former husband for the clothes she wore, the shoes on her feet, the food she ate – something she'd endured since that night in the kitchen of April Cottage, three years ago, when after packing his belongings, he had left her alone to return to London – and Lucia.

So what to do about it? Nothing, for the time being at any rate. In need of rest and relaxation, Kate returned slowly to the Crown Hotel to make the most of a soft, warm bed: deep sleep, before her dinnertime appearance in the dining room, sporting her brand new hairstyle. A feeble victory, perhaps. Nevertheless, a much needed boost to her ego, knowing that never again would she have to cope with that blasted French pleat of hers!

The man she thought of as "the Loner" was in the reception lounge when she came downstairs. "Ah, there you are!" he said, stepping forward to greet her. "I thought you might have checked out when I didn't see you at breakfast this morning."

"Really?" She frowned slightly, wondering what business of his it was anyway. "No, I breakfasted early and went out for a walk."

He suggested urbanely, "I thought we might dine together this evening. My name is Alex Arden, by the way. At least I'm properly dressed for the occasion tonight."

He had a direct way of speaking, shrewd, intelligent grey-blue eyes in a lean, suntanned face; greying hair brushed back from a high forehead. An air of authority about him, as if used to getting his own way.

Startled by the invitation, "That's very kind of you," she said, about to add that she would prefer to dine alone. But how could she, without offending the man?

16

Accepting the inevitable, she said, "My name's Kate. Kate Ford."

When asked which wine she'd prefer to accompany her choice of roast lamb, Kate, feeling gauche and more than a little naive and foolish in the presence of this stranger, admitted that she didn't drink wine. He was obviously a man of the world, a traveller judging by his suntan, now faultlessly attired in a dark-grey suit and tie.

"How wise of you," he commented drily. "So shall we settle for Perrier 'on the rocks' with a twist of lemon?"

Don would have said impatiently, "God dammit, Kate, what have you got against wine anyway? A glass or two would do you good! Loosen those bloody inhibitions of yours once in a while!"

She could almost see him now, standing in the kitchen of April Cottage, nursing a glass of red wine, breaking the news of his love affair with Lucia Keane.

"Kate," Alex asked concernedly, "is anything the matter? Are you feeling unwell?"

Staring at him, unseeing, she answered, "No, just a bit tired, that's all. I'm sorry. This – homecoming, after so long an absence, is not quite what I'd expected. But how could you, a comparative stranger, possibly understand?" She stopped abruptly, knowing she was speaking more to herself than her companion. Obviously, the man hadn't the remotest idea what she was talking about. Aghast, she said quickly, "Please forgive me. I didn't think what I was saying."

"No need to apologise. You spoke of a homecoming, a feeling of disappointment, a long absence from home, myself as a stranger. That's true enough, and it was insensitive of me to presuppose that you would want to have dinner with me when, I imagine, you would have preferred to dine alone. On the other hand, perhaps you need to talk to someone? More specifically, a – stranger. But not here and now. Tomorrow, perhaps, when you've had time to think about it."

Kate nodded. "Thank you. You're very kind – for a stranger!" She smiled suddenly, and the smile lit up her face.

Looking at her across the table, Alex thought what an attractive woman she was, and wondered why she didn't smile more often – why there was an underlying air of sadness about her, as if she had lost her direction in life and scarcely knew where to look for a signpost pointing the way ahead to happiness.

The thought occurred to him that he too was in search of a signpost

Louise Brindley

to, if not happiness, peace of mind – if such a thing was possible for him, knowing that he alone had been to blame for the loss of his wife and their son, Peter. Harm he'd inflicted as surely as if, holding a knife, he had ripped apart the fabric of their lives beyond repair.

18

Three

Next day, Alex suggested walking into town across the Spa Bridge. He had some business to attend to which shouldn't take more than a few minutes, then they might have coffee together at the Royal Hotel, if the idea appealed to her.

They met in the reception lounge at ten o'clock. Kate noticed that Alex was carrying a camera, holding the leather strap loosely in one hand, pushing a notebook into his jacket pocket with the other. "To do with my work," he explained, smiling as she came towards him.

"Work? Oh, I thought you were on holiday."

"A combination of the two, in a way. I'm writing a book on Scarborough's development as a seaside resort. At least, I'll start writing when I've found somewhere to live, which is what I am up to this morning. I've arranged to pick up a list of furnished flats to rent. Preferably something spacious and quiet, near the town centre – asking for the moon, I suppose."

"Not at this time of year," Kate said, "now the holiday season's over. I'm on the look out for somewhere myself, as a matter of fact. Not too spacious, just something small and self-contained for the time being, until . . ."

"Until?" he queried when she left the sentence unfinished.

"Until I decide whether or not to stay on here." She smiled. "Shall we go now? It's a lovely morning."

Alex obviously had a warm feeling for the town's unique situation and scenery: the magnificent sweep of the South Bay, the ruined Norman fortress on the windswept promontory dividing the South Bay from the North – a bay of equal size yet more rugged, lacking the tree-clad slopes of its neighbour.

He stopped several times to take photographs from the Spa Bridge linking the South Cliff to the town centre, apologising as he did so, explaining that he wanted to compare shots of present day Scarborough with archive photographs and paintings of the town as it was in its Victorian heyday so as to pinpoint the changes when it came to the nitty gritty of writing and compiling the manuscript.

"There's so much research to be done, it's difficult to decide where to begin," he said impatiently. "You see, what I'm after is a living portrait of the Victorian era, not a dry-as-dust text-book. I want to capture the period precisely: the kind of people who came here, with retinues of servants in tow, to drink the Spa Water, firm in their belief that it would cure everything from gout to chronic indigestion."

"Then perhaps you should think in terms of a novel," Kate suggested. "Unless you've been commissioned to write a text-book, that is?"

"No, I haven't," Alex said thoughtfully. "I haven't received a commission so far. I simply waved the idea of a book about Victorian Scarborough under my agent's nose, and he told me to go ahead with it. Its acceptance, or otherwise, is dependent on the first three chapters and synopsis."

Frowning slightly, regarding the slim figure of his companion – slender, possibly, because she ate scarcely enough to keep a bird alive – he said, "How come you're so knowledgeable on the subject of writing? You're not a writer yourself, by any chance?"

"No, I'm not. But my husband was a writer and freelance journalist by profession."

Kate hadn't meant to discuss her private affairs but, having started, she felt duty bound to offer a fuller explanation. She said hesitantly, "Don was the breadwinner, I was simply his housekeeper, trying my best to keep our marriage on course; failing utterly to do so, as it happened." She paused, looking into the past. "I should have known, should have realised all along that what my husband really wanted was not a – housekeeper – but someone much younger, far more attractive and much cleverer than myself. Well, that's all, really. He found that – someone. Need I say more? Now, I'd really rather not talk about it any more, if you don't mind."

"Fair enough," Alex conceded, thinking that Don Ford must have been a damn fool to part company with a woman of Kate's calibre. More to the point, he told her so.

"Familiarity breeds contempt," she said. "The fact is, I couldn't keep up with him. I never really tried. He was much cleverer than I. Meaningful conversations were held with other people. But I learned a lot about his work: agents, publishers, deadlines and so on. I'd have been a fool not to."

They had reached the end of the bridge, near the amazing bulk of the Grand Hotel, a mammoth red brick building standing as a kind of monument to the Victorian era. Infinitely larger and more imposing than the Crown, but not as old.

Kate said, "Greg – he's my brother – and I once walked inside, as bold as brass, to see how the rich folk lived. I thought we'd be collared and marched out by the scruff of our necks, but no-one took a blind bit of notice of us. I guess they thought we were staying there with our parents." She laughed. "Funny, I'd forgotten that until now."

"And what was it like inside?"

"Enormous. Frightening. Overpowering, smelling a bit 'foody'. I remember thinking that cabbage must be on the menu, and I didn't like cabbage."

They were in a pleasant open square with a central garden, the Grand on one side, a row of tall houses on the other, once privately owned when wealthy folk had servants at their beck and call, now mainly hotels.

Alex said, "Am I right in thinking this square has some connection with the Brontës of Haworth?"

"Oh yes. Anne Brontë died in a boarding house on the site of the Grand Hotel. Charlotte and a friend, Ellen Nussey, were with her at the time. The bridge we've just crossed was well known to them. The perfect place for a stroll and a breath of sea air, I imagine."

"Please, tell me more," Arden said persuasively.

"Well, to spare their father further distress – a third funeral in a short space of time – Charlotte decided that Anne should be laid to rest here in Scarborough. Her grave is in the churchyard near St Mary's, up yonder on the hill overlooking the Old Town."

"You obviously know a great deal about the Brontës," Arden remarked. "May I ask why?"

"It's quite simple, really. I read *Wuthering Heights* when I was fourteen – a birthday present from Greg. Difficult to explain the effect it had on me, a romantically minded, impressionable teenager, but it was mainly a strong feeling of kinship with Emily Brontë. From then on, I haunted the public library to borrow books about them. The more I read, the more fascinated I became."

Kate paused. "Greg and I had planned to visit Haworth one day. But the 'best laid schemes of mice and men . . .'" She smiled sadly. "Greg won a scholarship to Durham University, then our parents died suddenly within a year of one another. I met and married my future husband, Don Ford, within the space of a few months, and went with him to Wiltshire – a long way from home. But I took with me my dog-eared copy of *Wuthering Heights*, and if I were ever called upon to take with me one book to a desert island, that would be it."

They reached the far end of the square and crossed the road to the estate agent's office where Alex had arranged to pick up his list of accommodation. Waiting for him to emerge, Kate glanced in the window. Obviously this was an upper-crust agency. She would need something less pricey and might find what she was looking for in the "Accommodation to Rent" columns of the *Evening News*.

The coffee bar of the Royal Hotel was reasonably quiet. Finding a window table, Alex spread out the information leaflets, unhooked a gold-plated pen from the top pocket of his body-warmer and began ticking the possibilities, crossing out the improbables, drawing Kate into his game of noughts and crosses, letting his coffee go cold in the process, seeking her advice on the possibles, their situations and so on, saying he relied on her knowledge of the town to guide him in the right direction.

"You forget," she said, amused by his boyishness, "it's years since I lived here."

"I know. Even so, areas don't change all that much. Where is Weaponness, for instance?"

"Some distance away from the town centre," she told him, "and terribly 'posh', as I recall."

"Then that's out," he said decisively, crossing it from his list. "What about this? A superior self-contained furnished flat overlooking a pleasant central garden. Two bedrooms, lounge, dining room, bathroom and a large, well-equipped modern kitchen."

"Well, you did say you wanted something spacious," Kate commented drily. "Does it say where?"

He unearthed and popped on a pair of half-moon glasses. "The Crescent," he said, the spectacles perched half-way down his nose.

"The Crescent? But that's spang-bang in the town centre," Kate said eagerly, "directly opposite the old Sitwell house and Londesborough Lodge. You know, the former home of Lord and Lady Londesborough where Edward the Seventh contracted some loathsome fever or other on account of the drains, and very nearly died as a result?"

Arden shuddered slightly. "No, I didn't know, and I rather wish you hadn't told me."

"Now I remember. It was typhoid fever. But I shouldn't worry too much if I were you. I expect the drains have been fixed by now!"

Alex laughed at her teasing. "So you think this flat might be worth a visit?"

"Yes, I do. I mean, viewing costs nothing, and you'll know right away if it's right or wrong for you. When you've finished your coffee, why not go back to the estate agent's for a key to the flat?"

"OK, I'll do just that. On one condition – that you'll come with me."

"But surely you can make up your own mind? You don't need me."

"Of course I do, to point out the defects, if any; to give me the benefit of a woman's advice regarding the fixtures and fittings. Besides which, you came out with me at my invitation, and I'm not about to part company with you yet."

Kate sighed deeply. "All right, if you insist," she agreed reluctantly, wondering what she was letting herself in for, reminding herself that she had no part to play in Alex Arden's life, that it was her own future, not his, that really concerned her. Despite his charm, his quirky sense of humour and his mature good looks, she realised full well the necessity of standing firm and strong on her own two feet, within her own depth, not his.

They hadn't far to walk to the Crescent and there had been no problem about handing over the keys of the flat since, as Alex explained, he and the estate agent had met socially on several occasions, and the man knew he was unlikely to make off with the family silver.

"Is that the Sitwell house over there?" he asked.

"No, that's Londesborough Lodge. The Sitwell house is further along, behind that high brick wall." Kate felt on familiar territory here. Scarcely anything had changed at all. It was just as she remembered it.

The flat was certainly spacious. On the top floor of a tall house midway along the terrace, its front windows overlooked the garden and the honey-coloured façade of Londesborough Lodge.

Alex spent some time at the drawing room window, enjoying the view, before turning his attention to the rest of the flat. "Well, Kate, what do you think of it?" he asked when they had made a tour of inspection. "I sense an air of disapproval. Am I right? Come on, speak up. Tell me what you've got against it."

"It's too fussy," she said frankly, looking distastefully at the ornaments arrayed on the marble mantelpiece, the many side-tables adorned with bobble-fringed lampshades, the deep, obviously comfortable and expensive settee and armchairs grouped around the fireplace. "You couldn't write here, not in this room at any rate. The only sizeable table is in the dining room, and that's far too highly polished. I'm sorry, Alex, but what you need is something more functional, much plainer. Somewhere you could work without worrying about the furniture. A place with a good old-fashioned kitchen table, for instance, to spread out your notes and photographs, your typewriter and so forth."

"You are quite right, of course," he admitted. "I got carried away with the view. The practicalities escaped me. Now you can see why I needed your advice."

Kate wondered in what surroundings he usually did his writing? Don had always professed himself unable to write anywhere except his studio or his London office. There had been a spare room in the cottage which he'd refused to use because of "household distractions". She had known he meant her.

Alex said, "I'd better return the key to the agent, then we'll find somewhere to have lunch. Or am I taking too much for granted?"

When Alex had returned the key, explaining that the flat was not quite what he'd had in mind, after passing the Royal Hotel, they walked along St Nicholas Street, Kate glancing about her at the buildings, noticing the changes wrought by the passage of time, regretting the loss of Marshall and Snelgrove's department store in particular. The façade was still intact, but the shop itself had been carved up into separate units occupied by a variety of traders including a furniture retailer's, and a catering firm advertising "Coffee, Snacks, Hot Soup, and Fish and Chips"!

Alex said gently, "The old order changeth, you know, Kate?"

"I know," she said, "but that doesn't make it easier to bear."

"Perhaps you are looking at the past through rose-tinted glasses?" he suggested.

"You could be right," she confessed, "but isn't that the charm of youth? The ability to see the world through rose-tinted glasses?"

"I wouldn't really know," he said quietly. "The fact is, I was sent to boarding school, aged ten, by parents who couldn't wait to get rid of me." He smiled grimly. "They made no secret of the fact that I stood in the way of their full enjoyment of life. Their trips abroad, and so on. So no rose-tinted glasses for a little lad scared almost witless by the harsh school discipline he was faced with, with no one to turn to for comfort and support.

"You, at least, had a happy, fulfilled childhood with your parents and your brother, Greg. I envy you that, Kate. I really do!"

Kate said simply, "I'm so sorry, Alex. I had no idea."

"It really doesn't matter any more, does it? What matters is not the past but the future?"

Kate asked, on a sudden impulse, "Tell me, Alex, have you ever been married?"

He screwed up his eyes against the sunlight of the bright October day. "Once, long ago," he confessed wearily. "But, taking a leaf from your own book, I'd rather not discuss the matter further, if you don't mind! Just tell me, where do we go from here?"

They were standing at a crossroads: St Thomas Street straight ahead, Westborough on the left, Newborough on the right, St Nicholas Street behind them.

"Let's try Newborough, shall we?" Kate said, tucking her hand into the crook of his elbow, guiding him gently, as she might have done a little boy for whom she felt suddenly responsible.

"I thought we might walk down to the Foreshore," she said, self-consciously removing her hand, thinking, How ridiculous – a little boy indeed! "There's a fish restaurant near the harbour. At least there used to be."

Walking downhill towards the Old Town in the lee of Castle Hill, suddenly the old fortress seemed to dominate the skyline, appearing almost benign and friendly, gilded with October sunlight.

The thoroughfare was lined with modern shopfronts – shops geared mainly to the sale of goods likely to appeal to summer visitors, thin on the ground now that the holiday season was over.

Passing the old George Hotel, Kate paused to look at a gift shop window packed with mementos of Scarborough, with soft toys, baubles, bangles and beads, her eye caught by a series of hand-written adverts offering second-hand bargains for sale – prams, bicycles, washing-machines, cookers, job lots of furniture and other unwanted items – among which she spied a card: "Accommodation to Let.

Maisonette, fully furnished, two beds, bathroom, kitchen, sitting room. Sea views. Attic studio. Reasonable rent. Enquire Within."

Standing beside her, Alex read the card through his half-moon glasses. "Wherein lies the snag?" he asked. "There must be one."

"Only one way to find out," Kate reminded him. "Shall we go in and ask?"

"Lead on, Macduff," he laughed, "though it's probably chatty, with mouse droppings on the kitchen floor."

"O ye of little faith," she said light-heartedly, entering the shop.

They were directed to a private entrance round the corner from the shop. A long flight of stairs led up to a sitting room, kitchen, bathroom and bedrooms. More stairs, narrow and somewhat rickety, led to an attic studio.

"Ye gods," Alex breathed ecstatically, approaching a wide dormer window overlooking the South Bay. "Now that's what I call a view! This is *it*, Kate! Absolutely perfect! Just what I had in mind! What do *you* think?"

"I agree with you. It *is* perfect. And no mouse droppings on the kitchen floor. Oh, Alex, I'm so pleased for you. Now you'll be able to get on with your book uninterrupted!"

"I have you to thank. If it hadn't been for you . . ." He paused, then added, "You will have dinner with me tonight, won't you, by way of a celebration?"

"Dinner?" she said, tongue-in-cheek. "We haven't even had lunch yet."

Four

A lex's housing problem settled, it was time for Kate to give some thought to her own, to which end she approached various agencies and looked at several flats before deciding, the following day, on a sitting room and kitchen combined, with an en-suite bedroom, overlooking the Valley Bridge and the steep, wooded gardens below.

The sitting room, reasonably well furnished, light and airy by reason of a Victorian bay window and high ceiling, was divided from the kitchen by a kind of bar-counter, behind which stood a sink unit, cupboards and work surfaces, a small electric cooker, mini refrigerator, electric kettle and a stand containing various pots and pans. More than adequate, Kate reckoned, for the requirements of a single person who wouldn't be doing much cooking anyway.

She had hoped for a separate bathroom with a proper bath, not a shower unit. But this was the best accommodation she had seen so far, and she loved the view from the sitting room window: the feeling of space imparted by the bridge into town, and a sense of life going on around her from the constant flow of traffic and pedestrians crossing the bridge; the many criss-crossing paths leading down through a thickly wooded area of autumn-tinted trees to Valley Road – a wide thoroughfare running from east to west like an artery pumping life-blood to the town centre, the Spa and the seafront of Scarborough.

To her surprise and disappointment, Alex Arden had left the Crown Hotel without bothering to say goodbye to her. From a distance, she had caught sight of him stowing his luggage into the boot of a silver-grey Mercedes. She hadn't even known he owned a car. Scarcely surprising since she knew next to nothing about the man apart from his penchant for *The Times* newspaper, his literary ambitions, that he had once been married. Above all, that he had made use of her.

Well, she had been made use of before today, and in all probability she would be again, Kate surmised, as she waited for the removal of her own luggage, by taxi, two days later. Men, she thought bitterly, Who needed them anyway?

She felt lonely at first in her strange new surroundings. This was a sizeable house with broad landings and passages, carved up into various flats and bed-sits, but she didn't see a soul as she went upstairs to her third floor apartment to start unpacking. Well, what had she expected? A brass band, balloons, a "Welcome Home" sign?

Then, opening the door, she saw a letter on the carpet. Greg and Cindy had written to wish her luck in her new home: the letter was enclosed in a greetings card embellished with white heather and a silver horseshoe. Close to tears, she propped up the card on the mantelpiece. Then came a knock at the door, and an elderly woman handed her a bunch of flowers in Cellophane, tied with a red ribbon bow.

"These came for you, dear," the woman said, "and I've brought you a few teabags and a jug of milk in case you felt like a cuppa."

"Oh, how kind of you. Won't you come in?"

"No, dear. I don't want to intrude. But if there's anything else you need, my room's downstairs. Room six. Don't be afraid to ask. My name's Fanny, by the way. I'm what you might call the caretaker. Leastways, I clean the stairs and the front entrance. Keeps me out of mischief."

"I'm Kate Ford. And thank you so much for taking care of my flowers; for the teabags and milk. I'll put the kettle on right away."

"That's right, dear. I always says there's nowt like a good hot cuppa to make you feel at home."

That brief encounter with Fanny had made all the difference to Kate. Fanny, the card, the letter and the flowers Greg had sent her, cheered her enormously. And the flowers were lovely, a dozen long-stemmed red roses. Greg would have ordered them himself, Kate knew, by-passing the seasonal, common-or-garden chrysanthemums in favour of something special. "For Someone Special", was written on the card tucked into the bouquet.

Later, when she had unpacked and stowed away her belongings, she went up the road to the Ramshill Road shops to buy eggs, bread, butter, milk and cornflakes, planning a simple supper of scrambled eggs on toast – a far cry from the more exotic fare of the Crown Hotel, especially the "celebration" meal she'd eaten with Alex Arden a few nights ago.

She wondered how he was getting on in his new environment. Chances were, feeling hungry, he would eat at the nearest restaurant. Hardly likely that he would be bothered to cook for himself, a man accustomed to the good things in life. Unlikely they would meet again, except by chance. Bumping into each other in the street, perhaps?

Twilight was falling when she returned home. This was the time of day she loved best: street lamps springing into bloom against the encroaching darkness of night, the sky a greenish blue, translucent as a robin's eggshell, a slip of a moon, a scattering of stars.

Crossing to the window, Kate saw that the Valley Bridge was aglow with the head and tail lights of homegoing traffic, resembling rubies and diamonds strung on a slender gold chain. In the distance, the concentrated glow of the town centre lamps and neon shop signs lit up the sky as twilight faded and night swallowed up the remains of the day.

Going through to her bedroom, Kate undressed, showered, then put on her old favourite dressing gown, warm and comfortable with knitted cuffs and a stand up collar. Returning to the living room, she switched on her radio to the opening strains of Debussy's *Clair de Lune*.

The last thing she wanted was to watch television. The set squatted opposite an armchair drawn up near the hearth of what must have been an open fireplace when this house had been a private dwelling, with servants to clean the grates, riddle the ashes and bring up scuttles of coal from the cellars.

The fireplace was now boarded up, and the hearth contained an electric fire with a simulated coal effect. Suddenly Kate recalled April Cottage: open fireplaces and log fires, gazing into the heart of the flames, firelight dancing on walls and ceilings. All over and done with now.

Preparing her supper of scrambled eggs, she wondered suddenly what the hell she was doing here. A stranger in a strange place, virtually alone in the world apart from Greg and Cindy, and Fanny on the floor below.

Come Monday, she thought, she must try to find herself employment of some kind, however menial, to give herself some purpose in life, a sense of direction connected to precise time-keeping and getting up early to wash, dress and breakfast.

But what if nobody wanted her? How could she possibly spend her days confined within this circumscribed living space of hers, however comfortable and well furnished, or wandering the streets of Scarborough like a lost soul, tormented by memories of past happiness? She simply couldn't, and she knew it! On the other hand, how could she possibly return to the Greater Manchester area to spend her days in a mental and physical straitjacket?

Kate knew that Greg would welcome her return with open arms. She also knew that his wife, Cindy, was and always had been jealous of their brother and sister relationship, which made her feel like an outsider when their shared memories of the past came uppermost in conversation. And in no way would she, Kate, wish to drive a wedge of dissention between husband and wife, however innocently. She knew, for instance, that Greg would not have told Cindy about the bouquet of red roses he'd sent her, "For Someone Special!", for the simple reason that her dispassionate sister-in-law, brought up within the compass of a large family – seven siblings all told, had no way of understanding how close just two siblings, one brother and his sister, had grown towards one another in the halcyon days of their youth and childhood.

Switching on the electric fire and a red-shaded table lamp beside the armchair, she ate her supper seated on a high stool at the room-dividing counter, deriving comfort from the lights of home beyond the window, the flame effect of the fire, the glow of the red-shaded lamp; listening to piano music, Listz, Chopin, Rachmaninoff – a calming influence on her unsettled state of mind, wondering what she could do to make the flat more homely.

Tomorrow, perhaps, she would rearrange the furniture? Clean the cooker, sink and work surfaces, buy a Sunday paper from the newsagent's in Ramshill Road and, if the little supermarket was open, purchase washing-up liquid, other cleaning materials, plus cheese, macaroni – not spaghetti! She would never willingly eat spaghetti again for as long as she lived.

Kate missed her garden – the joy and physical exercise involved in weeding, planting and hoeing, imbuing her life with a sense of purpose when Don was away from home, as she missed what she would always think of as "her" wood where, often, when she stood quite still, wild creatures – baby rabbits, robins, squirrels – came close to her, betraying no fear at her presence in their midst.

She had never told Don about the wood, and so it had become her secret sanctuary at times of stress, especially after the loss of her first child, a son, almost perfectly formed, yet lacking a heartbeat. But that had not prevented her giving him a name – Roland. Her other two unborn babies she had named April and Jonathan, in her heart of hearts.

How strange that she had felt unable to share, with Don, those secret components of her life, just as he had felt unable to confess to his adultery with that "other woman" until Lucia's pregnancy had forced the issue into the open.

Then had come the bitter realisation that their marriage possessed little more substance than a sandcastle built within reach of the incoming tide, albeit a brave little sandcastle initially, with a deeply dug moat and little paper flags flying from the sand-pie parapets.

"Never mind, Sis," Greg used to say, drying her tears of disappointment, "we'll build a better castle tomorrow, just you wait and see!"

Now, that tomorrow was here! Her marriage was over and done with. She was no longer a starry-eyed girl but a middle-aged woman vaguely attempting to create a new life from the ruins of the old, with little or no guarantee of success unless she built the future ahead of her, not on sand, but solid rocks far beyond the reach of the incoming tide!

As she got ready for an early night, exhausted by the exigencies of the long day behind her, the doorbell connecting her flat to the world outside suddenly rang shrilly and repeatedly until, clad in her dressing gown and slippers, she hurried downstairs to answer the summons.

Alex Arden, the last person on earth she had expected to see, was on the doorstep.

"What on earth are you doing here, at this time of night?" Kate demanded fiercely. "In any case, how did you find me?"

"With considerable difficulty," he said urbanely. "In reply to your first question, I really need to talk to you, Kate. In any case, why 'at this time of night'? It's scarcely ten o'clock yet!"

"Can't it wait till morning?"

"Very well, then, if you insist. Shall we say ten o'clock, at my flat? No need to breakfast beforehand. I'll have coffee and croissants awaiting your arrival!" And then he was gone, swallowed up by the darkness of the October night, leaving behind him, on the doorstep, a bouquet of pink carnations and a bottle of Perrier water, which must have been there all the time, if she had taken the trouble to notice.

Kate scarcely slept at all that night in her stange new bed, wondering what on earth Alex wanted to talk to her about. At the same time she was faced with the realisation that she had been inordinately pleased to see him again despite her acid words spoken in the heat of the moment, and had been disappointed that she was looking far from her best in her dressing gown and slippers, her face devoid of make-up, her hair still damp from the shower.

His flowers she had arranged to their best advantage in a water-jug that she'd discovered in one of the kitchen cupboards and placed on her bedroom chest of drawers.

Up and doing early next morning, she moved a small settee nearer to the fireplace, the chair closer to the window – as a kind of "seat in the circle". Next to it, she placed a small round table, handy for library books, reading glasses and so on, for when she got around to joining the library, which she fully intended in due course, to catch up on all the books she had always meant to read. An exciting prospect. Never too late to learn, she thought, removing several gimcrack ornaments from the mantelpiece and stowing them away in a kitchen cupboard.

A woman of simple taste, a homemaker by nature, she deplored the "busy" wallpaper and carpet. Nothing to be done about the latter, but a couple of coats of emulsion paint would soon put paid to the jazzily patterned paper and create a more restful background, provided she could borrow a step-ladder. She must ask Fanny about that later. Not today. Sunday was probably the old lady's day of rest.

Thankfully, the paintwork would need nothing more than a good wash with hot soapy water, and the plain moss-green velour curtains did not clash too violently with the green and brown carpet or the dralon-covered settee and armchair. This, after all, was temporary accommodation, so no use spending a small fortune on redecoration until she knew for certain whether or not she would remain here for any length of time: the future dependent on finding work of some kind to obviate the necessity of delving into capital or the meek acceptance of Don's quarterly hand-outs.

At half-past eight, ready for action, Kate went to the small supermarket – open for business as she had suspected it would be – to purchase her cleaning materials, plus various items of tinned and frozen foods to store in her kitchen cupboards and the deep-freeze compartment of her work-top refrigerator, feeling guilty as she did so.

Never, in her April Cottage days, would she have even dreamt of buying convenience food! Frozen chips and fish-fingers, of all things! Ready-made stew and dumplings! Had she gone raving mad all of a sudden? But did it really matter what she ate nowadays as long as it proved sufficient to keep body and soul together? Why cling to worn out shibboleths and customs no longer valid in her present circumstances?

At a quarter to ten she set off to walk to Newborough for her meeting with Alex Arden, pondering the reason why he had proffered this strange invitation to have breakfast with him? Not lunch or dinner, but *breakfast*, of all things!

Reasonably she assumed it was because she had refused to talk to him the night before. But how could she possibly have invited him up to her flat in a state of dishabille? Standing on the doorstep, she had felt that she was being watched, had noticed the slight twitching of a net curtain at a ground floor window by someone anxious to get a better view of the grey Mercedes parked in the road outside the iron gate.

"Sorry about last night," Arden said laconically, by way of a greeting. "I didn't mean to embarrass you. I should have realised you'd be under surveillance by nosey-parkering neighbours." He chuckled. "I couldn't help noticing the twitching of the front room curtains.

"Make yourself comfortable," he continued, leading the way upstairs to the living room, "while I make the coffee and warm up the croissants."

Sitting down, Kate noticed that the table had been set with cutlery, plates, butter and a pot of marmalade. "Thanks for the flowers," she called out to him, wondering why he had put them on the doorstep instead of handing them to her. Better not to ask, she decided. Possibly he had felt it inappropriate to appear as a Greek bearing gifts after his hurried departure from the Crown Hotel without bothering to say goodbye to her. She had not forgotten or entirely forgiven his lack of sensitivity on that occasion.

"Mugs all right?" he asked, appearing from the kitchen.

"Fine. But if you mean you haven't any cups, why bother to ask?"

"The thing I like best about you, Kate," he said, setting down the tray, "is the way you speak your mind straight out. No prevarication, no archness or pretence, and let the barbs fall where they may."

"In which case, why am I here? You said you wanted to talk to me. What about?"

"Frankly, I need help with my research," he said bluntly, taking a leaf from her book. "We made a good team, I thought, and you are familiar with the town and its history, which would help me enormously. It could be quite fun, don't you think?"

33

Kate paused momentarily. "I'm sorry, Alex," she said. "The answer has to be no."

"No?" Arden frowned, surprised by her negative response. "But why not? I've said I'm sorry about last night. Surely we can discuss the matter further?"

"There's nothing to discuss. The fact is, I'm planning to find myself a job. I need to earn a living. If I were a lady of leisure, money no object, I'd enjoy helping you. As things stand, I can't afford the luxury of a 'fun' pursuit."

"I see." Alex poured more coffee from the percolator. "What kind of work are you looking for ?"

"Anything that's available. I'm not qualified for anything in particular. Housework, maybe. I'm quite used to that. Cooking, perhaps."

"Can you type?"

"No."

"Not to worry. That isn't important. You could easily learn. It's just a question of mastering the keyboard."

'I bet that's what Chopin was told by his music teacher!'

Arden laughed. "How about sewing?"

"What kind of sewing? Embroidery? Dressmaking?"

"Plain sewing. Curtains."

"Yes, I've made curtains." She frowned. "What is all this?"

"Well, it comes under the heading of an interview." Alex smiled, obviously enjoying being mysterious – a facet of his quirky sense of humour.

"An interview for *what*?" Kate demanded, losing patience.

"The job I'm about to offer you as my personal assistant cum cook-housekeeper and seamstress. I'll need new curtains throughout," he said matter-of-factly. "Plain curtains. I really can't live with all this chintz."

Kate looked at him in amazement. 'Is this some kind of joke?"

"Not at all. You need a job, I need help. It's a matter of supply and demand. Hours flexible, to suit both parties, excellent rates of pay, plus overtime as applicable. Well, what do you say?"

"I don't know what to say." It hadn't sunk in that she had been offered a job at all, much less one that she could cope with and would, in all probability, enjoy very much. It seemed too good to be true.

"Damn it," Alex said, "those croissants are still in the oven. I'd better rescue them before they're burnt black."

View from a Balcony

Kate guessed he had made that an excuse to give her time to think things over, and was grateful for the respite. But what, after all, had she got to lose? She could cook, clean and sew curtains standing on her head: second nature to a housewife of twenty years. It was the research aspect of the job that intrigued her most of all.

When Alex returned with the croissants, he said lightly, "Guess what? I forgot to switch on the oven!"

Kate said, "When would you want me to start?"

Five

A lex had been teasing her about making curtains, Kate discovered. He would take the measurements, then she could choose the materials at a shop specialising in the ready-made variety.

"Good lord, girl," he said, "you didn't really imagine I'd expect you to slave over a hot sewing-machine, did you?"

Frankly, Kate hadn't known what to expect in her capacity as general factotum to a quixotic character like Alex. The *un*expected most likely!

She'd felt embarrassed at first by the rates of pay he'd suggested over the croissants and coffee that Sunday morning. "I'm sorry, but I couldn't possibly accept that amount," she'd said quickly, decisively.

"Why? Isn't it enough?"

"Not enough? It's far too much!"

"Allow me to be the judge of that," he'd countered swiftly. "You'll earn every penny, believe me! Wait till you're on your knees in the kitchen with a scrubbing brush and a bucket of hot water!"

Knowing he was joking about that at any rate, she'd said, "I still think you are being over generous, and I'm not looking for – charity."

"The thought never entered my mind. Plainly and simply, I need someone to take care of me. Above all, to help me with my research. Someone of taste and discernment with a brain in her head and a depth of feeling for the place she still thinks of as home. You, Kate, are that 'someone'. Need I say more?"

The weather had changed abruptly. Wind and rain had put paid to the Indian Summer days which seemed almost dreamlike now that November was here.

Kate realised Alex would need new curtains, lined to keep out the draughts of cold air rattling the windows, particularly those of his attic studio which, to her surprise, now contained a business-like desk, swivel chair, several metal filing cabinets, bookshelves, wall-to-wall carpet, a divan bed, and two long, Dimplex heaters turned on at full blast.

"You've certainly been busy," Kate commented, wandering from room to room on her first day at work, noticing various other additions to her employer's living space: leather armchairs to supplement the sitting room furniture; a brand new electric fire in the hearth; thick rugs on the floor. In the kitchen, new pots and pans, cups and saucers and electrical equipment. In the bathroom, a heated towel-rail and a newly installed shower-unit. "You must have spent a small fortune."

"Money has never been a particular problem of mine," he said edgily, "thanks to my parents who left me well provided for when they had the misfortune to die together in a car crash on the Route Nationale." He paused momentarily, then continued, "They were on their way to Arles, at the time, to witness a bull-fight, so I'm told. My father was at the steering wheel of the car – most probably drunk, knowing him! At any rate, he pulled out to overtake the car ahead of him and smashed headlong into an oncoming lorry."

"I'm so sorry," Kate said. "How dreadful for you."

"Not as dreadful, I imagine," Alex replied bitterly, "as witnessing the death of a magnificent animal in a blood-soaked arena. Now, let's change the subject, shall we?"

"Yes, of course." At that stage, Kate put forward her idea of planning menus on a monthly basis; mealtimes and so on.

"Oh, to hell with all that," Alex interrupted wearily. "Feed me baked beans on toast! Pig-swill, for all I care! My main concern, right now, is getting to grips with the history of Scarborough's development as a seaside resort. If only I knew where to begin."

"Then why not begin at the beginning, with Scarborough's first ever custom-built hotel?" Kate suggested quietly.

"You mean – the Grand?" Arden asked.

Kate shook her head. "Oh no, not the Grand – the Crown. The Grand came later. The Crown came first," she told him, remembering her underlying reasons for wanting to stay there in a balcony room overlooking the South Bay: because of its uniqueness and because generations of Victorian families, long dead and gone, had stayed there way back in the mid-1800s, those inhabitants of a world distanced far from the present-day world of the 1970s, devoid of the horse and carriage, bustles and parasols.

At least she, Kate, had achieved a long-cherished ambition to keep company with the ghosts of all those people who had once stood on the balcony before her.

Next day, she and Arden went to the library to research the history of the Crown Hotel from bound volumes of the *Scarborough Gazette and Herald* dating back to the last century. They turned the brittle pages with great care, making notes, exclaiming excitedly when one or the other came across nuggets of information relevant to their quest. Like digging for buried treasure and finding it, Kate thought.

Glancing at Alex, she recalled the bitterness in his voice when he had spoken about his parents, and realised that, despite his veneer of charm, she still knew nothing about him or his past life apart from his lonely childhood and his, presumably, failed marriage. Not even his writing background, how many and what kind of books he had published, or where he came from. Nor was she likely to find out unless he imparted the information of his own volition.

But wasn't she in the same boat? A woman with her own secrets to keep, fearful of intrusion into her personal life? Or had she already revealed too much in confessing that Don had left her for another woman? Why had Alex's marriage failed, she wondered. Had his wife been having an affair? Or had *he*?

"Have you noticed, Kate," Alex said suddenly, "the many references to one John Fairgray Sharpin, the first tenant manager of the Crown Hotel? According to this, the Crown was built by a consortium of businessmen smart enough to realise that the old coaching inns and hostelries, beloved of Charles Dickens, would soon become redundant when the railways came into being."

"Yes, I had noticed. They must have had their heads screwed on the right way."

"What puzzles me is their choice of a manager," Arden continued. "A man in his early twenties, a Yorkshireman by birth, a wine merchant by profession, ambitious enough to open his own business in London – but it failed miserably by all accounts. Rather odd, wouldn't you say?"

"That depends on what he had to offer. Youth, flair, enthusiasm, imagination. Presumably his job as a warehouseman failed to satisfy his creative instincts. I came across a reference to him as a man of vision. I have it down here somewhere."

She riffled through her notepad. "Yes, here it is. 'A Man of Vision, small in stature yet possessed of an abundant energy and engaging in manner. By means of clever advertisement in certain prestigious London newspapers, extolling the excellent amenities of The Crown Hotel, the unparalled splendour of its position overlooking the South Bay and its close proximity to the Spa, notable for the health-giving properties of its mineral water, Mr John Fairgray Sharpin has successfully lured to our shores the *crème de la crème* of high ranking members of the aristocracy, Churchmen, Members of Parliament and many other distinguished personages.' "

Kate laughed. "Well, there you have it! Nothing succeeds like success! J.F.S. – as he was affectionately referred to by his peers on the Town Council when he became Britain's youngest ever mayor – must have been quite a man! A force to be reckoned with! Can't help wishing I'd been alive at the time to shake hands with him."

"Perhaps you were, "Arden said unexpectedly, "if, like me, you believe in reincarnation?"

"I don't, as it happens," Kate said levelly, suppressing a shudder, as if a goose had walked over her grave. "I think that one appearance on this merry-go-round we call life is more than enough for anyone to endure. I'm not into retrogression or whatever it's called. The here and now is quite enough for me to come to terms with." She paused a moment, then, "I've had enough of research for one day," she said lightly. "In any case, it's almost lunch time."

They spent the afternoon in the attic studio, collating the notes they had made earlier, making comparisons, putting various dates in order, beginning with the opening of the Crown Hotel in the year 1844, to create a precise framework of known facts vital to a history of Scarborough's emergence as a famous seaside resort. Yet Kate was far more intrigued by the personality of John Fairgray Sharpin.

Leaving Alex to type his notes, Kate went down to the kitchen to begin the shepherd's pie she'd planned for supper, having told Alex that she wanted to leave early that evening to decorate her flat. Peeling potatoes, she thought about those old copies of the *Scarborough Gazette* that she had looked at that morning; her joy of discovery as if the past had suddenly come alive, especially reading those lists of visitors to the Crown Hotel in its Victorian heyday. Among them earls and countesses, lords and ladies, high ranking politicians, generals, rear admirals and churchmen.

There had also been detailed descriptions of the food served at various banquets and dinner parties, balls and other functions: salmon mousse, quails' eggs in aspic, game, poultry, roast meats, rich desserts. Little wonder, she thought, that they needed the restorative properties of Spa mineral water to offset the dire effects of so much rich food; gargantuan breakfasts and five course luncheons into the bargain. The miracle was that women of that era did not burst out of their whaleboned stays in the face of such gluttony at table.

But what of the retinues of common-or-garden folk, the ladies' maids, footmen and coachmen in attendance on their lords and masters? Scarcely likely they would have stuffed themselves to repletion in the servants' dining hall. Possibly they had been too tired to care about anything but sleep once they had finished work.

The working conditions of the lower classes of that era touched Kate deeply. She hoped that the book Alex was about to write would not focus entirely on the leisure pursuits of the rich and famous. The more she thought about it, the more she wished that he would try his hand at a novel. She had a strong feeling, however, that he would go for the softer option of a non-fiction book.

At twenty to seven, she called up to him that supper was ready, anxious to get the meal over with as soon as possible. She was running late this evening, but there was still no sign of him and time was ticking away.

At this rate, it would be half seven at least by the time the meal was eaten. This really was too bad of him, she thought angrily, keeping her waiting unnecessarily when she had other things to do. Oh, drat the man! What was keeping him! Then she'd have the washing up to see to, the pots to put away – which meant she wouldn't be home till eight, at the earliest.

When Alex eventually put in an appearance, "I was just about to leave," Kate said, bringing the food to the table.

"But we haven't eaten yet!" Alex raised his eyebrows. "Is anything the matter?"

"Since you ask, I'm finding my working hours a bit too flexible for my liking."

"You mean I'm taking up too much of your time?" he lay down his cutlery. "But I thought you understood there'd be no hard and fast rules. I assumed that ours would be a working relationship based on friendship. Apparently I was wrong."

Kate said coldly, "You're missing the point. What you seem to forget is that I have affairs of my own to attend to."

"Such as?"

"My flat, if you must know! The sitting room's in a state of chaos. The curtains down, carpet turned back, paint rollers everywhere, not to mention the stepladder I borrowed from my downstair's neighbour. I *did* tell you! Apparently you weren't listening!"

"You mean you are decorating? Doing it yourself? But that's crazy! Why didn't you tell me? I'd have hired a firm to do it for you!"

"The reason *why* I didn't tell you! I happen to prefer doing some things myself, to retain a modicum of independence. And it would help if you came down to meals on time!"

"I see. So I'm being punished for keeping you waiting a few minutes? For keeping you from your blasted paint tins and rollers? Most women would want to go home to get on with their knitting; read a good book. But no, not you!"

"I'm not 'most women'," Kate retorted. "In any case, it wasn't a few minutes, but twenty!"

Arden sighed deeply, impatiently. "But nothing was spoiling, was it? After all, a shepherd's pie!"

"That's beside the point. For all you knew, it might have been a — cheese soufflé!"

"In which case, you'd probably have stormed upstairs and dragged me down by the hair!"

"Don't put ideas into my head!"

"All right, Kate," Alex conceded. "You win! So let's take it from here, shall we? Unless you're thinking of handing in your notice. *Are* you?"

"I'm not sure," she retorted, angry with herself for being angry, remembering the many occasions Don had gone missing at mealtimes, leaving the food she'd cooked for him untasted; disappearing in the direction of the village pub, staying there till well past closing time.

Intuitively, Arden said, "You'll have to let go of the past sooner or later, you know that, don't you?"

"I don't know what you mean," she snapped back at him defensively.

"Of course you do! You pride yourself on your honesty, so why not face up to the fact that, unlike Lazarus, the past can't be resurrected? However hard you try, it's gone, over and done with. Now, sit down and eat your supper, then I'll drive you home and give you a hand with the decorating."

"Oh for heaven's sake, Alex," she said wearily, "at least try to be practical. You know damn well what I'm up against. The twitching of the net curtains, remember?"

"So what is it you're afraid of?" he said bluntly. "Shocking the neighbours? Or are you too proud to accept help when it's offered? Independence is one thing, letting false pride ruin your life's a different matter entirely.

"Think about it, Kate! True independence means not giving a toss what other people think of you, and I should know. Why, do you imagine, do I behave so badly at times? I'll tell you why. Because, that way, I can't be categorised as a good guy or a bad. It's the best form of self defence I know. You should try it yourself sometimes.

"Look at it this way. In my experience, the bitchy women of this world fare somewhat better than the haloed variety. The meek don't always inherit the earth, you know?"

"And have *you* inherited the earth?" Kate asked coolly.

Arden laughed softly. "No, far from. But I've enjoyed building up my defence system against the holier-than-thou brethren of this particular planet!"

"I see." Kate smiled, heartened by the devil-may-care cheek of the man. "Very well, then, I accept your offer of help. So let's get started on the decorating, shall we?"

Six

This was a facet of Arden's character Kate had never suspected or would have believed existed had she not seen him on the step-ladder wielding the paint-roller with the panache of a professional decorator.

What a surprising person he was, and how quickly he was getting on with it, she thought, on her knees washing the skirting boards.

Later, she made coffee, which they drank near the uncurtained window. "You certainly have a lovely view from here," he remarked, coffee mug in hand. "We Londoners have street lights in abundance, no views worth mentioning. Lots of parks and open spaces, of course, but nothing comparable to the feeling of space and freedom I've discovered here in Scarborough."

He spoke softly, as if to himself. Kate remained silent, unwilling to break his train of thought, hopeful of further disclosures of his background. None was forthcoming.

At least she knew now that he lived in London, possibly within striking distance of some park or other. But which? Regent's, St James's, Green Park? Impossible to decide which, though she'd bet her bottom dollar on St James's.

Not that she knew London all that well. She had simply gone there occasionally with Don, in the early days of their marriage when, as a freelance theatre critic, he'd attended various matinée performances, leaving her to her own devices.

He'd been faintly amused that she had spent those afternoons sightseeing from the upstairs of double-decker buses. It was amazing how much she'd gleaned about that teeming city from those lumbering red vehicles. Changing buses frequently, she had revelled in the sight of famous landmarks: St Paul's Cathedral, Marble Arch, the Houses of Parliament, Westminster Abbey, the Albert Hall, the Tower of London.

A young bride, proud of her clever, successful husband, she had never stopped to wonder why she was not included in those theatre visits of his.

The reason why not seemed abundantly clear to her now. As long ago as that, there must have been other women in his life of whom she had been blissfully unaware. What a naive fool he must have thought her, a starry-eyed teenager content to lumber round London on double-decker buses whilst he was palm-paddling his latest female conquest.

When they had finished their coffee, Alex moved the ladder to begin painting the fireplace wall. "With luck," he said, "I'll have this finished in an hour or so. Then, tomorrow morning, when the paint's dry, I'll hang the curtains and re-lay the carpet."

"Thanks, Alex," Kate said, "I can't thank you enough."

"No thanks necessary," he assured her. "Anything to help a damsel in distress – to make up for the shepherd's pie hiatus. I'm really sorry about that."

He meant what he said; knew he behaved badly at times. His many faults and failings, of which he was acutely aware, included a degree of arrogance, shortness of temper, fondness of having his own way, inability to suffer fools gladly, an inclination to take down a peg or two the sycophants and the "pompous bastards" who crossed his path now and then.

But never, by word or deed would he willingly hurt or offend Kate Ford, whose friendship and plain speaking he valued as pearls beyond price. This woman was no fool, no sycophant, and he knew it.

They were talking and laughing when suddenly, without warning, the door was flung open and an elderly man, obviously angry, clad in pyjamas, a dressing gown and slippers, barged into the room.

"Fine goings on, I must say," he thundered. "But make no mistake, I shall write a letter of complaint to the landlord first thing in the morning!"

Rounding fiercely on Kate, who obviously hadn't a clue who he was, "I've warned him time and time again of the inadvisability of letting his flats to unsuitable tenants: flighty women such as yourself who bring in their 'fancy' men without a by-your-leave."

Perched atop the ladder, paint-roller in hand, Alex said – equably for him, "Tell me, sir, do you make a habit of bursting into other people's flats – without a by-your-leave – clad in your night attire? If so, I may

44

well write a letter of complaint to your landlord warning him against the advisability of letting his flats to evil-minded octagenarians such as yourself."

Dismounting from the ladder without undue haste, facing the old man and towering above him, Alex continued levelly, "Tell me, sir, have you a solicitor? I mean a really *good* solicitor?"

"Huh?" The old man's mouth sagged open, revealing his toothless gums. "I don't know what you mean. What would I want with a – solicitor?"

"I thought that would have been perfectly obvious to a clever fellow like you," Alex said coolly. "Or perhaps the services of a barrister would be a safer bet in a trial for slander when your case comes to Court.

"You see, old son, I shall make it my business to sue the pants off you for referring to Mrs Ford as a 'flighty' woman, myself as her 'fancy' man."

He added mischievously, "Needless to say, I shall look forward enormously to your definition of a 'fancy' man from the witness box; a 'flighty' woman, come to that.

"Do remember, my dear sir, that when your case comes to Court, you will have to swear, on oath, that upon bursting into Mrs Ford's flat, clad in your night apparel, you found myself atop a ladder, paint-roller in hand; Mrs Ford on her hands and knees washing the skirting boards. Scarcely a romantic situation, wouldn't you say?"

"Oh, very well then," the old man mumbled, "have it your own way."

"I fully intend to," Alex said grimly. "The trouble with nasty-minded people like you, they poison the atmosphere with the sheer filth of their warped imaginations.

"Now, I suggest that you get the hell out of here before I evict you forcibly with . . ." Arden's lips twitched upwards in a smile. "Well, that's up to you. I'll give you to the count of ten. Ten, nine, eight, seven, six, five . . ."

At the count of five, the old man hurried down to his own apartment as if the devil was after him.

Kate looked stricken. Alex said, "Try not to let it upset you too much. After all he's just a silly old man with a bit of a power complex in need of a lesson in manners. Don't worry, he'll think twice about bothering you again after the scare I gave him."

He paused, then asked, "You didn't take seriously all that stuff and nonsense I spouted?"

Kate shook her head. "No, it's just that I felt – safe – before. I don't now. Not any longer."

Arden knew what she meant, and no matter how hard he might try to persuade her otherwise, the damage had been done. Her privacy had been invaded.

He said, "Let's not wait till tomorrow, shall we? The sooner the decorating is done, the curtains hung and the carpet replaced, the better."

"But that could take till the early hours," Kate demurred, dreading a second confrontation with her downstair's neighbour.

"No matter how long it takes, I want you to wake up in the morning to find everything done and dusted. I'll take the empty paint tins away and dispose of them for you."

"Thanks, Alex." She felt like crying, he was being so kind to her, revealing the softer side of his nature, a deep concern for her welfare at odds with his usual brusqueness of manner erected as a barrier against the world. How had he put it? "A defence system". Yes, that was it. He was certainly not on the defensive now.

It would be wonderful to have the flat put to rights. Then, perhaps, she would begin to feel secure again, to put the incident of the old man into its proper perspective. What price the idea of standing on her own two feet if she fell at the first hurdle? What, after all, had she expected? That independence, peace of mind and contentment would be handed to her on a plate?

If so, she'd better think again! Life was not like that, and she knew it. There would always be problems to face, niggling worries, sleepless nights, haunting memories both happy and sad to contend with. And burning questions to be answered: "Where did I go wrong? When did Don stop loving me? What if our children had lived?" Except that there were no answers, simply the feeling that her life had stopped abruptly three years ago, leaving her stranded in a limbo-land somewhere between a ghost-ridden past and a future she had scarcely, as yet, come to terms with.

Kate returned the ladder to Fanny, who kept it in the cellar for general household use.

"I heard tell old Joe Updike had a go at you the other night," she said. "Huh, the trouble with him and his missis, they've been here that long they think the place belongs to them! The last woman moved out because of him and his complaints. The television was on too loud or she had too many callers coming and going at all hours.

"He's going ga-ga if you ask me! I called him Hitler to his face when he complained about the vacuum cleaner – said it was too loud. Well, I told him straight it weren't my fault if it was, an' what did he want me to do? Get down on my knees with a dustpan an' brush?"

"Oh, surely not in this day and age?" Kate broke in.

"He has it in for me 'cos I live here rent free. But dammit all, I only have the one room with a bit of a kitchen in one corner. No bathroom or loo. I have to go along the landing to the communal bathroom when I want to have a bath or spend a penny.

"I know what's bugging him! He thinks I should live in the cellar, not in a room next door to him an' that miserable wife of his. You know the kind? Enjoys ill health! Truth to tell, I wouldn't mind living in the cellar. At least I'd get a bit of peace and quiet down there!"

She laughed suddenly. "Hark at me! Grumbling my head off! Must be catching! But I'm not really complaining, just letting off steam! I think myself lucky to have a job at my age. I've been a cleaner all my life, like my mother before me. I worked at the Crown Hotel in my younger days. When I retired, they had a party in my honour an' presented me with a cut glass vase an' a lovely bouquet of flowers."

"How lovely for you," Kate enthused. "Then what happened?"

"The manager made a speech, an' I had my photograph in the paper. Eh, I were fair taken aback! Well, to cut a long story short, I got this job on the strength of that photo of me in the *Evening News*. Now, here I am and here I intend to stay, an' it'll take more than the likes of Joe Updike to get the better of me."

She concluded cannily, "An' you shouldn't let him get the better of you neither!"

Kate felt like kissing Fanny at that moment, a proud, invincible, gutsy old lady facing life squarely on her own terms, with not a sign of self-pity in her make-up.

Shakily, close to tears, she said, "Thanks, Fanny, I'll try not to!"

Unexpectedly, Fanny continued, "I've never been one to pry into other folks' business, but I couldn't help noticing how lonely you were the day you came here to live, an' I thought what a pity it was. I wondered if you'd lost your husband recently?"

Kate nodded. Strangely enough, she didn't mind the older woman's question or giving her a straightforward answer. "My husband left me for another woman some time ago. We'd been married a little over twenty years when he asked me to divorce him.

"I was born in Scarborough. When my parents died, I got married and went to the West Country to live. After the divorce, I sold my home and stayed with my brother and his wife in Manchester until I decided what to do next. So here I am, back where I started."

"But surely you have friends hereabouts?" Fanny said sympathetically. "People you knew before you left home?"

"No one close, I'm afraid, except a girl I went to school with. We wrote to each other for a while, then lost touch. You know how it is? She may not live here now for all I know."

"Aye well . . . But you'll make new friends, I'm sure, a bonny lass like you!"

"Lass?" Kate smiled. "Hardly that: I'm into my forties now."

Fanny pulled a face. "Huh, that's nowt to worry about. I'm into my seventies an' still going strong. Mind you, I never was what you might call good-looking, an' I never married. I wouldn't have said no, mark you, if anyone had asked me, only no one did. I was born Frances May Kiddy, an' that's the name that'll go on my headstone, I reckon."

Bidding Fanny a fond farewell, Kate hurried down Newborough in the teeth of a bitingly cold November wind. Kiddy, she thought. What an unusual surname. One that she had never come across before.

In boisterous, expansive mood, when Kate appeared on his doorstep, fully booted and spurred, awaiting her arrival, Alex announced cheerfully that they were about to go walkabout.

Teeth chattering, "Where to?" Kate asked suspiciously, longing for a cup of hot coffee to warm the cockles of her heart before setting off on a journey into the wild grey yonder.

"You'll find out soon enough! Just follow me," Alex adjured her, striding along King Street towards St Nicholas Cliff, then down the "Zig-Zag" near the Grand Hotel to the seafront. From thence to the Valley Gardens.

"Now, Kate, tell me what you see around you." Alex had stopped walking to survey the scenery, an air of excitement about him. "Take your time."

"What, on a day like this?" Kate grumbled, wondering what she was supposed to be looking at. "Oh, very well then, if you insist."

48

Breath whirling away like smoke she said, "I see lots of trees; trunks and branches, no leaves. Paths and shrubberies, the spandrels of the Valley Bridge, a few empty beer cans and cigarette packets . . ."

"No need to be facetious!"

"I'm not. You asked me to describe the scene, and that's what I'm doing!"

"All right. Get on with it!"

"Well, obviously there's the old duckpond over yonder, and a bit of a scummy pool under the bridge, with a rusted metal tripod as a centrepiece." She broke off suddenly, recalling her younger days when the scummy pool was afloat with waterlily pads, and a small fountain from the then gleaming tripod splashed water into the now derelict pond.

The equally neglected duckpond, edged with Victorian wooden railings in a criss-cross pattern, Kate remembered as a shining expanse of water alive with a flotilla of ducks swimming from their nesting places on the small island in the centre of the lake to gobble up the bread that she and Greg had thrown to them.

"I'm sorry, Alex," she said, "I'm not enjoying this very much."

"So I gathered. But never mind about that. Tell me what else you can see from where we're standing."

Gazing about her, she said, "The gardens of Londesborough Lodge on the right hand side of the road, far better maintained than the scrubby area opposite, I dare say, since the Lodge and its grounds are now the property of the local Borough Council."

"Anything else?" Arden peristed.

"Well, yes. Plantation Hill leading down past the old Sitwell house, with its arched gas-lamp brackets still in situ . . . How odd. I thought they'd have been relegated to the scrap heap ages ago."

Arden smiled mysteriously. "Thanks, Kate," he said. "Now I'd like you to imagine yourself walking down Plantation Hill wearing a long skirt, ankle boots and a wide-brimmed hat, to witness the opening ceremony of 'The People's Park'. The brainchild of your hero, John Fairgray Sharpin!"

"Really?" Kate's eyes shone. "I had no idea. You mean that he . . . ?"

"Was responsible for the duckpond?" Alex said, latching on to her train of thought. "Apparently so, plus the landscaping of the area as a pleasure ground for the working-class folk of Scarborough, who came here in their hundreds to watch the procession of carriages from the Town Hall."

He added dreamily, "The month was May. There was magic abroad in the air." Then, more matter of factly, he said, "I brought you here to gauge your reaction to the idea of starting my book with a chapter describing the events of that night, and the role played by Sharpin in Scarborough's development as a first-class seaside resort. Well, what do you think?"

"As a novel, you mean?" Kate asked hopefully.

"No, of course not," Alex said impatiently. "I'm not into writing romantic fiction. I thought you knew that! There are women writers enough engaged in churning out that kind of nonsense, in my opinion! Now, isn't it about time for some hot, strong coffee? Don't know about you, but I'm frozen stiff with all this standing about on a day like this!"

Of all the impossible men, Kate thought as, turning abruptly, he strode ahead of her up the Zig-Zag and along King Street to his flat.

Seven

"The month was May. There was magic abroad in the air. Darkness had fallen. Lamplights glimmered like fireflies, seeming to move and dance in the gentle breeze blowing inland from the sea."

Kate smiled reflectively. "The People's Park" had fired her imagination to the extent of wanting to write about it in her own way. Nothing whatever to do with Alex's more prosaic approach to the subject.

What had it really been like that night, she wondered, when throngs of working class Scarborians had trooped down Plantation Hill to the valley below to witness the opening of their very own pleasure ground?

Giving rein to her imagination, she visualised the scene in her mind's eye: colourful Chinese lanterns strung between the branches of the trees; sounds of music and laughter, the quacking of ducks from the newly established duckpond; children's swings and roundabouts; the bunting-bedecked platform awaiting the arrival of Town Hall dignitaries and their ladies, in open landaus, to add a certain weight and solemnity to the occasion.

Not that the onlookers would have cared tuppence about top-hatted, grey-bearded town councillors and their lady wives, in direct contrast to the "Man of the Moment" – the young, dark-haired, charismatic Mayor of Scarborough, John Fairgray Sharpin.

And when the carriage procession had returned from whence it came, what then? Kate wondered. What did people in celebratory mood usually do? Eat, drink and make merry, she imagined, as they had done since time immemorial. The Victorian women, despite their clothing – long skirts, ankle boots, high-necked blouses, tightly-laced corsets and layers of petticoats, their menfolk in their sombre suits, starched collars, and waistcoats and the married couples with children in tow would have made the most of that golden opportunity to revel in the many sideshows, beer tents and hot-food stalls.

She envisaged savoury ducks, pease-pudding, sausages and hot mutton pies; wide-eyed children staring up at a Punch and Judy show; hoop-la stalls, coconut shies; young couples walking hand-in-hand beneath lantern-lit branches.

People would have come from all areas of the town: off-duty chambermaids, porters and stable-lads from the Crown Hotel, more than likely; ganzied fishermen from the Old Town – keeping an open eye for pretty young lasses in muslin dresses and tip-tilted boaters, they on the look-out for handsome young men.

Kate imagined the kissing and canoodling that went on in the rustic shelters along the way on that warm, heady May night long ago, the scent of lilacs and May blossom borne on a breeze blowing in from the sea, the murmur of the tide washing in on the shore, the tinkling of water from the fountain into the lily pool beneath the bridge. Except, of course, there wouldn't have been a bridge spanning the valley in those days.

Her heart lifted suddenly at the possibility of writing her own version of Victorian Scarborough via a series of random jottings written purely for her own pleasure, so imparting a new sense of purpose to her finding out all she could about that particular era, if only to prove to herself that she possessed a mind of her own above and beyond her failed capacities as a wife and mother in what she now thought of as her "Don days".

Next morning, not hearing the usual clatter of typewriter keys when she arrived at Alex's, Kate went upstairs to his office and found him, in tetchy mood, kneeling on the floor surrounded by photographs, notebooks and newspaper clippings.

"Well, don't just stand there," he said abruptly, "go down and make some coffee! I've been up since the crack of dawn trying to make sense of this lot!"

"Why? What's the problem?" she enquired mildly.

"The problem is," he said sarcastically, "that I need some hot, strong coffee right now, not in the middle of next week!"

"You're wrong, Alex!" Kate said uncompromisingly, "Apart from a shave, a shower and a haircut, what you really need is a skivvy, not a so-called housekeeper. In which case, the sooner you find yourself a skivvy, the better!"

This said, shored up by her new-found purpose in life and sick and tired of the male gender in general, Kate marched downstairs to the side door.

Deeply shaken, Alex called after her, "Hey, hang on just a second! You can't simply walk out on me like this!"

"Oh, can't I?" she called back to him. "Just watch me!"

"At least tell me where you're going!" Alex demanded hoarsely from the upper landing.

"To the library, if you must know," Kate conceded, coming to terms with the realisation that her life would be much poorer without Alex Arden, yet unwilling to allow him dominion over her life lest she ended up a cipher once more, as she had done with Don.

"Very well, I'll see you there in an hour," Alex said urbanely, pulling up his defences, unwilling to admit to himself, or Kate, how much he had come to rely on her friendship. He added, "You really must stop taking umbrage the way you do."

"Perhaps I shall," she said coolly, "when you stop behaving like a bear with a sore head!"

At the library, using her recently acquired membership card, Kate chose several books pertaining to the Victorian era which she stowed in her shopping bag, after which she applied for, and received, permission to enter the inner sanctum of the Scarborough Room – an accolade accorded only to members of the public engaged in bona fide research connected with the history of Scarborough.

She was there, turning pages of the *Gazette and Herald* when Arden entered the room. "Feeling better now, are you?" he asked brusquely.

She glanced up at him. "More to the point, Alex, are *you*?"

"You know, Kate," he said, tongue-in-cheek, "I can't help thinking that had you treated your ex-husband as badly as you treat me, you might well still be married to him; based on the premise that a man would be more inclined to leave a boring woman; seldom, if ever, a troublesome one!"

Faced with the strong tide of feeling surging between them, yet unwilling to admit its existence, Kate suggested, off-handedly, "Well, shall we stop wasting time and get on with our research before you find out how troublesome I could be if I tried harder?"

The nature of the "tide" was not entirely clear to her. It seemed as changeable as the sea itself, a strange combination of admiration and irritation, liking and disliking, to do with the complex character of the man himself, coloured by her own refusal to accept male domination ever again.

She had come a long way since her "Don days", with every step along the road to recovery a hard-fought battle against despair and loneliness. And the battle was not yet won, nor would it be until she had learned how to stand, firm and proud, on her own two feet.

But could any human being become so insular as not to need companionship? Even the emotionally-challenged companionship of a man like Alex Arden?

Their morning's research concluded for the time being, he said, over lunch – hot soup and toasted sandwiches in the Royal Hotel snack bar – against a background of whirling snowflakes seen through the window, "By the way, Kate, I'll be spending Christmas in London. How about you?"

"*Christmas*?" Kate frowned slightly. "I don't know. I haven't really thought about it yet."

"But, my dear girl, it's only three week's away from now!" He paused, "Surely you'll be spending it with your brother, in Manchester?"

"Greg won't be in Manchester at Christmas," Kate said. "He and his wife, Cindy, usually spend Christmas with her family, in Bradford."

"So what's to prevent you spending Christmas in Bradford?" Alex persisted.

"First and foremost, I haven't been invited," Kate said defensively. "More importantly, even if I had been, I'd have turned down the invitation!"

"May I ask why?"

Kate countered his question with one of her own: "Tell me, Alex, how would you react to a houseful of spoilt children, running amok?"

"I get the picture," he said wryly. "In which case, how would you react to spending Christmas with me?"

"In London, you mean?" Kate asked warily.

"A strong possibility, since that's where my home is. Of course, I could hire a caravan north of the Watford Gap and commute daily, if you'd prefer."

Kate laughed. His quirky sense of humour was the thing she liked most about Alex. "Ask a silly question, you'll get a silly answer!" she said.

"Then how about a sensible answer? Think about it, Kate. I have business matters to attend to before Christmas, and you'd be a great help on the domestic front: opening the house, so to speak, doing the shopping and so on."

"I see. So this would be in the nature of a working holiday for me?" Kate asked, wanting to get things clear in her mind.

Arden frowned. "Only in the sense that you'd be shopping and cooking anyway even if you stayed here in Scarborough and, frankly, I'd rather you spent Christmas with me than alone in your flat."

What he said made sense. Even so, Kate needed to know exactly what she'd be letting herself in for. "Would we be alone in the house?"

"Yes, of course. Why? Is that a problem?"

"No. I simply thought you might be expecting – house guests over the Christmas weekend."

"No way," Alex assured her briefly. "I've had enough of house-parties, dinner parties, luncheon and cocktail parties to last me a lifetime!"

Glancing across at him, noticing and understanding, by the sudden air of weariness about him, that he too was ghost-ridden by past events – memories of a lost love, almost too hard to bear at times, she said quietly, "Very well, then, I accept your invitation."

Alex had elected to travel south, by rail, on the nineteenth of December, a much easier and more direct means of transport than road travel, he explained, hence his decision to garage the Mercedes pro tem, until their return from London ten days later.

In a whirl, Kate had sent presents to Greg and Cindy, and made up a hamper of treats – chocolates, biscuits, various tinned foods, glacé fruits and a Christmas pudding – for Fanny, before treating herself to various items of clothing – a couple of new sweaters, a hostess gown, high-heeled sandals, plus a cotton nightgown and matching peignoir, just in case she bumped into Alex on her way to the bathroom.

Alex arrived at the station ahead of her. The eight o'clock train was standing at Platform One. It was a bitterly cold morning. A hailstone-threaded north-east wind scurried along the platforms.

"Ah, there you are," Alex commented drily, "I'd begun to think you'd changed your mind at the last minute."

"Why? I'm not late, am I?" Kate asked anxiously, unaccountably nervous all of a sudden, wondering what she had let herself in for, feeling a bit like "Alice in Wonderland" about to disappear down a rabbit hole.

"This train's fairly crowded," Alex said, taking her by the elbow and urging her along to the front of the train. "Not to worry, I've booked

55

Louise Brindley

First Class seats from York to King's Cross so we should be able to get some decent coffee *en route*."

After heaving their cases into a luggage rack, he continued when they were seated, "We'll lunch at King's Cross then take a taxi to St John's Wood. I daresay the house will feel chilly to begin with, and the beds will need airing, but once the central heating and the electric blankets have been switched on, it will soon begin to thaw out, and so shall we!"

So Alex owned a house in St John's Wood? Not just a flat, but a whole house? Possibly a very large house, Kate reflected nervously, with an enormous kitchen and a cooker big enough to roast an ox, let alone a turkey. Well, so be it. Too late to turn back now!

The house, in a tree-lined avenue, was a three-storey building of Victorian vintage, with steps to the brass-letterboxed front door, a spacious vestibule set with richly patterned floor tiles, and with a half-glass inner door beyond which lay a wide hall and a broad mahogany staircase.

Picking up a scattering of mail which he stuffed carelessly into his valise, Alex led the way across the hall to the kitchen quarters where he fiddled briefly with the controls of the central heating system, while Kate, glancing about her new domain, felt somewhat nervous at the sight of an Aga cooker, stainless steel sinks and draining-boards and a towering refrigerator capable of holding and keeping fresh their Christmas food supply – when it had been purchased.

Daylight was fading. Alex was right about the house being chilly. Kate said, "Now might be a good time to do some shopping, don't you think? We'll need food for the morning, something for supper later on tonight."

"I'd thought of dining out. There's a decent restaurant in the shopping area," he said, having set the central heating controls to his satisfaction.

"No, Alex. I'd much rather settle in first, get my bearings, do the shopping, serve the supper, then have an early night." The last thing she wanted was to dine out in public before she'd had a bath or shower, and there wouldn't be any hot water for ages yet. Besides, she hadn't seen her room or switched on the electric blankets, and the Aga needed lighting and stoking in readiness for tomorrow, she pointed out to him.

"Of course, you are perfectly right," he admitted. "I had a man-servant in the old days, who took care of such matters for me after . . well, no matter. Suffice to say that he knew his job like the back of his

56

hand – an ex-army batman experienced in caring for officers and gentlemen. A veritable Jeeves to my ineffectual Bertie Wooster, if you like."

"What happened to him?" Kate asked.

"Oh, that? I pensioned him off when it became abundantly clear that the job was becoming too much for him," Alex said carelessly. "Found him a ground-floor room in a retirement home not far from here, where I knew he'd be well looked after for the rest of his days." He added, "Which reminds me, I must call round to see him before Christmas; take him a bottle of Scotch!"

In need of exercise and fresh air, Kate insisted on walking to the shopping centre, but before they left the Aga had been lit and fed coke from the fuel store, the electric blankets had been switched on, and the house had begun to feel marginally warmer than it had done before. It was a strange house, Kate thought: certainly spacious, even rambling, but lacking an atmosphere of homeliness – a so-called "woman's touch" – as if every reminder of the woman, once the mistress of the house, had been deliberately got rid of.

Finding a supermarket, Kate set about loading her shopping trolley with what she regarded as the necessities of life, as she had done so often in her "Don days". No shopping list necessary: she knew exactly what she wanted.

It hadn't quite dawned on her yet that she was actually here, in London, the world's most exciting city. Strange to think that, within striking distance of this common-or-garden supermarket lay the bright lights of Piccadilly, the Haymarket, Shaftesbury Avenue, the Strand, and Trafalgar Square. With luck, she'd be given the chance to explore the City to her heart's content whilst Alex was engaged in attending to the business matters he'd mentioned earlier. This time, not from the front seat of a double-decker bus, but on her own two feet.

At the supermarket checkout, Alex added to the contents of her trolley a bottle of malt whisky, smoked salmon, several boxes of chocolates, a roll of wrapping paper, and a large Christmas pudding.

"Not to worry, Kate," he said lightly, footing the bill, "I'll ring for a taxi!"

The house felt slightly warmer on their return. The central heating was obviously doing its stuff, and so was the Aga. Besides which, Alex had switched on the drawing room electric fire at full blast before they'd set out on their shopping expedition. Even so, the room still felt cold to Kate's way of thinking, robbed of a woman's touch – flowers and family photographs, chintz-covered armchairs and settees. Or perhaps the ex-Mrs Alex Arden had not cared much for chintz; had preferred leather settees and armchairs?

In the kitchen, unpacking the groceries, Kate placed bacon, sausages, milk, vegetables, a cold roast chicken and the smoked salmon in the refrigerator; tins of salmon, tuna, soup, baked beans and corned beef in the store cupboards above the laminated work surfaces. In the cupboards beneath the sink units, bottles of washing-up liquid, household bleach, and so on, necessities of life which most men assumed grew on trees.

Her bedroom at least had not been stripped bare of womanly touches: cretonne-skirted dressing table, triple mirror, matching bedside tables with pink-shaded lamps. But hardly likely that Alex would have bothered about guest rooms occupied by weekend visitors. There was Chanel soap and bubble-bath in the en-suite bathroom, fluffy pink towels and a basket containing small items such as hairpins, a spare toothbrush, shower-cap and body lotion.

Kate wondered if Alex occupied what had once been the marital bedroom, or if he had elected to sleep elsewhere when his wife went away?

The water was not yet hot enough for a bath, she discovered, running the washbasin tap. Washing her hands and face, she changed her outdoor clothes for a lightweight tweed skirt and one of her new sweaters, applied a modicum of make-up, combed her hair and went downstairs to get the supper ready.

Alex appeared in the kitchen to find her preparing salad, washing lettuce, slicing tomatoes, red and green peppers, de-stringing celery and grating carrots.

"I'll carve the bird," he said, "and we'll eat in the drawing room, near the fire."

"It's not exactly heart-warming food, is it?" Kate said.

"No, but there's plenty of it, and we can at least boil the kettle for some hot coffee – to soften the blow."

He was being kind, and she was grateful for small mercies. One never knew with Alex if one was in for a kick or a kiss, metaphorically speaking. In bad humour, he'd have probably said that she was to blame for turning down his dinner invitation at that "decent restaurant" he'd mentioned earlier.

"Quite honestly," she said, "I'm not in the mood for salad. I'll settle for a chicken sandwich and a cup of coffee, then have an early night, if you don't mind."

"Me too," he said unexpectedly. "You see, I'll need to make an early start in the morning. I've arranged several important appointments with my bank manager, estate agent, and literary agent. And, well, quite frankly, I feel that I'm giving you a raw deal, leaving you on your own all day – a stranger in a strange place."

"If that's bothering you, forget it," Kate reassured him. "I have plans of my own in mind!"

"Really?" He frowned slightly. "Such as?"

"Oh, visiting the National Gallery; looking up at Nelson's Column; standing on Westminster Bridge. You know the kind of thing I mean?"

"All by yourself?" Alex's frown deepened at the thought of Kate alone in London.

"Yes, of course. Why not? I've been 'all by myself' for some time now. I'm beginning to get used to it, to value my independence. One day, in the not too dim and distant future, I may even take a trip abroad, to Paris, for instance, to see the Eiffel Tower, Notre Dame – the Mona Lisa!"

They ate their chicken sandwiches and drank coffee in front of the drawing room fire. "Well, what do you think of the house?" Alex asked abruptly.

Sensing a mood change from the affable to the impossible, Kate replied cagily, "I don't really know; I haven't seen all of it yet."

"In which case, if you've finished eating, perhaps you'd care for a guided tour?" Arden suggested sourly. He added flamboyantly, "Might as well get used to catering to the curious since I've decided to sell it! And you *are* one of the curious, aren't you, Kate? So come with me, allow me to introduce you to my fine spacious dining room, the scene of more bloody awful dinner parties than I care to remember!

"My ex-wife had a penchant for parties, you see? Any excuse would do for the killing of the fatted calf! Note the mahogany dining table and twelve chairs, the marble-topped Georgian side table, the silver candelabrum. Impressive, don't you agree?"

"Please don't, Alex," Kate pleaded, suddenly afraid of his loss of control. As if years of built-up tension had focused suddenly on the storm centre of his life so that he could no longer hold back his intensity

59

of hatred towards a woman who, presumably, he had once loved enough to ask her to marry him.

"And this, Kate, is my study," Alex said, opening the door of a small, book-lined room with a central desk, typewriter, and piles of A4 paper. "At least it was in the dim and distant past when I knew how to write. A forgotten art nowadays, I'm afraid!"

It was there, in that room, glancing at the titles of the books on display, that Kate, adding two and two together, realised that the author Sandy Alexis, whose output of travel books had been published to great acclaim twenty years ago, and Alex Arden were one and the same person.

"Why didn't you tell me?" she asked.

"Because Sandy Alexis no longer exists," he said briefly. "He died and was buried; forgotten a long time ago."

Eight

Early next morning, Kate came downstairs and went into the drawing room to clear the remains of last night's supper. Crossing to the rear window, she drew back the curtains. There were French doors leading to a paved terrace, a long garden beyond: frost-rimed grass, stark trees, high brick walls, neglected shrubberies.

The house felt warmer. Crossing the hall to the kitchen, she refuelled the Aga, deriving a modicum of comfort from the performance of a task as familiar to her as breathing. Even so, the atmosphere of the house weighed heavily on her, and the sleepless night she'd spent worrying about Alex's state of mind had undermined her hard-won self-confidence, her pleasurable anticipation of the days ahead. Her so-called holiday.

She was washing up the coffee cups and plates from the night before when Alex entered the kitchen.

He said, without preamble, "I owe you an apology for my bad behaviour last night. Please, forgive me!"

Facing him, she knew that he hadn't slept either. His face looked grey; eyes haunted. The eyes of a man forced to look into the depths of his own soul; to hate and despise what he had found there.

"What is there to forgive?" she said.

"Bringing you here in the first place," he said tautly. "I should have known better! I knew, you see, what would happen the minute I entered this damned house again! And I was right! They were all here, awaiting my return, those bloody awful memories of mine!"

"Sit down, Alex! I'll make some coffee. I know what you're going through, believe me!"

"That's just it, Kate," he said despairingly, "you couldn't begin to know, how could you, the way I felt when my wife told me the child I adored as my own son, Peter, was not mine at all, but the result of a one night stand during one of those damnable weekend house

61

parties of hers, with a man whom I had regarded as my best friend!"

He continued hoarsely, "When Leonora finally told me the truth, not kindly but cruelly, relishing every detail of the telling, I lost control of myself completely! Told her to get out of the house; to go to the devil for all I cared. Her and her bastard son included!"

He covered his face with his hands. "If I had only known! I loved that child so much, you see? Had I kept control of my emotions, not acted so hastily, begged Leonora to leave Peter with me, things might well have worked out quite differently in the end."

Sitting opposite him at the kitchen table, Kate asked quietly, "So exactly what did happen?"

Uncovering his face, staring into the past, Alex said haltingly, "Leonora's car was parked in the road in front of the house. She got into it, dragging Peter by the hand. I made no attempt to stop her! I was so bloody angry, so bloody-minded, that I just wanted rid of her as quickly as possible. *Her*, not Peter! After all, an innocent child I had brought up and loved dearly as my own flesh and blood, until . . ."

"Go on, please," Kate begged him. "I'm listening."

Alex said tonelessly, as if drained of emotion, "I watched the car drive away. Leonora at the wheel, the boy beside her, his face wet with tears, not knowing what was happening, calling out to me, "Dadda, Dadda," over and over again until the car was out of sight.

"At midnight, the police arrived on the doorstep to break the news that my wife's car had been involved in a fatal accident at a busy roundabout on the outskirts of Oxford; that both she and her passenger, a child aged seven years or so, had died instantaneously when their vehicle had struck the bonnet of a ten-ton lorry travelling in the opposite direction."

Reliving the horror of that night, he said, "I nearly went crazy with grief over Peter. I should have kept him with me at any cost. Should have held my temper in check. I couldn't see beyond Leo's betrayal at the time; that Peter was no part of me. It was hearing him calling my name, the look of misery on his face that brought me to my senses. But it was too late then. I'd lost him, the only person I've ever really loved."

His face crumpled suddenly. Tears were close to the surface. Shoulders hunched forward, mouth trembling, he was fighting hard for self-control.

Understanding Alex's suffering, knowing that whatever she said would sound trite or inadequate under the circumstances, Kate made some toast and coffee.

"I don't want anything to eat," he said wearily.

"Fair enough. But at least drink your coffee," she said levelly. "What time is your first appointment, by the way?"

"Ten o'clock. And, thanks, Kate."

"For what?"

"Not smothering me with sympathy. I don't deserve it."

"I've learned that we don't always get what we deserve, in this life," Kate said wistfully, looking back into her own past. "In any case, sympathy isn't always the answer. A helping hand, a bit of common-sense advice is far more useful in the long run."

"Really?" Alex attempted a smile. "So what piece of common-sense advice are you about to offer me?"

"First and foremost, stop dwelling on the past and look to the future! Your advice to me, as I recall. What's done is done, and can't be undone. How did Omar Khayyám put it? 'The moving finger writes; and, having writ, moves on: nor all thy piety nor wit. . .' I'm sorry, I've forgotten the rest of the quotation."

" 'Shall lure it back to cancel half a line, nor all thy tears wash out a word of it,' " Alex reminded her.

"Well yes," Kate conceded, deeply aware of her dislike of the house, longing to get away from it as quickly as possible, sensing something unnerving about it. A vengeful watcher in the shadows, perhaps?

"Meaning what, exactly?"

"That you should cram all your business appointments into one day, if possible; that you – I mean we – should then catch the first available train home!"

"Back to Scarborough, you mean?"

"Where else?" Kate asked.

"But I thought you had your own plans in mind?" Alex demurred. "Shopping, sight-seeing and so on?"

"Oh, forget all that," Kate adjured him. "Frankly, I'd far rather spend Christmas alone in my own flat than stay here in this dreadful, ghost-ridden house a moment longer than necessary."

"Ghost-ridden?" Alex asked sharply. "You mean you've seen something that – frightened you?"

"No, not at all! Something far more subtle than that! A sense of –

brooding evil in the atmosphere, impossible to explain or to quantify. As if our presence here is unwelcome."

Arden shuddered. "I know. I've been aware of it myself. And I think you are right, that we should go back. I'll do as you suggest, make my business appointments as brief as possible. My bank manager had suggested lunching together. I'll make my apologies."

Drinking the last of his coffee, he stood up. "I could ring the estate agent I have in mind; ask him to look over the house this afternoon. That can't be avoided, I'm afraid. I'll explain it's a matter of some urgency; say I'm leaving London sooner than expected. At the same time, I'll arrange the removal of the furniture for auction."

"All of it?" Kate asked.

"Every stick of it," he said brusquely. "I hope never to set eyes on it ever again."

"But what about your books?" Kate spoke anxiously, not wanting him to act in haste, repent at leisure.

"You mean Sandy Alexis's books? The works of a dead and forgotten author? No, Kate, they can go on a bonfire for all I care!"

"They'll do no such thing," she protested vehemently. "*I* want them."

"*You*?" Alex frowned. "But why the hell should you?"

"For my brother," she said, "because they meant so much to him. Quite simply, you were a kind of 'folk hero' of his twenty years ago, along with T.E. Lawrence and 'Grey Owl'."

"Two other 'phonies' as I recall," Alex said sarcastically. "But if you want them, take them, they're yours!"

"You misunderstand," Kate said proudly, "I want to buy them, not have them given to me as a – load of rubbish! Because they are *not* rubbish, and you know it!"

"Very well, Kate, have it your way!" Alex glanced at his watch. "Before I go, what are your plans for the day?"

"I'm staying here," she said decisively. "Only right and proper, don't you agree? After all, I am your 'housekeeper', and it would seem a pity not to cook you a decent meal in the Aga – before it finally goes out."

When Alex had gone, alone in the house, Kate wandered from room to room – a fine, spacious house, worth a great deal of money, she surmised, albeit an unhappy house in view of the dreadful happenings that had taken place there.

And yet she was not sorry that she had come here. Doing so had given her a deeper insight into his past life, his difficult to understand personality; rapid mood changes, outbursts of temper, yet his underlying decency of spirit – witness his kindness towards his old retainer, for whom he had bought a litre of malt whisky as a Christmas present to take to him in the retirement home Alex had chosen for him, footing the bills for his upkeep himself, more than likely, Kate assumed. Correctly, as it later transpired . . .

She kept well out of the way that afternoon, in the kitchen, when Alex and the estate agent were together discussing matters pertaining to the sale of the property, busying herself in preparations for the evening meal.

When the man had gone, Alex said urgently, "Look, Kate, I really must visit my old friend Gabriel Owens before supper; take him his Christmas present. You do understand, don't you, that I couldn't possibly leave London tomorrow without saying goodbye to him?"

"Of course I do," she assured him. "In fact, I'd like to come with you, if you don't mind."

"Mind? Of course I don't mind. Why should I?"

And so they went together to visit Gabriel Owens, a still-handsome man despite his years; obviously frail now, yet possessed of a lively intelligence, who obviously adored his former employer.

"My dear Mr Alex," he said shakily, attempting to rise from his wheelchair, "how good it is to see you again! You've made Christmas for me, you really have!"

"Stop trying to show off, Gaby," Alex said huskily, kissing the old man's forehead. "Sit down and shut up! Just because there's an attractive woman in the room! This, by the way, is my – friend – Kate Ford."

Stepping forward to shake hands with Gaby, Kate explained, light heartedly, "Actually, I'm Mr Arden's current housekeeper."

Gaby's eyes twinkled. "Well, you're far better looking than the old 'un, that's for sure!"

He was obviously over the moon with the bottle of whisky Alex placed in his lap on the point of their departure. Tears filled his eyes when they bade him goodbye. He said proudly, choking back his emotion, "I'll never forget your kindness to me, Mr Alex. The peace of mind you've given me, in my old age!"

Tucking the old man's rug about his knees, hiding his own emotion, albeit unsuccessfully, Alex said brusquely, "The trouble with you, Gaby, you chose the wrong career! You should have been a parson, not a bloody batman!"

Bending down to clasp the old man's hands in hers, Kate murmured, "I'm so pleased to have met you, Mr Owens. Well, goodbye for now, and God bless!"

Retaining her hands in his, digging his nails into her palms, Gaby murmured fervently, sotto voce, "Please, promise me you'll stay with him, take care of him, for my sake, and his! You see, he really does need someone to take care of him!"

Kate murmured softly, in reply, "Very well, Gaby. At least I'll try."

She and Alex dined royally on their return from the old people's home, on smoked salmon and the chicken casserole she had prepared earlier. At least they might have done so had either of them felt hungry.

Kate asked warily, "Did you see your literary agent, this morning?"

"No, I cancelled the appointment. There was really no point since I haven't even got to grips with my book about Scarborough." He paused briefly, then continued, "Remember when you came upstairs that day to find me on my hands and knees trying to sort out my notes and photographs?"

"Shall I ever forget?" Kate murmured, tongue in cheek. "The day I walked out on you; told you that what you needed was a skivvy, not a housekeeper?"

"I was angry, that day," Alex said despondently, "because I knew that I was a spent force so far as writing's concerned! I'd been up since the crack of dawn, attempting an opening chapter which any sixth form schoolboy might have tackled far more successfully than I, a so-called professional writer, could ever hoped to have done, given the prevailing circumstances. Lack of self-confidence, for one thing, in my ability to string together two sentences, plus a synopsis which I knew damn well that my agent, let alone a hard-nosed publisher, would reject out of hand. And rightly so. Very kindly, of course. Nevertheless the bitterest pill of all to swallow!"

"But aren't you jumping the gun a little?" Kate queried intently. "Isn't it possible that, given time, you may well regain your old prowess as a writer?"

"No, I don't think so," Alex said briefly. "Too much water has passed under the bridge since my 'glory days' as Sandy Alexis, when, travelling the world in search of adventure, from the Gobi Desert to the rain forests of the Amazon, I somehow assumed the mantle of an explorer. I was nothing of the kind. A dilettante with a penchant for words would be nearer the mark.

"I made no discoveries of importance. I simply indulged a passion for travel, losing myself in far flung places, made observations, kept diaries which I extended and enlarged upon when I returned to so-called civilisation. This was simply a means of filling the empty spaces of my life – a rejected human being with money to burn. The success of my books went to my head like strong wine. For the first time in my life, I was in demand: feted, famous.

"Then I made the greatest mistake of my life. I married Leonora."

"Were you in love with her?" Kate asked quietly.

Alex shrugged. "I thought I was. She was very beautiful, incredibly sexy. Not clever, but smart, quick-witted. I soon discovered that she was also incredibly selfish: wanting the good things of life, clothes, money, jewellery. Not that I blamed her for wanting what most women want – beautiful women, that is. Above all, Leo wanted admiration, to be the centre of attention, and she was, believe me, on a seemingly endless merry-go-round of parties, dinner dances, cocktail and champagne parties, house parties. You name it."

He brushed a hand across his eyes wearily, a gesture Kate found infinitely touching, revealing as it did the little boy lost, lurking beneath a manly façade.

He said slowly, painfully, "I desperately wanted a child. Leo told me, in no uncertain terms, that a baby was the last thing on earth she intended to be lumbered with."

He continued awkwardly, "Nothing would induce her to . . ." He stopped speaking abruptly, not knowing how to express that his marriage to Leonora had been a precautionary tale from beginning to end.

"Throw caution to the wind, you mean?" Kate suggested mildly. "Then it must have come as quite a shock when she told you she was pregnant? I imagine she gulled you into thinking that, on at least one occasion, she *had* thrown caution to the wind?"

"Well, yes. Or so I believed at the time," Alex conceded, deeply grateful of Kate's understanding, her way of coming to the nub and kernel of a problem and finding a solution, as she had done in suggesting spending Christmas in Scarborough, not in this prison-house of his, with all its unhappy memories of a past best forgotten if the future was to hold any meaning at all for a man robbed of all that he had once held dear to him. His wife, his son, Peter, his writing career. Above all, Peter, the only person he had ever really loved . . . until now!

Nine

They arrived back in Scarborough to steadily falling snow; twinkling fairy lights strung between the branches of trees in Westborough; crowds of people thronging the main shopping centre in search of last minute presents; red neon signs and brightly lit shop windows dispelling the gloom of a wintry December afternoon.

Emerging from the station, Alex hailed a taxi, handed the driver their luggage to stow in the boot of his car, and gave his Newborough address as their destination.

Making no comment as the taxi sped into the traffic, Kate realised that Alex had taken for granted their spending Christmas together under his roof. Not that she minded. They could scarcely have taken separate taxis to different destinations.

This way, at least she would be able to fulfil her promise to Gaby Owens to "take care" of Alex to the best of her ability: to make certain he had enough to eat and drink over the Christmas period; a warm, comfortable bed to sleep in; holly and mistletoe; a Christmas tree in the sitting room; soft lights and sweet music; roast turkey plus the usual trimmings for Christmas Day lunch.

She would enjoy to the full all the shopping, cooking and planning involved, relevant not only to Alex's comfort and well-being, but hers also, as a woman in need of the fulfilment denied her so often during her "Don days" – when she had discovered, to her dismay, that Don regarded Christmas as a pagan, not a Christian festival. And yet they had been married in St Mary's Church.

But *why*? she had often wondered since then. Why the pretence of a solemn, Church of England wedding ceremony which the bridegroom, an agnostic, must have viewed, all along, as a sham, a kind of sick joke, even as he had uttered his vows of fidelity to one woman alone for the rest of his life?

Deep down, Kate knew exactly why. Because Don had wanted her physically – a desirable young girl on the threshold of life – and marrying her had seemed the only way of gaining entry to her bed.

Morality had been much stronger in those days. Girls of her generation had been taught to "save" themselves for their wedding night. The war had undermined morality to some extent, Kate realised, and it was easy to understand why. Young men on embarkation leave not knowing when – or even if – they would return home when the war was over. Young girls desperate to give the ultimate proof of their love before it was too late. Living for the moment with no thought of the future. There, but for the Grace of God . . .

Of course she had wanted, desperately at times, to give Don the ultimate proof of her love, before marriage. Head over heels in love with him, she had come dangerously close to forgetting her upbringing and her mother's strongly held views on morality. Not that she had ever preached sermons on the subject. A gentle person, she had stated simply her beliefs in what she'd termed "decency", the "honourable estate of matrimony", based on the happiness of her own marriage to a decent, forebearing man who had obviously not sought sexual favours from her until their honeymoon at a small hotel in Blackpool.

Would things have been different, Kate wondered, had she succumbed to Don's passionate desire to possess her during the days and nights of the courtship? More than likely, had he done so, their wedding might well have never taken place at all! Too late to wish, now that it hadn't!

That way, at least she'd have been spared the final humiliation of betrayal, the untold grief of three miscarriages, the wasted years of caring for a man who, obviously, hadn't cared a damn about her in the long run!

"Well don't just stand there dreaming, Kate!" she heard Alex saying forcefully. "Hadn't we better go shopping? Don't know about you, but I'm so hungry I could eat a horse!"

"Yes, of course," Kate said mildly, returning to the present, thankful to be home once more, well distanced from that ghost-ridden house in St John's Wood. "I'm ready when you are."

She had never enjoyed a shopping spree so much before. In expansive mood, he'd marched into the St Helen's Square Market Hall, a stone's throw away from his flat, to fill their shopping bags to capacity with fresh fruit and vegetables before turning his attention to a butcher's stall, when Kate had pointed out to him the inadvisability of ordering a twenty pound turkey which they'd never get through in a month of Sundays.

"Very well, then, you do the ordering," he said, "while I take a look at those Christmas trees over yonder!"

Amused by Alex's enthusiasm, at the same time Kate couldn't help thinking that he seemed a shade too excited, febrile almost, verging on impatience, as if he wanted Christmas organised, over and done with as soon as possible. On the other hand, it was good to think that his enthusiasm derived from the release from spending Christmas in London. And if he had taken for granted that they would spend Christmas together in his flat, so be it. Just as long as his present state of euphoria lasted long enough to ensure a happy and peaceful holiday together. So why the uneasy feeling that it might not?

Deep down, Kate had to admit to herself that she liked Alex's flat far better than hers. Well, his was not really a flat at all, but a house with a private entrance, no busy-body neighbours to twitch back net curtains or notice their comings and goings.

Privacy meant a great deal to her. A throwback to April Cottage, Kate imagined, set in a half acre of ground, far removed from the staring eyes of curious neighbours. The reason why she had never really cottoned on to Greg and Cindy's modern bungalow on a housing estate in the Greater Manchester area, the garden of which was overlooked by the owners of similar bungalows, within a mile-wide radius of neatly-mown lawns, bird-baths, fishponds, rose-beds, and herbaceous borders.

Now, on Christmas Eve, listening to the Service of Nine Lessons and Carols broadcast from King's College, Cambridge, making preparations for Christmas Day, baking mincepies and sausage rolls, Kate had seldom felt happier in her life then she did then, thinking that she had, perhaps, come home at last. She was finally acknowledging the strong tide of feeling running between herself and Alex Arden. If not love, then damn close to it, she realised. He was, after all, a man who had occupied the greater part of her life since their first meeting, without whom her life would scarcely be worth the living, or so she believed, pushing to the back of her mind that she had once felt the same way about Don, wondering if she had a penchant for charismatic men who treated her badly at times.

These past few days, at least, Alex had been utterly charming towards her; helping her to set up the Christmas tree in the sitting room and decorate it with coloured fairy lights; poking and prying about the kitchen when she was busily occupied in preparing and cooking their supper, obviously with something important on his mind by the way he looked at her, thoughtfully, intently, then dismissively, as if what he had intended saying to her would be far better left unsaid.

After Christmas Day lunch, he suggested taking a walk to Castle Hill to blow away the cobwebs from his mind. The bitter wind blowing in from the sea would certainly do that, Kate thought, as they battled their way to the headland overlooking the Marine Drive, a broad road at the base of the cliffs, linking the north and south bays, almost devoid of traffic and pedestrians on this cold December afternoon.

Families would be indoors on a day like this, gathered round the fire, children playing with their new toys, although a few intrepid individuals were on the north beach, walking their dogs – one individual, a tall man with grey hair and wearing a Burberry, apparently shell-gathering. Alex, on the other hand, appeared to be wool-gathering.

"You're very quiet," Kate commented. "Is anything the matter?"

"Yes, as it happens," he said, as if relieved that she had asked him. "I've been meaning to tell you."

"Tell me – what?"

"The fact is, I entered negotiation some weeks ago with the owner of my flat, with a view to buying the property outright, the gift shop included. This entered my mind when I decided to sell my London house. I didn't want to find myself homeless."

"Well, that's fine, isn't it?" Kate asked uncertainly, puzzled by his apparent lack of enthusiasm. "Unless the deal fell through?"

"No, it didn't. The owner was happy to accept my offer. He was on the verge of retirement anyway, and my offer was generous, to say the least."

"I see," Kate said bemusedly. "But what about the shop?"

"No problem," Alex assured her. "The manageress has agreed to keep it on as a going concern."

Then why her gut feeling that something was wrong? Kate wondered. Why her instinctive, sneaking suspicion that he was holding something back?

She said, shivering in the teeth of the cold north-east wind, "I've had enough fresh air for the time being. I'd rather like to go home now, if you don't mind."

Unexpectedly, Alex said, "I'm glad you regard it as such, Kate. Gull House as your home, I mean!"

She hadn't a clue what he meant – unless? Her heart lifted suddenly to the possibility that he had in mind a proposal of marriage. If not a marriage made in heaven, at least a deep and lasting relationship based on their need of one another.

There would be certain pitfalls along the way, Kate realised; heated exchanges of opinion; endless rows, soon over and done with. But above all, an underlying understanding of one another's past lives, which had shaped their present destinies beyond their power of control.

Unlike Don, Alex was not a womaniser, thank God. A little too rich for her liking, perhaps, whilst she was clinging on, for dear life, to her nest-egg from the sale of April Cottage. Even so, taking all these things into consideration, if Alex asked her to marry him, Kate knew she'd say yes. Why? Because she had fallen deeply in love with him. As simple as that!

Kate made tea on their return home from their wind-scoured walk to Castle Hill and back, rejoicing inwardly that Alex had possessed the foresight to purchase the property he now regarded as home. Hers also, one day, God willing. "Gull House" – she liked the name enormously.

"Could you be happy living here?" he said. "Leaving your own flat?" As if he had somehow read her mind.

"Moving in with you, you mean?" She had to be sure of her ground.

He frowned slightly, "That's not exactly what I had in mind."

"Then – what? I'm sorry, I don't understand."

"I asked you a question. You haven't given me an answer. Please, Kate, I need an answer. It's very important."

"An answer to what exactly?" She hadn't the remotest idea what he was driving at. An air of unreality had crept into the conversation.

"It's simple enough, surely? I asked if you'd be happy living here; giving up your own flat."

"That's two questions," she reminded him. "When I asked if you wanted me to move in with you, you said that wasn't exactly what you had in mind. So tell me, Alex, what have you in mind? I'm no good at guessing games."

A sudden thought occurred, a possible solution of the mystery, utterly ludicrous, and yet . . . She said disbelievingly, "Don't tell me you want a live-in housekeeper? Someone at your beck and call all the hours that God sends? If so, the answer is no! I'd rather keep my independence!"

"You misunderstand entirely," he said quietly. "What I'm in need of is not a housekeeper but a reliable tenant to look after the property. Please hear me out, Kate, before you climb aboard your independence bandwagon. What I'm offering you is rent-free tenancy of this house, plus expenses to cover the costs of maintenance – repairs, heating, and so on, plus an increase of your present salary to ensure your peace of mind during my – absence." He paused briefly. "Think about it, Kate. It's an offer worth your consideration, at least I hope so."

Kate looked at him disbelievingly. "During your absence?" she uttered bleakly. "You mean you are going away?"

"I have to," he said wearily.

"But where to? For how long?" She felt that her world had shattered suddenly like broken glass, as it had done so often before; when her parents had died, when she had failed so miserably to give birth to those dream children of hers. Above all, when Don had walked out of her life, leaving her alone in April Cottage to piece together the shattered fragments of her life as best she could. Now, she could scarcely bear the thought of losing Alex; of picking up the pieces of her life all over again.

"I can't answer your questions, I'm afraid," he said tautly, "for the simple reason that I don't know where I'm going or how long I'll be gone. That depends on how long it takes to find what I'm looking for, and where."

"And what *are* you looking for?" Kate asked him in a low voice, hoarse with emotion, in desperate need of reassurance that he regarded her as something more than an – employee. Or perhaps she was wrong in believing – hoping – that they had some kind of a future together?

"Peace of mind," he told her, speaking gently, knowing he had hurt her, at the same time realising how much more he would hurt her by staying on here in his present mood: an overwhelming restlessness of spirit, impossible to deny or to come to terms with until he'd had time and space enough to distance himself from the past, to try, at least, to make sense of his life.

How simple it would be to take the soft option, to tell Kate that he had fallen in love with her; ask her to marry him, and take it from there. And then what? He knew only too well. He would make her life a misery. Inevitably so, resultant upon his introspective concern with the past, those events: hatred of his parents, the faithlessness of his wife Leonora, the death of her son, Peter; the loss of his writing ability, which had changed him, beyond recognition, from the man he once was, to the man he was now – a sour, tetchy individual, incapable of either happiness or peace of mind, until he taken a journey into nowhere; a voyage of discovery, perchance, not into the past, but the future.

He had in mind, albeit vaguely, Afghanistan, Turkestan, Mongolia – wide open spaces far away from the pressures of modern day living: back-packing, carrying with him merely a razor, toothbrush, a couple of spare shirts and cashmere sweaters; wearing boots and an anorak; sleeping under the stars . . .

"Very well, then," Kate said coldly, "I'll think about it. But if I accept your offer, it will be with certain reservations. First and foremost that I may not still be here, if and when you decide to come back to Scarborough again. In which case, should I leave the property empty, or sub-let it to another 'reliable' tenant, such as myself?"

"Please, Kate," Alex implored her, "don't make things more difficult for me than they already are!"

"I'm sorry," she said, realising the futility of argument. "It's entirely up to you to make the necessary arrangements, to come and go as you please. It's your life when all is said and done. I just hope you'll find what you're looking for."

They had been sitting near the fire, by lamplight and the twinkling lights of the Christmas tree, in a shadowy corner of the room. When she'd brought in the food from the kitchen, the sandwiches, the cakes she'd made, the tea-things, placing then on the low coffee table drawn up between them near the hearth, she had experienced a thrill of pleasure in Alex's company. Getting up to clear the table, she wondered how she would feel, alone in the house, when he had gone away? Would the loneliness prove unbearable as it had done at April Cottage when Don had left her?

Alex's presence had filled the house, as it had filled her life. The place would seem empty without him. She might well feel nervous all alone in a house of this size. Besides which, how would she fill the empty days ahead of her with no one apart from herself to cook for?

But beggars could not be choosers. This way, at least she'd be spared the necessity of seeking alternative employment, she would have a safe roof over her head for the foreseeable future. Alex, she knew, could be trusted to secure, legally, the financial details of her future welfare, as only a rich man, with money to burn, possessed the power to do.

And yet, Kate considered wistfully, after carrying the tea things through to the kitchen, her hands deep in the washing-up water, had Alex been as poor as the proverbial church mouse, and had he asked her to marry him, without a penny to his name, she would not have hesitated to say yes to his proposal. Loving him so much, how could she possibly have said no?

When later, he followed her into the kitchen to ask what she had planned for supper, she said crisply, proudly, "Sorry, Alex, I've decided to go home, to spend the rest of the holiday alone."

Ten

S he needed space, time to think things through coolly and calmly. Above all, realistically.

She and Alex had been through a great deal lately. Their ill-fated trip to London, the atmosphere of the house in St John's Wood, discovery of the secrets of his past life, had heightened, intensified her feelings towards him. But was she really in love with him, or merely seeking security, as she had been when she married Don?

She could see it all clearly now, her desperate need of love and security after the deaths of her parents, so that she had not even stopped to consider what she might be letting herself in for, rushing into marriage the way she had done.

Greg had tried to warn her, to no avail. She hadn't wanted to listen, so certain of her love for Don that she had brushed aside her brother's misgivings as airily as a cobweb on a window pane.

Alone in her flat, looking out at the lights of the Valley Bridge, being brutally honest with herself, Kate recognised and accepted the similarities between the past and the present. Alex, like Don, had entered her life when she stood in need of help and support. Both were charismatic and clever, charming yet selfish.

Alex had been born rich. Don had become rich eventually by reason of his relentless, driving ambition to climb to the top of his chosen profession as a writer. Alex, on the other hand, had become a famous writer more by accident than design.

As for herself, Kate realised, all Don had really wanted from her was sex and children. Alex apparently wanted a dogsbody. A custodian. Obviously he harboured no deeper feelings for her. She was simply a handy person to have around to provide his creature comforts. A difficult man to understand or get close to.

Thankfully, she had betrayed no sign of her feelings towards him. And what did those feelings really amount to? Had she mistaken sympathy, physical attraction, his powerful presence in her life for love? Had she imagined that tide of feeling, running between them so strongly at times? Had she fooled herself into believing that they might find happiness together?

Common sense told her the sooner she relinquished hope of a future with Alex, the better. Reaching a decision about the future must be based on doing what was best for herself and no one else.

Two choices were open to her. She could stay on here in this flat, start looking for another job and put all thoughts of Alex out of her mind. Or, she could accept his offer of continuing employment as the custodian of his house, as such retaining her links with him, however tenuous they may be; living in hope that he would, one day, return to Scarborough.

Kate sat in her chair near the window till the early hours of next morning. When she finally got up, rather stiffly, at three a.m., switched off the lights and went to bed, she had reached her decision.

Alex had spent a miserable time since Kate's departure. Even so, he had recognised her need of solitude to think over the proposals he had put to her in his usual clumsy fashion, God dammit!

Somehow, he had never been able to express his feelings for her in words: clearly, simply and succinctly, as he had so often wished to do. Why not? he wondered.

Deep down, he knew the answer. Because he was afraid of commitment, of possible rejection by another woman, apart from his mother and – Leonora.

The desolation of his past life still clung to him as a shroud. Never had his mother shown the slightest degree of affection towards him. She had simply appeared to him as a glamorous, butterfly creature flitting in and out of his childhood on her way to some function or other, passing his nursery on her way downstairs without bothering to kiss him goodnight.

He had grown up taking wealth for granted – the opulence of the family home in Hampstead, richly furnished, with servants at their beck and call. Their riches were derived from various sources; tea plantations in Ceylon, timber mills in Canada, cattle ranches in Texas – handed down from father to son, from son to grandson and so on, originating with a long dead and gone forebear of his who had created the wealth of the Arden family in the first place. Alex's great, great grandfather, Adam Arden.

The plantations, mills and ranches had been sold off to other companies in the course of time; assets ploughed into other ventures closer to home. Alex's grandfather had established a chain of food-stores in major cities the length and breadth of Britain, had invested money in country properties going for a song, which he had upgraded and turned into luxury hotels.

With visionary foresight, he had also bought into a publishing concern, a race-track, several famous hotels and theatres in the centre of London, and a film company situated in Elstree, on the outskirts.

It grieved Alex to think that, after the death of his grandfather, his own father had chosen to squander the family wealth in high living: countless holidays abroad, to the Caribbean, the Seychelles, Turkey, Morocco, Sardinia, Corfu, Paris, Rome, Nice; drinking far more than was good for him, not giving a damn that his only child had been condemned to life in a boarding school he'd loathed and detested. Later to a public school, equally hateful.

And yet, after the death of his father and mother in that fatal car crash on the Route Nationale, there had been more than enough money left in the family coffers to assure his own lifestyle for the foreseeable future, his grandfather's solicitor had assured him, anxious, at the same time, to impress on him his responsibilities as the heir of the Arden family fortune.

But young Alex, at that stage of his life, could not have cared less about responsibilities. All he had wanted was freedom. And so he had gone off into the wild blue yonder, leaving business matters in the hands of those who understood them far better than he ever would; appointing the solicitor, Mr Daker, a man of the highest integrity, to act on his behalf, instructing him to sell the Hampstead property and its contents, which he loathed and wished never to set eyes on again.

All that seemed a very long time ago. Now, history was about to repeat itself. His urge to travel was as strong as it had been then, and for the same reasons: a need of self discovery, of escape from the complexities of life. Curiously, the sale of another property, the house in St John's Wood, was involved in this, his second bid for freedom.

Missing Kate intensely, he thought suddenly of his promise to let her have those old books of his she wanted to give to her brother, and remembered, ruefully, that she had likened himself to T.E. Lawrence – Lawrence of Arabia. If only . . .

Even so, perhaps there were similarities inasmuch as Lawrence had also sought escape from his own persona. He had based *The Seven Pillars of Wisdom* on his experiences of the First World War when, as a British Intelligence officer, he had dramatically led the Arabs against the Turks to capture the seemingly impregnable fortress of Akabar for his own compatriots, his own country, to his everlasting fame and glory. And yet Lawrence, turning his back on fame and fortune, had ended his days as a low-ranking member of not the army but the RAF, a partial recluse living alone in a tiny cottage, "Clouds Hill", frugally furnished, close to his RAF camp in Dorset, and had died tragically in a road accident when the motorbike he was riding had swerved suddenly to avoid two boy cyclists and hit a tree. A fine, brave human being.

That, thought Alex, was where the similarity ended. There had been nothing in the least brave or fine about Alex's own life, so far. Nothing uplifting or transcendental. The best he could hope for was that his future would be more settled, more rewarding than his past.

Meanwhile, so much depended on Kate's decision regarding her own future, somehow linked inexplicably with his. So why was she taking so long to reach that decision? Why didn't she come to him to put him out of his misery?

The sudden realisation that she might well not come to him at all added to his misery. After all, why should she? She probably hated his guts! He hadn't been very kind to her at times, and she was so deserving of kindness, a lovely, intelligent, caring human being, albeit with a mind of her own, a mile wide streak of independence inside her. She'd taught him lessons in good manners more than once during their brief relationship, he recalled, willing her to come to him, knowing that his life, his future, would be unbearable without her.

Moreover, he was worried about her physical requirements. She had left abruptly, taking nothing with her apart from an overnight case. She had no food. What was she living on? Fresh air?

He spent Boxing Day restlessly pacing the house, pausing now and then to make lists of all that needed doing in readiness for his departure early in the new year.

There were urgent letters to be written to his trustees – descendants of old Mr Daker, who had died some time ago, informing them of his intention to go abroad for some considerable time, his destination as yet undecided.

Unable to settle, to think clearly, he wished that Kate was here to bring light and common sense to bear on his present state of confusion.

How could he possibly proceed further until he knew her answer to his proposals concerning the tenancy of the house?

Only one way to find out! Putting on his outdoor things, he hurried downstairs. Opening the door, he jerked back a little in surprise. Kate was there on the doorstep. He said abruptly, "I was just on my way to your flat. Well, don't just stand there! Come in!" What he really wanted to say was: "Thank God you've come. I've missed you!" But of course, he didn't say what he meant. Old habits died hard. He sounded tetchy, irritable.

"I'm not stopping long," Kate said, beginning to wish she hadn't come at all.

"Don't be ridiculous. Of course you're stopping. There's enough food in the fridge to feed an army!" Alex led the way upstairs.

"Food's the last thing on my mind at the moment," Kate retorted.

"Then for goodness sake sit down and tell me what is!"

"Very well. I've decided to accept your offer."

"You have? Thank God for that!" His relief was evident. He actually smiled at her. "So why the nonsense about not stopping? We have a great deal to discuss."

"Not now, Alex. In any case, what *is* there to discuss? All I need to know is when you'll be leaving. Meanwhile, I intend staying on in my own flat. A period of unpaid leave, if you like, time in which to make my own arrangements, to visit my family in Manchester, if you've no objection? Frankly, I'm tired, in need of a change and a rest before taking on the responsibilities of my new role as your – agent – for want of a better word."

"*Agent?*" He looked shocked. "Dammit, Kate, that's the last thing I had in mind!"

"I'm sorry, Alex," she said calmly, "but that's exactly what you have in mind. Someone to act on your behalf when you're away. You spoke of expenses to cover the costs of maintenance, repairs, heating and so on. All well and good, but it will be up to me to decide what to do, who to send for if, say, the roof springs a leak or the brickwork needs repointing, with insurance claim forms to fill in."

"And *you* said there's nothing to discuss," he reminded her tartly.

"There isn't, for the simple reason that it is up to you to leave me explicit instructions how to act in an emergency beforehand, some higher authority I can turn to for help if faced with something totally unexpected. A break in, a burglary, for example, connected with the gift shop next door."

"My God, Kate, you really have been doing your homework, haven't you?" Alex said sarcastically.

"Yes, I have." She smiled briefly, "Now, it's high time you did yours, don't you agree?" Thinking, at one and the same time, how much she would miss this cut and thrust between them when they were far apart from one another.

When Kate had gone, taking with her her heavier suitcase in the boot of a taxi, Alex set about doing his "homework" as she had suggested. The trouble was, he couldn't concentrate on the task in hand. Her image, the very thought of her, kept on getting in the way.

Speaking her mind, as usual, she had brought to his attention the heavy burden of responsibility her tenancy would entail if things went badly wrong with the property; the necessity of covering every eventuality – Acts of God, fire, flooding, theft – the mood he was in, possibly the collapse of the whole bloody building from old age, he shouldn't wonder, beginning to wish he'd never bought the damned house in the first place.

Even so, he marvelled at her perspicacity, her grasp of fundamentals, her sense of self-preservation, akin to his own. At their first meeting, he had seen her as a nervous, lonely, lost individual. And perhaps she had been, then. No longer. Had his own selfishness somehow rubbed off on her? he wondered. Had she finally reached the hard-won conclusion that she was nobody's fool, but a clear-sighted, straight-thinking individual, capable of standing alone on her own two feet?

Alex might well have changed his mind on that score, had he realised Kate's true state of mind concerning her future, her desperate need of the only person in the world she could turn to for help, comfort and advice. Her brother, Greg!

"Of course, Kate," he'd said on the phone, "you know you're more than welcome to stay with Cindy and me any time, for as long as you like!" He'd added anxiously, "You sound a bit fraught. There's nothing wrong, is there?"

"Nothing that seeing you again won't put right," she'd assured him, trying her best to sound light-hearted. "I'm just a bit tired, that's all; in need of spiritual refreshment. In any case, it will only be a flying visit. A long weekend, if that's all right?"

Greg said, "Cut the cackle, Sis! This is *me* you're talking to, remember? Don't tell me, let me guess! Another sandcastle built within reach of the incoming tide?"

"Something like that," Kate confessed. "Some folk never learn sense, do they?"

"I take it, then, that your latest 'sandcastle' has to do with what's his name? Alex Arden? Your rich employer?" Greg asked gently.

"Yes, it has," Kate admitted, "but I'd rather talk about it in person, not on the telephone, if you don't mind."

"Fair enough, love," Greg conceded thoughtfully, "so just tell me the date and time of your arrival. I'll meet your train, and we'll take it from there, shall we?"

Meeting her at the station, he took her to a nearby pub for a brandy and soda, saying she looked in need of a warmer. In any case, they could talk better in a quiet corner of the bar parlour than a crowded station buffet.

Dear Greg, she thought, always on her side, doing what was best for her, still taking care of her as he had done when they were children. Not making a fuss, that was not his style. He was not nor ever had been particularly handsome. He had no outstanding physical features. His hair, thinning a little now, was brown in colour, his eyes a light hazel, twinkling eyes betraying a sense of humour and much more besides – an innate wisdom and kindness of heart. She said, "Oh Greg, I've missed you so much," and wondered, not for the first time, if he and Cindy were happy together? Difficult to explain, but he didn't look – cared for. His shirt collar needed ironing, and his loosely fitting tweed jacket had seen better days.

"I've missed you too, Kate," he said quietly. "Now, tell me what's wrong."

It was harder than she'd expected to put her feelings into words. When Greg asked her gently if she was in love with Arden, "I don't honestly know," she confessed. "I thought so, now I'm not so sure. In any case, he's not in love with me, and a one-sided love affair just isn't possible." Kate smiled ruefully.

"And yet you're willing to take on the responsibilities of his house?" Greg queried.

"For purely selfish motives," she said. "I need a job, and this is the only offer I've had, so far."

"Doing what, exactly? I'm sorry, love, but won't you feel lonely and bored without something positive to do each day? A sense of purpose in life?"

He continued thoughtfully, "You've always been such an active person: cooking, cleaning, gardening, caring for others. Remember how you looked after Mum and Dad, running that big, old house of ours single-handed? Then, forgive me for saying so, I know all the hard work entailed in turning April Cottage into a home. I've kept all your letters. Remember, you used to write to me daily in diary form then post the letters to me when they were almost too fat to fit into the envelopes?"

"Yes, of course I remember," she said mistily.

"I still read through them now and again," Greg admitted fondly. "They were so brilliantly funny at times! You up a ladder, a paint pot in one hand, a brush in the other; that bird trapped in a chimney! You'd just nicely finished your painting when down came the bird along with a downfall of soot which stuck to the wet paint as if it had been glued onto it! So what did you do?"

"After spending the best part of an hour cornering the damn thing and hustling it into the garden to rejoin its wife and babies, I can't honestly remember," Kate said, frowning.

"Then I'll tell you exactly what you did. You sat cross-legged on the floor not knowing whether to laugh or cry. The compromise you reached was laughing till you cried."

"Did I really do that?" Kate asked wistfully.

"Much more. Next day you climbed back up your ladder to begin painting the room all over again!"

"I must have had a lot more energy then than I have now," she commented drily, "and a better sense of humour."

"We both had more energy in those days," Greg reminded her, "but there's nothing wrong with your sense of humour—"

"Yours either," she interrupted.

"Thanks, love." He paused momentarily. "What I'm trying to say is this. Don't make the same mistake you made over Don in letting Alex Arden rule your life, the way Don did. Remember that you are a person in your own right with a life of your own to live. All right?"

"Yes. Fine. Message received and understood," Kate assured him. Glancing at her watch, she added, "Won't Cindy be wondering where we've got to?"

"No. She's having her hair permed this afternoon. She left me instructions to give you sandwiches for lunch; said she'd be home around five to start cooking supper. Sorry, 'dinner' as she prefers to call

83

it now she's rubbing shoulders with our rich new next door neigh-bours." Greg laughed. "The husband's in 'oil' by the way!"

"So are sardines," Kate said wickedly as she and her brother drained their glasses of brandy and left the pub, arm in arm, to find Greg's car, a battered Volkswagen, parked somewhere near the station, though he appeared to have forgotten exactly where.

"Not to worry, Sis," he said gaily, "it'll still be around somewhere or t'other. I mean to say, who, in their right senses, would want to pinch a clapped out Beetle? The bane of Cindy's life, by the way! She's always on at me to buy a better car, and I dare say she'll have her own way in the end. She usually does!"

At that moment, Kate knew beyond a shadow of doubt, that all was not well between her brother and his wife.

At the bungalow, Greg made "ham" sandwiches, as per Cindy's instructions, from a sliced white loaf of bread and a packet of moist luncheon meat.

Coming through to the kitchen from her bedroom where she had dumped her belongings, Kate could have wept at the sight of Greg cutting the crusts from the sandwiches.

"Here, let me help you," she said quickly. "You make the coffee – meanwhile, I'll slip the sandwiches under the grill to toast." At least toasting would dry out the limp luncheon meat to some extent, Kate thought, wondering, as she did so, what her lazy sister-in-law had planned for their so-called dinner? Something in oil? Sardines on toast, perhaps?

No wonder Greg's clothes were fairly hanging off him, Kate thought angrily, for the simple reason that he wasn't getting enough to eat! But what, if anything, could she do about it? Nothing, her common sense warned her. She was merely Greg's sister. Cindy, on the other hand, was his wife, the woman he had vowed to love and to cherish till death us do part, and in no way was she prepared to come between husband and wife, no matter how tempting the desire to do just that, to tell Cindy, in no uncertain terms, exactly what she thought of a woman too idle to iron her husband's shirt collars!

It was a fraught weekend, all told. When it was over and done with, Kate returned to Scarborough, to her own flat, to find a letter from Alex on her sitting room carpet, pushed under the door, most likely by her friend Fanny.

The letter read briefly:

View from a Balcony

Dear Kate,

   This to inform you that all the legal details of your tenancy of "Gull House" have been dealt with, hopefully to your entire satisfaction. Also that, my travel arrangements having been concluded after various delays, I shall be leaving Scarborough on 14 January, prior to which date I suggest a meeting between us to conclusively iron out the final details to our mutual satisfaction.

   Yours sincerely,
   Alex

P. S. There'll be documents to sign, requiring both signatures, yours and mine.

So that's it, is it? Kate thought sadly, crumpling up the letter in the palm of her hand, the end of an affair that had never even begun. But ah, how dearly she wished that it had.

Part Two

Eleven

She had lived through all this before, Kate thought. The circumstances were different but the feelings of loneliness and loss were every bit as acute now as they had been when Don walked out of her life.

She moved into Gull House the day before Alex's departure, thinking he'd need help with his last minute arrangements, plus a good breakfast inside him before catching the early morning train to King's Cross.

Knowing Alex, he'd probably say he wasn't hungry, but she would cook bacon and eggs anyway. Whether or not he ate it was up to him entirely. She couldn't force him to eat. A law unto himself, Alex would do exactly as he pleased. Men usually did, within her limited experience of the male gender.

As she had anticipated, the house was in an uproar upon her arrival: stacks of unwashed pots in the kitchen sink, dust everywhere, his bedroom a tip, clothes strewn on the floor, the Christmas tree still in situ in the living room, pine needles thick on the carpet, an unopened crate blocking the landing.

"As you can see, I'm in a bit of muddle," was his opening gambit as she followed him upstairs. "The crate, by the way, contains the books you wanted."

"Thanks," she said briefly, edging past it, wishing she possessed the leg power to kick the damn thing downstairs. Alex also, come to think of it!

Bitterly disappointed by his lack of enthusiasm at her appearance on his doorstep, marching into the kitchen, donning an apron and rolling back her sleeves, Kate made a start on the mess in the sink. A "bit of a muddle", she thought mutinously, a "disaster area" would be nearer the mark!

Every work surface was littered with biscuit tins, crumbs, bread and

89

cheese boards, empty milk and wine bottles, stained glasses and coffee cups. Mice, if there were any, would be having a field day.

Next she tackled the sitting room. Alex came in to find her struggling to remove the Christmas tree in its bucket of soil.

"I'll do that," he said. "Where do you want it?"

"The yard might be a good idea. I thought you'd have got rid of it by this time."

"I've had other things on my mind. I've sold the car, by the way."

"No point in keeping it, I suppose. When you've seen to the tree, there are some bags of rubbish in the kitchen to go down to the dustbins; left over food from the refrigerator, empty wine bottles and so on." Her anger was apparent. "When I've finished clearing up after you, I'll go shopping."

"Well, I did warn you that things were in a bit of a mess. Your fault for walking out the way you did on Christmas Day," he reminded her.

"Funny, I thought you'd end up blaming me. But then, no good keeping a dog and doing the barking yourself, is there?" Her anger evaporated suddenly. "I'm sorry, I shouldn't have said that. After all, clearing up after you is what I'm being paid for, and I'll clean the house from top to bottom after you're gone!"

"That's up to you entirely. I want you to feel at home. Oh, remind me to give you a spare set of keys." He picked up the tree which promptly parted company with the container. Soil showered on to the carpet. That's all she needed, Kate thought, feeling the way she had done at April Cottage when that bird came down the chimney along with a mound of soot, not knowing whether to laugh or cry. Suddenly, she laughed.

Might as well make the best of a bad job, she told herself. There'd be all the time in the world to clear up when Alex had gone. No use ruining the little time they had left together being angry or upset.

When Alex returned from his trips to the yard via the kitchen fire-escape, she asked him, as she made coffee, if he'd decided where he was heading for? His ultimate destination on his long trip abroad. Not wanting to pry, but needing some idea, for her own peace of mind.

Feeling more relaxed since her recent outburst of laughter which had lightened the atmosphere between them, he told her that he intended to fly from Heathrow to Saudi Arabia, from there to Tibet. He couldn't be more precise than that. He had no fixed itinerary in mind. He would play it by ear, as his mood dictated. The whole point and purpose of the excursion, when all was said and done.

They spent a pleasant if somewhat silent evening together. Kate had made a chicken and mushroom pie for supper after tidying his room, making his bed and bundling his discarded clothing into the washing-machine.

There seemed little left to say to one another. Both were physically and mentally tired: Kate from all the running about she had done that day and dreading the thought of tomorrow; Alex from the sheer volume of planning involved in his bid for freedom, which had irritated him past bearing at times these past few days. Going away entailed masses of red tape: inoculation jabs at his doctor's surgery; prolonged interviews at a local travel agency to ascertain that his passport and other documents were in order; sessions at his bank with regard to his traveller's cheques – far beyond their usual remit, amounting to not hundreds but several thousand pounds. Funds sufficient to underwrite the various expeditions he had in mind.

Importantly, at the back of his mind lay the dread of saying goodbye to Kate, the woman he loved, but lacked the courage to tell that he loved her. To what purpose, since she was so obviously not in love with him? And yet he could have sworn, in London, in the St John's Wood house, especially when he had shown her his study and those old books of his, that she had fallen in love with him, as he had with her.

Apparently he was wrong as he had been so often before during his chequered lifetime.

And yet, early next morning, on the point of departure, having stowed his luggage in the boot of the awaiting taxi, seeing Kate standing forlornly on the doorstep of Gull House, on a sudden impulse, he turned back to cradle her briefly in his arms, to murmur gently, "God bless you, Kate, and thanks for your friendship, which has meant more to me than you'll ever know."

Then suddenly he was gone. The taxi sped away, and Kate's lone-liness began.

Fanny was deeply upset when Kate told her she was leaving her flat. "If this has owt to do with old Joe Updike," she said, "I'll give him a good helping of 'tongue pie'!"

"No, it hasn't." When Kate explained the situation, Fanny said wistfully, "Will you come to see me once in a while?"

"Of course I will." Kate held the old woman's hand. "And you must come to see me whenever you feel like it. Promise?"

"Aye, I'd like that." Fanny smiled reminiscently. "Gull House, you say? I know it well. I used to play there as a kid with a schoolfriend of mine. Eh, the things we got up to in that there attic! Mekkin' tents out of bedclothes and an old clothes' horse! Having dolls' tea-parties an' suchlike!" She sighed deeply. "Happy days, they were! My friend's name was Clara Marshall. Her mother was a widow-woman who took in lodgers to make ends meet.

"Eh, how that poor woman worked to keep the cart on the wheels! Forever washing, cooking an' cleaning, she was, an' it weren't exactly an easy house ter foller, them stairs being so steep. But the house was all in one piece in them days, before what used to be the kitchen and the front room were knocked into one to make room for that gift shop!"

Fascinated, Kate longed to hear more. Talking to Fanny, listening to her reminiscences of Gull House which the old lady had known well, long before she was born or thought of, seemed akin to the pages of a history book being turned by the gnarled fingers of a woman who knew the Scarborough of long-ago as intimately as she knew the age-spots on the back of her hands. A vaguely formed yet thrilling idea had stirred in Kate's mind. Bidding Fanny goodbye, she walked back to Gull House to explore the possibilities of Alex Arden's typewriter.

The woman in charge of the York Place Business Agency, tall, spinsterish, grey haired, with horn-rimmed glasses, seemed nonplussed at first when Kate told her that she had no interest in learning short-hand or bookkeeping, that all she wanted was to learn touch-typing.

It seemed odd at first looking not at the keys but at a chart on the desk beside her, but Kate had every intention of getting up speed on Alex's typewriter, not prodding with two fingers when it came to writing the book she had in mind: a novel set against the background of Victorian Scarborough. The novel she had urged Alex to write, to no avail.

Researching her book would provide a new interest and impetus to her life, Kate realised, and learning the art of touch typing would add to her store of practical knowledge.

Furthermore, since Alex's departure, she had spent her evenings reading books, borrowed from the Vernon Road Library, on the lives of eminent Victorians – Elizabeth Barrett and her husband, Robert Browning, Charles Dickens, Lord Melbourne and the old Queen herself – with a view to soaking herself in the Victorian era, to reach a closer understanding of the shibboleths of that age, reading between the lines to discover that human beings had been every bit as fragile and vulnerable then as they were now.

Around midnight, switching off the sitting room lights and the electric fire in the hearth, after making certain that the house was securely locked and fastened for the night in fulfilment of her role as the custodian of Alex's property, Kate would go up to her room to make ready for bed, often to lie wide awake till the early hours of next morning, wondering where he was, imagining great tracts of wastelands beneath burning sun or starlight, eventually turning on her side to fall fast asleep from sheer mental exhaustion, and awakening, after a few hours of uneasy sleep, to review, over a cup of coffee and a slice of toast, the new day ahead of her.

On Mondays, Wednesdays and Fridays came her thrice weekly visits to Miss Murgatroyd to master the art of touch typing. Above all else she must keep busy, to which end she had begun decorating the kitchen and her own bedroom. At April Cottage she'd spent the long lonely days following Don's departure outdoors in the garden or in the greenhouse. Later, perhaps, here at Gull House when the weather was warmer, she would colourwash the yard's high brick walls and make a kind of patio with terracotta pots and hanging baskets of flowers.

Whether or not she would prove capable of writing a novel, Kate had no idea. To begin with, she would need several strong central characters and a gripping storyline. No use thinking she could cobble together a plot as full of holes as a threadbare blanket. Food for thought, and food for thought was something she desperately needed right now to keep her mind occupied with thoughts other than those centred on Alex.

Soon after his departure, she had opened and unpacked the crate on the landing and carried the books it contained upstairs to his study, where she arranged them carefully on the bookshelves he'd had built to house his collection of reference literature pertaining to the Victorian era in particular; the coming of the railways; Continental spa's and watering places; social habits and customs of that era, alongside a leather-bound volume of *The Seven Pillars of Wisdom*; paperback copies of the poems of Wilfred Owen, W.H. Auden, John Betjeman and Rupert Brooke – none of which she had felt inclined to peruse. To have done so would have seemed an intrusion of his privacy. Not the books so much as his personal choice of poetry.

The titles of his own books appealed to her strongly. Among them: *In Search of a Dream*, *My Brothers, the Bedouin*, and *Wide Rivers Run Deep*. These she would, perhaps, read in the fullness of time, but not now. Not yet.

Come next summer, she would invite Greg and Cindy to stay with her, Kate decided, when she would give her brother the books as a surprise birthday present, by which time, hopefully, her patio garden would have come to fruition, the tubs, hanging baskets and the terracotta Provençal pots burgeoning with lavender, night-scented stocks, colourful snapdragons, begonias and gloxinia.

Looking forward with hope, she reckoned, was far better than looking back in despair. Better by far to fill each waking moment with either sheer physical hard work or its mental counterpart, than to squander time feeling sorry for herself, as she had done when Don had left her.

But Don, after all, had been her lawfully wedded husband, whose defection had entailed the intervention of lawyers in the subsequent, unsavoury divorce proceedings. Alex, on the other hand, was nothing more than her employer, free to come and go as he wished. No promises made, therefore none to be broken. That he had chosen to leave her, albeit well provided for, Kate realised, was his prerogative entirely. Therefore, no legal lash-ups. No messy divorce proceedings. Equally, no – love. Just friendship.

In the Scarborough Room, Kate spread out a copy of the *Gazette and Herald* on the long oak table, her notebook and pen beside it, and knelt on a chair to inspect more closely the typescript, resembling a geologist examining a rock face in the hope of finding a vein of gold running through it.

Half an hour passed by. Nothing. No reference to the Crown Hotel. Her mind began to wander. Her thoughts strayed from the printed pages to Alex Arden. She wondered where he was right now, missing his tall, familiar presence in the room, his owlish appearance when he perched his glasses halfway down his nose, his habit of ruffling his hair with his hands when deeply preoccupied with the task confronting him, his occasional deep grunts of satisfaction when he came across nuggets of information relevant to his quest.

Then, suddenly, idly turning a page, Kate's eyes opened wide in surprise! She could have whooped for joy! There it was, in black and white, the name Albert Kiddy, of Newborough, Scarborough, winner of the May Day Horse Procession's First Prize of a blue riband and rosette in respect of the immaculately groomed and decorated team of dray horses, owned by his employers, Theakston Breweries, under his command.

The newspaper report continued in the fulsome fashion of the mid 1800s, not that Kate bothered to read on. All that really interested her was the name Albert Kiddy, almost certainly a forebear of Fanny's? Her great grandfather, most likely! Only one way to find out!

Next day, over a cup of afternoon tea in Fanny's bed-sitting room, "Oh aye, Albert were my great grandad right enough," the old woman said proudly. "I've got some cuttings and photographs in an old trunk of mine in the cellar. I keep it down there 'cos there ain't room for it up here. I could look them out for you, if you're interested."

"Yes, I am, very interested," Kate said. "I'd like to know more about your family tree."

"You would?" Fanny seemed doubtful. "But they were just ordinary working-class folk. Nowt posh, like me. Winning that there ribbon an' rosette was the highlight of great granda's life. Mind you, he was well thought of by the brewery, an' they gave him a grand send-off when he retired. A bit of a do, beer and sandwiches laid on, sherry wine for the ladies, a framed test – testawhat's it – an' a nice sum of money. Fifty guineas, an' that were a small fortune in them days."

Fanny continued mistily, "He kept that framed 'testament' of his over the mantelpiece till the day he died, which weren't very long after his retirement. Not that I remember owt about it. I wasn't born or thought of then. But he made good use of that money, the poor old fellah, setting up his son, John, my grandad, in his own cabinet maker's workshop in St Sepulchre Street."

"Look, Fanny," Kate suggested quietly yet eagerly, "why not come to Gull House for tea on Sunday afternoon? Bring your cuttings and photographs with you? I'll have a good old bake-up beforehand: make lots of cakes and scones. We'll have time for a proper chinwag, and I'd love to hear more about the house as you remember it from your schooldays."

"Oh yes. Thanks, my dear, I'd really like that," Fanny said gratefully. She added mischievously, "Just one thing, if you're thinking of mekkin' sandwiches, I'd rather you didn't. Truth to tell, I'm sick an' tired of sandwiches. I'd far rather have a slice or two of cooked ham on a plate any day of the week."

Kate smiled sympathetically. Looking round Fanny's bed-sitter with its limited cooking facilities, she well understood the old lady's need of a good substantial meal inside her apart from soup, sandwiches, biscuits and boiled eggs.

"Leave it to me," she said briskly, bidding Fanny farewell. "Till Sunday, then? I'll look forward to it enormously."

"So shall I," Fanny said fervently.

Fanny had mentioned cooked ham, but Kate wanted to give her guest something hot and sustaining, so, apart from cakes and scones, she made a substantial meat and potato pie, to the old lady's obvious delight when Kate produced it, piping hot, from the oven, along with a jug of gravy and a tureen of vegetables.

"Eh," Fanny said wonderingly, "I thought we was having afternoon tea, not a bust-up dinner! Not that I'm complaining, mind you! I haven't had a meat and tater pie since – I can't remember when. But what a lot of trouble you've been to!"

"No trouble at all, I assure you," Kate laughed, serving her guest a sizeable chunk of the pie. "I've missed having someone to cook for other than myself."

Kate had elected to serve the meal in the kitchen, where they would feel more at home. When they had finished eating, she would show Fanny the rest of the house. Later, they would sit near the front room fire where, hopefully, Fanny would reveal the contents of the carrier bag she had brought with her.

But first she must tell the old lady exactly why she had expressed so much interest in her family background: her intention of writing a novel with, possibly, Albert Kiddy as one of the key characters. To do otherwise was unthinkable. For all she knew, Fanny may well stubbornly refuse to give her consent to a fictionalised version of her family history. Not that Kate imagined for one moment that even if the book was written, it would stand a chance of publication. Even so, she must give Fanny the right of refusal on so delicate an issue.

To her surprise and delight, Fanny embraced the idea wholeheartedly: obviously pleased and proud that her great grandfather would receive the recognition he deserved – apart from his blue ribbon, rosette, "testament" and the lump sum of fifty guineas he'd received on his retirement from Theakston's Brewery.

Soon the low table drawn up to the sitting room fire was littered with the contents of Fanny's carrier bag, including the tattered remains of Albert's blue riband and rosette, and daguerrotype photographs of him as an old man, taken alongside an elderly woman whose right hand rested on his shoulder; plus an upright, serious-faced young man with fair hair whose head appeared to be held in a vice, and a slender young woman, dark-haired and wearing a white dress and a broad-brimmed hat.

"That's my great grandad and great grandma," Fanny said eagerly. "The young man's my grandad. Leastways he was. He'd dead now, of course, an' so is his sister, Lucy – the one wearing the hat. My word, the trouble that lass caused them you wouldn't believe."

"Really? How come?" Kate asked.

Fanny sighed. "Well, they do say there's one in every family, and she was it! A born troublemaker. Course, tales might have got a bit exaggerated in the telling. But she *was* a bonny lass, no doubt about that, as you can see for yourself. Trouble was, she knew it, and wouldn't settle her mind to anything.

"Her an' her brother were as different as chalk and cheese. When John left school, he started work as an apprentice joiner. No messing. He knew exactly what he wanted to be. Not so Miss Lucy! Oh no, not her! She wanted to be 'different' –" Fanny chuckled – "an' seemingly she got her wish in the long run."

Kate listened intently as Fanny got into her stride, running on like a stream in full spate, recounting the family history from hearsay, leaving gaps now and then, not unusual for a woman of her age.

"Ended up the wife of a rich man twice her age, by all accounts," Fanny went on, "who treated her like dirt an' made her life a misery with his 'extra-martial' relationships an' so on, till she finally ran away with a handsome young sea-captain, half *her* age, an' was never seen or heard of again, as if she had disappeared from the face of the earth. I've often wondered what became of her, poor lass. Perhaps they were shipwrecked on a desert island? Who knows?

"Summat I know for certain, leaving school, Lucy started work as a chambermaid at the Crown Hotel. It happened this way. My great grandad Albert knew the owner quite well by way of his drayman's job, delivering beer to the hotel vaults at regular intervals, an' he asked the man if he could find employment for his young daughter, as a waitress or whatever . . ."

Kate's eyes glowed. At last, her metaphysical hero, John Fairgray Sharpin, had entered the arena as a vital, living person in the Kiddy family's history, not merely as a name printed on the pages of a dusty newspaper in the Scarborough Room of the local library.

"What was the man like?" she asked breathlessly.

"Eh?" Fanny looked puzzled. "Oh, the owner of the Crown Hotel, you mean? Why, I can't say for sure. All I know is that old Albert was as pleased as Punch when he gave young Lucy a job as a chambermaid. Not that she stuck it for long, the daft cat! Next thing they knew, she'd run off with a cellarman old enough to be her father, and married into the bargain. What I mean to say is, the man was married to someone else, not Lucy. The father of four, no less. Well, you can imagine the schemozzle that caused! Then my great grandad went in search of them.

"Not that they took much finding! They'd landed up working in a posh hotel in Brighton, posing as a married couple. The bloke had been daft enough to leave a letter from the Brighton hotel in a wastepaper basket in his room."

"Then what happened?" Kate asked intently, deeply interested in the machinations of poor Lucy Kiddy, the undoubted heroine of her embryo novel.

"Well, Lucy was hauled home in disgrace. But had she learned her lesson? No fear! Six months later she was involved in a love affair with a young fisherman she'd met in The People's Park, or whatever it was called – a kind of fairground in the Valley, so far as I can make out, with all kinds of wickedness taking place there! A bad influence on the town as a whole, in my opinion."

"I'm certain it was never meant to be anything more than a source of happiness and relaxation for the ordinary folk of Scarborough," Kate said quietly, in defence of her long dead and buried hero, John Fairgray Sharpin. A man for all reasons . . . Then, smilingly, she suggested making another pot of tea to revive Fanny's flow of energy and good humour.

The tea made and more cakes consumed, Fanny said she'd best be getting back home. Putting on her outdoor things, she thanked Kate profusely for giving her such a grand time. Kate reminded her that she'd left her carrier bag in the sitting room. "I hadn't forgotten," Fanny said. "I thought you'd like to take a closer look at the stuff I brought with me." She chuckled. "That way I'll be bound to see you again soon, shan't I?"

When the old lady had gone, in a taxi Kate had ordered and paid for, and taking with her the remains of the meat and tater pie and a bag of left-over cakes and scones, protesting there was really no need but ta just the same, Kate went back to the sitting room to gather together the scattered photographs, various scraps of paper and the rest of the nostalgic reminders of the Kiddy family, which she returned carefully to the carrier bag and took upstairs to the attic studio.

Gripped with a strange feeling of excitement, she would be unwise to even attempt looking at the contents of the carrier tonight. Akin to a greedy child at a birthday party eating for eating's sake. What she needed right now was time to digest the mass of information she'd received so far.

Fanny's visit had been fun, but exhausting. When Kate had showed her round the house after their main meal, the old lady had recounted endless stories of her childhood days, fascinating but bewildering – a bit like listening to a switched on tape-recorder without a pause button, Kate had thought at the time.

Then had come her more interesting, slower-paced revelations of her family history, which Kate had found utterly absorbing, especially those snippets linked to Albert Kiddy's relationship with John Fairgray Sharpin, when suddenly the past had come alive for her, so that beyond and above Fanny's monologue she had imagined that meeting between Albert and Sharpin, when the drayman had asked the charismatic tenant manager of the prestigious Crown Hotel if he could provide employment for his daughter, Lucy.

Kate knew instinctively that Sharpin would have treated Albert as his equal, not patronisingly or high-handedly, but as a fellow human being. Possibly Albert had confided in him that Lucy was – in present day parlance – a bit of a problem child, with a will of her own and strong aversion to work in any shape or form whatsoever.

Nevertheless, Sharpin had taken the wayward Lucy under his wing, for friendship's sake, knowing full well the calibre of the man making the request: a decent, upstanding honourable man deserving of all the practical help that was within his power to provide.

And so young Lucy Kiddy had gone to work at the Crown Hotel as a chambermaid, against her will, more than likely. And what would it have been like for her, Kate wondered, an impressionable, discontented teenager, brushing shoulders with elegantly dressed women on their way downstairs to the dining room, whilst she was on her way upstairs to turn down their beds for the night?

Little wonder that poor Lucy had hopped it to Brighton with that cellarman, Kate conjectured as she made ready for bed. In desperate need of love and attention – romance with a capital R – she would have easily fallen under the spell of a man much older than herself: walking hand-in-hand with him beneath a moonlit sky; turning up her flower-like face to be kissed by him; listening to his lies, believing every word he uttered . . .

And she, Kate, should know. For hadn't the self same thing happened to herself at roughly the same age as Lucy Kiddy?

On the verge of sleep, there should be a law against moonlight, she thought hazily.

Twelve

" April, April, Laugh thy girlish laughter. Then, the moment after, Weep thy girlish tears".

The words of an old poem, learned at school, entered Kate's mind as she stood at the sitting-room window staring out at the pouring rain. Moments before, the sun had been shining, and it would be again once this rain shower had passed.

April! Almost four months since Alex had left Gull House, and she had heard not a word from him, had received not so much as a postcard. But perhaps they didn't sell postcards in the Arabian Desert? And it was likely there were no post-boxes handy!

All very well to view the situation with a wry sense of humour, to imagine a camel train hitting some twentieth-century oasis complete with postcard stands and pillar boxes; possibly even a bedouin supermarket selling pickled sheep's eyes and bottled beer? Utter and absolute rubbish, of course, and she knew it!

Deep down, she was seriously worried by Alex's lack of communication during the seemingly endless days since his departure into the wild blue yonder. But what, if anything, could she do to relieve her anxiety? The answer came pat, simply and clearly. Nothing! Nothing at all! All she could possibly do was to get on with her life in her own way, as best she could, to live in hope of some kind of message from him in the not too distant future.

She had at least learned how to touch type, and had begun writing, albeit tentatively, the first chapter of her novel. (Sod's Law, she thought ruefully. Now she could type faster than she could think!) At least the York Place Business Agency was doing a roaring trade in A4 paper and correction fluid.

The thought occurred that she was jumping in at the deep end in starting a novel without a clearly defined outline of the plot and the characters involved. And so, curbing her enthusiasm and getting down to the nitty-gritty, she had painstakingly set about typing lists of information relevant to her brain child, beginning with her notes on the history of Scarborough in particular; the Victorian era in general.

Next on the agenda came a series of thumbnail sketches of the characters involved: their appearance, mannerisms, backgrounds, social habits, and so on.

Fanny's "bag of tricks" had yielded several surprises in the shape of old letters and documents, school exercise books in John and Lucy's handwriting, household accounts kept by Mavis Kiddy, Albert's wife; John's indentures of apprenticeship to one Martin Gooch, a Master Cabinet Maker of Dumple Street; bits and bobs of jewellery, a coral necklace and a tiny gold ring such as a child might have worn. Lucy, most likely.

Kate's nucleus of main characters included Albert, Mavis, John and Lucy Kiddy and John Sharpin, very clear and real to her. But there were many others not so clearly delineated in her mind's eye: Lucy's elderly husband, for instance, the cellarman she'd run off with to Brighton; the sea captain with whom she had presumably ended her days, the young fisherman she'd met and fallen in love with in the People's Park.

Kate knew exactly where and when she would begin her novel – on that May evening long ago when the Kiddy family had trooped down to the Valley to witness the opening of the pleasure ground. How the story would end was far more difficult to decide. Readers of romantic fiction wanted a happy ending. Perhaps she'd settle for Lucy and her sea captain standing at the prow of his ship, gazing at the far horizon, contemplating their happy future together?

At least, doing the spadework beforehand, Kate found the intended novel had begun to assume shape and form. Whether or not she possessed the ability to breathe life into her characters, to write convincingly about the Victorian era, remained to be seen.

Meanwhile, life went on, and she had other things to see to: planning her patio garden, for instance; cooking, cleaning and shopping. More urgently, worrying about the shop below when the manageress, a Mrs Dorothy Paulson, handed in her notice unexpectedly due to family problems beyond her power of control: a sick husband on one hand, a cantankerous mother on the other, living under the same roof and fighting like cat and dog.

"I'm sorry, Mrs Ford," Dorothy said weepily, "but I'm needed at home right now! My husband has Parkinson's Disease, and my mother's in the early stages of senile dementia. So you see how it is? But I do really need the money!"

Kate thought quickly. Presumably Mrs Paulson had known the pitfalls ahead of her when she'd taken on the responsibilities of a manageress. "I'm sorry this has happened," she said, "but perhaps we can reach a compromise?"

"What sort of a compromise?" Mrs Paulson dabbed at her eyes with a hanky.

"Perhaps you could work part time?" Kate suggested, feeling sorry for the woman. "That way you'd still have some money coming in, and it would be a great help if you could stay on long enough to show someone else the ropes."

"You mean a replacement manageress?"

"No, an assistant saleswoman's more what I have in mind. I'm sure we could come to some satisfactory arrangement. Above all, I'd appreciate your doing the buying as usual, knowing the reps, the amount of stock to order, and so forth."

Mrs Paulson managed a smile, "Yes, I think I could manage that all right. Thank you, Mrs Ford."

"Call me Kate."

"And you can call me Dot, or Dotty."

"Thanks – Dot! Well, let's mull things over for a while, shall we? You work out how much time you can spare, meanwhile I'll advertise for an assistant, and we'll take it from there."

"Have you thought of working here yourself?" Dot asked. "That way there'd be no need to advertise."

"No, I'm sorry." The sooner that notion was knocked on the head, the better, Kate thought. She had quite enough on her plate as it was. Besides, the shop was not strictly her province. Dot's wages were paid by Alex's London-based firm of solicitors, who also settled the stock bills and various other accounts – light, heating, insurance, etc., on a monthly basis – at Kate's insistence before Alex set forth on his voyage of discovery. Kate thought she had made it perfectly clear to him that she wanted nothing whatever to do with the shop. And she had meant what said she'd said.

Frankly, she'd considered him mad to even contemplate keeping on the gift shop in the first place, although his reasons for so doing had made sense inasmuch as one day, perhaps, he might wish to restore

Gull House to its original state: an impossibility if ownership of the downstairs premises changed hands.

"Fair enough," she'd conceded, "just as long as you don't expect me to become involved in the running of it."

"You have my word."

Now, here she was up to her eyes in it! But not for longer than she could help. No fear! But then, business matters were one thing, human problems a different matter entirely. No way could she have failed to respond other than sympathetically to Dot Paulson's anguish over her domestic dilemma, to try her best to come up with a reasonable answer to a decent woman's *cri de cœur*.

In thoughtful, nostalgic frame of mind, Kate walked up to Westborough where she paused for a while, shoring up her courage before turning into Albemarle Crescent to re-visit the house she had loved so much in her childhood years – uncertain that she could bear to look at it without bursting into tears.

An impossibility, she realised, tears flooding her eyes as, looking up at the windows, she imagined her mother's face smiling down at herself and Greg as they had set off, buckets, spades and shrimping nets in hand, to spend carefree hours on the beach.

Things were different then from now, life lived at a slower pace. Children came on holiday with their parents for a week or a fortnight, staying in one place, usually in some small boarding house well known to them to which they returned year after year – the Albemarle Crescent house, for instance, where Kate's mother had taken in boarders during the summer months to help pay the rates, as had most other housewives in Scarborough with rooms to spare.

Standing on the pavement, she could see, in her mind's eye, the Saturday morning crop of new arrivals from the railway station, decent, ordinary couples with well-behaved children in tow: the husband, neatly dressed in a suit, collar and tie, his wife wearing a skirt, blouse and hand-knitted cardigan, the little girls in summer dresses, the boys in short flannel trousers. The father would be carrying the cases, his wife various brown paper carrier-bags with string handles; the children, buckets and spades.

How hard Mum had worked to give those people a good, carefree holiday at the seaside. Nothing had been too much trouble. "Eh, Mrs Harker," they would say, "it's grand to be back." And Mum had laughed delightedly and said there'd be a cup of tea on the go when they'd finished unpacking. Lemonade for the kids. And there'd be a good high tea ready for them at half-past five; a bite of supper around nine, before the children's bedtime.

Looking back, Kate realised whence her housewifely instincts had sprung, her love of cooking, of homemaking: traits inherited from her mother, whose joy in life had lain in keeping other folk well fed and happy.

If only it were possible to turn back the hands of time, to hurry down the corridor of years to find her mother standing there, smiling, arms outstretched to embrace her.

Turning away, blinking back her tears, fighting hard to gain control of her emotion at seeing the old house again, Kate walked downhill to Aberdeen Walk, a busy shopping thoroughfare close to the heart of town, drawn by a desire to find out what had become of her school friend, Jenny Laird, the bubbly, fun-loving girl who had been bridesmaid at her wedding to Don Ford that cold winter morning twenty-odd years ago. Who had, indeed, been instrumental in arranging that blind date which had brought herself and Don together in the first place.

She couldn't remember the exact address, but she knew the house well enough: the street in close proximity to Gladstone Road Infants and Junior School, the Lairds' house above a corner shop where Jenny's dad had sold sweets, tobacco and groceries.

It was a longish walk from the town centre to Gladstone Road, a trip down "Memory Lane" as she recognised old, familiar landmarks – a clothing shop with a clock above the entrance, a triangular patch of grass, red-brick public lavatories, a butcher's shop, a post-box; half-forgotten street names, rows of prim Victorian villas with narrow front gardens and a preponderance of laurel bushes, iron railings removed during the war she scarcely remembered. She had been far too young at the time.

Hardly likely, she thought, nearing the corner shop, that Jenny's father would still be there behind the counter, bluff and smiling, serving schoolchildren aniseed balls, Spanish bootlaces and acid drops from cardboard boxes on display in the window. He'd have probably retired ages ago, but it was just possible that the Lairds were still living in the house above the shop.

Entering the shop, noting the inevitable changes wrought by modernisation – laminated shelving in place of wood, a counter display unit revealing piles of ready-cut ham and luncheon meat, pre-packed cheeses and bacon slices, plastic trays of coleslaw, Waldorf and beet-root salad, Scotch eggs and frankfurters – with the strong feeling that she was wasting her time, Kate asked the man in charge of the counter if he knew the present whereabouts of the Laird family.

"*Who?*" he asked, frowning. "Sorry, love, never heard of 'em!"

"They used to own this shop," Kate explained patiently, "a long time ago, but I thought they might still be living in the area."

"Naw. Like I said, I've never heard of 'em! Why don't you try next door? The old lady there's been here since 'Dick's Days'. Going on ninety, I reckon, an' a right old busybody. If anyone'll know, *she* will!"

"Do you happen to know her name?" Kate asked.

The man laughed. "Mrs Parker! Mrs 'Nosy' Parker, we call her!"

"Thank you." Kate beat a hasty retreat from the delicatessen counter with its piles of pale spotted luncheon meat and sweating ham slices, as fast as possible without causing offence to the new owner of the premises.

Not exactly looking forward to her possible encounter with a ninety-year-old tittle-tattle, nevertheless Kate rang Mrs Parker's doorbell and waited, in a state of nervous tension, until, after much fiddling with bolts and locks by the old lady inside, the door finally opened to reveal, not a wizened crone, but a spry looking lady, white-haired, with sharp, intelligent eyes and the complexion of a schoolgirl, who said mildly, "If you're one of those 'do-gooders' from the Town Hall wanting to move me into an old folk's home, the answer's *No*! The only way I'll leave my home is feet first, in a wooden box! So there!"

Kate smiled, liking the old woman at first sight. "I'm not from the Town Hall, Mrs Parker. I'm just trying to discover the whereabouts of the Laird family – friends of mine from way back."

"You *are?*" Mrs Parker beamed like a sunburst. "Then you'd best come in, my dear. I'll put the kettle on for a cup of tea!"

"No, please don't bother," Kate protested weakly, not wanting to intrude on the old woman's privacy, at the same time following her into a neat little kitchen with an old-fashioned stone sink, wooden draining-boards and gleaming brass taps; a pre-war gas cooker; ceiling clothes' airer draped with celanese knickers, woollen camisoles and stout hook-sided corsets, two brushed-wool nightgowns and several pairs of lisle stockings.

"As you can see, I still manage to keep myself clean and decent," Mrs

Parker said chirpily, filling the kettle and applying a match to a ring on the cooker, "despite my years! Eighty-five next month, would you believe it? And still going strong! Except, I have to say that my eyesight isn't quite what it used to be, so I can't quite make out . . . Have I seen you before? What's your name, by the way?"

"Kate. Kate Ford, née Harker," Kate supplied. "Jenny Laird and I were at school together, and her parents were very good to me when — that is after the death of my parents." She paused painfully. "In fact, I was married from the house next door, and Jenny was my bridesmaid."

"Oh yes, of course, now I remember. Not very clearly, I'm afraid, but vaguely. The Lairds were such nice folk, and Jenny was as pretty as a picture, as I recall, in her pink bridesmaid's dress," Mrs Parker reminisced, warming the teapot and measuring into it two spoonfuls of tea from a tea-caddy commemorating the Coronation of King George the Sixth. Closing the lid of the caddy with gnarled fingers, she continued, "I was sorry when the Duke of York had to take on the job of King when his brother renounced his throne to marry that dreadful American divorcée, Wallis Warfield Simpson. And what a fluttering in the royal dovecote that caused!" Mrs Parker said disapprovingly, pouring boiling water on to the tea-leaves in a brown earthenware pot with a chipped spout and a cracked lid, indicative of its many years' usage as an eighty-five-year-old lady's dearest companion of the past four decades.

Sipping her tea, very delicately Kate asked the burning question: "Have you any idea, Mrs Parker, what became of the Laird family after their retirement?"

Handing Kate a plate of digestive biscuits, the old lady said confusedly, "They moved away to Warminster, as I recall, or could it have been Ilminster? I forget which, but Jenny stayed on in Scarborough, of that I'm sure — at least I think I am!" She wrinkled her forehead. "The last I heard of her, she'd started a second-hand dress shop somewhere in the Old Town, near the Market Hall, though whether or not she's still there, I can't say for certain."

Thanking her hostess, Kate got up to leave. Mrs Parker followed her to the door. Smiling sadly, she said, "I miss the old days. That's why I want to stay where I am, to keep things the way they were. Do-gooders tell me I'd be better off in a home. But I've got a home, and here's where I'm staying."

Kate said gently, "I envy you your home, Mrs Parker. I had one once. Foolishly, I let go of it. I often wish now that I'd clung on to it, the way you have done."

"You'll have a home of your own again one day," the old lady said perceptively. "Believe me, I *know*!"

Kate looked puzzled. "But how? I mean, how can you be so sure?"

Mrs Parker's cheeks flushed slightly. "I daresay you won't remember a fortune-teller's shop in Eastborough. A – Madame Zara?" She chuckled softly. "*I* was Madame Zara!"

Curiously, Kate did vaguely remember the shop, which she and Greg had often passed on their way to the sands. She certainly remembered her mother having consulted Madame Zara once or twice at times of emotional stress and indecision; the comfort she'd derived from her visits; the good advice she'd received from the bizarrely named clair-voyant, whom she had described as "a nice, ordinary little woman, not in the least bit frightening."

On an impulse, bending down, Kate kissed the old woman's soft pink cheek. "I'm so glad to have met you," she said warmly, "and I do believe what you told me about having a home of my own again, one day."

"You were wise to part with your cottage," Mrs Parker said. "It had served its purpose. Staying on there, you wouldn't have been happy. Too many unhappy memories; too many – ghosts. My advice is, forget about the past. Look to the future. Many people, some close to you, others not so close, are in need of your help right now. You'll need to be strong for their sake. And you will be, of that I'm sure!" She smiled happily. "And this will not be your last visit to my home. So, goodbye now, my dear, until we meet again."

Walking back the way she had come, Kate felt strangely comforted and uplifted, as if a strong link had been forged between the past, present and future. Incredibly, Mrs Parker had mentioned parting with her cottage, which she had not referred to directly as such. Kate had merely mentioned her home. An educated guess on the old lady's part? Kate thought not. After all, for all Mrs Parker knew, she might have lived in a flat, a maisonette, a modern house or a bungalow. Yet she *had* known, not just about the cottage but Kate's reasons for leaving it – too many unhappy memories, too many ghosts.

Deep in thought, Kate remembered Alex once asking her if she believed in reincarnation, and she had said no. Now she wondered what she *did* believe in? A life hereafter? Fate? Destiny? Ghosts? Almost certainly that the presence of those who had gone before possessed the power to live on, unseen, in places close to them in their earthly lives – as the spirit of John Fairgray Sharpin may well still live on in his beloved Crown Hotel; as the shades of Albert, Mavis, John and Lucy Kiddy lived on in her imagination, awaiting their rebirth, at her hands, on the keys of Alex Arden's typewriter.

Thirteen

H aving "mulled things over", Dot Paulson presented Kate with a list of what she termed "times of availability": Mondays, Thursdays and Fridays.

She had, apparently, persuaded her husband to attend a day centre three times a week, and a neighbour to keep an eye on her mother. Not that her hubby had needed much persuading to get shot of his frenetic mother-in-law thrice weekly, Dot confided to Kate, and vice-versa. Her mother had expressed satisfaction that her son-in-law would be "out from under her feet" three days a week.

"All this has blown up quite recently," Dot explained ruefully, "since Mum started losing her memory. Asking the same questions over and over again. Forgetting where she'd put things and blaming my hubby for hiding them from her. That's when the rows started. And there was I – pig-in-the-middle – trying to keep the peace between them. Not that I succeeded. Things went from bad to worse. That's when I decided to hand in my notice. I honestly didn't know whether I was coming or going between the pair of them!"

Kate understood completely. "Mondays, Thursdays and Fridays will suit me fine," she said. "And not to worry if you have to change days occasionally. I'll give you all the help and support I can."

Dot fiddled up her sleeve for a hanky, saying emotionally, "I'm sure I don't know what I'd have done without your help. You've been a tower of strength to me, you really have!"

Suddenly Kate thought back to her meeting with Mrs Parker. The old lady's words: "Many people, some close to you, others not so close, are in need of your help right now. You'll need to be strong for their sake."

Many people? Kate puzzled. So, apart from Dot Paulson, who else?

Why the strange feeling that Dot Paulson's problems were merely the tip of a very large iceberg indeed?

Only time would tell.

Raking the streets of the Old Town for a second-hand dress shop in the vicinity of the Market Hall, Kate reached the conclusion that it no longer existed – if, indeed, it ever had.

Evidently, "Madame Zara's" clairvoyancy had certain limitations in the area connected with Jenny Laird's present whereabouts. A pity, really, Kate had looked forward to a possible reunion with her old schoolfriend, the bright, bubbly blonde whose enjoyment of life had somehow rubbed off on to other people, teachers and pupils alike, all of whom had liked Jenny enormously because, quite simply, she was one of those rare human beings who radiated happiness and goodwill to all of her fellow human beings. Mankind in general. Men in particular, perhaps, Kate realised. And why not? With her looks, her personality, Jenny had only to smile, to throw back her mane of naturally blonde, curly hair, to glance teasingly at any member of the male sex with those innocent blue eyes of hers, to have them at her beck and call.

No one Kate asked remembered a dress shop in that part of town, even the shopkeepers she approached when buying chocolate, post-cards or newspapers she didn't really want. "No, sorry love," they said, shaking their heads.

In the Market Hall, Kate asked various stallholders, buying meat and vegetables which she did want, if they recalled a second-hand dress shop, and met with the same response, until one woman, weighing apples, said, "If it's second-hand stuff you're wanting, you could try that stall down yonder, near the exit. She often has a few bargains mixed in with the tat. But don't let her con you into buying summat you don't want. She could sell ice-cubes to an eskimo, that 'un!"

"Thanks. Might as well take a look." Paying for the apples, Kate walked between the stalls towards the rear exit.

The woman, powerfully built, with a mass of dyed blonde hair, serving a customer, had her back to Kate. The stall was crowded with what could only be described as junk oddments of china, gimcrack ornaments, items of brassware and cheap jewellery; knitted toilet-roll covers and tea-cosies; off-cuts of dress material, a few electrical appliances; piles of dog-eared magazines and paperback books. Suspended on hangers above the stall, a variety of out-of-date dresses,

111

suits, skirts and jackets. In boxes on the floor space fronting the stall, a jumbled mass of shoes, sandals and slippers.

When the woman turned towards her, "Hello, Jenny," Kate said mistily. "Remember me?"

Jenny's reaction startled Kate. Her cheeks flushed to the colour of beetroot, she held on to the stall to steady herself, then the colour drained away suddenly, leaving her cheeks deathly pale, and she burst into tears. Racking sobs shook her overweight body, rivulets of black mascara ran down her face. Staring at Kate with anguished eyes, she muttered hoarsely, "Well, go on, take a good look! No need to tell me what you're thinking! Why don't you go away and leave me alone!"

Deeply shocked by her friend's hostility, Kate said levelly, "I'm not going anywhere until you tell me what all this is about. I've been searching high and low for you. Now I've found you, you'll not get rid of me that easily. Here –" handing her a hanky – "dry your eyes. Your mascara's running. Now, give me a smile and tell me you're as pleased to see me again as I am you!"

"*What*? The state I'm in?" Jenny dabbed her eyes. "A fat, blowsy old tart like me? Well, go on, admit it!"

"Very well, then, if it will make you feel less sorry for yourself. So you've put on weight, dyed your hair. But not so much of the 'old', if you don't mind. We're the same age, remember? More importantly, I'm still your friend. Or have you forgotten how much we once meant to each other?"

"No, of course not," Jenny admitted reluctantly. "But oh, what's the use? Look at you, still slim and attractive; well off too, I daresay, not like me, a fat bloody failure, up to my ears in debt, eking out an existence at a – junk stall!"

"We need to talk," Kate said compassionately, "but not here. Could we meet later, perhaps, at your place or mine?"

"Sure. Why not?" Jenny said recklessly. "I'll give you my address. I'd really like you to see where I live: the depths I've sunk to. Just be prepared for a shock, that's all. You see, Kate, the Jenny Laird you knew and cared for no longer exists!"

A memory stirred in Kate. Seemingly she had a strange penchant for forming friendships with people whose former personalities no longer existed. First Alex, now Jenny.

She experienced some difficulty in finding Jenny's address that evening. Possibly that also was non-existent? She came upon it at last up a narrow alleyway off Queen Street, a small house in a state of decay with a sash window on the ground floor, two more on the first floor, and with two dormers above a length of sagging guttering, leaking water on to the doorstep close to where Kate was standing, looking in dismay at the peeling paintwork and grimy windows, wondering if she had come to the right place after all? Surely not? The place looked ready for demolition, if it didn't fall down of its own volition.

The door opened suddenly to reveal Jenny, bizarrely dressed in a voluminous ankle-length Indian cotton skirt, a black jumper strained tightly across her ample breasts, several strings of brightly-coloured beads about her neck, dangling gilt earrings, scuffed red slippers on her feet, and with her mane of bleached hair spread about her shoulders.

"Well don't stand there, come in," she said aggressively. "Welcome to my 'palace of delight'. What you'll see will amaze you! In fact, I've a good mind to charge you admittance!"

"Stop it, Jenny," Kate uttered hoarsely, unbelievably angry. "Make a damn fool of yourself if you like, but don't try making a fool of me! It just won't wash, that's all!"

"I don't know what the hell you're on about," Jenny retorted. "You said you wanted to talk. What about? The good old days? Now you're getting up on your high horse; telling me I'm making a damn fool of myself, if it's any of your bloody business!"

Kate's anger faded. Remembering a joyous schoolgirl of long ago, opening her arms, smiling, she said gently, "Come here, you daft ha'porth. I came here because I love you. I always have and I always will."

Next thing she knew, their arms were about one another, and Jenny was crying on her shoulder, saying, "I'm sorry, Kate. I really am sorry. Please forgive me."

"What is there to forgive? You've done me no harm," Kate murmured soothingly, drawing the weeping woman indoors, an arm about her waist. "Quite the opposite, in fact. Remember how you came to me after my parents died? None of our other classmates even bothered. But *you* did, and I'll never forget that." She paused to find the right words. "You gave me a – reason for living."

"You mean Don? Don Ford?" Jenny asked wistfully, her tears, pretence and aggression forgotten in memories of the past. "You know, Kate, I was a bit jealous of you and Don. The way he looked at you, especially on your wedding day. And there was I stuck with his flatmate, John Spivey. Oh, a nice enough bloke, but not half as handsome and clever as Don." She paused briefly. "So where is he now? Don, I mean."

Kate drew in a deep breath. "He's in New York," she said calmly, "with his new wife and their son. Don and I went our separate ways some time ago. The reason why I'm here now, trying hard to create a new life, a new future for myself."

"Oh, Kate, I'm so sorry. I had no idea," Jenny said sadly, leading the way to the kitchen, an untidy, cluttered apartment, to make coffee for her guest. "And there was I thinking you had everything in life you'd ever wanted. All that any woman could possibly want – a nice home, a handsome husband, children! The kind of things I've longed for all my life!"

Sitting down at the kitchen table, head in hands, close to tears once more, Jenny said dully, "The trouble with me, I was so vain, so sure of my power of attraction over men that, when John Spivey asked me to marry him, I turned him down flat.

"I thought he wasn't quite good enough for me, you see? I wanted excitement, admiration, a good time."

Raising her head suddenly, choking back her tears, Jenny said defiantly, "Well, now you see before you a woman who hasn't the sense she was born with! What price my attraction now? I'm fat, ugly, disillusioned, disappointed, and it's all my own fault! So for God's sake, Kate, face facts! I'm a whore at heart. I've had more men than you've had hot dinners! I don't deserve your love or your friendship. So why don't you leave now?"

"Because," Kate replied simply, "you are still – Jenny Laird."

The state of the house was appalling. There was junk, which Jenny referred to as "stock", everywhere. "I could just open the rooms to the punters and save myself the cost of renting a stall," she said ruefully, with a flash of her old sense of humour, "except that the landlord wants me out of here at the end of the month. I'm in arrears, you see?"

Jenny's stock derived from jumble sales. "First through the doors picks up the best bargains," she explained. "That's when my size comes in handy. 'Fat Jen, the human bulldozer', they call me. I try not to mind, but I do."

She paused to kick aside a box of hats in the middle of the sitting room floor. "My own fault for letting the weight pile on. Comfort eating, I suppose. Too many sandwiches, cakes and fish and chips. And the booze didn't help any! Whisky, beer, rum, gin. You name it!

"I'd get my men friends to bring a bottle with them when they came to call. A few drinks and they couldn't have cared less what I looked like!"

Kate remained silent, realising that Jenny needed to spill out her anger, hurt and disappointment at her own folly in spoiling her life the way she had done. If confession was good for the soul, chances were she'd feel a lot better in revealing the extent of that folly to someone who cared about her.

Even so, Kate could scarcely bear to listen to the sordid details of her friend's fall from grace: the men she had known who had used and abused her for their own ends, resorting to physical violence more often than not, enjoying her humiliation at their hands. A fat woman in need of not sex, but love, they had given her nothing but sex. Certainly not love.

"I told them, over and over again, that I wanted nothing more to do with them," Jenny said wearily, "but they just laughed at me; told me I should be grateful for the booze – and bed! The shameful thing is, I knew deep down that I couldn't do without either. Especially the booze! You see, Kate, downing a half bottle of whisky, gin or whatever to ease the pain of living, I couldn't have cared less about what would happen later, upstairs in my bedroom. And – well – having sex made me feel 'special' somehow. Like a real woman, not just a – whore!"

Swallowing hard, she continued, "I'm off the booze now, thank God, and those men friends of mine are a thing of the past. Don't ask me how or why it happened. I just woke up one morning to the realisation that what I was doing to myself was all wrong somehow. A bit too late though. Far too late to make up for the mess I've made of my life so far!"

Speaking at last, Kate said quietly, "That's where you're wrong, love. It's never too late to make a new beginning. If you really want to, that is."

"*Want* to?" Jenny's eyes filled with tears. "Of course I do. If I only knew how!"

"We'll think of something," Kate promised.

"*We?*"

"Remember, Jenny, you're not on your own now. You have someone on your side. First thing, how much rent do you owe?"

"A hundred quid."

"Right. We'll settle up with the landlord. But you'll be leaving here at the end of the month anyway. That will give you time to clear out your – stock." Kate smiled.

"But what shall I do with it?" Jenny asked, aghast at the thought of getting rid of so much junk.

"How about a jumble sale? Several jumble sales, if necessary. We'll hire a van, put the stuff inside and send it on its merry way. I'm sure the local vicars will be delighted at not having to beg for jumble, to find bags of it on their doorsteps."

Jenny giggled helplessly. "Like sending coals to Newcastle?" she suggested mischievously. "Oh, how I'd love to see their faces when they see what's in the bags!" She paused uncertainly. "And when I've got shot of the jumble, then what? What about my stall? How shall I earn a living when I've nothing left to sell? And if I leave here, I shan't have a roof over my head."

"Not *if* you leave here, *when* you leave here," Kate said briskly. "And having nothing to sell will present no problems since you'll be giving up your stall as soon as the house has been cleared, and coming to stay with me for a while until we decide what to do next. All right?"

Jenny looked puzzled. "I honestly wouldn't have believed it," she said.

"Believed what?"

"Time was when you couldn't say boo to a goose! Now look at you! Talk about taking the initiative! Telling me what to do!"

"High time someone did. So what do you think of my plan of action? Are you for it or against it?"

"You mean I have a choice?" Jenny felt suddenly trapped, resentful of Kate's well-meant interference in her life. But what alternative was left to her?

"Of course you do. I'm sorry, I had no right to assume you'd want to leave your home or give up your livelihood at my say so. But I would like you to accept payment of your arrears. Otherwise, you wouldn't have any choice about leaving here, would you?"

"I suppose not," Jenny admitted gloomily, "as long as the money is in the nature of a loan. I'm not looking for charity. I'll pay back every penny once I'm back on my feet."

"Fair enough," Kate conceded, "a loan it is then. Let's make it two hundred pounds, shall we? That way you won't need to worry about next month's rent." Opening her shoulder-bag, she produced her chequebook and pen.

Signing the cheque, she handed it to Jenny, then got up to leave, realising there was nothing more to be said for the time being, fully understanding Jenny's reluctance to accept charity, as she herself had been when Alex offered her the job as his housekeeper.

On the doorstep, dodging drips from the leaky guttering, she said, "If you should change your mind about staying with me, you'll find me at Gull House in King Street. I'll write it down for you."

Smiling brightly, she added, "Well goodbye for now, love, and good luck."

Afterwards, Kate thought how badly she had handled a delicate situation. Jenny had put it in a nutshell when she'd said, "Talk about taking the initiative. Telling me what to do." The "girl" had been resentful of her well-meant interference, and rightly so. (Strange, she still thought of Jenny as a girl, not a middle-aged woman.)

More to the point, how did Jenny see *her*? As a rich meddler, most likely, with her readily available chequebook and pen. Worst of all, a patronising rich bitch. Nothing could be further from the truth. All she had really wanted was to get her friend well away from her present environment, to offer her a ray of hope for the future. Apparently she had failed utterly to do so. And this was her own fault. Marching in where angels might fear to tread!

As she made ready for bed, an old adage of her mother's sprang to mind. "One may lead a horse to water. Twenty cannot make it drink!"

Next morning, in the kitchen making toast and coffee, she heard the rattle of the letterbox. Hurrying downstairs in her dressing gown, her heart skipped a beat. There, at last, was a letter from Alex.

Fourteen

The letter gave no clue as to Alex's present whereabouts. It was post-marked Turkey and had been written in Ankara over a week ago.

Dear Kate,

To let you know that I am staying here for a few days to catch up with overdue correspondence and make the necessary arrangements for the next stage of my journey. Where to, I haven't yet decided.

Have been away from so-called civilisation these past few months and I'm finding an overcrowded city difficult to come to terms with after the solitude of the Arabian Desert. My hotel suite, though quite large and air-conditioned, feels as claustrophobic as a shoebox.

But needs must, as the saying goes, and there are certain compensations – the benison of hot running water in my marble-tiled bathroom, a balcony from which it is possible to catch a breath of air and to look up at the stars at nightfall.

I think of you often, and hope that you are enjoying Gull House and coping well with the responsibilities which I, perhaps selfishly, heaped upon you.

Knowing you as well as I think I do, I could not have chosen a more reliable person to take care of my home during my absence.

Yours ever sincerely,

Alex

Bitterly disappointed by the contents of the letter she had awaited so long – "Yours ever sincerely", indeed – stuffing it into her shoulder-bag, Kate marched down the fire-escape to the yard to apply a second coat of whitewash to the brickwork, slapping it on with abandon, her disappointment laced with anger that Alex had not begun the letter, "My dear Kate", had not ended it "With love from Alex".

Except, of course, that he did not love her, and she was not and never would be anything more to him than "Dear Kate"; certainly not "My dear Kate".

Deriving a grim satisfaction from the task in hand, Kate thought angrily that Alex might have saved himself the trouble of buying a stamp, might just as well have not bothered to write to her at all to say – virtually nothing of importance. He might at least have told her where he was heading. He must have had some idea, some destination in mind. Presumably he would not simply drive to the nearest airport and toss a coin on the tarmac? Heads the North Pole, tails Timbuktu!

Deep in thought, slap-dashing away with her paint brush, she looked up sharply when someone called her name: "Mrs Ford? Mrs Kate Ford?"

Two young police constables were standing outside the back gate, looking into the yard at her. Startled, she dropped the brush she was holding, splattering the paving stones with wet paint. "Yes, I'm Mrs Ford," she said hoarsely. "Why do you ask? What do you want? Is anything the matter?"

"Just a word please, if you'll unbolt the gate for us."

"Yes, of course, if you'll hang on just a sec till I wipe my hands." She did so hastily on a paint-rag she had placed on the fire-escape next to a bottle of turpentine for that purpose, her mind racing, stunned by the appearance of the Law on her doorstep, wondering what she had done wrong.

She withdrew the bolts, facing them squarely. "Please, come in," she said as calmly as she could, "and tell me what all this is about."

"I'm PC Newton, and this is PC Warburton," the spokesman of the pair informed her, speaking quietly. "There's been an accident, I'm afraid, and your name and address was found in the woman's possession in the Casualty Ward of the hospital, where she was taken in the early hours of this morning, before being admitted to the Intensive Care Unit."

"*Woman*? What – woman?" Kate asked perplexedly, her mind a blank momentarily. "You don't mean Mrs Paulson, do you?"

Police Constable Newton consulted his notebook. "No, not Mrs Paulson, a Miss Jenny Laird, who suffered a fractured skull and other injuries after, apparently, falling down a steep flight of stairs at her home sometime between two and three a.m."

"*Jenny*?" Kate looked at the man in horror. "Oh my God! I must go to her at once. They will let me see her, won't they?"

"Are you related to her, Mrs Ford?"

"No, just a friend of long standing. We were at school together."

"Has she any next of kin?"

"I don't know. Her parents may still be alive but they left Scarborough some time ago. We, that is Jenny and I, had lost touch with one another till yesterday. She invited me to her home last evening."

"At what time?"

"Seven thirty." Impatiently, "Why do you ask? Is it important?"

"And what time did you leave?"

"I can't remember exactly. Around nine o'clock, I imagine."

"Did she mention expecting another visitor later on that night?"

"No." A dreadful thought occurred to Kate. "Are you telling me that what happened to her wasn't an – accident?"

"That's not up to me to say, ma'am. We are simply making further enquiries into the cause of the incident, based on the possibility of an intruder entering the house in the early hours of the morning."

"I see," Kate said bleakly, wondering if Jenny had been speaking the truth about ending her relationships with the men in her life? Probably not. The fact remained that she was lying, seriously injured, in hospital, in need of all the help and support that she, Kate, could provide.

"May I go to her now?" she said. Tears filled her eyes. Poor Jenny, she thought. Poor, dear, foolish Jenny. Her own worst enemy.

And, "Yes, of course, ma'am," PC Newton assured her. "Our car's parked just round the corner. We'll drive you to the hospital right away, if that's OK with you?"

"Thank you," Kate murmured gratefully, at the same time dreading what might confront her at the journey's end.

It was far worse than she had imagined. Never till her dying day would she forget seeing Jenny lying, still and pale, in a hospital bed, her head swathed in bandages following an emergency operation to remove a blood clot from her fractured skull.

Sitting beside her bed, holding her hand, Kate thought how young and innocent she looked with her face devoid of make-up, her eyes tightly closed against the pain of consciousness of a world which had treated her so badly.

View from a Balcony

There were hospital sounds all about her – the swish of curtains on metal rods, quiet yet purposeful footsteps, the movement of trolleys, voices; overlaid with smells peculiar to hospitals – of antiseptics and food, of cut flowers and sickness, recalling memories of her mother's final illness when every room in the house had smelt of . . . death.

What really had happened in the early hours of this morning to cause Jenny's headlong fall down a steep flight of stairs? And what were her chances of recovery from her injuries?

Please God, don't let Jenny die, Kate prayed inwardly. Give her a second chance to make something of her life.

The ward sister entered the cubicle at that moment. "I think you should leave now, Mrs Ford," she said kindly. "Leave your phone number at the reception desk on your way out. We'll contact you in case of an emergency."

Rising to her feet, relinquishing Jenny's hand, Kate said tautly, "Please be honest with me. What are her chances?"

"I'm sorry, Mrs Ford, it's too early to say right now. At a rough guess, about fifty-fifty. She's a very poorly lady indeed."

"May I come back this evening?" Kate asked wistfully.

"Yes, of course you may." Drawn towards Kate, realising the depths of her distress, the ward sister said sympathetically, "Come as often as you wish. You are the only one who has come forward so far to show even the slightest interest in her welfare. Apparently she has no next of kin, but surely she must have friends, apart from yourself?"

"I really don't know," Kate admitted despondently. "I just wish I knew what happened to her in the early hours of this morning."

The ward sister said, sotto-voce, "As far as I know, a neighbour rang up the police station around two a.m. to complain of a so called 'domestic' row going on next door, followed by a scream, then silence. Then, to the best of my knowledge, failing to alert Miss Laird, policemen broke into the house to discover her lying unconscious at the foot of the stairs."

"I see, and thank you for telling me," Kate said quietly, with a backward glance at Jenny as she left the cubicle, made her way to the reception desk to leave her telephone number, and phoned for a taxi to take her back to Gull House.

In restless mood, Kate returned to the yard to clean up the paint from the paving stones. She worked automatically to wipe up the mess

121

before it hardened, her mind centred not on the job in hand but on Jenny in her hospital bed with a fifty-fifty chance of survival.

The thought of her slipping away from life without regaining consciousness was impossible to come to terms with. Kate thanked God for the nosy neighbour who had called the police, otherwise Jenny would have stood no chance of survival whatsoever.

But who had been in the house with her in the early hours of the morning? It was almost certainly a man with whom she had quarrelled violently. Presumably one of her many men "friends", so called, whose presence had been unwelcome.

The only crumb of comfort, there would be a full-scale police enquiry into the matter to discover the identity of the man involved in the tragedy. Small comfort indeed if Jenny lost her battle for life. And if she did? Facing that terrible possibility, Kate, as her proxy next-of-kin, would do all in her power to ensure that her girlhood friend was accorded a fitting farewell, with a church service and lots of flowers. Jenny had always loved flowers, especially long-stemmed red roses.

And if she miraculously survived, what then? Impossible to cross that bridge till she came to it, Kate realised. "One may lead a horse to water, twenty cannot make it drink." Jenny alone would have the right to decide about her future, if she survived. *If?* Pray God that she would.

Having cleared up the spilt paint, Kate went to a florist's in town to buy flowers to take with her to the hospital that evening: a dozen long-stemmed red roses . . .

There had been no change in her patient's condition, a nurse advised Kate as she entered the cubicle to sit by her friend's bedside, clasping her hand until visiting hours were over and she had to return to Gull House, where, in a state of mental turmoil, she went up to the attic studio to attempt a return to normality, a sorting out of her muddled emotions in this, her favourite room of the house, where she felt closest to – Alex, no matter how far away from her he appeared to be right now. Or was she doing him a grave injustice in not having read his letter more carefully?

Seated at his desk, she took the letter from its envelope. Re-reading it, her eyes fell on the words "I think of you often", which she had scarcely noticed before, as if, reading the lines, she had failed to read between them.

A sudden feeling of warmth invaded her being, as though a small part of her had been with him even in the desert and that marble-tiled bathroom in Ankara, his balcony beneath the stars, if only as a recurring memory trapped within the recesses of his mind. And this, possibly, had been his reason for writing the letter, to let her know that she occupied at least a small corner of his life, if not his heart.

Darkness had long since fallen. The room was very still, very quiet; lamp-lit. Instinctively, Kate placed her hands on the typewriter keys, a kind of reaching out for – something. She scarcely knew what. Release from pain, perhaps; her mental anguish over Jenny? Forgetfulness of her present problems? An escape route into the past; make believe instead of reality?

Whatever the motivation, feeding a sheet of A4 bond, a carbon and a backing sheet of copy-paper into the machine, in that quiet, lamp-lit room, Kate began writing her novel: Chapter One. Page One.

Then suddenly, miraculously, the present day world ceased to exist, and she was one of a joyous crowd of folk trooping down Plantation Hill to witness the opening ceremony of John Fairgray Sharpin's "People's Park". She described the event in almost graphic detail: the heady scent of may blossom threaded with the tang of the sea washing in on the shore; the glimmer of gaslight from the arched, overhead brackets; the Kiddy family: the gentle giant, Albert, his pretty, shy wife, Mavis, their seriously minded son, John, and their problem daughter, Lucy, in search of enjoyment, fun and laughter, not knowing what the future held in store for them.

Totally immersed in the story, Kate's thoughts and imaginings simply flowed from her mind on to the paper by way of her quickly tapping fingers on the typewriter keyboard, until, at last, having completed the first chapter, totally exhausted, without bothering to undress, she lay down on the divan in a far corner of the room, and fell fast asleep.

In time to come, the long days and restless nights that followed would seem dreamlike to Kate, as they had done during her mother's illness when, alert to every sound and movement from the sick-room next to hers, she would get up to plump up the dear invalid's pillows, to gently sponge her forehead with lavender-water, to slake her thirst with sips of barley water from a feeding-cup, more often than not in the darkest hours before the dawn. A privilege, not a penance.

In time to come, Kate would also remember the pattern of her days during Jenny's fight for life. Morning and evening visits to the hospital, taking with her bunches of fresh flowers which Jenny could neither see

nor scent – roses, carnations, freesias – plus fresh, clean cotton night-
gowns, bottles of spray-on eau-de-Cologne to kill the hospital smells of
antiseptics, boiled cabbage and decay.

Afterwards, her return to Gull House to get on with the next chapter
of her book, forgetful of time, of the present, as she conjured up the
arrival of rich folk, gentry families from London, at the Crown Hotel,
in their horse-drawn carriages, to spend the summer months in pursuit
of pleasure in those balcony suites overlooking the panorama of
Scarborough's South Bay spread before them from Castle Hill to
the Flamborough Head cliffs in the distance, as far as the eye could see.

Immersed in the opening chapters of her novel, possessed of an
overwhelming fondness for the attic studio, Kate decided to sleep there
from henceforth, in close proximity to Alex's divan, desk, typewriter
and bookshelves. After all, the house was hers alone during his absence,
and she needed no one's permission to sleep where she chose. And she
had chosen to sleep here, as close as possible to the man she loved,
wherever he happened to be right now, halfway up Mount Ararat in
search of Noah's Ark, in a Tibetan monastery, in Mongolia, or down a
salt-mine in Siberia!

Frankly, she couldn't care less where, just as long as he came home
again one day, all in one piece, as large as life – and twice as difficult. A
more than likely possibility. After all, Alex without bite would be like a
boiled egg without salt and pepper; toast without butter and marmalade; rainy days without an umbrella!

Advertisements in the evening paper had yielded a crop of applicants
from whom she and Dot Paulson had chosen one Cora Clegg, a smart
twenty-five-year-old brunette, as the likeliest candidate for the job of
sales assistant: the only interviewee with experience of selling what Dot
referred to as "fancy goods". Not that Kate had cottoned on to Cora
entirely, though she couldn't for the life of her have said why. She was a
shade too smart in Kate's opinion, the type unlikely to risk breaking a
polished fingernail opening boxes in the stockroom, or dirtying her
hands dusting shelves.

On the other hand, she had worked in a Leed's jeweller's shop prior
to coming to Scarborough to "be with her boyfriend" – in the biblical
sense, one imagined. Hardly likely, Kate thought, that a smart cookie
like Cora Clegg would have remained inviolate in the rat-race of life,
especially not in Leeds.

Sensibly, Kate had left the final decision-making up to Mrs Paulson as the one responsible for showing Miss Clegg the ropes and in deference to Dot's role as the manageress of the shop below. Just as long as Dot was happy with her under-strapper, as she appeared to be, and as long as the shop remained open to cater to the requirements of customers during the busy summer season ahead of them, Kate saw no valid reason to interfere with Dot's decision to hire Miss Clegg as her assistant.

Later, Kate wrote to Alex's firm of solicitors in London, advising them of them of the changed situation regarding Mrs Paulson and the addition of Miss Cora Clegg's name to the payroll. She reminded them, at the same time, that she, Kate Ford, acting as their client's agent, had handled a tricky dilemma to the best of her ability on his behalf.

There would be no repercussions and no questions asked, due to her forethought in getting the legal aspects of her guardianship of his home and business affairs neatly sewn up before his departure for faraway places with strange sounding names.

She remembered his words at the time: "My God, Kate. I have to hand it to you. You've certainly got a wise head on your shoulders!"

"Well, at least I've got something going for me," she'd replied sarcastically. "Far better a wise head than a foolish heart, don't you agree?"

He'd laughed and said," You're right as usual, of course!"

If only she'd kept the sarcasm out of her voice. Why had she always felt the need to fence with him? A matter of pride, of self-preservation, she imagined, to keep her feelings towards him well under control. Now she wondered if, thinking of her often, he remembered her as a snappy, defensive individual, bossy and interfering? Her own stupid fault if he did.

Fifteen

A month passed, during which Jenny showed signs of physical improvement. Out of intensive care, she was moved into a side unit away from the bustle of the main women's ward, where she would receive the specialised nursing required after her close brush with death.

Now her mental state was causing concern, the ward sister told Kate. Not that she needed telling. Jenny's state of mind was apparent in her cavalier attitude towards herself and the nursing staff in general, fed on her deeply-rooted belief that there was nothing left to live for.

Making allowances, Kate understood why. Jenny's hair, her crowning glory, had been cut off – her head shaved prior to removal of the blood clot from her brain. A hard cross for any woman to bear, more so Jenny, who had taken a pride in that flowing mane of hers even as a schoolgirl, long before she had resorted to peroxide to "enhance" its fairness.

And it couldn't have been easy or pleasant for her when, regaining consciousness after the operation, police detectives, awaiting their opportunity, had begun asking questions about her so-called "accident". The name of the man with whom she had quarrelled so violently before her fall downstairs.

"I don't know! I can't remember!" had been her initial response to their questioning, the ward sister who had been present at the time, told Kate. "So I gave them their marching orders! Told them to clear off and give the poor lady a bit of peace. Asked 'em how *they'd* feel having questions fired at them after a brain operation!"

"Good for you! Then what happened?" Kate asked, liking the sister enormously for her gutsiness and courage in flying in the face of the Law.

The ward sister shrugged wearily. "Back they came next day. Well, I couldn't very well have stopped them, could I? Then Jenny admitted that her landlord had called on her the night in question, to collect the rent owing him – and more besides, if you get my meaning! Now I think she's scared of the repercussions, being forced to go to court to give evidence when his case comes up. The trouble is, she won't talk about it, she's bottling everything up inside. Even the counsellor who came to see her couldn't get through to her."

The sister paused. "We hoped that you, perhaps . . . ? After all, you are the one closest to her. In fact, the poor thing has no one else in the world – except you."

Kate shook her head. "Believe me, I've tried. She won't look at me half the time; just pretends to be asleep, or stares past me as if I were invisible. I don't know what to do about it. Frankly, I often wonder why I bother to come at all."

Sister Sheridan frowned. "That could be the answer! Stay away for a while. See how she reacts."

"Oh, I don't know," Kate demurred. "Wouldn't that be rather cruel?"

"Sometimes you have to be cruel to be kind," Sister Sheridan reminded her. "Another problem arises. What will become of her when she leaves hospital? She has nowhere to go that I'm aware of. Presumably she wouldn't want to go back to the – scene of the crime! It's a poor outlook all round. Apparently she had a stall in the market, but our welfare people discovered that it's been let to someone else. In any case, she'll be in no fit state to work for some time to come. So I guess she'll end up in sheltered accommodation: one of those state-registered homes for 'drop-outs', to put it bluntly."

"Not if I can help it," Kate said grimly. "The fact is, when I saw her on the eve of the accident, I invited her to live with me; offered to take care of her financially until she was back on her feet. She turned me down flat, I'm afraid. Her pride stood in the way of accepting what she thought of as – charity from a 'do-gooder'! My own fault entirely! I should have handled the situation more carefully, not charged in like a bull in a china shop! I've been kicking myself ever since!"

Sister Sheridan, christened Wendy, nick-named Dinah, a deeply caring person, said quietly, "We all make mistakes from time to time: say and do things we regret later." She paused momentarily. "The thing is, if, by chance, Jenny could be persuaded to change her mind about accepting your offer, would you still be willing to take care of her?"

Kate said hoarsely, close to tears, "Need you ask? Jenny was my childhood friend. I'd do anything – anything at all – to help her."

Sister Sheridan said understandingly, "Then take my advice, Mrs Ford, stay away from the hospital for a while. Give Jenny time to miss your daily visits, to switch her mind into other channels, to begin thinking in terms of the future ahead of her without your help and support. Above all, your – love."

"Very well, then, Sister, let's give it a whirl, shall we?" Clasping the ward sister's hand tightly in hers, choking back her tears, she said "My name is Kate, by the way. And yours is . . . ?"

"Dinah," Sheridan said wryly.

The shop appeared to be running smoothly, with Dot Paulson doing the ordering and keeping a watchful eye on Miss Clegg, who appeared not to need "showing the ropes", having a full complement of reef knots, bowlines and sheepshanks at her polished fingertips, Dot remarked, somewhat tartly, when Kate asked her how Cora was coping, to which complaint Kate turned a deaf ear. She had more than enough on her plate to contend with right then, without adding the shop to her list of worries.

All else had paled to insignificance compared with her anxiety concerning Jenny's future. Staying away from the hospital – being cruel to be kind – had left her weary from lack of sleep, guilt-ridden that she had, seemingly, deserted her friend at a time when she stood in dire need of her love and support.

And yet, weighing up the pros and cons, Kate realised how little her daily visits, her gifts of fruit and flowers, had meant to Jenny, who had seemed to despise, rather than welcome, her presence at her bedside. Even so, staying away from Jenny for a day, let alone a week, had proved a burden almost impossible to bear, until . . .

When Kate revisited the hospital on the seventh day of their separation, miraculously, propped up with pillows, with tears streaming down her sunken cheeks, hands outspread in greeting, Jenny uttered weakly, "Oh, Kate, I'm so pleased to see you again! I've missed you so much! I thought you'd forgotten all about me!"

Kate cradled the weeping woman in her arms. "Forgotten about you, Jenny? Never in this world, my love," Kate said mistily. "So let us make this a new beginning, shall we? Taking care of one another as we used to in the old days?"

"Yes," Jenny murmured drowsily against Kate's shoulder, "I'd like that. Taking care of *you*, I mean! Helping you in the house, anything at all. I'll find myself a job; pay back the money you lent me."

"All in good time. As soon as you're back on your feet," Kate said gently. "Try to rest now, and stop worrying. Everything will work out fine, you'll see."

Plumping up the pillows, smoothing the counterpane, kissing Jenny goodnight, Kate turned to smile at her as she left the ward, but she was already fast asleep; looking for all the world like a little girl.

Dinah was in the corridor, anxiously awaiting news of the encounter. "Well?" she asked, in a low voice. "How did it go?"

When Kate told her, "Oh, thank God," Dinah said fervently. "That's the best news I've had in ages. How wonderful to know she'll soon be going home!"

"How soon? At a rough guess?"

"A month or so," Dinah reckoned. "Of course, she'll still need nursing, but we'll give you all the help we can. We have a great team of district nurses. Best of all, she'll have *you*!" She paused, "Now, take my advice, go home and get a good night's sleep. You look all in!"

Up early next morning, like a giant refreshed, Kate walked briskly up Newborough to the town centre, a shopping list a mile long tucked into her shoulder-bag, feeling more alert, far happier than she had done for many a long day, as if a whole new future had suddenly opened up before her on this glorious, sunshiny June morning, with loneliness dispelled, and with so many plans in mind to give Jenny the welcome home she deserved.

Kate would continue to sleep in the attic studio, close to Alex's desk and typewriter. Meanwhile, she intended to make over her old bedroom as Jenny's special and private retreat from the world, if that's what she wanted, complete with brand new furniture – a deeply sprung single bed, rosy-shaded bedside lamps with matching bed-linen, and a triple-mirrored dressing table skirted with rose-embellished cretonne, its surface arrayed with crystal flagons of French perfume.

This, Kate realised, along with her plans to refurbish the double bedroom in readiness for Greg and Cynthia, whom she intended to invite for a visit sometime in July, during her brother's summer vacation, quite apart from the cost of the Provençal pots and the plants she had ordered to enhance the back yard of Gull House, would bite into her building society "nest-egg". So what if it did? What, exactly, was she saving up for anyway? A lonely old age?

Jenny came home on the second day of July, accompanied by two stalwart ambulancemen who helped her up the stairs to her room on the first floor, on the threshold of which, taking in the decor, the vase of red roses on the dressing table, alongside the elegant flagons of French perfume, she burst into tears, stumbling blindly towards Kate's arms, opened wide to receive, to comfort and caress her.

"It's lovely," Jenny sobbed. "I don't deserve it."

One of the men had gone downstairs to bring up a wheelchair. "Here you are, my duck," he said cheerily, "in case you feel like a spin!"

"If you think I'm going out in that thing," Jenny sniffed, "you think wrong!"

The man laughed. "No skin off my nose, my duck, but it'll come in useful about the house, if nowt else!"

Sensing an awkward situation, Kate asked the men if they had time for a cuppa, but felt relieved when they turned down the offer, saying they were running late as it was, and clattered downstairs, leaving her alone with Jenny, seated forlornly on the edge of the bed, tears streaming down her cheeks, staring at the wheelchair as if it were an instrument of torture. "Why did they have to bring that bloody thing?" she uttered hoarsely. "I can manage perfectly well without it!"

Kate's heart sank momentarily, faced with the realisation that coping with an invalid, no matter how dear to her, would not be easy: entailing both tact and determination on her part to strike an acceptable level of give and take. Not to allow her fondness for Jenny to stand in the way of doing whatever was necessary in her own best interests.

She said quietly yet firmly, "The bathroom's at the end of the landing. The wheelchair, I imagine, will come in useful should you wish to get there in a hurry!"

"Without bothering you, you mean?" Jenny asked sharply.

"No, not exactly that," Kate said levelly, "more as a means of retaining your spirit of independence! Now, love, it's almost lunchtime. Come through to the kitchen when you're ready. That's the door opposite yours. All right?"

Shock tactics had worked once before, hopefully they would do so again, Kate thought, peeling mushrooms and beating eggs in preparation for the simple omelette lunch she had planned, but what if she was wrong? She had been wrong so often in her life before,

What if, despite her good intentions, she proved inadequate to cope with Jenny as she now was, a tetchy, demanding, insecure invalid, no longer even faintly resembling her laughing girlhood companion of long ago?

Suddenly, Kate remembered her visit to "Madame Zara", and the old woman's words: "Many people, some close to you, others not so close, are in need of your help right now. You'll need to be strong for their sake. And you will be, of that I'm sure."

Strong? Kate had never felt weaker than she did right now, more uncertain of herself or her motivation in living – a far cry from the day she had walked into town so confidently to buy the new furniture and fittings for Jenny's room and the one intended for Greg and Cindy if they accepted her invitation to spend their summer vacation at Gull House.

If only she knew for certain that she was not "wasting her sweetness on the desert air". That the garden she had created in the back yard of Gull House would not bloom in vain; that Alex Arden was alive and well somewhere in the world; that the omelette she was about to cook wouldn't stick to the bottom of the frying pan! If only she could receive a sign, a signal, a message of some kind, to restore her flagging self-confidence, her faith in the future.

Suddenly, Jenny entered the kitchen, in her wheelchair.

"All right, Kate, you win," she said quietly, close to tears. "I'll behave myself from now on, and that's a promise!"

Hiding her emotion as best she could, Kate said, tongue-in-cheek, "Well, don't just sit there doing nothing! Set the table! The cutlery's in that drawer over yonder!"

The old rapport between them developed slowly at first. This Kate accepted patiently, knowing they both needed time and space to adjust to their altered circumstances. She had no intention of forcing Jenny to talk about the night of the accident or anything else for that matter, until she felt like it. On the other hand, she had her own life to live, her book to get on with.

One day, bursting with curiosity, sounding somewhat piqued, Jenny said tartly, "What I can't figure out is what you get up to in your bedroom for hours on end! Have you a secret admirer by any chance?"

Kate laughed. "Who, me? Hardly likely! No, something far more interesting. I'm trying my hand at writing a novel."

"You are? What's it about?"

When Kate explained, Jenny advised, "You'll need to spice it up a

bit, I reckon, otherwise it won't stand a chance of getting published."
Speaking as one who knew, she said, "People want sex nowadays, lots
of steamy bedroom scenes, naked bodies, flashing eyes and heaving
breasts!"

"You may be right," Kate conceded cannily, sensing Jenny's need to
talk, not about the novel, but herself, and what had really happened on
the night of the "accident". The kind of breakthrough she had hoped
for ever since Jenny came to live with her.

A long silence ensued, then Jenny said hoarsely, "I was upstairs,
getting ready for bed, when I sensed that I was not alone in the house. I
called out, 'Who's there?', but I knew it was *him*. It had to be him, the
only person who had a key to the front door!

"Oh, God, Kate, it was awful, hearing his footsteps on the stairs,
knowing he was bound to find me sooner or later. There was no place
to hide, you see? I was scared stiff of him, too scared to move, so I just
stood there, petrified, near the bed, knowing he'd be the worse for
drink, dreading what he might do to me when he found me!

"Then, when he opened the door of my room, swaying on his feet, I
ran past him on to the landing and started shouting for help. Next thing
I knew, he caught up with me, calling me names, threatening to kill me
if I didn't keep quiet, if I didn't give him what he wanted.

"But I didn't keep quiet. I couldn't. I just kept on screaming at him to
go away and leave me alone. Then he hit me in the stomach and I fell
back against the banister, gasping for breath, clawing at the rail for
support, only I couldn't get hold of it properly, and I fell backwards
down the stairs, with him on the landing above, watching me, doing
nothing to help me.

"I remember the pain when my head hit the floor, then everything
blacked out. The next thing I knew, I was in hospital and . . . " Jenny
stopped speaking abruptly.

"And?" Kate prompted her gently.

"When I opened my eyes, you were there, and there were red roses on
the locker."

"So you did notice them?" Kate smiled.

"Yes, but I was too upset about my hair to bother about flowers, and
then those detectives came to fire questions at me. It was awful, just
awful, lying there with all those wires attached to me and knowing I was
bald! I felt like a criminal – one of those women collaborators who had
their heads shaved for sleeping with German soldiers during the war!"

"I know, love, and I'm sorry. But your hair's beginning to grow now, and it looks quite charming, a bit like Ingrid Bergman's in *For Whom The Bell Tolls*. I saw the film on television a while back, and I read somewhere that her short curly haircut started a craze for a style named after her screen character, Maria. Apparently hairdressers were swamped with clients wanting short, 'Maria' hair-dos!"

"Oh, I know what you're driving at," Jenny uttered sarcastically, "You're just trying to make me feel better about my inch-long stubble! But you're wasting your breath!"

Kate sighed deeply. "In which case I'd better stop talking and start typing," she said lightly, determined not to let Jenny get the better of her; fast becoming inured to those rapid mood swings of hers – sweetly compliant one minute, irritatingly hostile the next.

Refusing to engage in a battle of wills and words, to succumb to emotional blackmail, Kate went upstairs to her studio to get on with the next chapter of her book. The chapter in which Lucy Kiddy had run away to Brighton with her cellarman lover, so madly in love with him that she couldn't have cared less that he was twice her age, married to someone else, and the father of four children, the oldest of which was a mere two years younger than herself.

And this, Kate recognised, immersed in her novel, was her means of escape from the exigencies of the present into the less stressful, shadowy world of the past, at her fingertips on the keys of Alex Arden's typewriter.

She loved Jenny with all her heart. Of course she did, but not to the extent of becoming her "whipping boy", spoiling her rotten, when what the girl most needed was the incentive to stand up, tall and proud, on her own two feet. She'd need to face the future ahead of her with all flags flying when it came to appearing in a court of law to give evidence against her former landlord.

Mulling over Jenny's advice to add steamy sex scenes to her novel, Kate decided not to. For one thing, she knew next to nothing about torrid bedroom encounters, flashing eyes and heaving breasts. All she really knew about was love – the finer feelings of a wife for her husband. In the early days of her marriage, there had been intense pleasure and delight in the act of physical intimacy with the man she loved. It was love, not sex, she wished to portray, to capture within the the pages of her book. Albert Kiddy's deep, unselfish love for his wife and family, for instance.

Above all, she had no intention of casting Lucy Kiddy in the role of a wanton, a whore, a home-wrecker. Rather as a romantically minded young woman desperate for the good things in life, glimpsed at the Crown Hotel, where girls not half as pretty as herself wallowed in the lap of luxury.

How easily Lucy must have succumbed to the blandishments of a handsome older man, earning good wages, who had promised her the earth if only she would go with him to Brighton to an even better paid job he'd applied for and accepted.

How could she have possibly refused that offer? Blinkered by love, seeing before her an escape route from her humdrum life in Scarborough, feeling herself to be the heroine of a romantic novelette, she had rushed headlong into an affair of the heart destined to end in failure: the humiliation of being hauled back to the bosom of her family by her caring father; the appearance also on the scene, in that Brighton hotel, of her lover's plain, middle-aged wife, the mother of his four children, of whom she had known nothing until the day of reckoning had arrived.

So what if her book received the thumbs down sign from potential publishers? Kate considered carefully. Frankly, she couldn't care less about publication. She was writing this book to please herself. "This, above all, to thine own self be true. Thou cans't not then be false to any man," she remembered.

Sixteen

The garden was looking quite lovely, Kate thought: worth all the effort she'd put into it. Apart from the flower-filled Provençal pots, she'd also splashed out on hanging baskets of trailing ivies and lobelia to enhance the colour-washed walls, and a wrought iron table and chairs, with Jenny in mind, thinking it would do her good to sit outdoors in the sunshine and fresh air, now that she was regaining the use of her legs and was able to negotiate the fire-escape, albeit slowly and clinging to the handrail for support.

In reply to Kate's invitation to her brother and his wife to spend their summer vacation in Scarborough, Greg had responded eagerly that they would look forward enormously to a holiday at the seaside. Above all, to seeing her again, which Kate took with a grain of salt, doubtful that Cindy shared her husband's enthusiasm for her sister-in-law's company. Somehow, she and Cindy could never quite see eye-to-eye, for the usual reason: that Cindy was jealous of Greg's close sibling relationship with his sister, resentful of their shared memories of growing up together.

Curiously, Jenny remembered Greg quite well from Kate's wedding day. "Is he as handsome as ever?" she asked eagerly.

"Handsome? Greg?" Kate laughed. "I doubt he ever saw himself as such. Certainly not as the dashing hero type."

"Well, nice-looking then," Jenny insisted. "Kind of warm and cuddly, with a lovely smile and charming manners."

"I'm sure his wife would agree with you," Kate said warily, "if you were daft enough to voice that opinion in her presence."

"Oh, I get the message! The jealous type, is she?" Jenny wrinkled her nose disdainfully. "But all's fair in love and war, and I should know!"

"If you mean what I think you mean, forget it," Kate retorted, irritated by Jenny's stupid remarks. "Remember that you are a guest here beneath my roof. Greg is my brother, and blood is thicker than

135

water! I'm warning you, Jenny, any of your fancy tricks and you'll be out of here faster than you can say knife!"

"All right, keep your shirt on," Jenny replied huffily. "The trouble with you is, you can't take a joke. I've had enough trouble with men to last me a lifetime."

"All right. Let's leave it at that, shall we?" They were in the garden at the time, Jenny holding a mug of coffee, leaning back in her chair, eyes narrowed against the sun. Glancing sideways at Kate, looking worried, she said, "That stuff about giving me the elbow. You didn't really mean it, did you?"

"Look at it this way," Kate, said levelly. "Hopefully, that's a decision I shall not be called upon to make."

The conversation had left a sour taste in Kate's mouth. For the first time she faced squarely the realisation that Jenny, as she was now, bore no resemblance to the girl she used to be. Some essential sweetness in her nature was gone beyond recall.

Scarcely surprising, Kate reflected, after all she had been through in her adult years. She had felt so certain that, given time, she might rekindle the embers of her friend's former kindness of heart, and there had been times when, in Jenny's gentler moments, she had glimpsed something of the tender young girl of long ago.

Now she wondered if she had ever really known Jenny at all? Or had she, along with teachers and classmates alike, simply fallen under the spell of the most popular girl in school? Blinded by her beauty, her bewitching personality, had she failed to recognise her underlying selfishness and shallowness of mind?

That day, for instance, when turning up on her doorstep, insistent on making up a foursome for a trip to the cinema with Don as her blind date, had she been concerned about Kate's welfare, or her own frustration at being lumbered with her current boyfriend's flatmate when she wished to be alone with – what was his name? – John Spivey! Ah yes, John Spivey, the man who had asked Jenny to marry him – who, in the long run, she had turned down flat because he wasn't good enough for her.

The truth struck Kate forcibly amidships! Lying sleepless in bed that night, she reflected that if it hadn't been for Jenny's interference, she might never have met Don Ford! There would have been no hastily arranged winter wedding, no April Cottage, no dead babies to mourn – no Lucia Keane, no divorce. And more than likely, no Alex Arden, no

Gull House, no Jenny Laird beneath her roof to pose even the slightest threat to her own peace of mind and, more importantly, that of her brother, Greg.

Peace of mind? Kate thought wearily, longing for the benison of sleep. Peace of mind had been at a premium since she had invited Jenny to live with her, since when she had been strung on a high-wire of emotional tension occasioned by her guest's rapid mood swings, from elation one minute to despair the next. Calculated? More than likely, Kate pondered, coming to grips with the realisation that the Jenny Laird she had so loved and admired in the days of her youth and girlhood, no longer existed. If, indeed, she ever had done so, beyond the realms of her own imagination. Well, Jenny had warned her that this was so.

And yes, blood was far thicker than water! Greg needed a holiday, freedom and relaxation away from the exigencies of his job. Teaching was no easy option. She had seen for herself the faint network of worry lines on his face at their last meeting, noticed the tenseness about him, the weary droop of his shoulders, the signs of a man growing old before his time, and her heart had gone out to him: wanting to ease his burden in some way. That was when the holiday idea had taken root and she had thought how much he'd enjoy a month by the sea, revisiting all the old familiar places he had known and loved as a boy.

Common sense told Kate that Cindy would have tried to talk him out of spending his summer vacation in England, much less a common-or-garden seaside resort like Scarborough. Knowing her sister-in-law, she would have plumped for Spain or Italy, Rimini or the Costa del Sol: one of those package holidays with sight-seeing tours included in the deal, hotels serving English food, rather than all that "foreign muck" – pasta and paella, pizzas, olives and anchovies, with not a decent cup of tea to be had. In which case, why bother to go abroad in the first place, Kate thought irritably. But this was typical of Cindy, in search not of culture but kudos.

Kate's assumption was correct. Cindy's resentment showed the minute she crossed the threshold. Obviously she regarded her holiday home for the coming month as below par, faced with flights of creaking stairs, narrow landings and passages, a far cry from her spacious, labour-saving bungalow on the outskirts of Manchester.

Greg, on the other hand, was over the moon with Gull House, and especially the bedroom, smelling of fresh paint and wallpaper, soap and water and sea air, with spotlessly clean linen and summer flowers from the vase of stocks and long-stemmed roses on the dressing table.

"You've gone to an awful lot of trouble," he said quietly. "I just hope you haven't worn yourself out, that's all."

Kate laughed. "I didn't do the decorating myself, if that's what you mean, and a dear friend of mine comes in twice a week to help with the housework." She meant Fanny Kiddy who came in on Tuesdays and Fridays to give the place what she termed "a good bottoming".

Cindy simply stared round the room with lack-lustre eyes, at loggerheads with her husband because he had refused, point blank, to spend his summer vacation on the Costa Brava along with a coach-load of British tourists wearing sun-glasses, shorts and colourful shirts, armed with cameras, and wanting bacon, sausages, fried eggs and baked beans for breakfast.

At the height of their quarrel, Greg had uttered wearily, "Very well, then, Cindy, make your own arrangements. Go to the Costa Brava if that will make you happy! But my mind is made up. I'm going to Scarborough!"

Changing her tune in a matter of seconds, she'd retorted sharply, "Not on your own, you're not. The very idea! To suck up to that precious sister of yours, I suppose? Well, I'm your *wife*, and don't you forget it!"

As if he could, Greg had thought despairingly. Chance would be a fine thing, wondering why he had married Cynthia in the first place. But of course, deep down, he knew why. Because she had been very pretty in her younger days and lionised him, a university student with a promising career ahead of him. Desperately lonely and unhappy following the death of his parents and his sister's departure to the West Country, in dire need of comfort, of release from his loneliness of spirit, he had seen a solution to his problems in the shape of a comely young woman more than willing to offer him the benison of a shoulder to cry on, with certain reservations, of course. Marriage, above all. A wedding ring placed firmly on the third finger of her left hand.

And so Greg had placed, unthinkingly, that band of gold on his bride's left hand, realising too late that, like Esau in the Old Testament, he had sold his birthright of freedom for a "mess of pottage".

Aware of Cindy's hostility, Kate pointed out the bathroom and the whereabouts of the kitchen, remarking that she had a friend staying with her at the moment, and that tea would be ready in the kitchen when they had finished unpacking.

Catching Cindy's look of disapproval, she said brightly, "We have all our meals in the kitchen. The old dining room was swallowed up some years ago when the property was altered to make room for a shop. Fortunately the kitchen is quite spacious, and remarkably handy for the person doing the cooking." She added, "My room is upstairs – a bedroom-cum-studio, with a view of the sea from the dormer window. I'll show it to you later. But first things first. I daresay you're ready for a cuppa."

Jenny had been into town yesterday, by taxi, to do some shopping, refusing Kate's offer to go with her, saying she could manage perfectly well on her own. She needed some new clothes, which was true enough. Since her dramatic weight loss, she had taken to wearing a dressing gown about the house, hardly suitable attire to wear in the presence of what she termed "company". And Kate agreed with her for once, dreading Cindy's reaction to a woman in a satin robe and slippers putting in an appearance at meal times.

Kate simply hoped and prayed that Jenny had not wasted the money she'd given her on anything too outlandish or bizarre. She'd have to wait and see, since Jenny had stubbornly refused to reveal the contents of the various carrier bags she'd brought back with her.

Setting the tea-table with cups, saucers, plates and cutlery, thinly cut egg and cress sandwiches, homemade scones and cakes, Kate had nervously awaited the arrival of her guests. Not Greg, but Cindy and Jenny, knowing that her sister-in-law would not take kindly to eating in the kitchen. As for Jenny, heaven alone knew how she would react to meeting the impeccably dressed Cindy. Not to mention Greg. Pray God she wouldn't fling her arms about him, smother him with kisses and chatter on inanely about having met him before on his sister's wedding day. But she wouldn't bet on it! Discretion was a word unknown in Jenny's vocabulary.

Preceding her husband into the room, Cindy glanced coldly at the well set table. Greg positively glowed. "What a lovely spread," he remarked, "and what a charming kitchen!" taking in the prettily curtained windows, gleaming paintwork, red geraniums blooming on the windowsills, and the fire-escape door, standing wide open to let in sunshine and fresh air. "Where does that lead to?" he asked eagerly.

"The garden," Kate said proudly, putting on the kettle to boil.

"Mind if I take a look?"

"Feel free!" Kate smiled at his boyishness, his enthusiasm as he stepped on to the fire-escape, his obvious pleasure in the small oasis she had created from a once dreary back yard. She could have wept when he said quietly, "'And yet the fool contends that God is not.'" A quotation from a half-forgotten poem of long ago. How did it go? Making the tea, suddenly she remembered. "Not God in gardens when the eve is cool? Nay, but I have a sign. 'Tis very sure God walks in mine".

"Oh, for heaven's sake, Greg, come in and have your tea," Cindy said irritably, destroying his moment of pleasure in a fraction of a second, wiping away his enthusiasm in less time than it would take to shatter a mirror with a well-aimed clod of earth.

"Sorry," was all he said, sitting down at the table.

Kate was pouring the tea when the door opened and Jenny appeared on the threshold, a slender figure wearing a pencil-slim grey skirt, a pink, lightweight, short-sleeved cashmere sweater, her face devoid of make-up, and with her newly washed, inch-long hair, curling gently on to her forehead, about her ears and on to the nape of her neck.

"I'm sorry if I've kept you waiting," she said breathlessly, "but I fell fast asleep. You see, I've been ill recently, and I haven't yet quite recovered my full health and strength. My name's Jenny Laird, by the way. Kate and I have been friends since our childhood days. As a matter of fact, I was her bridesmaid on her wedding day, all of twenty-three years ago. But we were friends long before that, at school, weren't we, Kate?"

Jenny Laird, a bridesmaid at Kate's wedding? Greg thought, casting his mind back to that day almost a quarter of a century ago, vaguely recalling a curvaceous blonde with waist-long hair, who had given him the "glad-eye" over a glass of champagne. But surely this could not possibly be the same woman?

"I gave my sister away, on her wedding day," he said hesitantly. "Don't you remember?"

Glancing at him coolly, Jenny said, "No, I'm afraid not," lying through her teeth, to Kate's infinite relief, "but it was a long, long time ago."

"Yes, I suppose so," Greg conceded. He added, feeling foolish, "Well, since you have so obviously forgotten all about me, my name is Greg, and this is my wife, Cindy."

"Oh, how do you do, Mrs Harker?" Jenny uttered solemnly.

"Quite nicely, thank you," Cindy replied frostily, suspecting some kind of liaison, however long ago, between this woman and her husband, which she would ferret out in due course, to her own satisfaction.

Oh God, Kate thought, pouring out the tea, handing round the cups and passing the plates of food, better by far a bizarrely clad Jenny complete with over-the-top make-up and long dangling earrings, or even wearing a dressing gown and slippers, than her understated alterego, all prunes and prisms, as if butter wouldn't melt in her mouth. So what, precisely, was she up to? Only time would tell. Or had she really turned over a new page in her life, at last?

After tea, Greg persuaded Cindy to take a walk to St Nicholas Cliff to look at the sea. Jenny had excused herself prettily, in the manner of "La Dame aux Camellias" about to suffer a relapse, and gone to her room for "a bit of a lie down", while Kate had elected to stay behind to make preparations for their evening meal: roast chicken with all the trimmings, followed by a substantial steamed pudding and custard such as their mother used to make in the old days, knowing Greg's fondness for custard, and jam sponge pudding in particular.

No doubt Cindy would jib at anything so fattening. But then, Cindy jibbed at most things nowadays, apart from holidays abroad, smart new clothes, tightly permed hair, and garden gnomes – with or without fishing-rods! In which case, she would be offered the alternative of fresh fruit salad or ice-cream.

Stuffing the chicken, preparing the vegetables, rubbing fat into flour, Kate realised that her brother had married the wrong woman, and he was paying the full price of his mistake, just as she had paid the full price in marrying the wrong man. But who could tell, at the beginning of things, lacking experience of life, what the end result would be?

Supper, or "dinner" as Cindy preferred to call it, was a fraught occasion. Jenny appeared, bright eyed and bushy-tailed after her nap, wearing a blue cotton dress which gave her the appearance of Alice in Wonderland.

Serving the food, Kate sensed Cindy's hostility towards Jenny, and vice-versa, and knew that Greg sensed it too, sitting there like a rose between thorns. At least he and Jenny did justice to the meal; Cindy merely picked at her portion of roast chicken, and pointedly pushed aside the runner beans and potatoes to the edge of her plate, declaring peevishly that she wasn't hungry, and felt like an early night.

"You *do* look a bit washed out," Jenny remarked, biting into a chipolata sausage. "Must be all the excitement and fresh air!"

Kate could have strangled her with her bare hands! Telling Cindy she looked "washed out" was akin to playing Russian Roulette with a fully loaded revolver. Oh God, she thought nervously, how would Cindy react to jam sponge pudding and custard? But, deep down, she knew exactly what her reaction would be.

Rising quickly to her feet at the appearance of the pudding, and despite Kate's offer of ice-cream or fresh fruit salad as an alternative, she stalked out of the kitchen in high dudgeon, closely followed by Greg, who, murmuring an apology, went after his wife, presumably in an attempt to pour oil on troubled water.

Jenny said virtuously, "I feel really sorry for a nice bloke like Greg married to a spoilt cow of a woman like that, don't you?"

"All right, Jenny," Kate said levelly, "you've made your point, had your idea of fun, plus a darned good supper. Now, it's high time you had an 'early night' too, before I wipe the floor with you!"

Greg reappeared in the kitchen an hour later, looking drained, by which time Kate had cleared the table and done the washing up. Cutting short his apology on his wife's behalf, she said lightheartedly, "I have a present for you, upstairs in my room. A belated birthday present. Something rather special!"

Greg smiled, grateful for her understanding. He'd spent a miserable half hour listening to his wife's accusations of not caring tuppence about her welfare, flirting with "that woman" – she meant Jenny – and sucking up to his sister, making such a damned fuss of her cooking, as if he never got a decent meal at home.

Eventually, tight-lipped, he had walked out of the room. And, "Where do you think you're going?" she'd called after him, infuriated by his lack of response.

Now, on the threshold of Kate's eyrie, he said, "What a marvellous room," taking in the desk and bookshelves, the neat divan bed, dormer window, pictures and paintings on the walls; shaded lamps, the piles of neatly stacked folders and reams of paper near the typewriter, thinking how happy he would be if only he had a bolt-hole like this where he could work and sleep undisturbed, far removed from Cindy's constant, grating presence in his life.

Recently, he had begun to wonder how much more of her he could take without telling her exactly what he thought of her. But old habits died hard. He had learned to bite his tongue rather than precipitate a full-scale row, knowing her propensity for tears bordering on hysteria at the least sign of resistance to her iron-clad will.

Knowing exactly what was going on in his mind, Kate said, handing him a box wrapped in coloured paper and tied with matching scarlet ribbon, "This is for you. Happy Birthday, Greg. A bit late, but better late than never."

"What on earth?" He laughed, his trauma of the past half hour forgotten in the pleasureable anticipation of opening his present.

"Why not open it and find out?" Kate suggested, thinking how eager, boyish and carefree he looked all of a sudden, just as he used to when building sandcastles in the days of their youth and childhood long ago.

Placing the parcel on the floor, he knelt beside it to remove its wrapping carefully, not wanting to crease the paper unduly. So like Greg, she thought, a careful, considerate human being in every respect. The reason why she loved him so much.

And now the moment of discovery had arrived! Never till her dying day would Kate forget the expression of joy on his face when, delving into the box, he held in his hands the books written by his hero, Sandy Alexis. First editions, signed by the author.

Greg said bemusedly, "These must have cost a small fortune. Where on earth did you find them?"

"In a house in London. The author was about to burn them. I persuaded him not to."

"You mean you actually met – Sandy Alexis?"

Kate smiled mysteriously. "Would it surprise you to know that this is his room? His house?"

Light dawned. Standing up, facing his sister, Greg said, "Alex Arden? The man you're in love with?"

"Yes," Kate said softly, knowing she spoke the absolute truth, "the man I'm in love with!"

The stairs creaked suddenly. Cindy appeared in the doorway. "I've been looking for you everywhere," she said angrily. "I might have known I'd find the pair of you together, as usual! Talking about me, behind my back, I daresay!"

"Not at all," Greg said restrainedly, "we were discussing the birth-

143

day present Kate has given me. Books by Sandy Alexis, no less. First editions, signed by the author."

"What? *More* books? As if you hadn't got enough of the damn things already! Well, do you intend staying up here all night?"

Stepping into the arena, Kate said pleasantly, "Of course not. I was about to suggest having coffee in the garden. It's such a lovely evening. You will join us, won't you, Cindy?"

"No! I have a splitting headache! Coffee's the last thing I need! Greg, I asked you specifically to pack that bottle of asprin in the bathroom cabinet. Apparently you neglected to do so!"

Kate said lightly, "Oh, if that's all. I've plenty of – pain-killers! Come with me Cindy, I'll have your headache cured in no time at all!"

Seventeen

C indy had not responded kindly to her sister-in-law's ministrations when, turning a deaf ear to her complaints about Greg and the missing asprin tablets, Kate had persuaded her to get into bed, handed her a glass of water and a couple of mild sleeping pills, wished her goodnight, and gone to the kitchen to make a pot of coffee.

The evening was silken soft, threaded with birdsong and starlight. The garden was heady with the fragrance of lavender and night-scented stocks. Greg was seated at the wrought-iron table, looking tired, Kate thought, and with good reason. Coping with Cindy was no easy option, as she well knew. Upstairs in the bedroom, listening to the woman's diatribe, she'd longed to tell her exactly what she thought of her constant whining and complaining, that she should think herself damn lucky to have a husband at all, a lesser man than Greg would have left her years ago to stew in her own juice. Of course she had not done so, for Greg's sake.

"It's so peaceful here," he said. "Like a different world. The kind of world we lived in a long time ago. Or that's how it seems to me. But how about you, Kate? Are you happy living here beneath someone else's roof?

"Forgive me for asking, but what will happen when Alex Arden comes home again? Shall you be prepared to stay on as his housekeeper? And where does Jenny fit into the picture? I don't understand the set-up! Is she here on holiday, or what?"

"It's a long story," Kate said, unmindful of the coffee pot and mugs she'd carried down from the kitchen, "and I'm not sure where to begin."

"No need to begin anywhere in particular," Greg said gently. "Just sit down and talk to me. I was always good at jig-saw puzzles, remember?" He poured the coffee; handed her a mug.

And so Kate talked, and Greg listened intently until, imperceptibly, twilight deepened into the darkness of night. The birdsong was silent, and the sky was filled with an amazement of stars: the Great Bear, the Pleiades; the Milky Way.

Talking to Greg helped Kate to come to terms with the problem of Jenny. Until that evening in the garden, she hadn't even realised the full extent of her frustration at Jenny's erratic behaviour, thinking one minute they were drawing closer together, having her hopes dashed the next, linked to a sense of failure that she had begun to lose patience with her, to doubt the validity of their girlhood friendship.

Loyalty forbade her revealing details of Jenny's sordid past. She simply told Greg about the incident leading to Jenny's brush with death, the arrest of her assailant, the forthcoming trial, the reasons why she had offered Jenny a home, a resting place at least, a kind of caravanserai until she was well enough to make decisions about her own future.

She added with a trace of bitterness, "I can't see her wanting to stay here with me when the court case is over and she's back on her feet again."

"In which case, problem solved," Greg said reasonably.

"I guess so," Kate admitted, "but I'll still feel that I somehow mishandled the situation."

"There are situations which are impossible to 'handle'," Greg reminded her, and Kate had known by the look on his face, that he was speaking from experience of his life with Cindy.

When Cindy had discovered the sitting room, which she referred to as the "lounge", she took to spending much of her time there, watching television. She was sulking, to put it mildly, muttering darkly that she couldn't see the point of eating in the kitchen when the lounge was big enough to contain a dining table and chairs, at which point Kate had begun taking "madam's" meals through to her to eat from a tray placed on the low table in front of the fireplace. A thankless task, as she had quickly discovered. A source of embarrassment for Greg; of some amusement to Jenny.

"I won't have you dancing attendance on Cindy," Greg said harshly. "If she prefers to eat in the sitting room, she should carry her own trays!" He paused. "Sorry. Here, let me take it!"

"I honestly don't mind," Kate said brightly, inwardly relieved at being spared her sister-in-law's company in the kitchen – as a kind of skeleton at the feast.

Overhearing the conversation, Jenny supplied innocently, tongue-in-cheek, "Perhaps I could help?"

"Thanks, Jenny, but that's not necessary," Kate assured her, imagining Cindy's reaction to her arch enemy's appearance in the sitting room, knowing full well that her sister-in-law had not forgotten or forgiven Jenny's "You *do* look a bit washed out" remark.

A fraught situation all round, Kate considered, especially since Jenny and Greg appeared to be hitting it off rather well together; talking over old times, drinking their after supper coffee in the garden, whilst Cindy sulked in the sitting room and she cleared away the supper things and did the washing-up prior to going upstairs to her room to get on with the next chapter.

One valuable lesson she had learned so far – that fate had a way of spinning its own complicated designs without the aid of human intervention.

Absorbed in her novel, she had now reached the stage of Lucy Kiddy's involvement and subsequent marriage to a rich man, twice her age; giving full reign to her imagination when poor Lucy, trapped within a loveless union, had begun seeking means of escape from her elderly, lecherous husband; curiously drawing a modicum of comfort from the trials and tribulations of a girl, long dead and gone, whose life, akin to Kate's own, had not been a bed of roses. A girl who had suffered the pain and misery of rejection, the hopelessness of unrequited love, as she herself had done.

The difference between herself and Lucy Kiddy was that Lucy's days were over and done with. Her own were not. The strong link between them was that the passage of time, the difference in dress, the social shibboleths of a century ago, had no bearing whatsoever on the emotional responses of women in love, either now or then.

She had told Greg about the book, and he had been up to her studio twice to read the opening chapters, until at Cindy's call, "Greg, where are you? What are you doing?" he'd hurried off to placate her. "Anything for a quiet life," he'd murmured wryly.

Later, helping Kate with the washing-up when Cindy was in the lounge watching television, referring to her brainchild, he said, "For what it's worth, Sis, and if the opening chapters are anything to go by, I think you're on to a winner! Well on your way to fame and fortune as a best-selling author!"

Kate laughed. "Pull the other one," she said dismissively. "Writing is simply a hobby of mine. Something I enjoy doing to fill in time." She paused momentarily, then continued, "When Alex went away, I knew I needed to do something positive to add a sense of purpose to my life, so I took a course in touch-typing. I might just have easily taken piano lessons, except that I hadn't a piano, only a typewriter! So what are you saying? That had I taken piano lessons, I might well be on my way now to giving Chopin recitals at the Wigmore Hall?"

"Knowing you, Kate, I shouldn't be at all surprised," Greg chuckled, entirely at ease and relaxed in his sister's company, as he had been all the days of their lives since he had first espied her as a small bundle in their mother's arms, whose tiny fingers, holding his, had placed a kind of hammerlock of love on the heart of a two-year-old toddler.

Fanny had taken a liking to Greg. Not so Cindy or Jenny. Kate detected a hint of jealousy in her attitude towards Jenny, whom she regarded as an interloper. Cindy she regarded as a stuck-up snob, undeserving of such a lovely husband. Not that she had ever voiced her opinions all that clearly. But Kate could read her like a book, and she sympathised with her to a great extent. "I know I *am* a servant," Fanny had blurted one day, "but I don't like being treated as such."

"When have I treated you as a servant?" Kate asked mildly. "So far as I'm concerned, you're doing me a favour helping me the way you do."

"I weren't meaning you or that nice brother of yours," Fanny muttered darkly, "but I can't say the same of others I could mention."

"I shouldn't worry about that, if I were you," Kate said placatingly. "It won't be for very much longer."

How could she have known, at the time, how prophetic her remark would turn out to be?

In retrospect, the unfortunate train of events to come had started with Dot Paulson's appearance at Gull House to lodge a series of complaints against Cora Clegg, whose behaviour was fast becoming intolerable.

Asked, "In what way, exactly?" Dot, obviously upset and bridling like a turkey cock, went into a long diatribe about Cora thinking she owned the shop. Several times recently, she'd found her entertaining her boyfriend in the stock-room and the office behind the shop.

"There he was, as large as life and twice as ugly," Dot spluttered indignantly, "his feet on the desk, drinking coffee and smoking cigarettes. The air was fairly blue with smoke. He didn't bother to get up neither, and what they'd been up to in the stock-room . . . Well, I ask you? I mean, it's just not on, is it?"

"No, it certainly isn't," Kate agreed. "In which case, the sooner we dispense with Miss Clegg's services, the better. Will you break the bad news to her, or shall I?"

"I'd rather you, if you don't mind?" Dot said tremulously. "I really couldn't face her or that beastly boyfriend of hers again. To tell the truth, I was scared stiff of him just sitting there, the cheeky young devil, as bold as you please, grinning at me: almost daring me to give him his marching orders! As for *her*! There she was, as bold as brass, standing behind him, her hands resting on his shoulders. And do you know what she said? 'Why, if it isn't old Dotty herself come to poke her nose in where it isn't wanted!' I ask you? That's why I'm here! What I mean is, you can't blame me, can you, for feeling so upset?"

And so it devolved upon Kate to give Miss Clegg the brush off – a month's wages in lieu of notice, to face the abuse showered on her as Cora marched defiantly out of the shop that self and same evening, towards the powerfully built young brute awaiting her on the street corner. A nasty experience, all told, Kate thought, turning the "Closed" notice on the shop door in the full realisation that the shop must necessarily remain closed for the time being, until a new manageress had been appointed to fill Cora's inadequate high-heeled shoes. Hopefully, not a sex-symbol next time, but a plain, intelligent ordinary woman in need of a job. Not necessarily a young woman with long fingernails, inimical to dusting and polishing. Someone like Fanny Kiddy, for instance.

Fanny Kiddy! Of *course*! Why not? Leaning back against the door, weighing up the pros and cons, she could at least ask Fanny if she would take care of the shop, even on a part-time basis, until the end of the season.

Fanny was over the moon. "Well, if you think I could do it," she said modestly, "I'll give it a go! Eh, I shall have to hev my hair permed and treat meself to a new jumper and skirt!"

One problem solved, Kate thought. Others were to follow in rapid succession.

Waking up suddenly in the early hours of next morning to the feeling that something was wrong, a light sleeper, Kate could have sworn she'd heard footsteps on the fire-escape.

Getting up, quickly shrugging into her dressing gown, not switching on her bedside lamp, she ventured on to the landing and stood there, listening intently, knowing that what she suspected was true. Someone *was* in the house! A burglar presumably.

Heart pounding, she tiptoed downstairs. The intruder was in the kitchen! Regardless of her own safety, sick at heart, angry beyond belief at this invasion of her home, switching on the landing light, she called out, "Who's there?" flinging open the kitchen door.

At the sound of her voice, the intruder ran full tilt down the fire-escape, a powerfully built young man whom she identified vaguely, in a split second of partial recognition, as Cora Clegg's boyfriend. No burglar but an arsonist! The air was smoke-filled; curtains and furnishings well alight from a pile of petrol-soaked rags planted in the centre of the room. The fire was spreading rapidly.

Miraculously, Greg appeared at that moment, alerted to a sense of danger by his sister's voice calling out, "Who's there?" Taking in the situation at a glance, he said calmly, "Ring the Fire Brigade, Kate! Tell them to hurry!"

"But what about Cindy and Jenny?" Kate asked anxiously, wondering how on earth he would cope with a hysterical woman and a semi-invalid at dagger's drawn with one another. The main priority, to get them out of the building as quickly as possible.

"Leave me to worry about that," he advised her, speaking more urgently. "Just do as I say, for God's sake, before the entire house goes up in flames!"

Kate fled to the sitting room to dial 999. Greg hurried to alert his wife and Jenny. The call made, Kate raced back to help Greg, by which time Cindy was on the landing in her dressing gown and slippers, complaining bitterly that she had known all along that something awful would happen, and what about her belongings?

"Where's Jenny?" Kate asked in alarm.

"In her room. I knocked on the door. There was no answer," Greg said, hustling Cindy towards the front staircase.

"She must have taken sleeping pills! I'd better find out," Kate said shortly, praying to God that Jenny hadn't also locked her bedroom door. "She's probably out for the count."

"I'll go to her," Greg said. "You take care of Cindy!"

"I'm warning you, Greg!" Cindy called after him as he hurried towards Jenny's room, at the same time shaking off Kate's hand on her arm. "Your place is with *me*, not *her!*"

Kate's patience snapped suddenly. "Tell me, Cindy, do you ever think of anyone but yourself? Well, don't just stand there like Lady Macbeth! *Move*, woman! There's a fire behind you, a staircase in front of you. So which is the better option? Since you don't want my help, make your own way for once in your miserable life! I'm going to help Greg!"

The fire brigade had arrived. Someone was hammering urgently for admission. Brushing past Cindy, Kate hurried down to let them in. Overwhelmed by the sheer physical presence of so many strapping men on the doorstep, she flattened herself against the wall as they crowded in, wearing breathing apparatus, to tackle the blaze on the upper landing where Greg was standing, holding Jenny in his arms.

"You'd best get out of here, mate," the fire chief advised him, "whilst the going's good! The blaze started in the kitchen, you say? Everyone accounted for?" Greg nodded.

Meanwhile, uttering a hoarse cry, Cindy had stumbled downstairs as if the devil were after her, her face a mask of fury as, looking up, she saw her husband carrying Jenny in his arms towards the safety of the street beyond.

Oh God, Kate thought, dreading the reckoning to come. Hell hath no fury like a woman scorned. No doubt about it, a full scale confrontation between Cindy and Greg was about to erupt once the fire had been brought under control.

It was far worse than Kate had imagined it would be. Greg listened to his wife's tirade in complete silence, saying nothing in his own defence, face haggard, trembling slightly as her cruel, whip-lashing tongue gave vent to her feelings of bitterness, scorn and disgust – the unjust accusations levelled against him.

The scene took place in the sitting room at five o'clock in the morning, after the fire brigade had left the premises and Jenny had gone back to bed, still woozy from the effect of the sleeping pills she had taken the night before. Taking her cue from Greg, Kate also remained silent for the time being, realising, as he had done, the futility of attempting to stem the flow of vitriol from Cindy's lips, resisting the strong temptation to throttle her sister-in-law with her bare hands.

"Call yourself a man?" Cindy screeched hysterically. "Take a good look at yourself, why don't you? All these years I've put up with you, and what have I to show for it? *Nothing*! The trouble with you, you have no drive, no ambition! You should have been a headmaster by now, earning a decent salary! But oh no, not you! And not a thought in the world for *me*! How do you think I've felt stuck away in that damned bungalow in Manchester as the wife of a bloody failure? And that's what you are, Greg Harker, a rotten bloody failure!

"I blame your precious sister for that, if you really must know! The truth is, you've always cared for her far more than you ever have done for me! Well, deny it if you can! The pair of you as thick as thieves – talking behind my back, kissing and fondling each other I daresay! I'm not blind, you know? A pretty peculiar relationship between brother and sister, I'd say! Bloody unhealthy, to put it mildly!

"Now, obviously you're having a hole and corner affair with that Jenny woman, aren't you? My God, the way you carried her downstairs made me feel physically sick! Not giving a damn about *me*. Only *her*! Well, admit it, if you are man enough to do so, which I doubt, knowing you, a poor excuse for a man!"

She paused dramatically before launching her final bombshell: "Well, I've had enough of you, Greg Harper, to last me a lifetime! I'm leaving here on the first available train to Manchester, and you'd better come with me if you know what's good for you! I'm warning you, I mean what I say! Otherwise I'll leave without you. Is that perfectly clear? Moreover, I shall institute divorce proceedings against you on the grounds of your adultery with Jenny Laird. Well, what have you to say to *that*?"

Breaking his silence at last, Greg said quietly, "I'll drive you to the station, if you like. Unless you'd prefer to take a taxi!"

Eighteen

For the first time, Kate felt sorry for Cindy, whose stupidity had cost her her marriage.

Sick at heart for Greg's sake, watching his face as his wife poured forth her venom, she knew that his strong sense of loyalty towards her, his belief in the sanctity of the marriage vows, had been damaged beyond pair, destroyed by her diatribe against him, shredding every vestige of his dignity and self respect.

"Look, Greg," she said quietly, "why not go for a walk; a breath of fresh air? I'll stay here with Cindy, help her to pack: make certain she's at the station in time to catch the eight o'clock train."

"Thanks, Sis." He nodded briefly and hurried downstairs.

Incensed, Cindy turned on Kate in a fury. "How dare you interfere in a matter between husband and wife? But if you think for one moment he won't be coming home with me, you have another thing coming! Greg knows which side his bread is buttered right enough!"

She sneered unpleasantly, "Oh, I know what's going on in your mind. You think you've got him back, don't you? Given the choice, that he'll stay here with you and that fancy woman of his?"

Kate said wearily, "Tell me, Cynthia, were you born a fool or, in your case, has practice made perfect? Hasn't it entered your head that your marriage is virtually over and done with, bar the shouting?

"Think about it, Cynthia, if you are capable of thought, that is. Ask yourself how any self-respecting, decent man on the face of the earth, would react to his wife's denunciation of him as a 'rotten bloody failure'; allied to his propensities to commit incest and adultery into the bargain. None of which allegations are remotely true, and you know it!"

"Now you listen to me, Kate Ford—" Cindy interrupted rudely.

"No, Cynthia," Kate riposted angrily, "*you* listen to *me* for a change. The fact is, and you'd better believe it, this is the end of the line so far as your marriage to Greg is concerned. Oh, he may well decide to return to Manchester with you. Knowing my brother as well as I do, and not in the biblical sense, I assure you, he will see it as his duty to make certain that you are well provided for, after the divorce."

"Pah! There won't be a divorce! Greg can't afford to leave me. He has financial commitments – mortgage repayments to meet, bills to pay. He couldn't afford to leave home. Where would he go? What would he do? In any case, he has no reason to leave me. *I'm* not the guilty party! *I* haven't done anything wrong!"

"Neither has Greg," Kate reminded her, "but this much is certain, you'll never live together again as man and wife."

Again came Cindy's sneering laugh. "Ha! If that's meant to frighten me, forget it! Greg and I haven't lived together as man and wife for years now! Not since he started harping on about wanting a family. Well, I soon put paid to that nonsense, I can tell you! The very idea! We'd only just nicely got back from our honeymoon when he started on about my getting pregnant! *Ugh*! The last thing I wanted was a baby messing up my life!"

"*Your* life? What about Greg's life?"

"Oh, *that*?" Cindy shrugged her shoulders dismissively. "He soon got the message when I told him I'd share a bed with him, but he'd best keep to his own side of it in future."

"I see," Kate said thoughtfully. "Now, isn't it about time you started packing? Meanwhile, I'll ring for a taxi."

"I shouldn't bother, if I were you," Cindy replied airily. "Greg will be back soon, his tail between his legs, as usual, to drive me back to Manchester where he belongs. With *me*, not *you*!"

Greg had walked slowly towards St Nicholas Cliff, where he stood for a while, looking out to sea.

Deeply shaken by the events of the past few hours, he could scarcely believe that they had all really happened – the fire, that moment of panic when he had failed to rouse Jenny; his fear that the fire might spread out of control and she might be trapped in her room.

Then, having got to her in time and realising that in her state of confusion from the sleeping pills she had taken at bedtime, she was incapable of walking downstairs, what else could be have done but carry her to safety?

And that had been the cause of Cindy's jealous outburst. Deeply shocked, he had experienced a sudden revulsion towards her, as if his life had swung out of focus, as though everything he had hitherto believed in, his marriage vows, his home, his responsibilities, no longer mattered a damn.

Cindy had always been jealous of Kate. This he had learned to live with and accept, as he had accepted her laziness and inate snobbery, her constant complaints at his lack of ambition, her refusal to bear his children.

A gentle man at heart, he had turned to books and music and pride in his work as a teacher as alternatives in a loveless marriage. But that she had imagined for one moment his relationship with his sister was in some way unhealthy beggared belief, as did her wild assumption that he had committed adultery with Jenny Laird.

He liked Jenny enormously, and why not? He was, after all, a full-blooded male, but not some blasted pervert engaged in a sexual relationship with his own sister. And Jenny was still pretty in a forced kind of way. Not as wildly pretty as she had been at Kate's wedding twenty-odd years ago, but exuding the same sexual aura as she had done then. Possibly the reason why Kate held certain misgivings about her and Jenny's present day friendship. Essentially, Kate had grown stronger throughout the passing years. Jenny had not.

In retrospect, there had been something faintly repulsive about Jenny's deviously worded invitation to take advantage of her room, her bed, her body, if he – how had she put it? – "If he felt the urge to release his physical tension once in a while." No such thought had entered his mind. He had simply enjoyed her company; talking over old times out there in the garden.

He loved this place, this town with its memories of happier times before the deaths of his parents had turned his own and Kate's lives topsy-turvy. As much as he longed to remain here, he knew this was impossible, a pipe dream until he had settled his marital affairs. He had his job to consider. Quitting the teaching profession without due notice would jeopardise his chances of future employment at, say, a private school, as a housemaster or a part-time tutor. Teaching was all he knew, and he was not prepared to throw away years of experience in his chosen profession without due care and consideration.

Leaving Cindy would be no easy option. Knowing her, she would fight tooth and claw to hang on to the bungalow, and him too, if he allowed himself to be bullied into submission, as he had so often done before. Divorce was an ugly business, he imagined, a possibility he had not even considered until, sick at heart, he had realised for the first time the depth of her bitterness towards him as she muck-raked their marriage in front of Kate. He had known then that it was over and done with at last – that sham edifice of his marriage to a woman devoid of humour, understanding or compassion. An edifice akin to a sand-castle built within reach of the incoming tide.

Returning to Gull House, finding Kate alone in the sitting room, he said wearily, "I'm sorry, Sis, but I have to go back to Manchester. To settle things once and for all. You do see that, don't you?"

"Yes, of course I do. And you are right. Just promise me you'll see a good solicitor as soon as possible. Tell him the whole story from beginning to end. And I do mean the *whole* story. Need I say more?"

"I guess not." He smiled awkwardly. "Then you don't blame me for wanting my freedom?"

"I'd be surprised if you didn't. And remember, if I can help in any way, all you have to do is ask!"

"It could be a long drawn out business," he said, dreading what lay ahead of him. "I have no valid grounds for divorce."

"I'm not so sure about that. The reason why you must choose the best possible solicitor." No use beating about the bush. "Cindy told me the reason why she has been your wife in name only for the past eighteen years."

Kate paused, understanding her brother's distress that his wife had taken her marital muck-raking far beyond the limits of acceptable human behaviour – his utter disgust that she had chosen to reveal, to Kate, of all people, intimate details of their non-existent sexual relationship since the days of their short-lived honeymoon period in a small hotel in the Lake District.

She said quietly, compassionately, "Don't you see, Greg, that you have valid grounds for divorce. But only you can decide if you want your freedom enough to fight for it fairly and squarely, just as I had to fight for mine and financial independence into the bargain, when I divorced Don on the grounds of his adultery with Lucia Keane.

"And Don's handing over the deeds of April Cottage to me was due not to his largesse, as I led you to believe, but to my persistence in refusing to divorce him, point blank, until he'd secured my own future to some extent. So now you know!"

Feeling suddenly much stronger and light-hearted, as he always had done in Kate's presence, Greg said, "So what if Cindy persists in retaining the deeds to the bungalow as a condition of my divorce proceedings against her?"

Kate laughed. "Then hand them over to her, by all means. With one proviso, that she also retains full custody of those blasted garden gnomes."

Cindy was in the front seat of the Volkswagen, staring straight ahead, when Greg, having stowed away their cases and Alex Arden's books in the luggage compartment, kissed Kate goodbye. Cindy had simply stalked past her without a word.

On the doorstep, clasping Kate's hands firmly in his, Greg murmured, "Please say goodbye to Jenny for me. Wish her well for the future; a happy outcome of that court case of hers."

When the Volkswagen had driven away from the side door, Kate went upstairs to face the ruination of the kitchen: smoke-blackened and virtually unusable for the time being, thanks to Cora Clegg's boyfriend, whose arson attack on the premises, she realised, had been in the nature of a wilful act of revenge levelled against herself for having given Cora her marching orders from the shop.

Bone-tired and weary from the exigencies of the night before, all Kate really wanted was to crawl into bed and sleep till the cows came home. An impossibility in the present circumstances.

First of all, she would have to inform Alex's solicitors of the arson attack and the fire damage to their client's property; also to report the break-in to the local police, and decide what to do about meals for herself and Jenny whilst the kitchen was out of commission. Moving into a hotel, for the time being, seemed the obvious solution to that problem.

Jenny appeared put out when she heard that Greg had gone without saying goodbye to her: "Huh, and there was I thinking I'd made a hit with him!"

"Unfortunately, so did Cindy. She accused him of having an affair with you," Kate said.

"*What?* Some fat chance! It wasn't for the want of trying, believe me." Jenny laughed. "If ever I saw a man in need of a roll in the hay! I'll bet he doesn't do much of that with the miserable cow he's married to!"

Common sense warned Kate not to mention the divorce threat hanging over Greg. Instead, she passed on his message and asked Jenny how she felt about moving into a hotel for the time being.

"Great," she enthused. "I could do with a change of scene, a bit of fun for a change now I'm getting back to normal."

"Just as long as your idea of fun doesn't include making a fool of my brother," Kate warned her, afraid that Jenny might take it into her head to further complicate Greg's life if she felt like it. She wouldn't put it past her.

"If that's what's worrying you, forget it," Jenny said carelessly. "Greg's a nice bloke, but as dull as ditchwater. And, well, to be honest, I bumped into an old friend of mine again, last week. John Spivey! You remember John? The best man at your wedding?"

"Yes, I remember. The man you turned down because you felt he wasn't quite good enough for you?" Kate reminded her.

Ignoring the remark, Jenny continued, "We had quite a long talk. As a matter of fact, I'm having dinner with him at the Royal Hotel next Wednesday. And why not?"

Why not indeed? Kate knew that she had not misread Jenny after all. She was just as selfish and manipulatative now as she had been all along.

She said quietly, "Your life is your own to live as you see fit from now on, and I'll not stand in the way of your independence. I'm glad that you feel able to tackle life on your own terms again. So what will you do when we have parted company? I am right in thinking that we have reached the end of the road? That you will not be returning to Gull House, even when the workmen have finished the redecorating?"

"No, I guess not," Jenny admitted reluctantly. "You see, John has suggested my moving in with him, to live, in a fortnight or so, when he has the keys to a penthouse apartment on the South Cliff."

"A – penthouse?"

"Well, a top floor flat," Jenny said, catching Kate's look of surprise. "I gather you disapprove?"

"What gave you that idea?"

"Because you have always disapproved of me, at rock bottom. That's true, isn't it? You've never accepted that I need men in my life; excitement; having a good time."

"And have you always had a good time so far as men are concerned?"

"No, but I can't stay cooped up forever, and John Spivey's doing really well now. I know he'll take care of me just fine."

"In which case there's nothing more to be said, except to wish you well." Kate added perceptively, "I take it that you won't object to being 'cooped up' with me in a hotel for the time being?"

"You really couldn't resist saying that, could you?" Jenny flung back at her. "So what do you want me to do? Fall down on my knees and thank you for picking me up out of the gutter? Or would you prefer a framed testimonial to hang on your wall?"

"Blessed are they who expecteth nothing, or words to that effect," Kate said quietly. "I helped you because I wanted to; because I valued your friendship at a time when I needed a friend to turn to. You, Jenny, were that friend! And so, perhaps, it is I who should provide a testimonial to hang on your wall? 'To Jenny. Friend of my formative years. With love and thanks for all the sweetness and happiness she brought into my life once, long ago.'"

Her eyes filled suddenly with tears. She said mistily, "I'll be lonely without you, Jenny."

But then, loneliness was something she had learned how to live with since Alex had disappeared from her life so abruptly. Yet never a day passed by without wondering where he was. And, whether or not he loved her in return, she knew that she would forever remain in love with him.

And so, Kate had booked rooms for herself and Jenny in a small hotel in West Square, near the town centre, but went daily to Gull House to find out how the repairs were progressing, and to pick up the mail, if any. She had not had word of Greg so far; had thought it best not to try to contact him, afraid of worsening the situation if Cindy answered the phone.

At a low ebb, physically and emotionally drained, beset by problems, worried sick about Greg, Alex and Jenny, her inability to get on with her writing, she felt that her life had suddenly ground to a halt, leaving her as stranded as a starfish in a rockpool, with no one to turn to for help or advice unless . . . It was then she thought of Madame Zara.

One morning at Gull House, having discussed with the foreman the paint and paper she wanted for the kitchen now that the fire-damaged units, furniture, floor covering and electrical equipment had been replaced, hearing the rattle of the letterbox, she hurried downstairs to find two letters on the mat. One from Greg, addressed to herself, the other addressed to Jenny.

Greg had written:

Dear Kate,

To let you know that I have found a solicitor willing to act on my behalf. Taking your advice, I told him the story of my marriage from start to finish. A bit daunting from my viewpoint, as you can imagine, but nothing compared to Cindy's reaction when I told her that I'd set the divorce wheels in motion.

Not to put too fine a point on it, she ordered me out of the house. When I refused to leave, she packed her bags and went off to Bradford to stay with her sister. The relief was enormous.

Sorry I can't write more fully at the moment, but I'll phone you as soon as possible. Truth to tell, I'm dog-tired. I know that you must be, too. But not to worry unduly, I see a ray of light on the horizon.

Ever yours affectionately,

Greg

Thank God. Thank God, Kate thought, for that ray of light on the horizon.

Jenny's letter contained news of her court appearance to give evidence against her former landlord, which she threw aside carelessly, saying that John would go with her to the York Crown Court when the time came. Kate made no comment. There was virtually nothing left to say. Jenny's eyes were firmly fixed on the future with her latest lover. Kate accepted the fact that she had no further role to play in her friend's life. She had, at least, played a small part in helping her over a rough patch, as Jenny had once helped her. Now, seemingly, those debts had been paid in full. No regrets.

Kate had been home for over a week when Fanny called to see her one evening after work. Thinking how tired she looked, Kate put the kettle on for a cup of tea and asked if she would like something to eat.

Fanny shook her head, "No," she said, "I just came to see how you were. I expect it's given you a bit of a shock, like. I know it did me. Not that I know the man. But, well, I couldn't help wondering what will become of all this, if the worst comes to the worst."

Kate frowned. "I'm sorry, I haven't a clue what you're on about. What man are you talking about? And what do you mean by what will become of all this? All what?"

Fanny looked stricken. "Oh lord, then you ain't read the evening paper?"

"No. It hasn't been delivered yet." Kate's bewilderment turned suddenly to fear, a cold feeling inside. "Why? What's in it? What's wrong?" But deep down, she knew the name of the man Fanny was talking about. She said hoarsely, "It's Alex, isn't it? Something has happened to him! He's dead, isn't he?" She sat down abruptly, trembling like a leaf, her face ashen.

"Eh, love, I'm sorry," Fanny placed a comforting arm about her shoulders, "I shouldn't have sprung it on you like that. But it ain't as bad as you think. He ain't dead, just missing. An' it mightn't be him at all. They're not sure yet – them Foreign Office folk, I mean."

"For God's sake, Fanny, *tell* me!"

"Here, you'd best see for yourself." Fanny fiddled in her shopping bag for her copy of the *Evening News*, and laid it on the kitchen table.

Kate read, with a kind of horrid fascination:

BRITISH CITIZEN BELIEVED KIDNAPPED. The Foreign Office today confirmed rumours of the capture by tribesmen in a remote area of Turkestan of a British citizen. The man, travelling alone and on foot, named as Alex Arden, better known as the author Sandy Alexis, is reported as being held to ransom somewhere in that area, for an undisclosed sum of money.

Foreign Office sources have also confirmed that a team of negotiators is being flown to the area immediately, hopefully to secure the release of the hostage as quickly as possible.

Kate buried her head in her hands. Oh God, she prayed inwardly, keep him safe. Let no harm come to him.

The distance between them seemed limitless, unimaginable. And yet she hoped and believed that wherever he was in the world, he would know that she was thinking about him; praying for him. Loving him.

Next day, she went to Gladstone Street to visit "Madame Zara", remembering the old lady's words: "And this will not be your last visit to my home. So goodbye now, my dear, until we meet again."

This time, the door was opened by a young pleasant-faced woman wearing a district nurse's uniform, who invited her into the hall. Kate's heart sank abruptly. Her fingers tightened suddenly on the bouquet of flowers she had brought with her.

The nurse said kindly, "It's bad news, I'm afraid. Mrs Parker suffered a stroke in the early hours of this morning. I'm awaiting the arrival of an ambulance to take her to hospital."

"May I see her?" Kate asked quietly.

The nurse smiled sympathetically, "Yes, of course, if you want to, though I must warn you, she is barely conscious, unable to speak properly, the poor old soul, and I doubt she'll recognise you."

"Even so, I'd like to see her," Kate said heavily, her eyes dim with tears as she followed the nurse upstairs to the old lady's bedroom.

Laying the flowers on the bedside table, looking down at Mrs Parker's twisted face on the soft feather pillow cradling her head, and gently stroking the withered hands lying uselessly on the counterpane, Kate whispered, "I'm so sorry, my love, but you were right in saying we'd meet again, remember? That I'd come here again, one day. Your prediction has come true."

Slowly, painfully, the old woman opened her eyes, the twisted mouth lifted in the semblance of a smile, the withered hands clinging to Kate's momentarily.

Bending closer to her, Kate caught her last, scarcely audible words: "Zara. Thirsty." And then she was gone from the world as easily and painlessly as a candle-flame puffed out by a breath of wind from an open window.

Part Three

Nineteen

Since Alex's disappearance, Kate's life had seemed frozen in a time-warp of memories, longing and regret.

Now November was here, and there was still no news of him. Foreign Office negotiators had failed to contact his captors. Efforts were being made to discover his whereabouts in a wild, remote region largely uninhabited apart from nomads – small bands of itinerant tribesmen lacking communication with the world beyond their own inhospitable territory.

At night, Kate had lain awake remembering the words of the poem "He Fell Among Thieves", the final terrifying stanza: "A sword swept. Over the pass the voices, one by one faded, and the hill slept". This was a poem she had hated even as a schoolgirl, conveying as it did the thoughts of a captive Englishman awaiting his dawn execution by a band of bloodthirsty brigands.

Possibly Alex had already paid the price of his bid for mental freedom. And if he had not, how could she bear to think of him denied the liberty he loved? Shackled hand and foot most likely, cold, hungry and dirty, faced with the realisation that each day that dawned may be his last.

Meanwhile, she must face each new day as best she could, gathering up the threads of her life as she had tried to do ever since leaving April Cottage.

More than a year had now passed since her return to Scarborough to make her brave new beginning. A year fraught with emotional problems: falling in love again; attempting to take care of Jenny, who, in the long run, had proved quite capable of taking care of herself, and with Greg in the throes of a prolonged divorce drama. Wife versus husband, with property, not love, at stake.

Love? A mockery more like. And yet . . .

* * *

On the day of "Madame Zara's" funeral in the old Dean Road Cemetery, according to the old lady's wish to be buried next to her parents, looking up through tear-dimmed eyes, Kate noticed a towering granite memorial erected to the memory of Jeanette, the beloved wife of John Fairgray Sharpin.

When Mrs Parker's coffin had been laid to rest, Kate walked along the path for a closer look at the granite obelisk in memory of Jeanette Sharpin, on which her face had been sculpted in bas-relief.

It was a strong face, striking rather than beautiful, and the lady had died young. Standing there in silent contemplation, the thought occurred that it was here, on this very spot, that John Sharpin had most probably stood on the day of his wife's funeral, head bowed, mourning the loss of a beloved person, just as she, as a young girl on the threshold of life, had mourned the loss of first her mother, then her father.

On the day of Madame Zara's funeral, the sun was shining and she placed on the old lady's coffin a bouquet of summer flowers: sweet-scented stocks, long-stemmed roses and carnations.

How could she possibly foresee then, that come November, the new life she was slowly rebuilding from the ruins of the old would suddenly crumble to dust beneath her feet?

Kate had lived with loneliness before, but never on this scale, with Alex dead, for all she knew, and Greg involved in a bitter divorce battle from which he might well emerge both penniless and homeless in the long run.

As for Jenny, she might as well be living on another planet. Kate had seen neither hide nor hair of her since the day she had announced her intention of moving into John Spivey's apartment to live with a man she had once turned down flat as being "not good enough" for her.

The final blow came when Dot Paulson, strung on the horns of her particular domestic dilemma, handed in her notice, closely followed by Fanny's.

"I thought serving in a shop would be a doddle," she explained tearfully. "Well, it ain't! Not at my age, anyway, with folk standing there firing questions at me, getting ratty at being kept waiting, an' me getting all confused; giving 'em the wrong change an' suchlike!

"Eh, I'm sorry to let you down, love, but I'd best stick to my caretaker's job in future. Summat I'm good at an' know like the back of my hand!"

And so Kate, having hung a "Closed" sign on the shop door, wrote to Alex's solicitors advising them that, in her present circumstances, she could no longer cope with the worry of keeping it open. But she missed Dot's appearances, regaling her with the latest news of her domestic troubles, and Fanny, she suspected, nursing a sense of guilt and hurt pride, would not be paying her usual frequent visits until she had come to terms with having "left her in the lurch".

All this at a time when Kate longed for someone to talk to, a reassuring smile, the comforting touch of a friendly hand to guide her through the dark days ahead.

Wandering the rooms of Gull House like a ghost, hearing the mournful sound of the fog-horn in the distance, she felt isolated, far distanced from her fellow human beings, her mind shredded with worry over Alex, wondering if he were alive or dead. And if he was dead, how could she face a future without him?

Slowly, painfully, she reached the conclusion that she must do something positive to fill the empty spaces of her life. But what?

Alex's typewriter beckoned, but she had lost the thread of her novel since the night of the fire, that cataclysmic event which had sparked off a chain reaction of disasters.

Feeding on memories, she recalled the morning she had come to Gull House to find Alex kneeling on the floor of his study surrounded by the material he had collected for his book on Scarborough's development as a seaside resort.

How angry he had been that day, frustrated because he had lost the ability to express his thoughts in the written word and he knew it.

She had not understood the depth of his humiliation at the time, that any sixth form schoolboy could have done better. How could she have done so, not knowing that here was a man whose former literary output had become classics of their kind?

If only she had taken the trouble to talk to him quietly on that occasion, to help him sort out the untidy piles of paper on the floor. Instead of which, nettled by his temperamental outburst directed against herself, she had told him, in no uncertain terms, that what he needed was not a housekeeper but a skivvy, prior to marching out of the room and downstairs to the side door.

What a fool she'd been! What a jumped-up, self-righteous idiot not to have realised that he stood in need of help, laced with sympathy and understanding, not condemnation.

The folders containing his notes and photographs were still on his desk, alongside his typewriter, just as he had left them when he'd reached the bitter conclusion that his glory days as a writer were over.

One night, unable to sleep, propped up with pillows in what had once been Alex's bed, reading the contents of the folders by the light of his bedside lamp, Kate derived comfort from the completeness of the past – laid away like love-letters, lavender-scented and tied neatly with the faded ribbons of a bygone age. All passion spent. A consummation devoutly to be wished: the pain and passion of living soothed by the long sleep of forgetfulness after death.

But what if Alex's belief in reincarnation was true? What if, having faced the traumatic events of one lifetime, heaven decreed a return to earth for countless rides on the merry-go-round of life? On the other hand, even as a child faced with her initial concept of a heaven somewhere in the sky, filled with haloes and harp music, she'd thought how boring it would be there without beaches to play on, donkey rides, and sandcastles to build: just being desperately good all the time, with nothing to eat except Ambrosia Creamed Rice!

A smile touched her lips as she recalled her first ever secret childhood companion, a figment of her imagination, though it – he, she – whichever – whom she had christened Reginald Missy (what would Sigmund Freud have made of that innocent slip-up? she wondered) – had always been with her, by day and night, to talk to whenever she felt lonely: especially in the middle of the night when the night-light in the saucer of water beside her bed had flickered and gone out.

Then he, she, it would tell her not to be afraid of the dark, that darkness was just a blue velvet curtain drawn down to separate dusk from dawn: a curtain pierced with holes to allow the stars and moon to shine through.

Often they had sung nursery rhymes together: "Baa-baa black sheep" and "Mary had a little lamb". Then suddenly, in the way of things, growing up, her strange hybrid guardian angel had flown away, never to return. How odd that she should think of it now, when what she most needed was a guardian angel to take care of her in her present darkness, loneliness and despair.

Up and dressed early next day, Kate walked along King Street to St Nicholas Cliff and stood there, near the Grand Hotel, looking out to sea. The air was cold and thin, like a whip's lash. The fog had lifted but no rays of light penetrated the greyness of the sky.

Chilled to the bone, she hurried down the zig-zagging paths to the seafront and turned in the direction of Valley Gardens; once the setting of John Sharpin's People's Park; of Lucy Kiddy's romance with a young lad from the fishing community based near the harbour whose dwelling places flanked the narrow, twisting streets and alleys of the Old Town in the lee of the ruined Norman fortress and the jutting headland separating the north and south bays of Scarborough.

The name of the lad Lucy had fallen in love with was lost in the mists of time, but Kate saw him clearly in her mind's eye as a strapping, broad-shouldered youngster, proud of his muscular physique, with a deeply tanned complexion from his days at sea in all weathers, wind, rain and sun; imagined him as blue-eyed and fair-haired in accordance with his Viking heritage – genes passed down the ages from father to son from the Danish invasion of Scarborough in the dim and distant past.

Scarcely likely that Lucy Kiddy, young, pretty and already sexually awakened from her abortive affair with that cellarman at the Crown Hotel, would have given so much as a second glance at any other than an equally sexually aware, handsome young male capable of satisfying her lust for love. Or – sex.

Poor Lucy. How difficult, at her age, and with her beauty, to differentiate between the two. Impossible to blame or condemn her for wanting to make the most of her youth and beauty for as long as they lasted.

Except, of course, Kate pondered, staring into the past, that in the flush of youth, the possibility of growing old never enters one's mind.

How strange to think that this place, these gardens now sadly neglected, had once rung to the sound of happy laughter, of music and stall vendors shouting their wares. Yet all those sounds must be trapped somewhere in the endless galaxies of time and space, if, as she had been led to believe, nothing in the world is ever lost beyond recall. Such were her mother's words, based on her unshakeable belief in the natural laws of life; witness the emergence of springtime after the long sleep of winter – frail snowdrops and crocuses pushing up through the frozen earth of January to proclaim their messages of rebirth, of renewed hope to the human race. And perhaps she was right.

But what about unrequited love? Neither flesh, fowl nor good red herring, Kate wondered, and the souls of unborn, or lost children, whose lives had ended before they had even begun?

Tears filled her eyes and flooded down her cheeks. If only she possessed the power to turn back the hands of time to that summer evening, long ago, when brilliantly coloured Chinese lanterns, strung between the trees of The People's Park, had shone down on the faces of a multitude of Victorians, men, women and children, all dead and gone now, yet somehow more real, more important to her than those living people she had loved and lost along life's way – Don Ford and Jenny Laird, for instance, who had accepted and used her love to their own ends, then turned their backs on her deliberately without a word of regret for the heartbreak they had caused her. All over and done with now. She would far rather live in the past than a present devoid of love and understanding.

Returning home by way of Plantation Hill, passing the now stagnant duck pond, littered with discarded cigarette cartons and empty crisp packets, deeply regretting the loss of the aviary of singing birds remembered from her childhood days, now sadly demolished and forgotten, as if it had never existed, and the scummy pool beneath the iron stanchions of the Valley Bridge from which once, long ago, on the opening night of The People's Park, a sparkling central fountain had splashed on to an abundance of lily pads and white, cup-shaped blossoms, Kate thought about John Fairgray Sharpin, who had master-minded The People's Park well over a century ago, that young, charismatic first-ever tenant manager of the Crown Hotel, from whose influence, by means of cleverly worded advertisements in the London papers of that day and age, extolling the virtues of Scarborough as an up-and-coming fashionable seaside resort, the town had reaped rich rewards in luring the *crème de la crème* of London society away from the Continental spa's, such as Chamonix and Baden-Baden, to partake of the health-giving waters discovered by a Mrs Farrer on the beach at Scarborough in the 1600s.

John Sharpin's advertisements had included indications of the first-class cuisine available: freshly caught local fish, Scottish salmon and beef, Welsh lamb, English venison, grouse, woodcock and pheasant, in season; fine imported wines from France, plus details of the stabling available for horses and carriages to the rear of the hotel.

Yet, amazingly, catering to the snobbish elite of that day and age, he had remained a man of the people, the ordinary working-class folk of Scarborough – the reason for his success as politician, Kate thought. Glancing up at the high wall bordering the Sitwell estate on her right-hand side, she was rocked by a sudden, overwhelming feeling of *déjà vu*, as if the present day world had ceased, momentarily, to exist, and she was listening, not to the sounds of motorcars streaming across the Valley Bridge, but the steady clip-clop of horses' hooves – not crossing the bridge – there was no bridge for them to cross – it hadn't been built yet . . .

Pulling herself together, trembling from head to foot, gulping in deep breaths of air, Kate wondered, Was she losing her mind, her grasp on reality? Or had her momentary lapse of consciousness been to do with too many sleepless nights, her lack of interest in the food which she shopped for, prepared and cooked religiously, then consigned, untasted, to the kitchen pedal-bin?

Possibly, but how could she be sure? She longed, night after night, for the benison of deep, dreamless sleep, which never came, and the simple enjoyment of home-cooked meals, which, despite a deep down hunger inside her, a desperate longing for sustenance, she could not begin to swallow for the continual lump of misery in her throat.

Walking on up Plantation Hill towards the town centre, deeply shaken by her psychic experience, she wondered where to go, what to do next.

Then suddenly, miraculously, out of the blue there came to her the sound of a familiar voice: "Mrs Ford! Kate! Remember me? Dinah Sheridan. We met at the hospital when your friend, Jenny Laird, was so poorly."

Remember? Of course Kate remembered this charming woman who had been so kind to herself and Jenny in the springtime of the year.

Dinah frowned concernedly. "Are you all right?" She clasped Kate's arm. "You look as if you'd seen a ghost. And you're trembling."

"I'm all right," Kate said faintly.

"All right, my foot! Here, come with me," she said, taking command of the situation. "There's a coffee shop in York Place."

Kate allowed herself to be led, glad of Dinah's supporting hand beneath her elbow, her lack of small talk, which she could not have borne at that moment, glad of the woman's silent sympathy and concern for her welfare, expressed not in words but positive action.

"Mind the steps," was all she said when they reached the café. Then, "Now, sit down. I'll fetch the coffee. Do you take sugar?"

Returning to the table from the counter, setting down the cups and sitting opposite Kate, she said briskly, "I've ordered scrambled eggs on toast. Don't know about you, but I'm starving, and they do nice scrambled eggs here, not all watery with hard knobs floating about in it. I often pop in for a bite to eat when I come off night duty, it helps me to unwind before going home to bed. Not that I sleep all that well during the day. Seems all wrong, sleeping during the day. A bit like living life in reverse. But one gets used to it in time I suppose, the way that one gets used to anything, in time."

"Do you really think so?" Kate said bleakly, staring into the past, "I wish I did." She paused to pick up her coffee cup, at least she tried to, and couldn't. Her hands were shaking too much. "I'm sorry," she whispered, "I've slopped it in the saucer."

Dinah thought how poorly she looked. She said, "So? It's cold out, and the cup was too full anyway!"

Kate said in a low voice, "No, it's more than that. I think I could be going out of my mind."

Twenty

S ister Sheridan's flat was in Bar Street, a narrow but busy thoroughfare linking St Nicholas Cliff and the town centre.

"It isn't very big, but it suits me fine," she said, leading the way upstairs. "The rent is reasonable and it doesn't take much heating."

Worried about Kate's state of mind, realising that she needed someone to talk to, she had persuaded her not to return to Gull House alone.

"But you've just come off night duty and need your rest," Kate demurred. "Not to worry," Dinah said briskly. "I never go to bed right away, just sit near the fire for a while to clear my mind, otherwise I'd never get to sleep at all."

The flat *was* small, but uncluttered and restful. The sitting room walls were pale green, hung with one or two gilt-framed watercolours and grouped-together etchings of nineteenth-century Scarborough by Turner.

Green velvet armchairs flanked the fireplace; the mantelpiece was decorated at either end, with trailing ivies in colourful Portuguese pottery containers. There were red-shaded lamps on the occasional tables near the armchairs. On the far side of the room, a dark oak china cabinet, cheek-by-jowl with a record-player. On the wall opposite the window, an elegant antique French escritoire, on top of which had been placed a cut-glass vase of dark red roses.

Glancing about her, Kate quoted softly, "'To make one little room an everywhere,'" remembering her favourite poet, John Donne.

"Look, Kate," Dinah said quietly, "why not stay here with me for a little while? Talk to me if you feel you can trust me enough to confide in me. If not, there's a spare bedroom next to mine where you could sleep till the crack of dawn, if you feel so inclined."

She added, "And if you've got it into your head that you are going out of your mind, all I can say is – join the club!" She paused. "None of us is an island. We all need help occasionally. I know I do."

Switching on the electric fire, she continued quietly, "Tell me if I'm wrong, to mind my own business if you want to, but I'll hazard a guess that you haven't been eating or sleeping much lately, for whatever reason, and lack of food and sleep can play funny tricks on the nervous system, believe me."

"To the extent of losing one's grip on reality?" Kate asked fearfully. "When we met this morning, you said I looked as if I'd seen a ghost, and that came close to the truth. I can't begin to explain, but suddenly, walking up Plantation Hill, I had the strange feeling that I . . . that I had gone back in time to the days of horse-drawn vehicles. I heard the sounds of horses' hooves quite plainly, and I remember thinking they couldn't be crossing Valley Bridge for the simple reason that it didn't exist. Now, can you look at me and tell me truthfully that I'm not going crazy?"

"I'd say that depended entirely on your reason for walking up Plantation Hill in the first place, at that hour of the morning," Dinah said levelly, "whether or not you slept last night and if you'd had anything to eat before setting off on your early morning walk on a bloody freezing November day such as this. You hadn't, had you? I thought not! In that state, the wonder is you didn't see St Peter at the Pearly Gates with a 'Welcome Home' notice slung round his neck! You daft ha'porth! You're suffering from insomnia and malnutrition pure and simple, in my experience. In other words, lightheadedness from lack of food and sleep.

"Well, that settles it! The spare room bed's made up, and I keep it well aired just in case my kid brother turns up unexpectedly, in need of a place to kip whenever he feels like it, to eat me out of house and home and use up all my hot water. He's a student, you see? But I love him." She added, "Now just you snuggle down, and try to get some sleep. Promise?"

Too weary to argue, Kate nodded, and followed her hostess to the spare bedroom where, shedding her outer clothing, she lay down thankfully beneath crisply laundered cotton sheets and a puffy green-silk covered eiderdown, her head resting on lavender-scented pillows, against which she fell immediately into a deep, dreamless sleep.

Looking in on her, Dinah smiled, then went to her own room to sleep away the cares of her long, fraught hours of night duty, thankful of the muted sounds of humanity beneath her bedroom window: reminders that she was not alone in the world, either. Darkness had fallen when Kate emerged from her room. Dinah was in the kitchen preparing supper. "Well?" she asked in that forthright way of hers. "Feeling any better?"

"Much better, thanks." Kate smiled. "What are you cooking?"

"My *specialité de la maison*. Beef casserole, made yesterday before I went on duty. I think stew tastes better anyway the next day, don't you?"

"You are an amazing person," Kate said.

"Oh? In what way – amazing?"

"The way you cope with life, your job and your home. Managing both successfully. I wish I knew how. I just seem to muddle through. Especially now."

"Why – especially now?" Dinah asked, returning the stew to the oven. "Do you want to talk about it? If so, I'm listening."

"It's a long story."

"I'm in no hurry," Dinah said. "Sit down, I'll put the kettle on for a cuppa."

Slowly at first, the floodgates opened. With a sweet feeling of relief, trusting Dinah implicitly, Kate told her about Don's affair with Lucia, April Cottage, the breakdown of her marriage, her meeting with Alex Arden, the fire at Gull House; Jenny's defection, Greg's divorce proceedings; Alex's disappearance, her fear that she may never see him again; speaking softly, simply, unemotionally, her inner tension betrayed merely by the clenching of her hands on the kitchen table and the gathering of tears in her eyes now and then which she brushed away resolutely with the back of an unclenched hand before they spilled down her face.

A very lovely face, Dinah thought: heart-shaped, with a generous mouth, and eyes the colour of forget-me-nots. Grey-blue forget-me-nots, if such a species existed. More like love-in-a-mist perhaps? But then, botany had never been her favourite subject.

She simply found it hard to believe that anyone, especially Jenny Laird, could have treated Kate so badly after all she had done to help her after she'd left hospital. She said grimly, "At least that ex-landlord of hers got his come-uppance! Seven years in gaol, the brute, and serve him damn well right!"

Jumping up to rescue the casserole from the oven an hour later, Dinah said, "Look, Kate, I suggest that you spend the night here with me; go back to Gull House tomorrow morning, or whenever you feel up to it. No hurry!

"Meanwhile, am I right in thinking that the last thing on earth you need right now is a dollop of stew and mashed potatoes? So how about a couple of boiled eggs and bread and butter 'soldiers'?"

Kate's smile lit up her face. "Oh yes. How wonderful that would be! And thank you, Dinah. Thank you for – everything. Above all, for being my friend."

At breakfast next day, over porridge, toast and coffee, Dinah said, "I've been thinking, I have Christmas leave due to me, four whole days! Can you imagine? I'll be free on Christmas Eve, and I wondered if you'd care to – come with me?"

Pouring more coffee, she assured Kate, "You may not care for the idea, but I'd like you to think about it. What I have in mind is a Christmas weekend at the Crown Hotel. No, don't say anything just yet.

"We both need a break, to relax, have a bit of fun. No shopping or cooking beforehand; being with people in pleasant surroundings. Plenty of sea air if we feel like it. I've made enquiries; tentatively booked a twin-bedded room on the first floor. A balcony room.

"I'd thought of going alone. I wouldn't have minded in the least. Last night, it occurred to me how much nicer it would be to share the room with someone whose company I enjoy. You were the obvious choice. The reason why I'd like you to think about it."

She continued quietly, "I know the Crown has strong associations for you with – Alex. I'm not being insensitive, at least I hope not. Oh, it's difficult to put into words, and I'm not very good with words . . ."

"No need to explain," Kate said gently, "I think I know what you are trying to say, that I'll be thinking of Alex anyway, no matter where. And you are right in your belief that I might feel closer to him in spirit, at the Crown, than anywhere else on earth."

Dinah said bemusedly, "You mean you will come with me?"

Kate smiled. "Yes, and thank you for asking me."

Dinah asked, "How did you know what I was thinking?"

Kate replied, "I don't know. I just did, that's all."

The third week in December, Greg phoned to say that Cindy had gone to Bradford to spend Christmas with her family, leaving him alone in the bungalow. Not that he minded, he was glad of the peace and quiet, the "cessation of hostilities" as he put it, with a brave attempt at tongue-in-cheek humour.

Kate said decisively, "If you think you're spending Christmas in that blasted bungalow with garden gnomes for company, well you're not, that's all! You're coming home to Scarborough for a holiday at the Crown Hotel with me and my friend, Dinah Sheridan. I'm sure she'll be pleased to meet you. So just pack your bags and get over here right away. Tomorrow or the next day! Oh, Greg, I'm so longing to see you again after all this time. I've missed you more than you'll ever know! Please, *please* say you'll come!"

Greg breathed a deep sigh of relief. "OK, Sis," he said brightly, holding his weariness of spirit, his physical bone-tiredness and deeply etched mental suffering of the past few months in check for her sake. "I'll be there and, by the way, I've missed you too – more than *you'll* ever know!"

But Kate *did* know. And his pretended blitheness hadn't fooled her one iota. He was a man faced with the ruination of all his quiet hopes and dreams for the future if Cindy emerged triumphant from the divorce proceedings to establish her claims of non-consummation of her marriage, based on her husband's refusal to accept or assume the responsibilities of parenthood, which had, or so she had lied, been made abundantly clear to her on their honeymoon, when he had utterly refused to engage in the normal sexual intercourse – expected by every young bride on her wedding night. Her word against his! If only he could prove otherwise.

Now, Greg was coming home to her, and nothing else mattered a damn! Whatever the future may hold in store for them, they would make this a Christmas to remember – herself, Greg, Dinah, and someone else besides . . .

Hanging up the phone, Kate whispered into the silent air surrounding her, "Oh, Alex, my darling, if you are still alive in this world, *please* come back to me. Whether or not you love me as much as I love you doesn't matter at all. My life just seems so lonely and meaningless without you."

Waking suddenly in the early hours of next morning, as alert as she had been the night of the fire when she had heard footsteps on the fire-escape, getting out of bed, Kate crossed the room to the tallboy, in the bottom drawer of which she kept a few very private and personal belongings, including the dog-eared copy of *Wuthering Heights* Greg had given her on her fourteenth birthday, her mother's wedding ring, her father's silver pocket-watch, and a bundle of old letters, Christmas and birthday cards she had never felt able to part with.

Kneeling down, she opened the bundle of letters. She and Greg had been great correspondents during her "Don days", when she had written letters to Greg almost daily, in diary form, describing in detail her life at April Cottage, which he had kept beside him all these years, just as she had kept his less frequent, much shorter letters, revolving around his life in Manchester with Cindy. Letters which had deeply troubled her at the time. Certainly not those of a recently married man overjoyed by the prospect of future fatherhood of the family of children he longed for.

Re-reading Greg's letters, at last Kate came upon the most important one of all, in which he had written: "I have begged Cindy to seek medical help and advice, to no avail. Obviously, the poor girl has a deep-seated fear of childbirth, common to most women, I imagine. But enough of my troubles for the time being. Suffice to say that I live in hope of fatherhood one of these fine days . . ."

Going back to bed, tucking that all-important letter beneath her pillow, Kate thought, come Christmas Eve at the Crown Hotel, she would give her brother possibly the best Christmas present he'd ever received. Proof positive of his innocence in the forthcoming divorce case between himself and Cindy.

Dinah had been warmly welcoming of Greg's inclusion in the Christmas celebrations, and, thankfully, there had been a single room available due to a last-minute cancellation when Kate had rung up the reception desk to book Greg into the hotel.

Then suddenly, it was all happening: the beginning of the festive season, and Greg's arrival at Gull House, looking pale and strained – the rapturous reunion of brother and sister prior to their departure, by taxi, to the scene of the festivities.

Obviously Kate didn't know, and Greg hadn't the heart to tell her of a newspaper report concerning the discovery of a decapitated body, in Turkestan, believed to be that of Alex Arden, more famously known as the celebrated author, Sandy Alexis.

Twenty-One

K ate and Dinah had been shown to their room on the first floor, with long windows leading to the balcony beyond.

Dinah was over the moon. "I've always wanted to stay at the Crown," she said mistily, looking out at the lights of Scarborough springing into bloom as the evening shadows fell. "Oh, I daresay it's been modernised to a great extent, but there's still an aura of the past about it, a feeling of history, don't you agree? Kate, are you listening?"

"Yes. It's rather charming, isn't it? 'Bluebells of Scotland.' How odd! There must be a piano in the next room."

"Huh?" Dinah frowned, "What – piano? I can't hear a thing!"

"But surely," Kate began, then stopped speaking abruptly, knowing that her time-warp experience had happened again, that her mind was still playing tricks, as it had done that day on Plantation Hill.

Dinah said concernedly, "Kate, love, are you all right?" wondering if she had made a mistake in returning her friend to the scene of her first encounter with Alex Arden in her present precarious state of mind. Or was it possible that Kate was imbued with second sight? There were fancy medical terms for it nowadays, none of which she could remember off-hand. The only term which sprang readily to mind was – clairvoyance.

Kate said quietly, "Yes, I'm fine. Just a bit tired and confused, that's all – trying to come to terms with what I imagine to be a legacy handed down to me by my friend, Madame Zara. A legacy I had rather have done without, I might add. Which begs the question, is it really possible for a dead person to enter the mind of the living?"

"But doesn't that happen all the time?" Dinah asked. "It's something more commonly referred to as – memory. In your case, I imagine, linked to your research into the Victorian era. How's that book of yours coming along, by the way?"

"It isn't. Not at the moment," Kate admitted. "I'm suffering a 'writer's block'."

"Hmmm, sounds painful," Dinah commented, hanging her clothes in the wardrobe, speaking lightly for her friend's sake. "Is it?"

"Yes, it is. Extremely painful, since you ask. You see, I can't make up my mind what happened to my heroine, Lucy Kiddy. Was she really drowned at sea, I wonder, or did she survive the shipwreck?"

"That depends on how you want the book to end," Dinah reflected, "happily or otherwise." She added, "I guess most people are in need of a happy ending in the long run. At least a glimmer of hope for the future." Finishing her unpacking, she said, "I like your brother, by the way. Strange, isn't it, that really nice people are often called on to endure the most suffering? That wife of his should have thanked her lucky stars to be married to a lovely man like Greg. Why she wants rid of him, I can't conceive. Oh, sorry! I didn't mean to imply . . ."

"That my sister-in-law refused to conceive? But that's the nub and kernel of the divorce proceedings. Cindy claims that Greg refused to consummate the marriage, but I know different. What's more, I can prove it. You see, I found this letter the other day . . ."

The hotel looked spectacular with its wealth of scarlet and gold decorations and jardinières of flowers in the public rooms. They had arranged to meet Greg, at the bar, for pre-dinner drinks. Kate's eyes misted over when she saw that he had bought a new suit for the occasion.

He had met Dinah briefly on their arrival at the hotel, and Kate had introduced them, before signing the visitors' book and being shown to their rooms; had known instinctively that they had "taken a shine" to one another. Come to think of it, Greg must have slung out his old clothes, crumpled shirts and threadbare jackets before leaving Manchester, and not before time.

On his arrival at Gull House, he'd been wearing a well-tailored tweed jacket and slacks, plus a brand new anorak, bless him. "My word, aren't you looking handsome?" had been her opening gambit, prior to giving him a bear-hug of delight at seeing him again.

"Well, I didn't want to let the side down," he'd responded cheerily, hugging his sister in return. And this was so typical of Greg, a rare human being incapable of letting anyone down. She had desperately

wanted to show him the letter there and then. To have done so would
have lessened the impact of a surprise packet on Christmas Day.

In his room on the top floor of the hotel, Greg wondered how he
would break the news of that decapitated body discovered in a remote
area of Turkestan when the time came to do so. Kate was bound to find
out about it sooner or later. Hopefully later. It would be too cruel, too
unkind to spoil the celebration of Christmas in such a way.

Approaching the bar, shrugging aside his misgivings, he pinned a
smile to his lips for the benefit of his sister and her friend awaiting his
arrival, warmed by an appreciation of this unexpected holiday far
removed from the exigencies of his Manchester-existence, a life devoid
of warmth, love and laughter – surely the birthright of every human
being, especially at Christmas?

Slowly, he began to relax, to smile naturally once more, charmed by
the hotel atmosphere, akin to stepping from the cold world beyond the
windows into a cosily-padded red and gold brocaded jewel-case of
Victorian vintage in which rich women, of that era, had kept their most
precious belongings.

Curiously, even in this present day world of the 1970s, he had sensed
the presence of long gone generations of men and women who had once
celebrated Christmas here in the last century. He guessed that Kate was
also aware of the ghosts in their midst, of laughter borne on other
winds, the faint rustle of silken ballgowns on the curving staircase
leading to the upper landings, the lingering scent of expensive French
perfume in the air about them. Not Coty's "l'Aimant" or Bourjois'
"Evening in Paris", but richly blended essences of jasmine, frangipani,
musk and sandalwood, attar of roses, lavender water and eau-de-
Cologne, belonging to a bygone age.

Memory drew Greg back to the days when he and Kate, as children,
had often looked up at the balconied rooms of the Crown Hotel, and
made up stories about all the rich folk who had once stayed there for
months at a time, arriving by horse-drawn carriages, with retinues of
servants in tow to do their slightest bidding. Then, eventually tired of
the game of make-believe, they had raced down the Spa gardens to the
seashore.

Entering the dining room, Greg placed a hand comfortingly beneath
Kate's elbow, understanding her feelings at returning to the scene of
her first meeting with Arden.

The room was packed, the food excellent, the waiters attentive. The

two single tables near the window, Kate noticed, had been pushe
together to accommodate a party of four. Thankfully, they were show
to a table for three at the far side of the room at which she elected to s
facing the wall, not the windows.

Dinah and Greg ordered roast duck and a bottle of Chablis. Kat
settled for grilled plaice and Perrier. Keeping a watchful eye on he
friend, Dinah noticed that Kate appeared to be enjoying her compara
tively simple meal, and thought how attractive she looked in th
midnight-blue chiffon dress and matching jacket she was wearing.

By the same token, glancing across the table at Dinah, Greg though
how nice, how wholesome she looked in her white silk blouse and blac
velvet bolero, with her long fair hair curling softly about her face. Not
young face, but animated, with clear blue eyes and a smile like
sunburst breaking through rain-clouds. A woman inured, by he
profession, to the pain and suffering of others, who had nevertheles
managed to retain her own identity, warmth and sense of humou
despite the rigours of her work involving, as they did, matters of li
and death.

Above all, he appreciated the loving care and attention that she ha
bestowed on his sister, which he had heard from Kate's own lips on h
arrival at Gull House. He thought how different his life might hav
been had he met and married a woman of Dinah Sheridan's calibre i
the springtime of his life. But too late now for either fantasies or regret

The meal ended, over coffee served in the reception area of the hot
Dinah mooted the idea of attending Midnight Mass at St Martin
Church, a mere cock-stride away from the Crown.

And so, at a quarter to midnight, the three of them, Greg, Dina
and Kate, ventured out into the cold night air, suitably clad in war
clothing, arms linked, Greg in the middle, savouring the quiet feelin
of happiness which had suddenly touched his heart with a sense
springtime not winter, the possibility of better times to come whe
the spectre of the divorce hearing had ceased to overshadow his li
as it had done these past months. Then he would be free, whatev
the outcome, to reshape his future closer to his heart's desire: fin
himself a new job; shake the dust of Manchester from his feet on
and for all. Cindy could have the bungalow, and she was welcome
it. He no longer cared a damn about that. All he wanted was h
freedom.

Her hand tucked securely into the crook of Greg's right arm, Dina thought how wonderful it would be to walk through life with someone like Greg beside her. Oh, who the hell was she kidding? Not someone *like* Greg, but Greg himself. Whoever said that love at first sight was an impossibility was utterly and entirely wrong, and she knew it. There was puppy love, of course, experienced in the blossoming days of one's youth and childhood, the object of one's desire some lanky, blazered schoolboy. In her case, a Sixth Form High School lad, whose desperately longed-for kiss, duly delivered, had resembled mouth to mouth recusitation hampered by the length of his tongue halfway down her throat, which she had spat out with difficulty and a great deal of disgust.

There had been other men in her life since then, some of whom she'd imagined herself to be in love with. But her feelings towards Greg were entirely different from any she had known before. This time she knew, beyond a shadow of doubt, that he was the one and only man in the world for her. Not because he was particularly handsome or prosperous. Simply because he was warm-hearted and kind, with a lived-in face, and he needed someone to love and take of him, just as she needed someone to love and take care of her.

Deeply aware of the rapport between Greg and Dinah, Kate rejoiced in her heart that this had happened between two people near and dear to her, so deserving of happiness. They were so right for one another. She had known that the minute she had introduced them, the moment she had seen the wondering expression on Dinah's face when she looked at Greg, the softening of Greg's features, and that uptight, worried look of his when he'd smiled at Dinah. Almost as if they had met before – long ago and far away.

Entering the church, gazing at the softly-lit crib, she wondered again about Alex's belief in reincarnation. Was it really possible that lovers could meet again in another lifetime, another existence, to an instant awareness that they had met before in the corridors of time? And if love ended in failure during one lifetime, given Alex's belief in reincarnation, might there not be a second chance of happiness in some future incarnation?

Deriving comfort from that possibility, Kate knelt in silent prayer until the congregation rose to the opening notes of "Once in Royal David's City".

After the service, in their bedroom, Dinah said quietly, "I'm so glad we went to church tonight. I felt it – set the seal on things, somehow.

The real meaning of Christmas. Not just eating and drinking and making merry. Something far deeper and more meaningful than just having a good time. Not that I'm knocking having a good time, believe me. It's great to let one's hair down once in a while." She smiled wistfully. "Well, I think you know what I'm trying to say?"

"It's Greg, isn't it?" Kate asked softly. "You've fallen in love with him?"

"Oh Lord, is it so obvious?" Dinah bit her lip. "Have I made a complete and utter fool of myself? Thrown myself at him? Well, they do say there's no fool like an old fool!" Her face clouded suddenly. "I couldn't bear it if he thought that! Not that I'd blame him if he did!" Her lips trembled. She was close to tears.

"I'm sure he thought nothing of the kind," Kate said. "Knowing Greg, he's probably upstairs in his room asking himself the same questions. Wondering, I daresay, what a man in his position has to offer you – a woman he fell in love with at first sight."

"Do you really think so?" Dinah, asked tremulously.

"I don't think so. I *know* so!" Kate assured her. "And I can't tell you how glad I am that this has happened. Greg means the world to me. I knew from the start that he and Cindy were never meant for each other. I don't want to go into all that, there's really no need." She smiled reflectively. "But you and Greg are – meant for each other. So no doubts or fears. Just have faith in your feelings for one another and lay hold of all the future happiness life has to offer the pair of you. Promise?"

"Yes, Kate. I promise. I just feel so selfish thinking of you and Alex. Knowing how you must be feeling now, without him."

Standing near the balcony window looking up at the stars, Kate said softly, "But you see, love, there's really no comparison. Alex went away not knowing how I felt about him. Pride got in the way. In any case, I knew that my feelings were not reciprocated, and I couldn't have borne being told so. Rejection is a bitter pill to swallow. It had happened to me once, I had no desire to go through it again."

"I'm so sorry," Dinah said compassionately. "So what will happen when he does come back?"

"*If* he comes back, I imagine he'll want me to stay on as his housekeeper, but I couldn't, I know that now."

"Then what would you do? Cut off your nose to spite your face? Wouldn't you rather be with him than without him?"

"I honestly don't know. Being with a man you love who doesn't love you is a no-win situation in the long run. I'd far rather make a clean break. I have a little money put aside for a rainy day. I could afford to buy a small property of my own somewhere in town, take in summer visitors for a living, the way my mother used to do." Kate shrugged her shoulders dismissively. "Only time will tell. Now, isn't it time for bed? So good-night and God bless. See you in the morning?"

"In case you hadn't noticed," Dinah chuckled, "morning's already here and has been for some time. Almost two o'clock! I wonder if Greg's asleep yet?"

Christmas Day dawned frosty and clear. Up bright and early, Kate and Dinah went downstairs to find Greg standing in the reception area – buttons and eyeballs polished – awaiting their arrival. How long he had been there was anyone's guess – most probably since seven o'clock when the chef had come on duty to start cooking the eggs and bacon, Kate reckoned, to cater to the needs of the residents wishing to attend the eight o'clock Mass at St Martin's. Not that communicants were supposed to partake of bread and wine on a full stomach, but what other people did was their own concern, not hers.

Aware of a slight hiatus between Dinah and Greg born of the knowledge, so far unexpressed, that they had fallen deeply in love with one another, Kate suggested that they went out for a walk together along the Esplanade, as far as the Holbeck Clock Tower and back, to work up an appetite for breakfast, saying she would wait in the reception area until their return.

Dinah went upstairs to fetch her coat. "Kate," Greg said, "there's something you should know."

She laughed. "I already do. Why do you think I want rid of you? I imagine you have things to say to Dinah that you wouldn't want anyone else to hear?"

Greg flushed slightly. "I haven't the right to say anything to her. Not yet at any rate, until I know what my future prospects are likely to be." He spoke wistfully. "Until this divorce case is settled one way or another. If it goes against me, I shan't have much to offer any woman."

"Perhaps this might help." Finding the letter in her shoulder bag, she gave it to him. "Merry Christmas, Greg. And remember, Dinah isn't 'any woman'. There are things she needs to hear from your own lips,

185

and if you have the sense you were born with you'll tell her the way you feel about her and let the future take care of itself."

She added, as Dinah appeared on the stairs, "No, don't open the envelope now. Wait till you're alone together. It isn't a cheque, by the way. Something far more precious than money.

"Right, off you go now. Sure you'll be warm enough, Greg? Or should you nip up and get your anorak?"

"No, I'll be fine. This tweed jacket's quite thick, and I've a sweater on underneath, of the 'Polo-mint' variety, as you can see, not to mention my thermal underwear."

"All right, all right, no need to go into the gory details," Kate laughed as she saw them off from the front steps and watched them walking hand-in-hand along the Esplanade, deriving comfort and happiness from the thought that, God willing, they would walk together, hand-in-hand, for the rest of their lives.

It had been a wonderful holiday, Kate thought on her return to Gull House with Greg, who would be leaving for Manchester that afternoon.

He looked worried, she thought, putting the kettle on for a cup of tea: sad, vaguely withdrawn, as if he had something on his mind. Only natural, she supposed, having kissed Dinah goodbye, not quite knowing when they'd meet again. But no, it was more than that. She had the gut feeling that something was seriously wrong. Nothing to do with Dinah but – herself. She hadn't seen Greg look like this since that dreadful day at the hospital when their father had died and he had broken the news to her very gently, and held her in his arms to whisper soft words of comfort, to stroke her hair back from her tear-stained face and dry her eyes with his pocket handkerchief.

When he came into the kitchen prior to his departure for Manchester, switching off the kettle, turning to face him, she said, "It's Alex, isn't it? He's dead, isn't he? Please tell me! I need to know! Have they found his – body? Is that what you're trying to tell me?"

Carefully framing his words, Greg said quietly, "A body has been found, yes, but whose body has not yet been established. You see, love, difficulties of identification have arisen to cloud the issue." No way could he bring himself to utter the gruesome word "decapitation". Wild horses would not have dragged out of him that the body of the nan had suffered the indignity of mutilation at the time of his death, or afterwards.

Curiously, Kate seemed to know instinctively what he meant. Her reaction puzzled him at first. Her softly uttered words: " 'Over the pass the voices, one by one, faded. And the hill slept'."

Much later he remembered the source of the quotation.

Twenty-Two

B eside herself with worry, Dinah telephoned Kate repeatedly begging her to stay with her for a while, knowing what she mus be going through – the horror of not knowing whether the body foun in an icy wilderness far removed from civilisation, was that of the ma she loved, or not – the grim reality of the lack of identification of th corpse.

All Kate would say in reply to the phone calls was: "Thank you, but must stay here. I need to be alone. Besides, I have work to do." It wa uttered in a cold, calm tone of voice, which Dinah recognised as that a woman in a state of shock far beyond tears or hysteria, therefore a the more frightening to someone inured to various manifestations grief. Some suddenly bereaved women became angry to the point violence, swearing, screaming, shouting, others sobbed uncontrollabl The few, the very few, stared into space, saying nothing at all, froze faced, inarticulate with grief, shrugging aside offers of help, flinching the touch of a comforting hand on the arm.

And this, above all, was the most dangerous manifestation of shoc in Dinah Sheridan's experience. The thought that this was happenin to someone she cared for was unbearable. Even worse, the knowledg that she was powerless to help Kate in this present crisis of her life, b the simple expedient of giving her warmth, shelter and love beneath he own roof, close to but far removed from the ghost-ridden rooms c Gull House.

All she could possibly say, over and over again, on the telephon was: "Remember I'm here, Kate, if ever you should need me." Anc "Yes, thanks, Dinah, I'll remember," came that cool, measured repl "but I must stay here. I need to be alone. Besides, I have work to do. '

Re-living the past, Kate discovered, provided the only solution t blotting out her present desolation of spirit; writing her only means o escape from the here and now, to that world of yesteryear that sh envisaged as neatly packaged as a bundle of love-letters tied with the faded ribbons of a bygone age, all passion spent. It was a comforting premise that, with the passage of time, the present would be laid to rest as surely as the past had been. Then, there would be no more heartbreak or despair, no futile hopes for the future, only as yet unborn generations poking round old graveyards, reading the inscriptions on the headstones, not knowing or caring tuppence about the life stories of the long dead and forgotten buried there in the quiet earth, along with all their human faults and failures, shattered hopes and dreams and unfulfilled love affairs . . .

Every day, come hail, rain or shine, Kate went in search of not the Scarborough she had known in the days of her youth and childhood, but the town as it must have appeared to long gone generations of men and women of the Victorian era, rich and poor alike, who had witnessed, in the last century, the birth of the railway, the demise of the horse and carriage as a means of transport, along with the old coaching inns reminiscent of Charles Dicken's *Pickwick Papers*.

Absorbed in her research, she came across old buildings, seldom noticed before in the springtime of her life: The Talbot Hotel in Queen Street, for instance, a coaching inn of the seventeenth century, and The Bell, in Bland's Cliff – a steep hill linking the town centre to the seafront.

All these discoveries, and many more besides, were grist to her mill when she returned to Alex's typewriter to get on with the next chapter of her book in this very special place where she felt closest to him, as though he were still alive and watching over her now as he had done in the past. And wasn't that the simple truth of the matter? That love, however hopeless it may have seemed at the time, never dies?

Whether or not Alex had loved her during his lifetime scarcely mattered to her now that he was dead and gone. All that she really cared about, right now, was writing a book worth reading, in his honour, dedicated: "In Memory of Sandy Alexis. A Man For All Reasons".

Greg had wanted to stay on with her for a while longer after the Christmas holiday, but Kate wouldn't hear of it. "I'll be fine," she'd told him, "and I want you to keep your solicitor's appointment tomorrow. The sooner you show him that letter the sooner he'll know what to do about it."

"Kate, I'm truly sorry about – Alex. I wish now that I hadn't told you, but there's never a right time to break bad news, and I wanted you to hear it from me, so there was really no choice. I couldn't bring myself to tell you sooner, to spoil Christmas for you."

"I know, love. No need to explain. Now, isn't it time you were on your way? You have a long journey ahead of you."

"But I can't just go and leave you alone, like this."

"Of course you can, and you *must*! I'll be better off alone. It's what I want, Greg, believe me!"

Driving back to Manchester, Greg pondered Kate's cryptic response, "Over the pass the voices, one by one, faded, and the hill slept". Racking his brain, the source of the quotation suddenly dawned on him. Of course. It came from Sir Henry Newbolt's poem. "He Fell Among Thieves", the last lines of which began, "A sword swept!"

Sick at heart, he realised that Kate had known the reason why the body of the man discovered in an alien landscape had been unindentifiable, and yet she had not given way to tears or turned to him for comfort. She had simply stood there, as white as a ghost, her eyes a brilliant blue, wide open and staring in the colourless oval of her face.

Then, for the first time in his life, he had sensed an unbridgeable gulf between himself and his sister, as if her spirit had somehow left her body and all that remained was the remote shell of her, as brittle as glass, as if she could scarcely wait to be rid of him.

At home in the bungalow, dumping his luggage in the hall, he dialled Dinah's phone number, desperately in need of her support, help and advice.

"Sorry, darling," she replied, "I've rung Kate twice already this evening: invited her to stay with me for the time being, to no avail. She simply doesn't want to know."

Greg said hoarsely, "You don't think she'll do something – foolish, do you?"

"No, I don't think so. She spoke of having work to do. The fact is, I honestly don't know what she has in mind right now. All that I can possibly do is to keep on pestering her with phone calls in anticipation of a reply, no matter how dismissive that reply might be."

"And if she fails to answer? What then?" Greg asked wearily.

"Well, then, if necessary, I'll either alert the police, or batter my way into Gull House unaided! And you'd better believe it! You see, my love, I think the world of your sister, and I'd like her around as my matron of honour on our wedding day! So stop worrying unduly. Trust me to keep an eye on things this end."

John Sharpin had remarried in due course. His second wife, Mary, was much prettier than Jeanette, a graceful, petite woman with neatly braided brown hair arranged in a coronet above a sweetly smiling face.

Kate had scarcely believed her luck one day, in the library, when she had come across an exhibition of old photographs and memorabilia relevant to the lives and times of eminent local dignitaries of the Victorian era mounted, behind glass, in the library foyer.

Gazing intently at the exhibits, she saw the studio portrait of Mary Sharpin wearing a black velvet, bustled gown trimmed at the neckline and wrists with white lace, smiling not at the camera but into the middle distance. It was the face of a happy, contented woman in love.

Another, less formal photograph, apparently taken in the Sharpins' apartment at the Crown Hotel, revealed John Sharpin seated at a desk, Mary standing behind him, her hands resting lightly on his shoulders, as though, without those gently restraining hands of hers, he would have leapt up from his chair and rushed out of the room like a whirlwind.

That photograph spoke volumes about the man, young, dark-haired and vital. The way he was sitting, for instance, one leg clear of the desk, the other stretched out awkwardly, bent at the knee, reminiscent of an athlete awaiting the firing of a starting pistol. Somehow, the photograph had captured the magnetic vitality and enthusiasm of the man who had masterminded The People's Park and had left the imprint of his vivid, unorthodox personality on Scarborough for all time – whether or not future generations would even remember his name, as few, if any, would remember that of Alex Arden.

The thought occurred that she was, perhaps, beginning to imbue both men with similar characteristics, and she wondered if – writing about Sharpin – she had begun to imagine him as a living person whose strength and vitality seemed akin to a torch handed down to her to guide her through the darkness of her present existence.

Greg's phone call one evening a week later, came as a surprise when he told her that the court hearing was over and he was a free man at last.

"The date was brought forward unexpectedly," he explained, sounding apologetic. "I didn't tell you because I didn't want to worry you.

The great news is, that letter you gave me made all the difference. The judge believed me, not Cindy, when the letter was read out in court.'"

Kate's eyes filled with tears which ran down her face, unchecked. "Oh, Greg, my love, I'm so glad for you," she murmured, feeling as if a burden had been lifted from her shoulders. "I'm just so sorry that I wasn't there for you when you needed me. Can you ever forgive me?"

"There's nothing to forgive," he said gently, "nor ever will be, between us."

"But you wanted to stay with me, and I sent you away when I should have turned to you for comfort. The person closest and dearest to me in all the world!"

"I understood the reason why, Kate, believe me. You needed solitude, not comfort, at the time, and I respected that. All in the past now. Thanks to you, I have a future ahead of me, a roof over my head and a secure job. Not that I'm planning to stay on in Manchester once the decree absolute has been granted. I have no wish to stay on in the bungalow, for obvious reasons. Much depends on Dinah, what *she* wants me to do." He paused. "I really do love her, you see, and she promised to marry me whatever the outcome of the divorce, even if I ended up a pauper."

He added anxiously, "But how are *you*, Kate? I can't bear the thought of you alone in Gull House, not eating or sleeping properly. Not getting enough exercise or fresh air. Not always answering the telephone, and I should know."

"I'm sorry, but I've been busy writing: getting on with my book. Please don't worry about me. I'm coming to terms with what happened in the only way I know how."

"I understand, and so does Dinah. But please, Kate, don't shut her out of your life. Promise?"

"Very well, Greg, I promise, and I never meant to. I just couldn't bear the thought of seeing or talking to anyone a while back. I couldn't have borne sympathy – or being away from home. I needed to feel close to Alex, to remember everything about him, to face the probability that we will never meet again."

Twenty-Three

On his retirement from the Crown Hotel, John Sharpin had built himself a villa in a cul-de-sac overlooking the railway, a splendid, turreted edifice with long, ground-floor windows leading on to a small lawn, with trees and flower-beds, which he master-minded in every architectural detail down to his J.F.S. "coat of arms" emblazoned in the landing casements and on the outer walls of his domain.

Staring up at those walls one chilly February afternoon, Kate imagined the ageing entrepreneur striding restlessly about his new home, regretful, perhaps, that his glory days at the Crown were over and done with forever.

Possibly, here was a man whose talents had blossomed too early and withered too soon? It seemed decidedly odd that he had chosen a site overlooking the railway, the coming of which had virtually put paid to the era of the horse and carriage.

Researching his background in detail, Kate had learned that as a young man he had begun his career as a grocer's assistant in his native town of Ripon, before transferring to London to set up, unsuccessfully, as a wine merchant.

Then, his spirits at a low ebb, he had seen in a London paper that the Crown Hotel, Scarborough, recently completed in the year 1844, stood in need of a young, energetic man of vision to become its first tenant manager. The rest was history . . .

In need of a hot cup of tea, walking down town towards home, suddenly Kate came face to face with Fanny Kiddy. The first time she had clapped eyes on her since she had left the gift shop, although they had exchanged Christmas cards, and Kate had sent her a small Christmas hamper comprising hand-made chocolates, tins of asparagus, red salmon, satsumas, a box of dates, and a watch-shaped bottle of eau-de-Cologne, for which she had so far received no thanks, nor even the faintest indication that Fanny had received her gift.

Perhaps leaving the shop had affected Fanny more than Kate had realised at the time. She should have taken the trouble to find out. Fanny had pride, and that pride had been stung. She said, "Hello, Fanny, it's good to see you. Have you time for a cuppa?"

"Well, if you're sure you want to see me."

"Of course I do. Why wouldn't I?"

"Oh, I don't know. You just seemed to change all of a sudden when that Jenny moved in with you, as if you couldn't be bothered with me any more."

So that was it. Kate said, unlocking the door, "Come upstairs, I'll put the kettle on."

Fanny, loosening her coat so she would feel the benefit of it when she went out, said, "You weren't exactly fat before, but now you're like two boards nailed together. Have you been fasting?" She mean dieting. "Or have you been poorly?"

"Something like that," Kate said, thinking that what she'd been through recently had been a kind of illness, both mental and physical. Then, for the first time in ages, she knew that she needed someone to talk to; to mend bridges, remembering how kind Fanny had been to her when she moved into that flat overlooking the Valley Bridge. And so she talked, and Fanny listened.

"Eh," she said eventually, "you've had a rough time of it an' no mistake. And there was I thinking – well, never mind what I thought. But you can't go on like this, living alone in this big house, not looking after yourself properly. That's why I'm coming in twice a week to give the place a good bottoming an' see you get some good grub inside you. And don't you try and stop me!"

"Fanny, I wouldn't dream of it," Kate said shakily, thinking she might as well try to stop a runaway train as Fanny in one of her decisive moods.

"That's settled then," Fanny nodded, re-buttoning her coat. "I'll come in Tuesdays and Fridays. It'll be like old times!"

Like old times, Kate thought wistfully, if only . . . At least she had taken a step in the right direction towards a more hopeful outlook on life. Meanwhile, there were other bridges to be mended.

Dinah welcomed her with open arms. "Come in and sit down," she said. "Isn't it wonderful news about Greg? We hope to meet again quite soon, to talk things over. Telephone calls are a bit inhibiting at times,

I've discovered. We're thinking of a long weekend in York, staying at the Station Hotel. Occupying separate rooms, incidentally." She chuckled softly. "We're old-fashioned enough not to want to spoil the thrill of our wedding night; daft enough to want to wander round the city hand-in-hand, and canoodle on the back row of the cinema like teenagers."

She added quickly, apologetically, "Oh, I'm sorry, Kate, I wasn't thinking . . ."

"About Alex, you mean?" Kate tilted her chin proudly, speaking his name without flinching. "You needn't be, not any longer. You see, I've accepted the fact that he won't be coming home again. I had to. My father used to say, 'Face the worst that could happen, the fact that it has happened, and take it from there.' And that's what I'm trying to do now."

"Yes, I can see that, up to a point," Dinah responded quietly, "but what about – hope? Surely you haven't given up hope that Alex may still be alive?"

"All I can say, it's easier for me not to build up false hopes, just to make the best of what I have left to me: tangible things I can touch, hear and see with my own two eyes."

"Like 'Bluebells of Scotland'?" Dinah suggested. "I'm sorry, love, I shouldn't have said that. But you were so certain of piano music in the next room that evening at the Crown. And I'm not doubting for one moment that you *did* hear it, just as I'm certain that you had heard the sound of horses' hooves that morning on Plantation Hill.

"What I'm trying to say is, the tangible things of life that most people take for granted, things they can touch, see, hear and scent – like flowers – are not everything for those gifted with second sight, as you are, and to deny that gift of yours is tantamount to tethering a race-horse to a muck-cart. Just as attempting to live without hope is tantamount to denying the spiritual messages of Christmas and Easter."

She stopped speaking abruptly. "Oh, God, me and my big mouth," she uttered despairingly. "I should have been a bloody Salvationist, not a Staff Nurse!"

Kate made no reply, but she knew, deep down, that Dinah was right, that she had not given up hope that, one day, Alex would come home again.

* * *

Reading through her manuscript, Kate felt hopeful that she had managed to capture something of the Victorian era: the careless ostentation and flamboyance of the very rich, the drudgery of the working class called upon to serve their lords and masters from dawn till dusk.

Weaving together the threads of the story had been difficult at times, and yet she had experienced little difficulty in breathing life into her characters, as if she knew them all as intimately as she knew herself, from the rich, vain women visitors to Scarborough, parading along the Spa promenade in their fine clothes, to poor Mavis Kiddy, Albert's wife, taking in washing and sewing to supplement the family income and to give her children, the studious John and the "fly-by-night" Lucy the best possible start in life.

Lucy, the complex heroine of the book with her many and varied love affairs, an endless troublemaker, a constant thorn in the flesh of her decent, ordinary hard-working parents, Kate had treated with compassion throughout the pages of her novel, understanding the girl's need of admiration, pretty clothes and sparkling jewels. Above all – love.

She was faced with the ending of Lucy's story. Strung on the horns of a dilemma, most likely, Kate thought, Lucy had never set out on a sea voyage at all, however dashing and handsome the captain of the vessel might have been. It was more than likely that poor Lucy had stood on the quayside watching the vessel go out of sight of land, and returned home to Scarborough to find the sailor lad she was really in love with. And this was how she intended to finish the novel.

Running throughout her book like a golden thread, was the life story of John Fairgray Sharpin – the catalyst linking the fortunes of both the rich and the poor people he had known so well during his lifetime.

So how had his story ended?

Writing about it, Kate could scarcely hold back her tears. She had, beside her on the desk, as she typed the penultimate chapter of her novel, a cutting borrowed from that exhibition in the public library, referring to the death of "The late Mr Sharpin, J.P.", on June 11th, 1895, aged seventy-five years.

The villa overlooking the railway lines had long ago been sold, and the Sharpins had moved closer to the town centre. Their new home in York Place, far less spectacular than the old, was perhaps better suited to an ageing couple in failing health.

No. 10 York Place was nevertheless a handsome residence, one of a terrace of similar houses, tall, with curved bay windows and steps leading to the front doors.

Looking at No. 10 one bright but cool and windy April day, Kate imagined the interior lay-out of the rooms. There would have been a long, spacious hall with an imposing staircase, red carpeted with mahogany banisters, a ground-floor drawing room, dining room, and kitchen quarters at the end of the passageway. On the upper landing, the master bedrooms; above these, the servants' rooms, one of which was occupied by a maid servant who, roused from sleep by the urgent ringing of a housebell at around ten thirty one night, had hurried down to the drawing room where she had found her master on the floor in a pool of blood.

Doctors had been sent for, to no avail. John Fairgray's seemingly indestructible life force had no longer existed in the body of a worn-out old man who, at the height of his manhood, had brought fame and fortune to Scarborough.

His widow, Mary Sharpin, had told the inquest jury that her husband had been in failing health for the past three years, but he had gone out daily as usual and refused to see a doctor, saying there was no point, that his time had come and he was worn out. She added that he was a man who quite understood his constitution, and had a great aversion to doctors.

A verdict of death from natural causes was recorded. The presiding coroner had paid tribute to a remarkable man whose vision and enterprise had earned him a well-deserved place in the annals of the town's history, and offered his sincere condolences to Mrs Sharpin and her daughter, Miss May Sharpin.

Kate wrote:

> The route to the Scarborough Cemetery was lined with silent onlookers, the men bareheaded, many women in tears, as they watched the passing of the cortège: the last journey of a man they had loved and admired, to his final resting place.
>
> The sound of the horses' hooves drawing the glass-sided hearse, and the jingling of their harnesses could be clearly heard in the warm air of that summer afternoon.
>
> The passing of the cortège reminded the older folk among the silent bystanders of the opening of The People's Park when their

hero, the young Mayor of Scarborough, dark-haired and hand-some, had bounded from an open landau and on to the flag-draped platform in the valley, like a jack-in-the-box, to declare the enterprise open.

How they had laughed, clapped and cheered him then, on that never-to-be-forgotten night, long ago, with brightly coloured lanterns strung between the branches of the trees in Valley Road; to the background music of the town's silver band, the quacking of ducks from the duckpond; the singing of birds from the aviary. And now . . .

But it was not just the older folk who remembered. A plump, middle-aged woman among the crowd of mourners, also remembered the night she had walked down Plantation Hill with her parents and her brother John, filled with an insatiable desire to show off the pretty new dress her mother had made for her, to attract the attention of the opposite sex in particular, knowing that she was beautiful because the swing-mirror on her bedroom chest-of-drawers had told her so. .

Now, glimpsing John Sharpin's flower-decked coffin through tear-dimmed eyes, the plump middle-aged matron standing on the pavement, her husband and three children beside her, knew that even the rarest beauty is destined to wither and die in time, as hers, Lucy Kiddy's, had done. Then, the only thing that mattered in the world was – Love.

Her book finished at last, Kate lay down to sleep, emotionally draine too tired to think any more for the time being. But sleep would not com As she tossed and turned, eyes aching with fatigue, her brain still ale writing about the death of John Sharpin, she realised, had been tant mount to writing about the death of someone close and dear to her, as she had been present at the passing of his cortège on its way to the De Road Cemetery, leaving her alone in the world, with nothing left to cli to. So how to fill in the rest of her days? Tomorrow and the day aft tomorrow, now that her manuscript had reached its fruition?

And she still hadn't thought of a title for it, a title that would captu precisely and convey her feeling of the past: neatly tied and laid loving aside like love letters, beyond change or alteration – out of reach of t tide. And there she had it. The title of her book. *Out of Reach of t Tide.*

Sleep came at last, albeit a troubled sleep threaded with dreams of a resence in her room, a ray of light from the landing beyond, the figure f a man beside her bed, looking down at her, speaking her name softly, ver and over again: "Kate. Kate darling. Wake up. Please, wake up."

Opening her eyes, she discerned painfully the light from the landing, he tall figure of the man beside her bed. A ghost? A figment of her nagination? And yet there was no mistaking his voice. She would have nown it anywhere.

"Alex?" she murmured disbelievingly.

Then suddenly the "ghost" had his arms about her, and he was olding her tightly, kissing her cheeks, her hair, finally her lips; telling er softly how much he loved her, had always loved her from the noment they had met; asking if there was the faintest hope that, some ay, she would come to love him in return.

"Some day?" she whispered. "Oh, Alex! That 'some day' is here, is ow!"

Twenty-Four

Alex's appearance had changed dramatically. His shoulder-leng hair was liberally streaked with grey, he had grown a beard, an his body bore the marks of the savage beatings he had endured in h days of captivity, scars that would remain with him for the rest of h life.

Less obvious were the mental scars of his suffering, yet Kate kne they, too, existed, that it was up to her to ease that suffering in the on way she knew how, simply by expressing her love for him in littl ordinary ways – making certain that he had good, nourishing mea inside him, a decent haircut and shave, clean clothes to wear, plenty rest, peace and quiet beneath the roof of Gull House. Not questionin him about his captivity, knowing he would speak of it if and when l felt able to do so, and not before; respecting his privacy; putting up wi his moods and occasional outbursts of temper, reminiscent of the o days.

Frankly, she couldn't have cared less, knowing that he loved her a much as she loved him, expressed not merely in words but his gifts flowers, expensive flagons of French perfume, silk scarves and, final one day, a small morocco case containing a flawless diamond engag ment ring accompanied by a somewhat unorthodox proposal marriage – as short and sweet as a donkey's gallop: "Well, do yc want to marry me or not? If not, just say so and have done with it

Kate replied teasingly, "The thing I most admire about you, Alex, your sublety and charm when it comes to romance. You might at lea have asked me to marry you first and fished out the ring later."

Alex chuckled softly. "All right, Kate, you win," he conceded. "§ how's this? I love you, Kate Ford, and I'm asking you most humbly marry me as soon as possible, for the simple reason that my life wou be meaningless without you. So please say that you will, and make n the happiest man alive."

Smiling up at him, Kate said, "Put that w

refuse?

"So how soon?" He was laughing now, excited as

The week after?"

"Next month would be nearer the mark. I have thi

"What – things?"

"Arrangements to make. Alex, I want my brother at our

"I should jolly well hope so. I'm looking forward to meet

Did you give him those books of mine, by the way?"

"Yes, and he was over the moon. He was staying here at the

with his wife – or should I say ex-wife? They were divorced recently.

was all a bit fraught. They had a blazing row over Jenny the night of the

fire, and that was the beginning of the end . . ."

"Just a minute, you've lost me," Alex broke in. "What fire, for God's

ake? And who is Jenny? Why haven't you told me this before?"

"There hasn't really been time. My mind's been on other things, in

case you hadn't noticed. Waking up to find you standing beside me,

and coming to terms with not only your reappearance in my life, but the

fact that you loved me seemed like a dream come true after all the

waiting and wondering, not knowing if you were alive or dead."

"Yes, of course," he said contritely. "I should have known. We have

lot to catch up on, haven't we?"

Kate nodded. "Yes, darling, we have, and I think it important that

we should begin our future together with no secrets between us. The

reason why I don't want to rush into marriage on an impulse, just

because I happen to be head over heels in love with you, the way I did

before. You too, I imagine?"

He said heavily, "That's all in the past now. Over and done

with."

Kate disagreed with him. "You're wrong, Alex," she said quietly, "if

that's what you think. We are both victims of our past lives to some

extent: events which shaped our destinies and made us the people we

are today. Our only hope for the future lies in not forgetting the past,

but learning to live with it – not without regrets. That would be

impossible. But relying on one another for sympathy and understand-

ing when the bad times come uppermost. When you, for instance,

remember the deaths of Leonora and the child you loved, and I

remember the so-called birthdays of the three babies I miscarried

during my marriage to Don."

murmured, "Oh Kate, my love
...ry."

...captivity. They were sittin...
...fell, the rest of the room

...aid, "I was treated as a...
...it was money they wanted
...of watching me suffer. The...
...d with execution. Thei...
...ne, 'Tomorrow, maybe
...movement with his right han...
...eh?'"

...Alex continued, "Then one day they brough...
...er captive to the camp. A much younger man than myself, name...
Yuri. A Russian most likely, who quickly became their latest source o...
amusement. That's when I began to plan my escape, the Russian's als...
when the time came.

"I had devised a rough cutting tool from a jagged piece of rock, t...
free myself of the rope binding my hands behind me, taking advantag...
of the hours of darkness, the drunken stupor of our captors gathere...
round the camp-fire in the clearing beyond our tent.

"It was a simple plan, born of desperation, with little or no chance o...
success. I knew that, so did Yuri, with whom I communicated in sig...
language to indicate the slitting of the tent canvas when we were free o...
our bonds and, either sliding or rolling down the hillside away from th...
camp to make our escape."

Alex covered his face with his hands, reliving the horror of th...
moment when a couple of drunken tribesman had entered the tent, i...
the early hours of the morning, to drag the Russian from their prison t...
his place of execution in the clearing near the camp-fire. "It was s...
brutal, so unnecessary," Alex whispered hoarsely.

"No need to go on," Kate said compassionately, "I can guess wha...
happened." Kneeling beside Alex, she held his trembling body close t...
hers, imagining that terrible downward sweep of an upraised sword

Alex said urgently, "Promise that you'll stay with me forever, Kate?...
love and need you so much. More than you'll ever know."

Kate promised. She had lost Alex once. She could never bear to b...
without him again.

* * *

She showed him her manuscript with some trepidation, explaining that writing the book had been a form of mental therapy to fill in what would otherwise have been time wasted in idleness.

"I'm impressed," he said. "I thought you said you couldn't type."

"I couldn't. I took lessons."

"What is it? A – romance?"

"In a way, yes. Why not read it and find out? Only don't be too critical. I'm no Emily Brontë." She couldn't decide if he was pleased or not by her literary aspirations. Knowing Alex, he might take exception to her having written her own version of Victorian Scarborough.

Alex's first meeting with Fanny was not an unqualified success. Startled by his presence, she said forthrightly, "So you've come back, have you? About time too. Well, now you are here, what are you going to do about that pesky gift shop below?"

"What do you suggest I do about it?" Alex asked coolly. Kate groaned inwardly. Trust Fanny to march in where angels might fear to tread.

"What any sensible body would do," Fanny went on. "Get rid of it. Have it put back to its original purpose. I used to come here as a child when there was a proper ground-floor sitting room, dining room an' kitchen, where they should be. Not a kitchen stuck upstairs like this 'un is.

"Another thing, that there fire would never have happened if it hadn't been for that there fakey shop an' that arse— arse— arsonite wanting to get back at Kate for sacking his girlfriend! Huh, fine goings on, I must say!"

Feeling that Fanny had said quite enough for the time being, Kate reminded her that Alex had bought the property as a going concern – the gift shop included – and that it was time, perhaps, to drop the subject. To her surprise, it was he who wished to explore the matter further.

"No, please, I'm interested in what – Fanny has to say," he said charmingly. "Do you mind if I call you Fanny, by the way? So you think that I should restore Gull House to its original state? So what should I do to set the wheels in motion?"

Flattered by his charm of manner and deference to her opinions, Fanny's initial hostility towards him melted away like mist on a summer morning. "Why, if I was you," she said confidingly, "I'd march right down to the Town Hall Planning Department for a reconstitutional order or some such!" She added girlishly, "An' yes you can call me Fanny, if you like. Everyone else does."

Turning his attention to Kate, he asked, "What do you think? After all, as my wife to be, the future mistress of Gull House, the final decision rests with you."

Fanny's eyes fairly started out of her face with surprise at this nugget of information. "Eh," she burst forth excitedly, "you mean you've pledged your plight to one another?"

"Something like that," Kate laughed, showing Fanny the sparkling engagement ring on the third finger of her left hand. "We're planning to marry quite soon, at the registry office in Dean Road a week next Saturday, followed by a blessing of our marriage in St Martin's Church, and a small reception at the Crown Hotel. Nothing fancy, just a buffet luncheon; smoked salmon sandwiches, salmon and asparagus mousse, mushroom vol-au-vents and so on, you know the kind of thing I mean? Nothing too formal.

"And, of course, you are invited to join us, to help us to celebrate the happiest day of our lives. So please, dear Fanny, do say you'll be there to grace the occasion."

"*Be* there? Just you try an' stop me!"

Later, caught up in the romance, the excitement of it all, waiting ages for the electric kettle to boil for a mid-morning cuppa -- her thoughts centred on a new hat for the wedding, something really smart with lots of veiling and an artificial rose on the brim, she realised, at long last, why the kettle was taking so long to boil. She'd plugged in the toaster by mistake.

One evening, after supper, drawing Kate into the circle of light shed by the dancing, simulated flames of the sitting room fire, Alex said intently, "I've read your manuscript, and—"

Hunching her shoulders against his expected harsh criticism of book, she interrupted, "And you're thinking up kind words to tell me how much you disliked it?"

"Well yes, in a way," he conceded, "because, reading it, I had to admit to myself that I could never have hoped to better it in a thousand years! And I don't accept defeat easily, as you well know.

"Frankly, I felt angry at first that you had plagiarised my idea for a book about Scarborough in the Victorian era. Then, reading on, marvelled at your depth of understanding, not only of an era, but of the characters you so brilliantly portrayed in the cleverly woven strands o the novel. I was in tears by the last page. Sad and uplifted at the same time, if that makes sense? The way you felt, I imagine, when you first read *Wuthering Heights*."

"Then you are not too angry with me?" Kate asked wistfully. "For trespassing on your territory, I mean?"

"No, and to prove it, when we go to London I intend to take your masterpiece to my agent and rub it in that at least one member of the Arden family is capable of writing a potential bestseller."

"Oh!" Kate's head was spinning. Everything was happening so fast that she couldn't take it in all at once. He'd been to the town hall earlier in the day to see about the "reconstitution" of Gull House, and foresaw no problems on that score. Indeed, the planning official he'd spoken to seemed amazed that permission for the gift shop had been given in the first place. Now Alex was enthusiastic about her book, and they were, apparently, going to London. The first she'd heard of it.

"You mean we're spending our honeymoon in London?" she asked.

"Good God, no! It's just that I have business affairs to attend to, and I want to see my old batman before taking you to Paris, then on to Venice and the Italian lakes – if you'd like that, of course. Otherwise we could spend a month or so in Skegness, Bootle and Worksop. Entirely up to you, my darling."

"You *idiot!*" Kate laughed, throwing a cushion at his head, knowing that this was the Alex she loved most of all, a man capable of tenderness and humour, deep down kindness and sensitivity. The man she would be more than proud and happy to marry in ten days' time. Which reminded her – she hadn't yet bought her wedding outfit or trousseau. In which case, the sooner she got cracking, the better.

"Just one more thing," Alex said. "I thought it would be rather nice to spend our wedding night at the Crown Hotel; to invite Dinah and Greg to dine with us before calling it a day. Would you like that?"

"Oh yes, Alex. That would be wonderful. The perfect start to our honeymoon."

Twenty-Five

D inah accompanied Kate on her shopping spree, bearing in mind that she too would soon be needing a wedding outfit, when Greg's final decree had been granted.

"I can't believe all this is happening," she said. "It's so amazing, so wonderful, Alex coming home the way he did, and with Greg a free man once more. That happy ending in view at last, like a pot of gold at the rainbow's end!"

"I know. It takes some believing." Kate smiled, happier than she had ever been in her life before. In love, really in love for the first time, with a man who loved her.

She had asked Alex about that during one of their firelight trysts. "You said you loved me from the first moment we met," she reminded him. "So why did you go away and leave me?"

"Because I needed time and space to think about it," he explained, "to face the possibility of rejection. Remember, darling, I had no reason to believe that you were in love with me? You never gave me the faintest inkling of your feelings towards me. In fact, more often than not I had reason to suspect that you disliked me intensely."

"Well, what did you expect me to do? Throw myself at your feet? Beg you to stay? You were not the only one afraid of rejection. I'd been through that once before, when Don left me. I couldn't have borne going through it again." She smiled knowingly, "But there was more to it than that, wasn't there? Even if I had told you I loved you, begged you to stay, you'd have gone anyway, wouldn't you?"

"Yes," he admitted quietly. "You see, darling, I had a kind of restlessness inside me, a strange longing to recapture my – lost youth – if you like. To prove that I was still capable of repeating the exploits of Sandy Alexis. You must remember, Kate, that I'm older than you are. In retrospect, I wanted to prove, if and when I returned home to you, that I was worthy of your consideration as a husband."

He added, tongue-in-cheek, "It came as something of a shock to me, reading your manuscript, that you had not been entirely faithful to me during my absence."

Kate frowned, uncertain of his meaning. "I'm sorry," she said bemusedly, "I haven't a clue what you're on about!"

"Forgive me," Alex held her hands in his, "I was referring to your hero, John Fairgray Sharpin, whose life story you portrayed so lovingly in the pages of your novel, and whose death affected you so deeply. I had the feeling that you regarded him as a living person who had somehow taken my place during my absence. Am I right?"

Kate smiled wistfully. "Yes, I suppose so. You see, I needed someone to cling to to help me through the dark days when I believed that you were – dead and gone forever.

"Quite honestly, and I admit it, I drew strength and courage from a man, albeit a ghostly figure, conjured from my admiration of his vitality and down-to-earth humanity during his lifetime. But falling in love with a ghost is scarcely possible, wouldn't you say?"

Trying on one outfit after another, Kate finally decided on a slim fitting, cream-coloured jersey-silk dress and a matching jacket, which suited her to perfection.

Then, moving to other departments of the chain-store in Westborough, she chose pale-tan high-heeled shoes, a matching handbag and gloves, and a wide-brimmed hat in a deeper shade of caramel – the colour of brandy snaps, to complement the wedding ensemble and the simple bouquet of deep-orange tea-roses and lilies of the valley she intended to carry with her to the registry office on her wedding day.

Cream, pale-tan and orange, Dinah considered admiringly, and there she was thinking that the bride-to-be would have plumped for the blue outfit, white accessories, and a bouquet of pink roses, which went to show how little she really knew about her future sister-in-law. No longer a reclusive creature, repining the loss of the man she loved, but a strong personality in her own right, now that the man she loved had come back to her.

Meanwhile, Greg had been in touch with Kate to reassure her that he would be more than happy to participate in the wedding ceremony in any capacity whatsoever: to give the bride away, walk down the aisle with her at the blessing, even to make a speech at the reception if called upon to do so. "Greater love hath no man," he laughed.

Kate deserved her new-found happiness. He had never admired her more than he had done when she'd told him of her decision to return her nest-egg from the sale of April Cottage to Don Ford. Her way of laying her past to rest once and for all. And Greg knew she would have done the same had she been marrying a poor man.

Kate spent the night before the wedding at Dinah's flat. Greg had stayed at Gull House with Alex, getting to know his future brother-in-law, a man he had long admired and respected from a distance.

The four of them had enjoyed a quiet dinner in a York Place restaurant before going their separate ways – Alex's idea – as a preliminary to their wedding day, he'd explained to Kate, anxious to meet her brother and his fiancée beforehand. "Nothing too formal," he'd added. "Just a chance to chat to one another, to let our hair down, as the saying goes. The reason why I chose the Georgian Grill, so we needn't wear our best bib and tucker."

It had proved a highly successful occasion, with Alex at his most charming, Kate and Dinah starry-eyed, and Greg slightly in awe of the host initially, discovering to his relief that the man his sister was about to marry was much easier to get on with than Don Ford had been. Ford was a man he had never liked or trusted, from the moment they'd met – in his view, self-centred, far too ambitious, and utterly ruthless. Moreover, his judgement of Don Ford's character had proved to be entirely correct.

He held no such inhibitions concerning the character of Alex Arden. With the unmistakable air of a gentleman about him, not a shred of conceit or pretence in his warm-hearted, generous personality, he obviously adored Kate. And that said it all, so far as Greg was concerned.

At the same time, he could scarcely take in the fact that he was sitting opposite the celebrated author Sandy Alexis, his kid sister's future husband. That future a matter of a few hours away. Twelve hours, to be exact.

The wedding day dawned fair and clear, with a scent of springtime in the air. He and Alex would arrive at the registry office a few minutes ahead of Kate and Dinah, who would share a taxi to the somewhat grim-looking venue in Dean Road.

"How are you feeling?" Greg asked Alex as they entered the building.

"The way you'll be feeling when your turn comes, I imagine," the bridegroom chuckled, "when I shall ask you the same damn silly question."

Dot Paulson and Fanny were in the reception hall awaiting the arrival of the wedding party. Fanny's hat had to be seen to be believed. Carmen Miranda, eat your heart out! Mrs Paulson's navy blue titfer paled to insignificance beside it.

Dismounting first from the wedding car, Dinah thought how wonderfully serene and lovely Kate looked as the chauffeur of the sleek limousine helped her to dismount.

A small crowd of onlookers had gathered on the pavement, among them a thin, haggard looking woman whom Dinah recognised immediately as Jenny Laird. Oh lord, she thought, had Jenny come to make trouble? A so-called friend who had caused Kate so much misery in the past. It would be too cruel of her to upset Kate on her wedding day. But there was nothing she could do about it. Detaching herself from the crowd, Jenny was coming towards them.

"Hello, Kate," she said in a low voice, unsmiling, looking far from blooming, Dinah thought, as one might have expected a woman who had left her friend in the lurch to pursue a more glamorous lifestyle with her current male admirer.

Kate looked startled, then, "Hello, Jenny," she replied quietly, "you are the last person I expected to see."

"I know, but I *had* to come. I heard it through the grapevine that you were getting married today, and I just wanted to see you again, to wish you well, and to say how sorry I am that I caused you so much grief after all your kindness to me. Believe me, I've lived to regret it." Tears sprang to her eyes. "Please say that you'll forgive me. Not that I deserve your forgiveness."

"But there is nothing to forgive," Kate said warmly. "All I ever wanted was your happiness." She added perceptively, "But you are not happy, are you? Tell me, Jenny, what's wrong? I really need to know!"

Oh God, Dinah thought wildly, why all this? Why *now*? Time was ticking away. The registrar would not be best pleased by the delay. "Please, Kate," she said urgently, "it's high time we went inside. We're five minutes late already."

Jenny said, smiling through her tears, "Of course I'm happy. It's just that John and I will be leaving Scarborough soon to live abroad, in Canada as a matter of fact. He's been offered a fantastic job there. It's just that I haven't got used to the thought of leaving England. All the old familiar places, and *you*, Kate. Above all, you!"

Clasping Jenny's hand in hers, Kate said, "But we all have to move

209

forward sooner or later, and memories never die. I shall always be here for you, loving you as much as I did when we were schoolgirls together. We'll still keep in touch. Now, I really must go. I have an important appointment to keep." Leaning forward, she kissed Jenny's cheek. "Thank you for coming, for being here on my wedding day," she murmured. Then, plucking a rose from her bouquet, handing it to Jenny, she whispered softly, "Goodbye, darling, and good luck!"

The civil ceremony was necessarily formal and uninspiring; the church blessing in St Martin's Church, quite simply breathtaking. The church itself was so beautiful to begin with, aglow with the coloured lights from the stained-glass windows dappling the aisle; the altar massed with white arum lilies and gardenias – the latter flown in from France, at the bridegroom's behest, to grace the occasion; the organ softly playing "Jesu, Joy of Man's Desiring" as the bride entered the church on her brother's arm, to walk the length of the red-carpeted aisle towards her newly-wed husband.

Never would Dinah forget the expression of sheer joy on Alex's face as he turned to welcome his bride, a radiant figure in her cream silk wedding dress, his wedding ring already placed firmly on the third finger of her left hand during that brief, formal ceremony at the registry office.

Now the pair of them were standing together on the steps of the altar, receiving a blessing on their union as man and wife, so utterly and obviously in love with one another that they seemed oblivious of their surroundings, the priest in charge of the ceremony, the organ music, the scent of flowers, or anything else for that matter, save their absolute joy in one another. The radiant bride and her handsome husband.

It had been a long, exciting day. Talking about it over dinner, they recalled the highlights, one of which was Fanny's hat and her enjoyment of the wedding reception, during which the hat had begun to tilt to one side a little.

"What a lovely idea of yours, Alex," Dinah said, "to invite the vicar and the church warden. I noticed that Fanny was making quite an impression on the latter. Is he married, by the way?"

Kate said, "I liked your speech, Greg. It was just right. Not too long, and delivered with a great deal of panache." She smiled teasingly. "How many sentences?"

"At least four, but who's counting? 'Always leave 'em wanting more,' is my maxim. Don't wait till they bring on the hook!"

"I shall have no such inhibitions at your wedding reception," Alex laughed. "My speech will make Lincoln's Gettysburg Address seem short by comparison."

"The church looked wonderful," Dinah said mistily. "All those flowers. There was a song once, wasn't there, something about gardenias?"

" 'For I bring a little white gardenia, as refreshing as a day in May. You may wear it if you care, or toss it away,' " Kate quoted softly. "It was Mum's favourite song, remember, Greg?" Her face saddened momentarily, thinking of the rose she had handed Jenny from her wedding bouquet, wishing she had not let go of her so easily, not really believing that all was well with her.

Now the conversation switched to talk of the future. Greg said, "The house in Manchester is already on the market, and I'll be leaving my school at the end of the summer term. I've already applied for teaching jobs in other places. Ideally, I'd like to settle closer to home, within striking distance of Scarborough."

"That shouldn't prove too difficult, a man with your qualifications." Alex suggested, "Have you thought of private tutoring? By correspondence course, if necessary? Working from home?"

"No, but it's certainly worth considering," Greg responded eagerly. "What do you think, Dinah?"

She smiled encouragingly. "Sounds great to me," she enthused. "By all means, give it a whirl. Not that I mind much where we end up, just as long as we're together."

Her voice faded as Kate stood up abruptly, eyes staring into the distance. "I'm sorry, I must go to Jenny at once," she uttered hoarsely. "Something's terribly wrong. I know it!"

There was a doctor's car, an ambulance and a police vehicle in the road outside the tall house where Jenny lived with John Spivey. Taking the initiative, Alex told the others to wait in the car until he found out what had happened.

He was gone some time, talking to the proprietress of the apartment building. It was a sad story. John Spivey had left for Canada some four or five weeks ago, leaving Jenny alone in the flat.

A sizeable amount of rent was owing, the proprietress, a Mrs Flynn, told him, which she had overlooked at first until it became apparent that "Mrs Spivey" had apparently no means of repaying the debt when, reluctantly, because she felt sorry for the woman, earlier that day, she had asked her vacate the premises as soon as possible.

"If I'd known what was in her mind," Mrs Flynn said shakily, "I wouldn't have been so hard on her. I knew how upset she was when her husband went away. Leastways I *thought* he was her husband. Mind you, they hadn't been getting on very well for some time: quarrelling and such-like. Not that I blame him entirely, far from. Not to put too fine a point on it, she'd been drinking a lot recently, staying out till all hours – seeing other men, I shouldn't wonder. But then, one shouldn't speak ill of the dead.

"I had the shock of my life, I can tell you, when I found her the way I did, the poor soul, lying there in the bedroom, as peaceful as a sleeping child, a rose clasped in her hands, a suicide note on the bedside table, propped up against an empty whisky bottle and the painkillers she'd taken."

"I see," Alex said grimly. "Thank you for talking to me."

Taking out his wallet, he asked, "Will this be enough to settle her rent arrears?" determined that poor Jenny's reputation should not suffer further harm at the inquest into her death.

"More than enough," Mrs Flynn replied, counting the wad of notes he'd handed her. She added nosily, "Were you a – friend of hers?"

"No. I never met the lady," Alex said briefly. "Now, if you'll excuse me."

He walked slowly towards the car. Kate got out of it and came to meet him. He put his arms round her and held her silently.

She said, "Jenny's dead, isn't she?"

"I'm afraid so, darling."

"Why? Why did she do it? If only she had told me. I might have been able to help her. I knew she was unhappy. I could tell by her face. She said she was sad at the thought of leaving Scarborough: going abroad to live."

"She told you that? When did she tell you?"

"This morning. She was outside the registry office. She came to beg forgiveness, to wish me well on my wedding day. I told her there was nothing to forgive. I kissed her, then I gave her a rose from my bouquet." Tears streamed down Kate's cheeks. "I told her I'd always be here for her. So where was I when she needed me?"

"Perhaps you were with her in a way," Alex said tenderly. "You see, she died holding the rose you gave her."

They walked back to the hotel very slowly. Dinah and Greg had gone back to her flat after a brief word with Alex who had outlined the situation and promised to phone them the following day. There was nothing they could do for the time being. Nothing anyone could do. His only concern lay in helping Kate come to terms with her grief, to cancel their honeymoon plans if necessary, just to be there if she needed him.

Walking back to the Crown had been her idea. "It's such a lovely night," she'd said, looking up at the stars. "So – peaceful."

After a while, she said, "You believe in life after death, don't you, Alex? Remember you once told me you believed in reincarnation. But I can't accept that. I'm not even sure that I believe in a hereafter any more."

"Because of Jenny?" he said simply, not a question but a statement of the truth as he saw it. "Perhaps she took her life as a means of escape from this world in the hope of something better to come?"

Perhaps, Kate thought wearily. If only she could bring herself to believe that this was true. Poor Jenny deserved a second chance of happiness in a world beyond the stars, if such a world even existed.

Reaching the hotel, she said wistfully, "Poor Alex. Not at all the kind of wedding night we'd planned. I'm so sorry, but I'd like to be alone for a while. Will you give me an hour or so?"

"Of course, my darling," he responded quietly, understanding her need of solitude to come to terms with the death of her friend. Not that he imagined, for one moment, that this would happen within the space of an hour. Possibly never, not knowing how much Kate had loved her, how deeply Jenny's death had affected her, as if she was somehow to blame for it.

Arden's deep-seated fear lay in the thought that he might prove inadequate, in the long run, to offer Kate the comfort she needed, to convince her that death was not the end. That life went on.

Very slowly, Kate went upstairs to their room. Opening the windows, she stepped on to the balcony and stood there for a while, breathing in the scent of wild flowers drifting up from the Spa gardens below; hearing the faint wash of the sea on the shore, remembering the first time she had stood there, a lonely woman facing an unknown future, unable to see the lights of home for the veil of fog obscuring her vision.

No fog tonight, and yet she couldn't see at all clearly the future ahead of her. Jenny's death had somehow put things out of perspective. A matter of a few hours ago, she had been part of the living world, now she was gone, and yet there was no sense that her life had been tidied away like an old, forgotten love letter – all passion spent.

Alex had told her of John Spivey's defection, that he had gone to Canada without her. Kate could only imagine Jenny's depth of suffering, which had led her to take her own life. If only she shared Alex's belief in life everlasting.

And yet, was there not clear evidence of that in the miracle of springtime? Her mother had told her, a long time ago, that nothing possessed of life ever died. Words of wisdom to comfort the sad heart of a child devastated by the loss of a kitten she had loved. She had been too young to understand at the time. All she knew was that some vital spark of life had been extinguished forever, beyond recall.

Now, deeply troubled, trying desperately to make sense of her confused thoughts and emotions, reaching out for *something*, she scarcely knew what – a shooting star, perhaps, or the passage of a lighted ship on the far distant horizon – suddenly there came the strange feeling that she was not alone.

Slowly turning her head, she saw at the far end of the balcony, the figure of a young man, dark-haired, not very tall but broad-shouldered, wearing a strangely-cut evening dress suit, a wing collar and a silk cravat, and heard somewhere in the background the music of a Chopin Nocturne played on a grand piano.

She would have known that man anywhere by the photographs she had seen of him, and something more important, an aura of restless energy about him, apparently directed towards herself, as if to prove to her the validity of life everlasting. The survival of the human spirit over which death held no dominion.

An amazing feeling of lightness and relief swept through Kate like a tide, as though a weight had been lifted from her shoulders; her vision miraculously restored so that her view from the balcony had broadened suddenly to encompass the past, present and future as one glorious whole. Indivisibly linked, not separated, by the passage of time.

Then suddenly the man on the balcony was gone, if he had ever existed beyond the realms of her imagination. But Kate knew that he *had* existed, and he would continue to exist in this place he had loved best on earth. His beloved Crown Hotel.

But what of Jenny? Resting her hands on the balcony, looking up at the stars, Kate knew that the death of her friend had, perhaps, been inevitable, and she had chosen to die, with dignity and grace, having come to terms with her destiny – beyond the stars.

And what of her own destiny? Kate wondered. This time, had she built her brave little sandcastle out of reach of the incoming tide?

Of one thing she was entirely certain, that she would love Alex Arden from here to eternity.

Looking up at the sky, suddenly she saw a brilliant shooting star; on the distant horizon, the passing lights of a ship at sea, and knew that she had not reached out for that unknown something, in vain.

It was then she heard the opening of the door as Alex entered the room, walking quietly so as not to disturb her, uncertain of his power to find the right words to comfort her.

Turning her head to smile at him, she held out her hand, and he stood beside her on the balcony, his arm about her, her head resting against his shoulder.

"Remember that letter you sent me from Ankara?" she said. "About your marble-tiled bathroom and the balcony from which you looked up at the stars."

"Shall I ever forget? I couldn't find the right words to say to you then, either." He paused. "Why do you ask?"

"Tell me, darling," she whispered, at peace with herself and the world, "could those stars have possibly been more brilliant, more beautiful than the ones we are looking at tonight?"